THE DISSOLUTION OF NICHOLAS DEE

THE DISSOLUTION

OF NICHOLAS DEE;

HIS RESEARCHES.

MATTHEW STADLER

GROVE PRESS

NEW YORK

Published simultaneously in Canada
Printed in the United States of America

FIRST GROVE PRESS EDITION

Library of Congress Cataloging-in-Publication Data

Stadler, Matthew.
    The dissolution of Nicholas Dee : his researches / Matthew Stadler.
        p. cm.
    ISBN 0-8021-3696-6
    1. Guardian and ward—Netherlands—Fiction.   2. Illiterate
persons—Netherlands—Fiction.   3. Historians—Netherlands—Fiction.   4.
Boys—Netherlands—Fiction.   5. Netherlands—Fiction.   6. Authorship—
Fiction.   I. Title.

PS3569.T149 D57 2000
813'.54—dc21   99-055784

Grove Press
841 Broadway
New York, NY 10003

00 01 02 03   10 9 8 7 6 5 4 3 2 1

THIS BOOK IS DEDICATED TO DINEKE VAN HUIZEN,

FOR HER HUMOR, KINDNESS,

AND GENEROSITY OF SPIRIT.

LIST OF ILLUSTRATIONS

Matthew Stadler's *The Dissolution of Nicholas Dee* is a member of that most endangered of species, the experimental novel, and the fact that I feel reluctant to apply such a damning term to such a good book says much about the times in which we live.

Right now, at the start of the twenty-first century, a modest and traditional little novel that fully realizes its aims is far likelier to be critically praised and widely read than a novel of such grand ambitions that it cannot, by definition, fully realize them. I have seen, in more than one review, the term "experimental" applied either as an outright pejorative or, at best, as a warning to the reader. About the farthest most reviewers are willing to go right now is to assure us that although the book at hand appears to be experimental it is not, in the end, all that bad.

I suspect that we, as a collective if highly various body of readers, writers, and critics, are not so much opposed to innovation as we are in love with success. We want our books to be flawless, unimpeachable; the messier specimens that flirt with excess in pursuit of the ineffable are not particularly welcome at present. Questions regarding any given book's scope and scale tend to go unaddressed, and the measure of a book's success is rarely weighed against the breadth and depth of what it attempts.

Innovation has never, of course, been eagerly received by large numbers of people, but during other periods a book that attempted more than it could possibly attain had at least slightly better chances of attracting attention. It's difficult to imagine what sort of careers writers like Barthelme, Hawkes, Coover, or Pynchon would have if they were starting out today. Novelists who test the limits of the form, who dare to be obscure or difficult, are not half as likely to be congratulated for their courage as they are to be consigned to the waiting room along with the rest of the kooks and crackpots, the people who seek patents for machines they've invented in their basements and those who insist they've been experimented on by extraterrestrials. The lot of the unorthodox writer is further complicated by the current fashion for Balkanizing books into a network of small territories within the larger territory: gay books for gay readers, African-American books for African-American readers, et cetera. This may be a good idea from a marketing standpoint, it may even be helpful to readers who want to read books that depict lives more or less like their own, but it also helps reduce literature to a lesser art form, one devoted to delivering the comforting and familiar to a body of readers trained to expect only that.

So the presence of a young writer like Matthew Stadler, which would be good news in any era, is particularly important now, as is Grove Press's publication of this definitive edition of his third novel. *The Dissolution of Nicholas Dee* was originally published in 1993 by another house, which mistakenly printed the book without Stadler's final rewrites, additions, and deletions. Novelists are rightfully nervous about a number of potential disasters, but surely near the top of any writer's list of terrors is the notion that readers will receive his or her book in something other than its finished condition. Grove Press's decision to give this book another life, in its final form, is practically unheard of in publishing.

The Dissolution of Nicholas Dee contains enough material for a half dozen more conventional novels. It is mainly concerned with the story of a young academic named Nicholas Dee, who has become convinced that the history of insurance, with its implication that all losses, no matter how devastating, can be somehow redressed, is an essential and overlooked development in human history. It also, however, incorporates the story of Nicholas's deceased father, John Dee, a celebrated historian whose fragmentary records of his research into sixteenth-century alchemy are sought after as if they were the relics of a saint, by people who hope to turn them into a popular book with movie potential. It involves as well the story of an angelic, dispossessed young man named Oscar; the story of another young man named Alton Motley who, a hundred years earlier, undertook the building of an immense opera house in a remote, swampy region of Holland; and the story of the theater troupe assembled to perform Motley's first opera, based on Shakespeare's *The Tempest*. That is only a partial accounting of what goes on in these three-hundred-plus pages.

Stadler's novel is structured around three different versions of *The Tempest*. In addition to the Shakespeare play there is Henry Purcell's operatic adaptation of the 1690s, which was based on Restoration "updates" of the Shakespeare play that eliminated aspects considered rough or crude, expanded the roles of the women, and added new characters. Stadler adds to that a second version of the opera, ostensibly written by Alton Motley, who took liberties with the Purcell version and had no knowledge of the Shakespeare. In these pages, Shakespeare's play undergoes more than one sea change of its own.

The Dissolution of Nicholas Dee is a vast meditation on literature and music, on history, and the ongoing human struggle not only to leave behind something significant but to make sense of what's been left behind by members of previous generations. It offers, as part of its many simultaneous and interrelated narratives, sections of the score of Purcell's opera. It leads a band of characters through adventures that do and do not resemble *The Tempest* and makes it clear that these people are and are not Prospero, Miranda, Aerial, and Caliban. It reveals new depths, new circles within circles, right up to its concluding page, and until the reader reaches that page it would be impossible to say, precisely, what the book is about. If *Nicholas Dee* is unapologetically experimental, it is also experimental work of the very best kind, in that it takes the form it takes not for the sake of unconventionality but because this story, with its resonances and repercussions, its multiple layers, could not be told in any other way.

To me, *Nicholas Dee*'s literary grandfather is Kafka's *The Trial*. Its parents are Nabokov's *Pale Fire* and Delillo's *White Noise,* and it does not particularly favor one parent over the other. Like any work of art, however, it is more than anything itself, as is any individual produced by parents and grandparents.

Matthew Stadler's career, still in its relatively early stages, is cause for hope among those who might be prone to despair about what can and cannot happen to writers who aspire to give us something other than more of what we've already got. With this new edition, Grove Press makes a serious and entirely laudable contribution to that future.

—Michael Cunningham

But no mind ever grew fat on a diet of novels. The pleasure which they occasionally offer is far too heavily paid for: they undermine the finest characters. They teach us to think ourselves into other men's places. Thus we acquire a taste for change. The personality becomes dissolved in pleasing figments of imagination. The reader learns to understand every point of view. Willingly he yields himself to the pursuit of other people's goals and loses sight of his own. Novels are so many wedges which the novelist, an actor with his pen, inserts into the closed personality of the reader. The better he calculates the size of the wedge and the strength of the resistance, so much more completely does he crack open the personality of his victim. Novels should be prohibited by the State.

—Elias Canetti, *Auto Da Fé*

I

THE CITY

ONE

I BEGAN BY LEAVING my small apartment, closing the heavy metal door and slipping the lock shut. The bright winter air was clean, and the vista (our city is situated amongst mountains by the sea) was crisp and clear—broken only by the beating blades of the police/news "choppers" which seemed always, these days, to be hovering over our neighborhood. It might have been the university they were watching. It sits above us on a hill. I have no television so cannot know what it was the choppers watched, but there they were, and I began by leaving.

Insurance had lately been on my mind, perhaps because of the precarious state of my income and the uncertain future of my researches; I am a professor of history. Who can account for these things? The narrow streets that snake below the university ring at night with shouted curses and screams; by day, deals are made and drugs ingested without shame, in full sight on the sidewalks. Strangers murder strangers. There are fumes and radiations, toxic shocks, unidentified discharges, disappearing children, and deadly viruses (not to mention widespread attacks on the funding and future of my discipline). At night in my bed, at the edge of falling into sleep, when I am most honest with myself, I sometimes tremble for a moment, and realize I've never been so afraid. The butcher below me recommended an agent whom he knew, and I called for an appointment.

Unbridled vice may be part and parcel of daily life here, but so it is in every city. One must accept the fact and live with it. I have my habits, and my customary caution, but I don't let them keep me from the pleasures of our beautiful metropolis. On winter days (as on that day when I left my apartment to arrange a policy of insurance against personal loss) the city sparkles like a jewel set in the rim of the sea. I am a brisk and eager walker, and have no car. Most of my life is contained within a small purlieu and I am content to walk, traversing the city center to the fish and vegetable markets, or heading up the hill to my job at the university. The rest of the city is bunched up around its seven hills, largely unknown to me, save for the occasional tram ride to the municipal park and my restless wanderings to the harbor and the ruins of the old factories.

On that day I boarded a northbound tram and rode it some distance to a neighborhood I rarely visited, a quiet residential area where the agent lived and did business. I found the office easily, on a small street of narrow houses built in rows, and was met by a pleasant woman of forty or so.

"Is it possible," I asked (after the procuring of coffee and biscuits) "to insure against personal loss?" The room was cluttered with thick vinyl binders and postcards. She was courteous and competent, buttressed there amongst her towering stacks of information.

"What sort of personal loss?" The depth of her question was both frightening and unfathomable. What had I lost? Nothing, really, except people, the ones who had died, and time. Nothing cataclysmic or "biblical," like Job. But each day, and everything in it, would be lost, just by the last silent turning of the clock. It was exactly this persistence and inevitability that rankled me. At least Job knew what he was up against. The only thing obvious or certain about loss in my life was its slow invisibility. I kept quiet a moment longer, and fished for a useful reference point to offer the agent.

"I think accidents, or theft. Anything I guess, if it's been lost unjustly." She scratched some notes onto a pad. There seemed to be no windows in the room, or none that I could see through the clutter. My request puzzled her.

"Do you want a quote for physical damage?"

"Well, I don't know the damages. I haven't had any yet."

"Or stick-'em-up insurance? Do you rent?"

"Yes, I rent an apartment." She relaxed visibly, and pulled a binder from the stack to her left.

"Address?"

"Marginal Way, below the university."

"Your age and the age of the building please, approximately."

"I'm thirty-three. I believe the building is late nineteenth century. "

"Frame or brick construction?"

"Brick."

"Is there a dead bolt or police lock?"

"A dead bolt."

Pages flipped and cross-references were made. Unit size, window locks, and precautions against fire were considered. A button was pushed and her large beige printer clattered to life and produced a page of figures. It looked like what I wanted. The two columns of evenly spaced numbers blocked the page off nicely.

"Is that comprehensive?" I asked, surveying the figures.

"Comprehensive?"

"I mean, if a natural disaster happened, lightning, or, say, an aircraft plummeting. Would these numbers cover the loss?"

She scratched her ear with a pencil and pointed. "Any loss in the unit is covered under this plan. You'd have to add earthquake if you wanted earthquake. As for life and health I suggest you begin by checking with the university. Other than that it's total."

I left the office with a small parcel of pamphlets and brochures, saddled with the task of sorting through my arrangements with the university. The wide variety of "premiums" and deductibles (and the burden of choosing from among them) cast a shadow of risk over the whole enterprise; I searched among the pages for the safest gamble, noting the lower rates for "secured units." It was, after all, insurance I sought, not another risk.

The December sky, so blustery and blue when I first set out, had clouded over considerably by the time I emerged from the agent's small office. I hurried along the narrow pavement toward the tramline. It was quite late already. Lights were coming on all across the city, muted by mist in the dusk. I could see the downtown in the distance from where I stood, peering right and left, up and down a street I did not recognize. There was no tram, though the metal tracks and suspended wires were there, slack and brittle in the cold. The iron smell of snow was in the air, and I hurried up the street looking for a sign.

I say that I "began" that day because the trip to the agent, and my possible insurance policy, took me in the end to a bookshop I'd never before seen, and an unexpected rendezvous with a woman whose appearance in my life properly stands as the beginning of my story. "She," as she was known to me for several weeks thereafter, emerged like a crushed star, and occupied an invisible position of gravity around which my life soon began spinning.

It was with some small relief that I spotted the bookshop sign and the warm glow of light through the two windows. I could certainly watch for the tram from there, and maybe get some better information from the shop-owner. The first small flakes began falling, buffeted by an icy wind. I thought I could see the searchlights, radiating like bright spokes from the hovering "choppers," still lingering over the university. The machines themselves were invisible from this distance, but the narrow bands of light came clear in the darkness and snow. I admired their steady searching for a moment, and ducked in under the bookshop's torn awning.

A clutch of little bells rang as I pushed the heavy door open. Warmth came mingling out into the cool evening air to greet me. I stepped inside and stood still for a moment, bathing in it, the sweet decaying smell, old musty books, the hard wooden shelves, an acrid smoky trace of cigars. From off my coat, the freshness of a December storm, the tiny flakes melting, their dampness evaporating into the shop's still interior. There seemed to be no one else there. "Hello," I called, singing the word softly. "Hello?" Nothing. No one. "Hello," I whispered once more. Sweet silence. It would be simple enough to just listen for the tram. I slipped my shoes off, setting them by the radiator, and made my way in to the books.

I could trace, perhaps, the history of this pleasure. Find its contours and depth, the echoes and sympathies, the shifting repetitions of this moment for me: once, with my father, on a day when the winter cold lay thick in my woolen jacket, my soft and tiny fingers held tight in his hard, smooth hand; and I, watching the motion of his long legs, the gabardine trousers moving softly with each step forward along the frozen walk (the empty blue winter sky), could imagine the warm, close air behind his working knees, the small hollow where the trousers hung loosely, holding the heat and odor of his strong legs; and he, looking down at me asking what it was I was thinking then, and would I like to stop for a moment, the small bells ringing as he pushed the heavy door open, the sweet smell of books mingling out into the cold air to greet me. The moment inside the door, the pause upon entering. I feel it closing behind me, its slow progress back, the slip of the latch, and the silent puff of air, the door fit neatly back in its frame.

I had a little list in my pocket, a scribbled note. Titles I might never find. Boyish fantasies of the intellectual: Bruno, Causabon, Fludd. Older now, too big to be led around by my father. And the hours that passed, my list lost on the floor unnoticed. The drift of my attentions through the windowless interior rooms—the simple etchings of flowers, pistil and stamen enlarged, names of tropical birds, stones of the glacial plateau, the English manor house, methods of instruction in the time of Charlemagne, a chart I once saw and could never again find chronicling bridge disasters, the mint, its history and manufacture, disorders of the brain, furtively and for several hours Welsh bundling (fearing that any practice with so intimate and blowsy a name must be obscene), maps, of course, islands and river deltas, a boat, once, that sailed over the Angel Falls, a woman's death by fire, fleeing Paris and the plague, the comparative sweetness of regional waters, the tongue and teeth, a sensitivity to cold, its touch upon the heart, the impossibility of Maxwell's demon, meaning and song, speech impediments. My legs asleep, the book upon my lap.

Impossible to judge the time, all light of day lost among the twisting walls of books. My sudden fear that time had come unhinged, whole lives drifted past, my mind having fallen so far. I rose too quickly, older still, a terrible ache in my knees. Difficult to find my balance. The muscles of my legs were still unwinding. A pile of books stood beside me, an accusation. I rubbed the backs of my knees through the warm gabardine and sat down, thinking to select one or two titles with which to appease the owner.

A woman, that is "she," appeared, suddenly, snow dusting her shoulders, smelling of the fresh winter storm. She shuffled forward, and I turned. Her eyes engaged with mine so strongly, right on the level. Was she so short? The bones of her face were strong; Scandinavian, possibly Dutch. The cold gave her cheeks a lovely blush. (Had mine lost their blush? I was so proud of them when I was young. Each morning I'd slap them with my open hand to bring the color up.) I looked up again and didn't see her.

"Do you have the time?" It startled me. Her voice, speaking from somewhere close behind me.

"Excuse me, I. Just a moment."

"No, no. No need to get up. I just wondered if you had the time. I'm afraid it's getting late."

Still seated upon the floor, I turned and faced her, eye to eye. She was barely three feet tall.

"Excuse me," I blurted, unthinking. "No, I'm sorry. Is it late, do you know?"

She weathered my awkwardness with calm and tact, maintaining both clarity and engagement. "I believe it *is* late," she assured me. "I thought you might know exactly. Haven't we met?" She extended her hand in warm greeting. Such a face, as though from stone. The eyes, ice blue above the strong bones, and that enormous head. I took her hand.

"Very pleased," I said, feeling both charmed and awkward. "I don't believe I've ever been to this shop before."

"Nor I," she replied easily. "It's a bit out of the way."

Was she very old? Sixty? Seventy? One hundred? Perhaps as young as forty? I couldn't guess, having never met a dwarf before, of any age.

"Yes," I got out. "Off the beaten track. Maybe at the university. I teach there." Her face brightened. Evidently I'd hit the mark.

"Yes of course. At the pool."

"The History Department."

"And you swim at the pool."

"The pool. Why yes, I do. Each Wednesday."

"Sometimes I watch." I couldn't recall having seen her there.

"Watch?"

"From the gallery. It relaxes me. The splashing, the repetitions. The steam is good for my complexion." She blushed. We nodded and clucked, as any two will do when reaching the end of pleasantries. Glancings at the shelves, a furtive touching of the book spines. "Well," she exhaled. "I still must know how late it is."

"Yes," I agreed. "And I, if there's still a tram. Perhaps by the desk?"

"Excuse me," she now called out, walking away toward the desk. "Do you have the time?"

I gathered myself, brushing dust off my trousers, and wondered after this strange woman. Where had she come from? Had I heard bells at some point, church bells marking the hour? Was she a supplicant, or some sort of nun? She did not seem to be "of our city." Was there a trace of an accent, or was it simply the shock of her appearance that made it difficult for me to place her? I listened for her voice, or the gravelly answers of the terse proprietor. Nothing. Dust stirred at my feet. I felt a chill, a sudden draft catching my pants leg.

"Hello," I called weakly. Silence.

And then the little bells, ringing madly with the jiggling of the door. I rushed to the front, feeling the lovely wooden floor under my stocking feet, and saw the door slamming shut, a shadow's form slipping out into the night, and no one at the desk. A small scrap of paper blew in on the last gust of wind and settled by my shoes.

Had she left me, just like that? With no parting words? And where was the proprietor? The heavy door rattled in its frame, still animated by her hasty exit. I would have liked her help with the tram, or gladly shared a cab home. "Hello?" I called, straining over the desk. I looked for some trace of human activity, a lit pipe, a coat, the light of a warm back room. "Hello? Have you the time?" The bookshop gave back nothing. I looked out the front window, out into the foul weather. The night was black. The storm blustered around the street lamps, obscuring the empty trolley tracks under fresh fallen snow.

I took the scrap of paper from the floor. "Nicholas Dee," it read. "Philosophies of Innundation in Early Dutch Dijkage."

But I am Nicholas Dee. That is, I mean, my name. Snow had melted, obscuring some addresses. There seemed to be a list of bookstores, most of them neatly checked off. A faint ticking could be heard.

Unmistakably the even progress of a clock marking time. It was so slight. With each gust of wind outside the storm obscured it, swallowing the mechanical sound in deep, distant howling. Then the wind would subside, shifting into silence. Again the ticking, like a metal blade. Where was it? The wind blew hard and rattled the windows.

I could see no clock, no watch left lying on the blotter. The storm kept calling, whistling along the narrow stone streets, playing thick white flakes against the dark glass. Was it so late? I pressed against the cold window, looking up and down the street for a sign, or the warm light of an illuminated clock. That welcome face one sees so often in our city, upon turning a corner, or entering a public square. Always at that moment when one is wondering, is about to inquire of a stranger, "What is the time?" and there, hanging perhaps by the clockmaker's sign, appended to the church steeple, or aloft by the entrance to the trains, a public clock. Accurate, large, always so softly lit. Up and down the little street all I could see were houses. Street lamps, battered by the gusts, blinked off and on, their wires loosened by the violence of the storm. There was no clock. And then the faint sound. Coming from the desk, it seemed, the soft, terse ticking marking off each second.

"Hello?" I called once more, agitation in my voice. "Hello? Is there anyone here?" I paused to listen. Only the silent books. And then the ticking. It touched me inside, repeatedly, tapping some inner sensitivity, ticking on the bottom of my brain. I tore at the desk drawers, pulling them out with some force, scattering papers and pens desperately, as though searching for a weapon. One side and then the next, dropping each drawer empty to the floor, piling them up in stacks. The mess of contents lay spilled upon the desk top. I sifted blindly, feeling for the beating heart, the tiny mechanical clock.

Chocolates, cigars, rubber stamps, and snuff. Papers thick with inky scribbles, dried pens, their ends chewed down to nothing. Rubber bands, cracked and dry, pencil grit, the grimy tailings of erasers. Postage stamps, pennies, flakes of old adhesive. Torn pages, tape and glue, clips and tacks. Crumbled tablets that tasted of sour orange. My fingers touched them all. A hat, crushed under books, once, I believe, a homburg. The tram appeared, rounding the far corner. Cash, in the hat, and cards listing books to be bought, and the names of customers who wanted them. Socks and shoes. I slipped into mine and reached for my coat. The trolley was drawing near.

I got into my coat and took my few things. Pushing the door open I left the little bookshop and went out into the storm. I could not look at what I had done, the havoc I'd strewn in my panic. My head down against the wind, I walked briskly to the tram stop and stepped up to the waiting door.

"Ticket, please," the driver said warmly. The clean interior light of the tram filled me with relief. I listened to the solid rubber door frame slapping shut behind me.

"Ticket, please," he repeated. The warmth of his voice was simply a habit. I reached into my coat pocket, feeling blindly for the slip of paper, and wrapped my hands around a small mechanical ticking. It was a watch, still warm from the hand that placed it there. It smelled of her, all fresh and northern. Behind the glass face two thin hands, steadily marking time around the circle. And behind the circle, gears. Tiny metal teeth, turning within, ticking to me.

"Ticket, please," he said again. And the trolley moved forward through the storm, returning to the university.

Who was this mysterious messenger? And what purpose had been served by her delivery of the watch? Clueless and overtired I rode the tram back home, cradling the softly ticking round of brass in my palm, and staring out into the diminished storm. The night gave back nothing but my reflection in the black glass. At last we passed my apartment and I rang the small bell and got off.

I live, have always lived, above a butcher's shop on the busy market street below the university. There are three apartments and mine is at the top. The stink of meat and garbage can be smelled in summer, but only on those few languid, sticky days of August when the winds have ceased and the air lies thick and heavy in the streets. In winter everything is fresh and clean. The butcher's blood freezes in the gutter. What scraps there are disappear with the dogs or turn to ice. My little cat could be heard atop the narrow stairs, calling my name. Snow blew in through the opened door. It dusted the carpet and quickly disappeared.

My three rooms are small and oddly shaped. The windows look out across the neighborhood toward the city's downtown and the harbor. A mantle of snow graced the buildings, partly obscured in clouds. Threads of colored light danced on the black water: beacons, and ships' warnings. I could see best with the lights off and left it that way for some time.

My family's furniture, what of it I could fit in here, made a fortress of my home. All of it was too grand for the apartment, giving the rooms some of the menace and sorrow of a broken graveyard (crowded with mossy obelisks and mausoleums, dirt and fallen leaves obscuring any messages left by the deceased). A network of paths wended among books, giving me access to the kitchen and the windows, principally. The dressing cabinet was big as a boat. It loomed in the darkened room like a storm cloud or ghost, filling most of a wall. My father's desk, made from black oak and pearl, took up another corner. It was no collector's piece—for he'd managed to disfigure its surface with butterfly pins and a dissecting knife—but obviously it meant a great deal to me. He was a brilliant man, and a brilliant historian, and everyone seemed to know it. Today, seven years since he died, I am still asked more frequently to speak about his work than about my own. I can't claim to have ever understood it completely.

The cat was swatting pens off the desktop. I don't know why she does this. I set my bundle of pamphlets by the bedside, and cleared space for the pocket watch beside her. She rumbled a bit and sniffed it, passing her cold nose along the glass. I sat down at the desk and turned the lamp on.

The face was a simple faded white. The numbers were Roman. Two thin metal hands emerged from the center, each straight and true. They appeared to be black. I turned the watch slowly, observing through a magnifying glass, and scrutinized the hands. Light and color swirled across their thin width, playing optical gymnastics, as if from the face of slick oil. It wasn't black but blue, a hard metal blue, glinting in the bright light. The shallow glass dome was unmarked. Only my prints dirtied its face, oily maps of my fingertips left by my cradling it the whole journey home. I fogged the glass with my breath and wiped it clean with a cloth. A name was inscribed on the white face. "W. A. Williams & Co.," it read. "St. Louis, Missouri." The brass was tarnished on its edge where it had been touched, so often, by nervous hands. At its crown a simple knob extended, a delicate round of ridged metal. It wound easily, each tightening of the coil marked by clicks. I turned the treasure over and found an inscription: "To my small Prospero. Pen and sword. J.L.D."

"Pen and sword"? Was it some sort of secret society? And J.L.D. Those were my father's initials. Could the watch have been stolen? Her note bore my name and a list of bookshops. The watch was an announcement, a provocation. It could not have been simply a gift or accident. What did she know of me (and why couldn't she have come to me during office hours . . .)? I turned the lamp off and hurried to bed, exhausted, and unwilling to struggle with her mysteries any longer.

Sometimes the choppers came by night and shone their search-lights on the street. Some sort of regulation kept them higher off the ground than in daytime (excepting in case of emergency or other ex-treme danger). They rarely came low enough to wake me, and I rather liked the sound of them then, the rapid trilling thump of their distant rotor blades, like a heart sped up and racing. While I slept, or lay in bed not sleeping, there were heartbeats everywhere, afloat in the air of the city. It was the searchlights that woke me sometimes. They would flood the window casings when trained on my block. I don't like curtains and living at the top I don't need them. But morning or the police choppers always woke me with their light. That night there were no searches, and I slept well.

TWO

I'VE PRAISED THE SITUATION of the city, with its vistas and fresh air, but one should not overlook the architecture and history of the place itself, the character and shape of it. We are the largest city in our region, the oldest and most cosmopolitan. When the founders first landed, it is said, they sang excerpts from Monteverdi's *L'Orfeo* standing knee-deep in tidal mud, as a gesture of greeting, and to calm the fearsome native population. A hundred or more half-naked young men with torches and crude scythes are said to have surrounded the boat as it bottomed out in the mud. The music pleased them, and a deal was struck. No other city in our region can boast a civic opera, nor a university of the size and reputation we enjoy here. The libraries and museums are "first-rate," and public life has long been enlivened by its rich contact (via the sea) with other continents. We are a seaport, and the harbor is busy with both commerce and cultural exchange. I go there often on walks, to take the air and to watch people.

Traveling first past fabric stalls and news vendors, along the busy market street near my apartment, north toward the opera house and its large public square, then heading west downhill, through a maze of steep cobblestone lanes, often slick with fish slime or rain, I can reach the harbor and its wharves in ten minutes. The breeze is touched with creosote, diesel, and the rank, salty ocean. Jobless men and tramps line the metal fences there, sleeping in boxes, or standing in lines drinking. Schoolboys give the men trouble, throwing bottles and rocks, while above them families in tour groups are rushed along plastic catwalks to the sight-seeing boats. There are docksmen too, with rope and hooks, wearing bright coveralls and metal hats. No one bothers with me. I am purposeful and regular in my habits. I usually buy fried fish from a vendor by the state ferry. All languages can be heard in the harbor, and some good stories too, if one has a hunger for that sort of thing. The public wharves offer a pleasant view back of the city bordered by the mountains which rise up suddenly behind it.

The city is dominated by the university on its hill to the south (featuring, especially, the twin spires of its neo-Gothic library, from which purchase, it is said, bombs were once hurled), and the iron and stone tower of the police, rising in the north above a blighted neighborhood of decrepit warehouses. That tower, which sports a tall and elaborate transmission needle, rises fully forty stories and glows red at night. Matching the university with its tremendous height, the police tower completes a "frame" of sorts, enclosing the busy downtown. Under the gaze of these twin sentinels the city conducts its business.

I grew up here and my father taught at the university. He was chairman of the department where I now work. They played shuffleboard in the halls then, Hank Shuntley, Marge LeBlanc, and my father. Marge usually won, and Hank and my father got drunk losing. The department was less formal or nervous in those days. Demography had not yet taken over the top two floors of the building, and these were still filled with books kept as a "Graduate History Research Collection." Parties (called "receptions") were held there at least once a week, and the afternoons were spent napping on old couches set in the window bays. I'd read there, or play Chinese checkers at a table behind the gray metal map drawers, whenever I'd come to campus with my father.

I remember each Saturday, when we'd go to the pool together. I was a timid boy, and spent more time sitting by the water than actually in it. I'd play for a while with the buoyant kickboards, and always spend long minutes agonizing over the high dive. But mostly I sat, dangling my legs in at the edge of the water, watching.

I remember my father diving and kicking swiftly to the bottom, and pausing there. He'd let go a brace of pearly bubbles through his nose and sink farther till he was lying flat against the tiles. He was so blue down there, through the blue water, and so peaceful. It was remarkable how long he could stay before coming back up. The sight of his body, made wobbly and insubstantial by the water, amazed and terrified me as I sat mostly naked at the pool's edge, looking down at him.

When I slept I had dreams of submersion, but never drowning; they were like flying dreams, except it was breathing water that was made miraculously possible. These days, when I go to the pool, I swim laps.

My father, John Dee, is remembered principally for his social history of the sixteenth-century inventors who called themselves alchemists. Three volumes of work, completed largely in a span of ten years, were enough to secure a reputation, his chairmanship, and support for the rest of his working life. The high regard for this work protected him from ridicule when the later monographs about plants, submersion, and "acardiochronic" history were published. You might imagine I would have learned from him, but in fact I never saw him working. I sat with him for hours in his office at home while he prepared butterflies, inspecting their beautiful wings with a magnifying glass, and fixing them (temporarily) to the desk with pins. Even at school he never worked. Part of my interest in the profession came from this false image of patrician ease. History, I thought, was the product of an ongoing conversation among friends, usually conducted over tea or drinks in warm, cluttered offices. This, in any case, was the impression my father gave.

THE TEMPEST.

OVERTURE.

Henry Purcell.

This was the page of music I stared at the next morning, with some pleasure, having at last received the score from the library. I had the album at home but wanted the score, to look at the sounds, as it were. There, clearly drawn, like a map on the page before me, were the somber first steps of Purcell's overture; the carefully measured introduction of themes, full, slow, and menacing, like lines of infantry taking their places, each on the empty battleground that will soon be drowned in blood. Of course there would be little blood in this *Tempest* (but plenty of drowning). I stared at it, delighting in the several layers of the opera's opening themes.

Purcell's *Tempest,* a bizarrely deformed and distant cousin to the Shakespearean original, was the music of my childhood. It hangs over those heavy afternoons like sleep. We listened to it nearly all the time. With its heavenly Ariel, fathers turned to coral, and continual talk of drowning, those several arias I could understand and remember took on greater meaning in my life. Sometimes, it seemed, the songs were sung as comment on my own trials.

I had the record on, and the winter sun brightening my room, with the score laid out on the desk. Kitty was there, asleep in a thick band of sunlight, and I followed the overture point by point along the pages. In the pauses between, that watch could be heard, still ticking, on the desk beside the cat.

I'd woken feeling unreasonably vigorous and flung my covers nearly to the wall, aroused by the sunlight. Its brightness was doubled by a heavy mantle of snow which had fallen overnight. The city sparkled and shone outside my windows. The sky was clear now, clear as crystal, and ice blue over the bright white hills. Though I could recall no dreams, I felt the sort of ease and calm which often follows vivid dreaming. Something had sorted itself out in sleep, possibly something to do with the dwarf. The watch intrigued me. The mystery of it, so vexing just twelve hours earlier, now was tantalizing, like a scab or wart which appears on the tender inside of a thigh, at which one keeps picking. I looked at it, ticking on the desk in front of me, and waited for the hands to move.

It was possible I'd see her again, if not at the pool then elsewhere. She must have some affiliation with the university to get access to the pool. I'd be on campus all afternoon. I had an appointment with the bursar, to check my existing policies, and plans to spend time in the library sketching out my ideas for a research grant.

Who knew where money would come from these days? Recent funding went to the most outlandish projects. Enacted "simulations," televised investigations shot on location from helicopters and boats, elaborate fictions, novels really, conjured from small shards of fact; all of them seeded with cash from government and industry. Our old chairman (my father's successor) cautioned me not to miss the boat and suggested we "team up" on a seven-part history of mathematics "TV docudrama/book package" (with guaranteed distribution to the Whittle Schools, plus foreign backing), but I could not. Cameras unnerve me, as do the dangers of electronic media generally. (A colleague of my father died, I am told, on camera, above a spectacular cliff on the Aegean Sea, clutching at an artifact that was improperly wired.) Was there grant insurance? The failure to secure a grant was certainly as natural and predictable a disaster as any storm or flood. I couldn't recall ever seeing a "history of insurance," and certainly not a definitive one. However regrettable, one's career often came down to finding odd gaps in the field, empty places where fallow soil had not yet been tilled:

"The History of Insurance: the Insurance of History." (The thought had occurred to me on the day when I "began," and I made a note of it, with plans for some preliminary investigations in the library.)

I turned the record over and took a small pill (a mild stimulant prescribed for me by my doctor). My new agent's brochure and her numbers stared up at me from the desk. While the day's bright sun washed any gloom or menace from the far corners of my apartment, it also (I now saw) revealed certain weaknesses in the superstructure. There were small cracks visible in the plaster, around the light fixtures and the windows especially. Blistered paint revealed a film of rusty water, trickling from the lattice of wood where the falling plaster clung. The joints in the frame around the door seemed to be pulling apart.

I must have seen it all before, a thousand times, but never through the eyes of an insurance agent. I made a quick inventory (listing especially those damages which made the unit more vulnerable to theft), reinked my jotted note "The History of Insurance: the Insurance of History," and gathered my papers for the day ahead.

THE TEMPEST.   ACT II.

Henry Purcell.

DUET *(Two Devils)* and CHORUS. WHERE DOES THE BLACK FIEND AMBITION RESIDE?

20

* * *

Vast patches of mud marred the pretty snow on streets near to campus, circular, as if from bombs or a flamethrower. Flashing lights and barricades indicated some sort of police/news action. It might have been floodlights that made the muddy pools, or the hot exhaust of the chopper engines. Evidently, they had landed here and everything was taken care of (By the time I passed going home the barricades were gone and fresh snow had been shoveled in to cover the scar. I was glad to see they'd finished their business.) The paper said something about drug rings and the swooping down of the choppers, and that was explanation enough.

At this hour the university was just beginning to stir. All across the broad white lawns, undergraduates shuffled toward class with colorful knapsacks hung lazily off their shoulders. Sculls coursed the waters of the inlet, far below. The heavy eights took practice in winter as in summer, barring a prohibitive thickness of ice.

Originally the university was a ramparts, and after that a pageant ground. The infantry and horsemen marched here, feathered and bedecked in colorful cloth, with their fabulous banners waving in the breeze. The plan of the quadrants is a remnant of that time. The army (stationed at the ramparts since the founding of the city) began instruction in the original buildings one hundred and fifty years ago, hoping to create greater refinement and guile among the officers. This became the university. It was not, as some have claimed, a monastery or place of worship. That idea is attractive enough to have become commonplace, but it is, alas, not true. Undeniably the university is pervaded by quasireligious pomp and ritual: the dogma, the rote repetition of accepted truths, the humility of the acolyte, elaborate hierarchies among the faculty, and a pervasive paternalism, to name but a few. But these are all strictly military in origin and intent. (While many will argue that the cruciform structure of our central library is suggestive of the church, it must be remembered that the crucifixion was, in fact, a police action.) Ostrander has documented the absence of any conventional due process standards in the university's disciplinary procedures, rightly implying a link to the military tribunals which preceded them.[1] Atten-

1. Kenneth Ostrander, *A Grievance Arbitration Guide for Educators* (Boston: Allyn and Bacon, 1981), pp. 73–79.

dance at even one of these "callings-to-the-woodshed" is enough to convince one utterly of the truth of this thesis.

History had its own building, until Geography and Demographics encroached, taking over almost two and a half stories. That still left us with the basement, first floor, and most of the second, of what everyone agrees is a little jewel of a building set very near the center of the old campus. Few are able to navigate the baffling warren of tunnels and passageways that unfold in History's lowest floor, where I work. I know them well only because of constant practice throughout childhood, trying to find my father.

The key turned nicely in my lock, letting the heavy door loose again from its frame. My office was empty and still. Low winter sun passed easily through the two windows, illuminating the dust I'd stirred. My work had settled here in layers, over the walls, the bookshelves, the desks and chairs, covering much of the floor. Old monographs, scattered drafts, books left open, their faces pushed down into the dust, an umbrella. I slipped my shoes off, placing them by the door, and set my things on the couch. The window casing certainly seemed rotten, the way the tired paint had chipped from it. Probably lead, and deadly if swallowed. I pried at the loose hardware. A crowbar was all that would be needed, from inside or out, and God knows what would happen to all my effects. I made a note of it, to ask the bursar that afternoon if the offices could be secured. Surely the university would see to the security and insurance of their own buildings.

The small red light on my phone/console was blinking, meaning someone left me a message. It was from our new chairman, Abbott Weathered. Could I come up now, this morning if I was free, and have our get-together over coffee? This would be our first meeting.

Abbott was found after a lengthy search and two years spent with no one "at the rudder." He was no Thucydides, it was rumored, but his mediocrity as a historian was more than made up for by his alacrity as a businessman. The department hoped his appointment would mark a bold step into a brighter future, and I hoped I would be among those to feast on the fruits of his expertise. He was a large man, too big for the dowdy pants that rode below his belly. He had the bulk and carriage of an ex-athlete, an ingester of anabolic steroids who'd grown into middle age by collapsing—all that meat and muscle gone to fat. His tightly buttoned vest held the chest and stomach up, while the pants clung to his narrow hips with a cinched belt. He was all right with a desk in front of him, but when he stood, the imbalance of his form made me fear he might topple over and be left helpless on the floor until a crane or strongman could be found to right him. Entering his office, I was glad to find him seated behind the big desk, fiddling with the drawers.

"Christ," he grumbled when I came in, "Almighty Christ on a stick." All I could see was his rounded back. He'd bent over, reaching deep into the bottom drawer, as if digging for clams. "Gorillas, useless." I shuffled a bit in place and coughed loudly.

"Professor Weathered?"

"Dee?" He popped up, surprised and blushing red from the exertion. "Sit, just . . . I'm in a bit of a crisis." He disappeared again from view. "My pipe is gone. Damned moving men left everything in a mess." I stole a peek at his enormous desktop, reading letterheads upside down: "I.C.A.," "Yale," "U.S.D.A.," "F.S.G.," and one in Cyrillic script, before he shuffled and cursed, reappearing with a pipe.

"How terrible for you, Professor, Dr. Weathered." I stood and extended my hand in greeting. "If there's anything I can do, anything at all." I wondered if his grant "manuals" or what-have-you had also gone missing in the move. "I hope I've not caught you at a bad time." He was sweating, even at nine on a winter morning.

"Now's no worse than ever, Dee. You're a good man to ask, but I've got a kid in a boat at six A.M., for Christ's sake, ice thick as my fist and some yo-yo of a coach calling. Do you smoke?" He offered the pipe, absently, while looking to the desk for another.

"No, not really." I nodded my apology and sat down.

"Dee. Don't be silly." He banged the pipe gack loose with a strong swat of the bowl against his hand, then reached again for the bottom drawer. Tobacco, a second pipe, and a package of those thin impossible papers were gathered. "Pipe, Dee? Pipe or papers?" The paraphernalia cheered him up considerably; he beamed at me like a boy with new toys and a friend to show them to.

"Really, it doesn't agree with me." I smiled weakly.

"Dee, it's the finest tobacco; it's Turkish. The aroma will do you good, bring that color up." He wheedled the extra pipe toward me, pushing it along the desk with his hand. I made no gesture toward it. Abbott blinked, then sighed. "I'll just put the flame to both of them, and leave it up to you then."

I sat and took in the room while he fiddled. His office was such a bare discomfort. The sheer enormity of it, the height of the ceiling, and the empty shelves, the grand extensions of space (prettified with faux-baroque trim) all mocked the man behind the desk. Even our huge new chairman seemed tiny here. He could fill it: hang his diplomas neatly on the wall; uncrate and arrange the books; shelve the boxes of manuscript pages; install the hanging files, and place the busts of Hegel and Carlyle. But the room would always feel empty. It's designed that way, to make one feel small. Abbott unrolled a soft leather pouch filled with gleaming dental instruments (or so they appeared to me) and began an excavation of the pipes.

"Lovely child," I offered, admiring the desk photo of a boy.

"Yes, Francis. He'll be thirteen in January. You're from here, isn't that right, Dee?"

"Yes, a native, actually. Born and raised."

"I can't figure this place," he stammered, leaning toward me across the desk. "We paid one-fifty on a three-bedroom, not five blocks from here, thinking Francis should attend Heights, and, you know, after that who knows; and because our water hookup or some such nonsense comes off Beacon we get a printout, a goddamned printout in an unsealed envelope no name or what-have-you, nothing but this carbon printout saying they're busing him over the hill to Valley; and we paid one-fifty, which you and I know is steep, even for a chairman. And . . . what do you make of that? I mean, as a native, was this . . . did this happen when you were a kid?"

"I, we lived by Valley. I was sent away to school."

"Military?"

"Preparatory; boarding school."

"So, you think we should send Francis away?" He put the pipe and tools down, and picked at his teeth in worry.

"Well. Actually, I wasn't very happy."

"Maybe to military school then, except the discipline. I've got a brother in the Army . . . I mean, if we lived near Valley, would they send him back to Heights?"

"I really can't say. You mentioned coffee?" I was still hoping to avoid the pipes.

"Yes, of course. How stupid of me. It's in the jar. One teaspoon, two if you like it strong." He pointed to a crusty jar of crystals. Powdered creamer was stacked in packets beside it. "I could use your advice on the school thing, Dee. It's been hanging over me like a monkey tree. Plus now the department wants a report, and I'm not even unpacked yet, as you can see."

"You mean our department?"

"Yes, our department. Tell me, Dee, how does it look to you?" I thought for a moment and looked at the room.

"It's a shame about your, your 'things.'" I dipped my head in commiseration. "I'm sure it will all seem much more comfortable once the books are unpacked."

"Yes, of course, of course it will, Dee. I was asking about the department. How does the *department* look to you these days? How *is* it? Lately, I mean?"

"Well, calm. Adrift, I'd say. 'Rudderless,' some have called it, over the last few years."

"Lacking direction?"

"I'm not unhappy," I countered. "My teaching, my researches. All of that couldn't be better." I nodded, hoping to sound convinced.

"Let me reassure you, Dee, about my commitment to this department." Here Abbott shifted. "I'm a strong believer in the value of good scholarship." He paused to suck on the dry pipe. "I don't have time for 'short-termers' who complain it's a bad investment. Good scholarship is good business, Dee. You and I believe that in our hearts. That's what makes us a good team."

"I think of it as a department, Professor, that is Doctor, Abbott, more so really than a team."

"A department is a team, Dee, any decent department is. If we all do our job, each pulling for each." He scooted closer like an anxious coach, and began making diagrams on a cluttered piece of paper. "The game plan for our department," he continued, gesturing with his pipe and instruments, "is written on what I like to call 'the spreadsheet of a thousand years.' You probably recognize the phrase from my book."

"I don't believe I've seen it." He produced a copy from a side drawer. It was bright green and sported a gold medallion below its title, *Investment in the University*. I turned the sturdy paperback over in my hands. It had a nice weight to it. Could this be the famous grants manual? "This book will help me with my grant?"

"It will broaden your horizons beyond grants. The university is part of the world economy, it's a major player in venture capital, high-risk investment, junk-bond sort of things." He'd managed to form two ample plugs and was already patting them into place in the pipe bowls. "The sooner we recognize these facts the sooner we can tap into speculative markets in private and public sectors, and bring really big dollars to the department. You get my drift, I trust." I wasn't following him too well, but flipped through the book looking for some of the interesting phrases he used. "History is no Sunday hobby. Look at television, Hollywood, or this wacky nostalgia kick that's got America back into big convertibles. Where would they be without history?"

"I'm not sure."

"The question's rhetorical, Dee. I'm stretching a bit to make a point; there's no denying the high return research investments bring, and our department can be as big a player as any other." He handed me the lit pipe with bright eyes and a smile.

"How, exactly, can this help me with my, my project?"

"You may be sitting on a cash cow Hollywood agents would kill for, Dee. This department is stepping into the twenty-first century and you could be among those who profit from it." The desk rattled and the boy's picture fell over, upset by the vigor of Abbott's enthusiasm.

"Hollywood?" I asked, curious. He looked at me for a moment, frowning slightly, and put the pipe down in an ashtray beside me.

"I'm sorry. Rhetoric, Dee, just my rhetoric. I get carried away sometimes." Abbott stared into space, blank as the morning clouds, then put the flame to his plug again and sighed. "Did I ask you about the buses? What's with this screwball town and all these buses? Who stuck buses into subway tunnels anyhow?"

"I'm sorry, I, mostly I walk to work . . . But tell me, this 'cash cow.' What exactly do you mean?"

"Well." Abbott paused and leaned back from the desk. "Let's be realistic. A book contract. I can see a major book contract, with maybe author tours, a couple of lists. There's only so much we can do first time out. Your name is worth something, anyway."

"My name?"

"Dee, Nicholas Dee. Your father's good as god."

"Gold. Good as gold."

"Whatever. Incredible man, Dee. Incredible work. I'm drifting that way myself, now, I mean scholarshipwise. The plants, the notions of time, and all that. Amelia's to thank of course, for the idea I mean, the little nudge, the suggestion." He tilted back into a cloud of smoke. "Behind a good man, and blah, blah, blah. I barely have time for it, what with my consultations and the chairmanship." My pipe smoldered in its holder, miraculously sustaining its ember without me. Abbott sucked lustily, putting the flame to his broad black bowl with every draw. My coffee had gone cold.

"Tell me more about the plants, Abbott." I rose and ambled to the hot plate for a warm-up. "I've never really understood that period in my father's work."

"As I say, it's hard to find the time for it. I've only just started on the monographs, the later monographs where he develops the example of the plants more fully." He paused to refurbish his pipe. Something was missing. He bent down into the bottom drawer again and fumbled, continuing almost inaudibly. "I want to apply the model, the metaphor of the plants, or what-have-you, to a teleological historiography, maybe Marx, or someone ancient."

"Asian?"

"Ancient." He reappeared, fiddling sheepishly with the pipe. "I don't mean to be so vague but it's all very preliminary. I've been so busy with the department, meetings, such as ours, speaking engagements, all that sort of thing. Amelia can only do so much. Actually I thought you might be able to help me."

"I can't imagine how. I've no idea what he was on to in those monographs." I felt some resentment he'd steered our conversation to my father's work. It happened all too often.

"No, no. I don't mean help with the scholarship. It's simply that I'm so unfamiliar with the archive, all the papers he left to the university. I thought maybe you could point me to anything in there about the plants."

"Well, that. Certainly I could keep an eye out. I was going to make time for that this winter, for cataloging more of the letters and whatnot."

"You could drop me a note, that is if anything turns up."

"Yes. I can't say it's likely anything will."

"I can help you with that 'book' of yours," he added eagerly. His offer had all the urgency and neatness of a playground trade.

"My book?"

"That book contract we were talking about. No one knows the players in New York like I do. I can have you under contract in a cat's turn. Where is that proposal?"

Had I mentioned a proposal? Certainly I'd asked him for help, but I couldn't recall ever mentioning any proposals. Still, it seemed silly to let his fleeting eagerness fall on fallow ground. After all I did have a proposal, of sorts, as yet unformed, embryonic, but a "proposal" nevertheless. "Well," I began. "There is something." I paused and stirred some creamer into the oily coffee. Abbott brightened and shifted his weight in the chair.

"I knew there was, I knew from that sharp look of yours. Tell me then, Dee, tell me what terrific project you've got cooking for my New York agent?"

"A History of Insurance, Abbott. *The* history, really. There's been no definitive work in the field." The new chairman stared at me across the tremendous distance of his desk. "Fresh ground, Abbott, I'll be breaking fresh ground." Abbott blinked, waving his pipe in some mute gesture, searching, it seemed, for the right reply.

"Crackerjack, Dee, just terrific." He scribbled a small note. "I don't believe I've ever heard of such a thing."

"It's always been near the center of my work."

"Top notch."

"A catalyst, I think. A key by which to unlock the mysteries of the modern condition." Abbott's enthusiastic silence was difficult to read. He scribbled a few more notes, and looked back up at me, surprised.

"Get it down on paper, Dee. Get those gems down on paper and bring 'em to me by Friday. And I'll have no truck with slouchers; this could be your meal ticket. I want at least three pages, four if you've got the stamina. We're talking full treatment. Synopsis, chapter titles, the whole nine yards. Am I being clear?"

"Oh very clear. I'm afraid I'm just not used to the chairman taking charge like this."

"I'm trying to help, Dee. You'll be helping me in turn."

"I understand and I, well thank you. Four pages? Are you sure that's . . ."

"Possible? Push yourself, Dee. Make it three if you find your-self petering out. No use filling pages with drivel."

"Enough. Are you sure that's enough to, uh, secure a, financing for the, the 'project'?"

"With your name? Which is not to mention that terrific proposal you're wrestling with? The modern, the insurance thing. It's all of it very, very contemporary, I would even say ahead of its time." Abbott sucked once more, grinned and rose from his chair, signaling me to do the same. "Friday, Dee. Bring it along to my house. You can meet my wife and kid."

> *Academics, generally, are such voracious and hasty readers. They have no patience for the pleasure and surprise of it. They plow through documents as if through a department store, looking only for the items on their list.*
> —John Lewis Dee [2]

The bursar turned up nothing but health insurance, and even that inadequate in its coverage of my teeth. His functions have all been computerized so the office is much cleaner and more spacious than my agent's. He entered my policy options and within moments returned

---

2. This typed note was among my father's papers. He left very little of interest, but aphoristic asides, like this one, are scattered throughout the chaos of pages.

with some advice. I'm to refit my "unit" (to qualify for certain bargain theft-and-loss premiums) and consolidate my university health plan with a new accident policy. I've engaged a carpenter to work on my home over the holiday; I'm having no visitors, and will be spending a great deal of time in the library anyway. Insurance aside, the home improvements (better locks, strengthened window casings, new door frames, etc.) are long overdue. I may engage a painter too, and someone to touch up the plaster. All that leaves is my teeth. (Sometimes, sitting among the dusty stacks of the library or lingering late in my office over a rare text I've found, when I begin to envy Huygens or Descartes their dilettante lives of scholarship, their travels by boat or carriage to well-appointed Parisian rooms, banquets and absinthe, groggy talk on fainting couches until dawn, wealthy urbane patrons, and their manuscripts penned on vellum—when, in short, I envy them the pleasure of being glorious figures in a richly imagined history—I stop and remind myself how awful their teeth were. Constant pain and the stink of a mouth full of decay [vainly countered by cloves, the oily nubs having been jammed into the loose bloody gums and replaced every hour or so] make them less enviable. Even without regular flossing, without the proper slow-scrub of a medium bristle pressed at an angle to the gum, professors today can maintain a fresh mouth [and a healthy one] simply by a regular rinsing from the city's fluoridated reservoirs.)

THREE

THE POOL HAD LAP-SWIM AT NOON and I went there, hoping "she" might be in evidence, or at least have left a message. I was up to fifty laps (which I know is nothing compared to certain iron-men, marathoning triathletes, and so forth, but it kept me fit and drained me, which is all I wanted from it). The building itself reminds me of a lung. Not the dull brick exterior, but the damp living interior. Expirations and slime; the busy staff, passing towels and fixing the flow of liquids; silent swimmers, washed and goggled, taking patient turns in the divided lanes. Films in primary school showed the lungs this way, peopled by hundreds of identical fat figures exchanging gases along a wet interior surface.

I took my towel and offered a gruff hello to Schloss (Chemistry, I believe). He always seemed to be there when I arrived, getting ready for a dip.

"Afternoon, Dee," he replied, fiddling with a hangnail. We each had our own metal cage. Schloss had hung his clothing neatly on the crude pegs and stood naked beside me. I could feel the air all over him touching me, and shrunk away. His body both revolted and fascinated me. "Missed you yesterday," Schloss allowed, picking something from the netted crotch of his swim trunks. "Ill?" The locker room was always warm and damp. My bare soles adhered minutely to a thin film of dew, a wet invisible mucus that occupied the entire floor. It was like treading after snails.

"No, no. Busy. I've got a grant to write." The way he stood, so thoughtlessly casual, filling up all that space beside me. He looked like a baboon, thin legs a little too widely spread, the enormous belly jutting forward. He practically touched me, or would have if I'd not slid away with haste.

"Damned annoying," he commiserated. "After a life of decent work you'd think they'd see fit to just keep the money coming. N.E.H.?" I bent down to fiddle with my lock. I could hear him struggling into his trunks.

"I'm not sure yet. Actually the new chairman has some clever ideas about money I might pursue." Schloss would leave soon, and then I could relax and slip into my bathing suit.

"Some sort of history foundation?" he asked, showing polite interest in what he liked to call "the useless art." A last tug pulled the string of his trunks tight to his big waist. I cleared my throat before speaking.

"I'm not sure. It's all very twenty-first century. Very new, really. Abbott outlined so many options." I looked up, bravely hoping he was done with his preparations. His trunks were on, thank God. And he'd tossed a big towel over his sloping shoulders, covering the ugly scattered hair.

"Well, if there's any help I can give you," he offered. Schloss was a generous man.

"There is something." I hadn't thought of it, until he asked. But if "she" was there, lurking maybe, in the gallery or by the diving boards. "Just a trifle really; nothing to do with grants. If you could just look and see if there's someone by the pool, on the sly I mean, not letting her notice you." I could always catch her by surprise, if I knew her station. Schloss perked up visibly at my request.

"Certainly, Dee, why of course. A sweetheart is it?"

"Actually, no. It's an acquaintance, someone I'd like to surprise. She's a woman, uhm, not tall. She might be in the gallery, I think, watching."

"Not tall, you say?"

"No, not at all. A dwarf, actually. She's a dwarf."

Schloss, good scientist, registrar of facts, didn't blink an eye. "A dwarf then. You don't mean a midget, or a pygmy?"

"I don't think so, Schloss. Though I can be stupid about these things."

"The layman can be quite easily confused."

"Yes, yes of course. Tell me, then, if there are any, you know, any dwarfs or midgets or pygmies, anyone at all. I'd be much obliged to you."

"Gladly, Dee. I'll only be a minute."

Schloss withdrew. The steamy tile room was almost empty. A murmur of water and scattered conversations echoed along the metal lockers. I looked at my bare feet and relaxed, happy to have an empty row of benches. What must other men think of me, my body? Everyone seems so curious and brazen. How they stand and chatter, swatting one another, gesturing and picking with unself-conscious ease. It was some relief for me, too, to be let loose from my clothes and engulfed in the cool blue water of the pool. I enjoyed the near-nakedness, the undoing, but only with privacy, or at a distance.

My legs were strong enough and quite big around the calves. The hair was funny though. It disappeared for long stretches. The bare skin was pale and shiny, as if my pants legs had rubbed it clean in spots. Maybe that's what happened to the hair. I had no veins to speak of, neither the ugly blue splotches of old age, nor the pulsing, virile worms of the young athlete. There was one vein, in the hollow behind my knee, which pleased me. I could feel its pulse easily, even through the cloth of my trousers. My arms and trunk were normal enough, pale because I avoid the sun, but fit and trim. I stood and stretched (careful, first, to double-check my solitude) and enjoyed the air on my body for a moment.

"No one, Dee," Schloss shouted loudly down the row. What a fright he gave me. I struggled quickly into my shorts, and turned to him with a smile and a thankful nod.

"Much appreciated, Schloss."

"Not at all. To the pool then, Dee."

My laps were disturbed by the absence of "her." Rather than forgetting, I kept watch, glancing up on every turn (and frequently during the passages between) to see if she might be in the gallery "watching" (as she termed her surveillance). It was hard to forget the startling eyes, so blue above her blushing cheeks. I felt the other swimmers, their lapping wakes rocking me gently on my course. Pausing in the deep end I let go, bending toward the bottom. Then there was nothing, no one; only the aquatic clanking of valves and drain plates, the blue light wavering above me. Pigeons nested among the lattice-work, by the thick glass high above. I sank deeper and relaxed.

Sometimes the sky can be terrifying, as that afternoon, when clouds gathered and split, resolving into chasms, vertical canyons as rough and varied as rock. Walking toward the library, looking up, I felt I might fall into it. My fear was unreasonable, but I could not take my eyes away. Watching, I felt, was all that would save me. The force of my vision against the sky was all that kept me pinioned to the ground. Such thoughts cannot be reasoned with but merely shaken from the head like sleep, and I did that, gradually lowering my eyes along the delicate line of the library's spires, to the heavy building itself, and at last to my feet. It was nice to see them safe against the ground. I started forward again, toward my researches, and kept my view inward.

My accustomed spot for study was empty. It was a desk, large and wooden, in the upper reaches of the library's vaulted reading room. A procession of arches boosted the building's stone ceiling to unrivaled heights along its nave, chancel, and transepts. The library was enormous, lit through vaulting windows of colored glass. A slim balcony clung to the upper columns of the chancel, and there my desk could be found. It was reached by an unlikely series of narrow stair-ways hidden in the stone walls of the chamber. A clever network of pneumatic tubes allowed me to send messages directly to the circulation desk, from which point books and the occasional snack were delivered.

Fact and anecdote are the coin of the historian's realm. One chases after them everyday; dates and deeds are collected like butter-flies, or recorded, like birds whose single, unremarkable note is heard and cataloged. That day I wanted an incident, an exemplary case that could serve as the pretext for my investigation. Abbott made it clear he'd no patience for slouchers. I thought a précis could be set spinning, if only a spindle of fact were found on which to pin it.

An unlikely reference in Saunders's *Treatise on Theaters*[1] gave me what I was looking for. It was an opera house, attempted in the Dutch province of Groningen, in the 1680s. Built on boggy land in the great estuary of Den Dollard, it was either never completed or it was destroyed. It failed, in any case, and a "policy of assurance" (O'Donnel) was made good on. The reference gave me hope, and a mildewed box of documents from the Dutch filled things out. (After the war and the liberation of Holland, we received two troop vehicles full of boxed documents, junk really, from a province where most attics turned up papers as valuable or interesting—warrants, certificates, letters, and pronouncements, stored for three centuries in the *stadhuis* of Groningen. When Allied troups drove the Germans out, they sent the documents to Canada, a gift for the liberators; it came to us as part of a government deal involving wheat subsidies.)

I remembered a clutch of papers from an "Andries Verweerd" and made my way down to the microfiche to have a look. Indeed it *was* Verweerd, an inventor of sorts, who had some involvement with the construction of a *muziektheater,* and whose name appeared at the bottom of a document which I here paraphrase roughly as follows: In consequence to the signing of this certificate and the payment annually of a fee (here the figure is obscured) the safety and integrity of a theater for the presentation of musical entertainments to be built in Finsterwolde, as located and described herein, by Mr. Andries Verweerd acting for Mr. Alton Motley, an Englishman, is hereby guaranteed and insured by the estate of Mr. Johannes Drop with the promise to put all damages right promptly and without cost. Loss of any part or function shall be compensated by Mr. Drop in accordance with the figures inscribed herein, and blah, and blah blah, etc.

The certificate was signed and dated (17 November 1682) and no further documents, in that small sheaf, yielded information about the building or its history. A check of reference books confirmed that such a theater would have been the earliest opera house of any description in the Netherlands, and among the first in Northern Europe.

---

1. George Saunders, *A Treatise on Theaters* (London, 1790). (It was, in fact, a scribbled note someone made in the margins of p. 79, regarding the construction of an opera house which Saunders had failed to mention.)

Somehow it had disappeared. I was curious about the building's fate, but more, I thought the policy and its collection could anchor my project in a rich story.

It was night and the snow had begun again by the time I left the library for home. The streets were busy with students traveling in packs and many of them drunk or boisterous. My nostrils bristled, frozen by the cold air. Between low drifting clouds, the night could be seen, empty and black, punctuated by a few brilliant stars. I doubled up my coat, pulling it tight around my shoulders, and hurried past the shouting students.

The opera house of Andries Verweerd hovered before me, partly obscured by the imagined fog of a Dutch winter morning. Its skeletal frame of stone and timbers rose into the mists. Whatever could possess a man to begin such a project? In Utrecht, perhaps, or Antwerp. But in Finsterwolde? The town was nothing more than a row of houses clinging to the ridge of a sleeping dike. The sea came up that far, and farther, with each winter storm. Groningen, the nearest city of any size, could not have been expected to support such a venture. Certainly it was philanthropic, though all I knew of Venweerd told me he was not wealthy. At that time, only the Italians had designed *teatri dell'opera,* those expensive palaces that cities would soon wear as badges of sophistication. Was there any interest in Dutch opera? Was there any such thing?

Excepting the monstrous concrete towers erected for students by the university, our neighborhood presents a pretty sight to pedestrians coming down the hill. The rooftops, fairly even in height, are varied and chaotic in their materials and pitch, giving the impression of a crazy, lumped-up quilt laid over the sleeping valley. With snow the impression is trebled, and wisps of smoke from chimneys and pipes seem even more like the exhalations of some slumbering giant. My windows can be seen, and I like to leave the desk lamp on to give the impression (in case a burglar or thief is watching) of someone home, probably studying or in prayer. Also the cat likes the warmth. From halfway down the hill one is close enough to see her, a dark circle in the wash of yellow light. I enjoyed the fantasy, each evening, that I was a vagabond, cold and hungry, drawn by the beacon of soft light to that small apartment where Kitty lay. Will the door be open? If not, will the mysterious key fate has placed in my pocket fit? Abandoned and alone, I trudge downhill harboring a last desperate wish that I might be given entrance to that sacred, warm place. (And, of course, my wish was always granted.) She greeted me, as often, with a dead insect, dropped from her mouth and swatted across the floor. Nothing in the mail bore news of the dwarf, nor had any message been slipped under the door. I left my shoes by the bed, embarrassed by the stink, and went to the kitchen for some tea.

The carpenters were due the next morning, and I had the task of arranging the rooms so they could begin their work unimpeded. The foreman suggested I move all my furniture away from the walls, ("compacting" as it were), and I did this. The dresser and desk exhausted me. Carting the tea around, and stopping for long stretches to sketch some notes (re: my project—which is not to mention forty minutes, give or take, inspecting the odd figures my father carved on the backside of his desk), it was nearly midnight when I finished. Everything was in its new and proper place. Kitty had a great deal of work ahead, sniffing all the shifted furniture (checking on something), and I was famished. I gathered my pile of scribbled notes and the newspaper, slipped into my shoes, and made my way to the Eichelberger.

The snowbound walk was still busy with people, mostly patrons of the moviehouses just now letting out. Some ducked into the café, calling out orders for hot chocolate or coffee. Warm light spilled from the windows, and a pleasant blast of heat came from the door when I turned from the street and entered. Miss Eichelberger emerged from the kitchen cooing greetings in her rich baritone. She directed the chef with a wave of the hand to prepare my usual: toasted cheese sandwich and soup.

There were headlines about the police in the municipal section of the newspaper. I extracted the pages, folding them neatly for easy reading, and observed the blurry photo labeled "perpetrators." Seven or eight men gathered in the glare of the searchlights. Two helmeted sergeants and a detective in a trench coat faced off against them, wielding guns and badges. The entire scene was obscured by snow the choppers whipped up, and made blurry by the swiftness of the "perpetrators'" actions. A crowd could be seen in stark relief behind the scene, held back by policemen linking arms. A uniformed news team was visible, filming. The unruly crowd held scrawled signs of protest and wore the telltale fashions of the student left— oxymoronic fatigues, puffy flak jackets, and bedouin scarves. One boy, dressed in just a T-shirt and jeans, lay in the snow beside the detective. He appeared to be making snow angels. His pretty face was graced with a smile, and an empty gaze skyward. He couldn't have been a day over fifteen, so soft and girlish were his features. Because choppers blew snow in all directions but his, the whole scene appeared to pivot around him—black and white in the snow, arms and legs spread, making angels. It wasn't clear if he'd been arrested or was just lying there. So it was in the photo marked "perpetrators."

The article that accompanied it gave the following information:

Police last night arrested seven members of an organized drug ring alleged to be bringing two to three tons of opiates each year into the city. According to the police, the opiates, largely un- processed, have passed through the city's harbor in cargo con- tainers falsely registered with a Catholic relief organization. The deadly drugs, which police say command a street value of ten to fifteen million dollars each year, have been shipped under- cover as food and medical supplies, candles, robes, and 'pub- lished matter.'

While the arrests mark a significant victory in the three- year-long battle by police against the drug merchants, Senior Detective Allen 'Shark' Clausewitz reminded reporters that the shipments make up only a small portion of the drug trade passing annually through the city. 'We've seen drastic increases in the last year, in the area of narcotics, barbiturates, and opiates especially. Two tons is just the tip of the iceberg.' Clausewitz went on to explain that police efforts would be shifted onto the shadowy network of street dealers, delin- quents, and users that populate the areas around the harbor, and in the city's poorer neighborhoods. 'Kids on the streets are the real victims here,' Clausewitz explained, 'and the sooner we can get them into jail the sooner these big dealers will pull up and move on.'

School administrators and counselors from around the city echoed police concern about the drugs, calling perpetrators 'the lowest kind of scum . . . dealing death in a sleeping pill' to school-age children and others. Clausewitz cautioned citizens to keep an eye out for drug-users. 'If you see someone sleeping in a public place, someone who looks like they should be else-where, or nodding, as if they're unable to wake up, call the police immediately.' A special hot line has been created for call-in tips, and for teens seeking help and counseling. Police will be man-ning the hot line twenty-four hours a day.

The article struck me with its uselessness. What could I possibly do with such information, except be frightened by it? The detective's warnings stuck with me, pointing nowhere and everywhere. That night, alone in the silence, the sky empty of choppers and devoid of sound, I tossed in bed like a victim unable to find his own heartbeat. Hovering between sleep and waking I half-dreamed beating circles in the snow, whirling my arms to stay aloft above that boy making an-gels. He lay there in black and white, but alive and smiling up at me. The detectives were angels too or choristers in golden robes floating slightly off the ground, and I hovered among them, bending toward the boy.

The room, when I swam toward waking in the deep middle of the night, was closed in around me, all the furniture pushed in too tight. It was hard to breathe. I curled under my covers and turned toward the window, wanting at least the view out, but the view was empty. There was no illumination from the searchlights or the build-ings, which had either been turned off or were blocked by clouds. I saw nothing, and my dream kept returning, like ghosts swimming toward me through the black glass. Now the boy was larger, bigger than everything else, and the police were cowboys on a shirt he wore. It was a western shirt I had when I was little, summer blue with lariats and bucking broncos, and cool silver snaps that clicked shut instead of buttoning. It may have been me wearing the shirt, for I could feel the cold touch of the snaps up and down my belly, and the snug fit of the blue cloth where it crowded my armpits. My father dressed me in it on Saturdays when we'd go walking through fields to an orchard with horses tethered to the trees, two horses. At home he slipped my arms into the tiny shirt and then buttoned it by pressing his thumb against each snap in turn. I loved to feel him pressing me that way, one snap after another from my belly button on up to the top. I'm sure they weren't horses at all, but ponies, ponies nearly as tall as my father, and docile enough to take sugar from my hand each Saturday when I wore the soft blue shirt.

Such reveries were confined to my sleep, bordered by evening work and morning waking. Between, the night welcomed me like a deep blue pool, like boundless water connecting everything each to each. My body burned hotter in sleep. My thoughts traveled farther and at much greater speed. I didn't know what to do with it except try to remember, and note what I'd found. That night it was the metal snaps and my father.

FOUR

"SHE" MADE HER NEXT MOTIONS toward me the following day when a package arrived under my office door, slipped in among the usual thick submissions to *The Journal* (editorship of which had been thrown to me, like a gnawed bone to a dog, after the dismissal of Abbott's predecessor). I presumed it *was* a submission, albeit mystifying. The envelope bore the conventional markings: "attn.: The Editor" "S.A.S.E. Enclosed" "Fourth Class: Printed Matter," and etc., etc. Its format and size were correct. There was a title page with an epigraph:

OSCAR VEGA

Their understanding begins to swell, and the approaching tide will
shortly fill the reasonable shore, that now lies foul and muddy.

It was Shakespeare's *Tempest,* though I could not recall the lyric from Purcell's operatic version. Odd that he would leave out so fine a line as this one. In place of an author's name were initials, "F.Y.I."; and the promised S.A.S.E. was missing. These clues were not enough for me, and I took it in with the rest, intending to give them all a quick read before my afternoon lecture on Huygens. Who was Oscar Vega, I wondered, and why the absence of dates or some clever lengthy subtitle (as was conventional)?

It was not until several weeks had passed (bringing a handful more submissions), that the real authorship was revealed, and it emerged that "F.Y.I." was in fact "she." My failure to recognize her sooner can only be due to my solemn pledge, made to *The Journal*, to read objectively, with no care about authorship. It was in just such a frame of mind that I laid "F.Y.I."'s pages open before me and began to read the story of Oscar Vega. I include the text here entire, together with my admittedly naive notes scribbled that day, at the foot of the disturbing submission.

"By the fence of the harbor in the evening Oscar Vega stood, delicate as an angel, watching the lights of boats departing from the city. The cold evening came from the east. It settled over the buildings and hills,[1] and Oscar felt it coming down, damp and icy on his bare arms. Oscar was too young to work at the docks, but he liked to watch through the metal fence. Fifteen, he was lanky and graceful. His dark eyes were startling, and his wide mouth was usually left open, as though he were about to speak. The docksmen never noticed him, except when he fell asleep by their fence, wearied by the hour or the warmth of a fine spring sun. Today, before the cold came, Oscar[2] slept by a vent near the fence of the harbor and dreamt of airplanes and flowers—a wood and canvas biplane landing in a field of heather.

"The plane bounces along the dusty field, filling Oscar's nostrils with the smell of dirt and gasoline. It rumbles to a halt beside him, rattling, and Oscar waits. No pilot is aboard, and no passenger. The plane rumbles in place, empty and unwelcoming. Oscar notices the torn heather, the terrible mess that's been made. The field is barren, strewn with dry, dead flowers. He wants to pick them up, to gather them in his arms, but finds it is hard to move. The airplane holds his attention. Its impatience and vacancy feel like an accusation. Oscar ought to climb aboard but that too seems daunting. He is stuck, as if in a room with a dangerous animal. He can neither approach nor turn away.

1. This account is pleasingly accurate in its evocation of our city (particularly the phenomenon known locally as "the evening drop"). Though unconventional, this kind of narrative approach to history is experiencing something of a renaissance lately.

2. It is unclear at this point whether "Oscar" is a real person or merely a fictional device.

"Waking in the cold, Oscar remembered nothing of his dream. Brick dorries splintered crates under their metal wheels. Oscar listened to them snap and crack. He leaned into the box where he'd been sleeping, stretched some, and thought of dinner. A bright moon caught in clouds bruised the sky iron above the bay.[3] Oscar felt the bruise like an eye watching him. He got up in the snowy air and shivered hot and cold. Warm fingers ran along his skin. The bay was a wide back, the city its nape and neck. Oscar tucked his shirttails in and made his way along the harbor. It was almost seven. He would go to see the doctor.

"'Have you had any dinner?' the doctor asked. She always asked first if he'd eaten.

"'No.' The doctor turned from the desk and crouched by a small icebox. Oscar imagined their distance from the ground, seven stories, and felt the empty air below them. Cold and then warmth made his cheeks burn and blush. His soft flat nipples tingled and touched his cotton shirt. Oscar saw his heart beating, through the shirt, and pressed a finger to his navel, wanting to feel further inside. He didn't get very far. His belly button was too taut and shallow.[4]

"'Where have you been today?' she asked. Oscar knew he didn't have to answer or could lie. He always felt very happy sitting by her desk. He enjoyed the cramped, close room, and the tall window behind him. Snow blew against the black glass, tacking too soft to hear. The doctor was looking at him.

"'Today, Oscar. Where were you today?'

"'Was Jesus skinny, or really muscular and strong?' Oscar asked.

"'Why, Oscar? Why do you ask that?'

"'In some pictures He's thin and then sometimes He's big and strong. Why do they do that?'

"'Did you see pictures in school today?'

"'I didn't go to school.' Oscar blushed. He drew his knees up to his chest and held them, looking at the doctor over his clean blue jeans. The doctor gave him a stern look back. There were his arms, hands clasped together, and the divinity of his eyes. She was charmed by his

3. I have seen such a moon, especially common in winter.

4. A curious detail.

gesture. 'I saw the pictures at the museum,' Oscar explained through his legs. 'I woke up late.'

"A small plate of cheese and fruit sat on the desk between them. The doctor poured Oscar a glass of milk. 'Do you go there often?' she asked, settling back in her chair. The question made him blush more furiously. Oscar drank the milk and feigned relaxing. In fact, he went to the museum all too often. 'Well,' he stalled, fishing for an answer. 'Hardly.' The lie felt clumsy coming out. He took the plate of food and set it resting on his lap. Oscar was silent, and the doctor simply sat and looked at him. Her attention always pleased him, even when her questions made him blush.

"She took a book from behind her and placed it on top of the cluttered desk.

"'Don't you study paintings at school?' she asked. Oscar leaned forward, taking an apple, and looked at the big book. A puzzled woman took a letter from her maid in the cover painting. The maid had a superior look, and seemed to know everything.[5] Oscar ran his finger along the line of their arms.

"'Yeah,' he answered. 'There's pictures in the history book, and the library has big painting books, like this one.'

"'I'd like you to look at some of these.' She opened the book of paintings and pushed it toward him.

"Oscar could not read or write.[6] Though he never told the doctor, she knew this. It was part of his gift, she thought, his illiteracy. That lack gave rise to a remarkable sensitivity: because he could not read words, Oscar became a supremely gifted reader of the world. She used the paintings so he could keep his 'secret,' and because his gift for reading the paintings was so extraordinary. The book was called *The Golden Age of Dutch Art*. Below the title was a woman's name.[7] The snow was gentle now and the wind had stopped. Oscar

5. To judge by the book's title (below), possibly Vermeer's *The Mistress and her Maid* (1665).

6. A consummate turn in F.Y.I.'s allegory—history is illiterate. It cannot write itself, but must be made orderly and written by the historian/doctor.

7. A thorough search in the university's collection turned up four books with this title, none of them written by women. Inquiries to publishers turned up no reports of out-of-print editions.

looked away from the book to the buildings on the hills and the harbor lights. There were boats on the black water. The loading cranes
were still. Metal-caged street lamps made bright pools of light along
the fence and lit the falling snow. No one was out walking. Oscar
looked at the light of windows in buildings scattered over the hills
and imagined the scenes behind them. Someone was being hit with a
frying pan, no doubt. Surely a television was on. There were sleeping
bags and books, and probably an argument at a card table. There was
sex, and a boy sneaking through a door in his pajamas to touch someone else in the dark when they were both supposed to be sleeping.
Oscar took the book onto his lap, glancing at the pages flipping past.
There were churches with dogs in them[8] and drunks with rotting
teeth.[9] Women held babies by the fire and threw fishbones into the
flames.[10] He thought again of the boy sneaking into someone's bed.
Cotton sheets were cool on your skin, and then warm if you moved
your body around. Soldiers drove spikes through children and ripped
bellies open with swords,[11] or the children were fat and demonic, rich
laughing brats with black shoes and lace.[12] Oscar stopped at a pale
oval. In it a doctor[13] stood over a dead body. The arm was slit open.
The doctor stretched the muscles out, holding them tight with his
forceps. An audience had gathered beside him.[14] 'Tell me about that
one,' the doctor asked. Oscar stared at the pale green form. The heavy
chest had collapsed and the face was lifeless and waxen. The painter

8. Probably Saenredam or de Witte. though they're hardly alone in depicting church
interiors with dogs.

9. Jan Steen, of course, springs to mind, but as with the church dogs, the ubiquity of
this image in Dutch painting makes identification impossible.

10. Another common image; Steen is the most likely here.

11. The elder Brueghel was a master of this imagery, and scores of painters imitated
his style. Any of them (really the historians of their time, given the prevalence of
illiteracy) might have depicted such a scene. A popular volume on the period would
certainly feature Brueghel.

12. I'm unfamiliar with this image.

13. Again, the allegory of "the doctor." This meta-reference (doctors looking at
doctors) points up the modern historian's necessary concern with historiography.

14. Rembrandt's *Anatomy Lesson* of *Dr. Tulp* (1652). The original is rectangular.

had taken pains to fill each living man's eyes with sharp black pupils. The eyes of the corpse were empty and dull.

"'They cut his arm open,' Oscar said. 'I guess he's dead and this is like the autopsy or something.' The arm held his attention. 'Look.' Oscar held his own arm out and wiggled his fingers. A small ripple of muscles played across the forearm. 'I like how you can see inside him.'

"'Who are those men?' the doctor asked. She leaned closer to see the details. Oscar looked at the bearded faces and broad white collars. Their postures were strange, so they could all fit in the picture. The doctor stood apart from them, behind the cadaver.

"'They're not very interested in the guy's arm,' Oscar observed. 'They're all looking this way, like they'd gone hunting or something. Maybe they're the police and the dead guy's a murderer.'[15]

"'Is the doctor with the police?' The boy looked again, admiring the distance the doctor kept from the other men. He was the only one with a dignified posture, and he was much livelier. Like the maid on the cover, the doctor seemed to know everything.

"'No. He's a scientist I think, or an inventor. He's a lot smarter than them anyway. They're just standing around all proud because this guy's dead, you see. But the doctor there, he's like it's a new thing. Like it's all just started, all the new stuff he can find out from the body. The police think it's all over 'cause they killed the guy.'

"'How would you change the picture, if you got to paint it? Is there anything you'd want to change?' Oscar let the book rest in his lap. The doctor watched and waited, taking the empty plate from the desk and wiping it with a dirty cloth. She wouldn't have chosen the picture if she'd been asked. But that's why she never asked it of herself. Oscar always surprised her.

"'I'd get the police guys out of there. They're just show-offs anyway, and you can't see the body enough because of them. The guy

---

15. In fact the man on the table *was* a criminal (typically the source for most anatomists), but the other men were not the police. They were doctors. Oscar's confusion is understandable. Group portraits were usually commissioned by officials eager to have their profession memorialized. The group paid a fee and each person was portrayed, either in full face or profile, according to price. Dr. Nicholas Tulp, the surgeon here, commissioned this work, together with the onlookers, fellow members of the Guild of Surgeons (and not a far cry from the police).

should be alive, I think, and not so pale. That way he can watch the doctor. Like if the guy was able to be alive and see the arm parts and everything without passing out or whatever, 'cause the doctor's so smart and so good he can do it exactly right so the guy can watch. That'd be perfect, if you could clear out the dumb police and let the doctor and this guy find everything out from his body."[16]

What had at first seemed entirely unsuitable for *The Journal,* began to loom as a manifesto of sorts, a seminal essay which could mark the beginning of my stewardship by articulating a call for the "New Old Historiography" (as I thought I might call it). I put my thoughts down on paper and set them aside in a freshly penned folder ("The N.O.H."), together with the one existing "chapter" of F.Y.I.'s essays. Never one to rush, I thought it best to let the idea stew awhile before announcing it to Abbott, or anyone else.

16. The commentary on historiography is, by now, unmistakable. A doctor inspecting a corpse symbolizes (albeit naively) the Positivist view. as it developed in the nineteenth century. It is impossible today to embrace the notion that the soulless corpse contains all the information we need to understand the life of the body now dead. Perhaps the image is well chosen: the doctor suffers a similar frustration, searching in the dead remains for some elusive clue. Whether the methods of the doctor offer an appropriate prescription for the historian is open to debate. Oscar articulates the dream of many in my field when he suggests the body should be alive, guiding the doctor and sharing each new discovery. His prescription is a call, a manifesto of sorts, announcing a new historiography reuniting the doctor with his patient, the historian with the past. But who are the police?

-port. His cru-el-ty does tread On or-phan's ten-der breast _____ and bro-thers dead.

Can Heav'n per - mit such crimes should be At - tend - ed with fe - li - ci-ty? No! ty - rants their

No! ty - rants their

scep - tres un - ea - si - ly wear, In the midst of their guards their con - scien - ces fear.

scep - tres un - ea - si - ly wear, In the midst of their guards their con - scien - ces fear.

49

* * *

My jambs and window frames had been laid bare by the workmen, leaving the apartment looking rather like a skeleton, or a dental patient with lips drawn back and gums bared. The jawbone protrudes in lumps and bumps beneath the pink glistening skin. White teeth break from the gum, crowding close into the warm, moist cavity. You can imagine what it was like. My windows and door were surgical sights. "Terminal weakness uncovered in frames," a scribbled note informed me. "Will return in the morning." The workmen left piles of sawdust like carpenter ants, and carelessly failed to cover my books. I took it upon myself to drape heavy tarps over the dresser and shelves, and swept up the conical piles with a broom.

Flyers had been slipped under the door with the day's mail ("Stay Alert!" they read in bright green letters. "A message from your police.") It was part of the antidrug campaign I had been reading about. I threw them in the trash and made coffee, settling in for an afternoon with my project. Further research (and no small amount of conjecture) produced the following pages for Abbott (and, I dreamed, his "agent"):

The History of Insurance   Nicholas Dee

The History of Insurance: The Insurance of History

A Historical Inquiry by Professor Dr. Nicholas Dee, B.A., M.A., Ph.D.(Provisional Outline—Eyes Only!)

I. THE BEST OF TIMES, THE WORST OF TIMES
The development of Insurance (its modern practice, as we know it today) was directly tied to the developments in mathematics and physics known commonly as the Newtonian Revolution. These foundations of modern science in Europe and the West offered a mathematical description of events that became an instrument for control and the mitigation of loss. Among these were the actuarial tables and probability theorems. Descartes, Leibnitz, Pascal, Newton—the fathers of modern physics—were thus midwives to the birth

The History of Insurance   Nicholas Dee

of insurance. While the work (and worldview) of these men
gave us the blessings of a fully functioning system of
insurance, they also made possible the modern constellation of a mechanistic physics with a barren, dualistic
metaphysics and the expansionist economy of world capitalism with its tendency toward a totalizing police function.
Thus it was the "best o' times and the worst o' times,"
positive- and negativewise, and blah, blah, blah.

   What else developed at this time? Maps, Dutch still
life and landscape painting, physics, first world—economy
of colonial exploitation, and etc., etc. . . . *Anatomy Lesson of Dr. Tulp*? Coffee?—Lloyd's of London, history reminds us, began as a coffeehouse in the seventeenth century.
Patrons drank the black drink thick as syrup from heavy
porcelain cups and gambled all day long. It evolved quite
naturally into an insurance house, one of the first and
most famous. Boyle, Newton, and other alchemists of the
era gathered at the nearby Athenium every day, drinking
numberless rounds of the same heavy black drink until their
hands jittered and they could not halt their speech. Like
Lloyd's, this gathering became an "insurance" firm of sorts,
the Royal Society. Who can say what part caffeine played
in propelling us toward a mechanistic universe in which
the vagaries of necessity and chance could be profitably
bet upon, that is, insured against? Explore links.

II. "LOOMINGS"

The Exemplary Case: The Opera House of Alton Motley
Beyond Holland's grim northeastern bogs (so thick with water
and peat, tangled brush and mud, no mapping was possible
until well into the nineteenth century), beyond the strips
of cultivated farm, hewn from bogs by drainage and guile
. . . the land gives up again to the ocean at Den Dollard,
a shallow fetid estuary at the mouth of the river Eems.

The History of Insurance   Nicholas Dee

Towns are scattered along the coast, built behind dikes
which block the sea. Each generation extends further into
the sea, reclaiming another crescent of land from the curving
shore. Many winter storms breach the dikes, inundating towns
and killing hundreds.

Rising from the mud and grass of the shallow marsh, a
monstrous, skeletal frame extends into the fog. Its tim-
bered pinnacles scrape the low gray clouds, while the incoming tide ripples against its stone foundations.

The Policy of Insurance:
Working under instructions from Alton Motley (his patron
and benefactor), Andries Verweerd secures a "policy of
assurance" (O'Donnel) for the "great and glorious endeavour." The policy is offered by Johannes Drop, a wealthy
merchant with a monopoly on Spanish salt shipments in parts
of the Baltic. Drop, a clever humanist, is fascinated by
the new sciences, eager to turn knowledge into profit, a
correspondent of Huygens; wife, mistress, etc., drinks to
excess. Insurance? Nature of Insurance? (Insurance of Nature?) Describe his houses.

(Their story, thus introduced, will unfold as the spine
of the book throughout.)

III. COME LET ME CLUTCH THEE
The practice of insurance as a manifestation of "Dutchness."
Geography and the physical environment, one could
argue, are the irreducible facts around which human activity must arrange itself. Whatever we endeavor to build
or practice must answer, finally, to the reality of the
weather and land on which we live. Taking this geological
or meteorological determinism as a starting point, Dutch
culture can be traced to the precarious geological base
on which the country rests. The Netherlands is a collec-

The History of Insurance   Nicholas Dee

tion, really, of dry islands hewn from swamps by hard labor.
The sea has repeatedly claimed great chunks of it. Dutch
resilience, their appetite for practicality and sensible
planning, their clever facility for juggling losses and
gains, derive, perhaps, from this fact of nature. These
are precisely the qualities that lie at the heart of the
practice of insurance.

In Dutch history, where are the forefathers of modern
insurance? Andries Vierlingh, dikemaster to William the
Silent? Simon Stevin, mathematician and engineer? Gerard
Mercator, hermetist and mapmaker? Try Vierlingh, *Tractaet
Van Dijkagie*, 1582.

IV. INSURANCE: THE MODERN ERA
Brief History of the practice of insurance since 1690. (Pending further research.)

It all seemed solid enough; and "sample chapters" aside, it gave me
confidence and something to offer Abbott when we met again on
Friday. I put the pages together in a folder, and turned the desk lamp
off. The apartment was a shambles.

Night had fallen, and my room was dreary, shrouded in tarps.
Light from the street made queer shadows on the ceiling. Evidently
the window glass was flawed. It was imperceptible to the naked eye
looking out on a normal day, but magnified and made grotesque by
the garish yellow street lights shining back at night. There were
ghosts in the shadowy forms above me. They shuddered with life
whenever the wind would rise and make the light posts tremble.
There might have been vandals manhandling them, or a light crew
at work, but I took the pitching and rocking to be the fault of the
wind, and I heard it, whistling between buildings. A tiny, clear bell
sounded, delicate as the phantoms on my ceiling, and repeated itself, three, four. Was I drifting? Where was the invisible sound coming from? Seven, eight, I scrambled from the bed and pulled the desk

drawer open. It was the watch "she" gave me, still running and now ringing ten (though I could not remember it announcing any other hour before). It was ten. Someone was knocking at the door.

I pulled my robe tight, and made my way past the workman's tools to answer it. "Yes, who is it?"

"Police News Team, sir," a pleasant man's voice answered. "We're here to check on your subscription." I opened the door a crack, and had a look at him. He was a tall man in a clean blue uniform, sporting the insignia of the Police News Team on his sleeve. "To Protect and Inform," the badge said.

"My subscription?"

"That's right," he answered, checking a list. "Are you wired for cable?"

"Isn't it a little late, uh, Officer? I mean for a door-to-door."

He smiled sheepishly. "Well, yes, it is getting on, Mister, is it?"

"Professor. Professor Dee."

"Professor Dee." We shook hands. "But access to the building has been difficult you see, and we were eager to catch you when we could."

"I see." Two chairs, my only two chairs, were empty and stacked by the door. I set them up and invited the officer in. "Please, sit." I gestured. "I'm afraid I don't even have a television." I turned the bedside lamp on.

"Well, Professor, there you go. It's a good thing I made the extra effort, then, isn't it?"

"I'm really not very interested in it. I have a lot of work to do, and very little time for entertainments." The kind blue man shifted in his seat, nodding. The apartment seemed especially dreary and undone with a visitor in it.

"I'm sure you're right, Professor, and you'll be glad to know I've not climbed the steep flights of stairs to bother you with frivolous entertainments. I am, as you can see"—here he gestured to his uniform—"with the Police News Team. I'm here to hook you into an information system which could save your life." He paused for effect. "You've probably seen us working, on the streets, at crime scenes. We're out there covering it all."

"Yes," I agreed. "I've seen several actions, and of course the choppers."

"That's right. The choppers are our swiftest, most effective tool."
He said it proudly. "Between them and the ground crews we can offer
the most penetrating coverage of the city. Anywhere, any time."

"I can't see why I'd want such a program broadcast into my
home, Officer." Even now the swallowed screams of violence could
be heard, drifting up from the streets.

"The program gives you twenty-four-hour access, Mr. Dee."

I shivered at the very thought. "It's disturbing enough to have the
neighborhood taken over by this sort of nonstop thievery. I certainly
wouldn't want to spend my time sitting here at home, monitoring it all."
I had little interest in his service, and was about to tell him so. The concerned officer noticed my tone and stalled me with the rest of his pitch.

"I guess I've not made it clear exactly what the Police News Team
is offering you, Mr. Dee, and if I may . . . " He shifted again in his chair,
and cleared his throat. "We broadcast encapsulations created from live
footage to show the average citizen real crime, and what he or she can
do to spot it. This isn't some sort of unedited surveillance, Mr. Dee,
but carefully crafted stories made useful and comprehensible for the
average citizen. You know as well as I that the honest citizen has a great
deal of trouble reading the chaos of strange behaviors, solicitations, and
weird drug effects that assault us every day. There are some things that
only the trained eye can see clearly, and that is our function. The Police
News Team looks at the city through a trained eye, and by watching,
you can see it too. It's probably the most effective crime-fighting tool
we have. Taking the policeman's point of view helps clarify things. I
think you'd not feel so queasy, Mr. Dee, about the streets out there, if
you had this service brought into your home." I paused and watched
him wind down for a moment. The cat cowered under the desk, upset
by our strange visitor.

"And do you also publish books?"

"We have writers, young novelists mostly, but their work is simply an adjunct to the broadcasts."

"I'm not sure I get it, exactly, Officer. You have writers, or was
it editors you said, clarify the crimes?"

"Well, the stories sort of write themselves. We edit and comment on the footage. Rather like annotation," he ventured. "Or foot-
noting, Professor, illuminating the text, as it were."

"So, you edit."

"That's right."

"Leaving out the confusing parts." My visitor put his hand to his hip, and lowered his stare.

"I see what you're driving at, Professor, and I can assure you the police and news are fully commited to complete disclosure. The modern police force has no secrets, Mr. Dee." He'd become a bit overheated.

"Of course they don't." I smiled, weakly, and fiddled with my robe.

"To Protect and Inform," he recited, indicating the motto on his sergeant's patch. "Useful information is the policeman's most powerful tool." He nodded emphatically.

"Yes. I, I sometimes share that, uh, belief."

"Of course you do, Professor. The university is a partner in our efforts."

"That's right. And, as a, a professor, I feel my, uhm, training, my university training, has given me enough tools, albeit primitive ones, to help me through these troubling times."

"I think it's hardly an adequate substitute for the police and news programs." He shook his head.

"Perhaps so." I got up from my chair, indicating that he do the same. "I'll just have to rely on it, Officer, because I'm in no position to start in with so far reaching, and, uh, total a program as yours." I saw him to the door. He handed me a card.

"Anytime, Mr. Dee. Night or day."

My unexpected visitor disturbed me with his information. I found myself unable to sleep now, tossing and turning with worry about the treacherous currents through which my life was taking me. So many possible worlds had opened up. I had begun to lose myself, ever so slightly, in the handful of stories my life was generating: the opera house of Alton Motley beckoned me; the outline loomed like a familiar portal through which I might soon pass. I was eager. It was why I loved research: this promised disappearance into a rich and distant life. Memories of my father were gathering thick and fast. At night, especially, they'd begun to coalesce, making a world as compelling as Alton Motley's. There was no outline, but the world of my father seemed total when I slept. And what of that woman, "she," and the mysteries of our new chairman, and "Oscar Vega"? Alive in the middle, I kept silent and observed the conduct of my researches into each of them.

The next day's dawn was a cruddy, muted thing marked more by the black overcoats of workers crowding along the narrow streets than by any discernible increase of light in the sky. I scuttled through the last day of classes like a frightened crab, terse and distracted (and made doubly anxious by the continued absence of "she" from the pool and my grasp). By late afternoon my anxieties had exhausted me. I crept home avoiding the familiar faces of students wanting a farewell chat before leaving.

I cannot blame the day, for it was typical. Something in my life had delivered me to a position of risk where every intrusion, even the unremarkable weather, touched me like violence. I hurried home to find the apartment further stripped, with just a small island of safety in the middle where all my furniture was gathered. "Secure doors and window frames," the foreman's note said, "are no guarantee if the walls in which they hang are weak. Will strip completely by Thursday." I threw the heavy bolt closed, tossed my papers onto the desk, and climbed into bed. I'd be among friends that evening, and until that time I was not leaving the safety of my covers.

THE TEMPEST.

AIR. *(Bass)* ARISE, YE SUBTERRANEAN WINDS.

Henry Purcell.

A - rise, a - rise, ye sub - - - - - - -

- - - - - - - ter - ra - nean winds,

A-rise, a-rise, ye sub- - - - - - - - - - - -ter-ra-nean winds, More to dis-tract their guil-ty

59

60

fix'd, all, all but the fix'd_____ and

so _ _ _ _ _ lid cen - tre shake;

Comedrive these

61

62

FIVE

Reading is an act of engagement, and of control.

—John Lewis Dee[1]

VALLEY SCHOOL ASIDE, the Weathereds had done quite well. Their large townhouse was reached easily by a walk across campus to the quiet enclave of older houses where they lived. The weather had thickened while I slept, and snow returned in earnest. It fell evenly in the dusk, lightly dusting my shoulders and hat. The small lane wound away from the street, too narrow for cars, and I entered in, passing the pretty gas lamps. I quickly found number 7. Holly and pine framed the door, red berries bright against the green. A servant answered (which was unexpected) and took my "things."

The room was already busy with people. It was some comfort to feel the door close behind me, and recognize the faces filling the room. Freddy and Earl were there, and their families. The secretaries too, gathered around the hors d'oeuvres. Was our department so big? There seemed to be at least ten or twelve more couples, and a gaggle of kids tumbling underfoot.

"Dee." Abbott called out, announcing my arrival to all within earshot. "Dee, Dee. So glad you're here." He embraced my hand. "Is it just you, alone then?" He looked solicitously over my shoulder. Abbott

---

1. John Lewis Dee, *Miscellaneous Papers*, undated.

couldn't keep still. He swiveled and danced as he looked, tipping up on toe-points as if it were difficult for him to see. I smiled dumbly.

"Amelia," Abbott now called, looking back into the throng. Our friend Dee has arrived." My heart fluttered. Abbott's wife. Wasn't she a doctor, or a therapist did he say? Perhaps she could be a steadying force on this difficult day. All around the room conversations paused, interrupted by Abbott's energetic calling of my name, and then they resumed. I looked but could not see her. Abbott picked at my lapel, straightening the fold, and cleared away some lint. I looked nervously past him, still searching the floor. "We'll just go in, shall we?" he suggested, leading me by the arm. "Drink?"

The furniture was all shifted to the perimeter. Two strong tables stood by the windows, one with a punch bowl and liquor, the other with food—shrimp and thin-sliced meats, cheesy canapés, fresh vegetables and dip. I took a small, crustless sandwich off a crowded tray, sad that it was cucumber and butter. Had they lived in Britain? I'd forgotten Abbott's specialty. Was it the Restoration? Children played among the table legs, fencing with carrot sticks. The men were gathered in a tight knot by the punch bowl, talking sports no doubt. Perhaps she'd left already, too tired to sparkle the entire evening, away to bed for a nap. Sickened, perhaps, by a bad shrimp. Abbott disappeared into the crowd, searching.

"Evening, Mr. Dee." It was Miss Benifica, in charge of copies.

"Good evening, Miss Benifica. Or may I call you Rose?" She giggled at the informality.

"Of course, Nicholas. You may call me whatever you like."

"Have you come alone tonight?"

"No, I haven't. I've brought a lady friend. From my dance class." She always had such vim, and a strong backbone. I often enjoyed a secret pleasure, watching her "handle" those machines in the office next to mine.

"Ballet?"

"Actually, dear, it's polka. I'd love it if you joined us sometime. The steps are very easy, and . . ."

"Dee." It was Abbott. "Here she is."

I excused myself to Rose and turned. The little knot of men opened up, tall somber figures arrayed like fences. The glowing red tips of their lit cigars hung from their bearded faces, pointing down into the center of the circle. And there in the middle stood a boy. Francis. I recognized him from the photo. His soft young face blushed bright below his dark eyes and a thick shock of brown hair. Healthy and angular, he bore no resemblance to his father.

"Francis," Abbott exclaimed, surprised to find the embarrassed child standing there at the center of all attention. "Where's your mother?"

The boy seemed to be suppressing giggles. He looked around at the circle of glowering men, their glowing wands pointed toward him. "I think she's gone. She was here just a second ago."

"And what are you doing with that drink?" Abbott passed deftly from one parental concern to the next.

"It's her gin," Francis explained. "I'm holding it for her."

"Damn it all. That woman's always giving the boy liquor." Abbott strode forward and took the perspiring glass from his son's hand. "Find your mother and bring her back here. Tell her Dee is eager to meet."

"She's not feeling well. She asked that I meet him for her." Francis held his arm out stiffly, as instructed. He was a charmingly awkward boy, just at that age where the hands and feet are too big and the body has begun growing in its slender frame.

"Very pleased," I said sincerely. I stepped up and took his hand. Francis blushed again, smiling.

"May I go play in the snow after I look for her?" he asked, imploring with his eyes. Nervous pony; he seemed to be almost prancing already. "She said I could. Michael and David already got to go out." Indeed the other children could be seen, not yet "out," but already digging woolens and hats from a big wooden box, tugging at mufflers and gloves. Abbott released him with instructions to carry his search throughout the house before adjourning to the snow.

"Lovely boy, Abbott. I had no idea you'd been married that long." Children were my favorite feature of departmental gatherings.

"Francis is twelve," Abbott reminded me, washing the thought down with a drink, as if it were trouble, "but he's not mine, Dee. He's Amelia's. Some mysterious beau in her past. I got them both, a little more than a year ago."

"You've met his father?"

"No, Dee, I haven't." Evidently this was a sore point. "There is a great deal about my little Amelia that remains unknown to me. I think that's why she s so fascinating; her past is a total mystery. Francis is one of the few visible clues."

The boy could be seen rushing into the vestibule. His pals were still pulling on their woolens, almost bundled for their run in the snow. He'd lost little time in the search, evidently unsuccessful. I let Abbott drift away to the drinks again, and watched the three boys tumble out the door and into the falling snow. The uneven light of dusk hung over the city. I sat down by the broad windows of the children's playroom and looked out into it. There was Francis, and his two friends; small dark figures rolling on the white lawn. The trail of their disturbances could be seen leading away from the door, out into the storm.

It mimicked a picture I have of my grandfather's land under a heavy snow. It was once a farm (though my grandfather let it all go fallow). The picture shows the long flat field that rolled down to the riverbank behind the house. The field is white and featureless, and the river is a wide black ribbon across the top. Some tall trees laced with snow are silhouetted against it. My father and his grandfather have made a trail trudging to the middle of the field where they're a dark blur. Only their feet are clear and solid. They must have been throwing snowballs. The wool trousers my father wore were the same that I wore, with small metal buckles at the bottom of the pant leg for keeping the snow out.

Why wasn't I out there now? Cold air bright against my face, jostling in the snow, a trip and fall down the long rolling hillside. The horizon disappears in degrees of gray. I'd wrap strong arms around Francis, taking him down in a tug, and we'd roll and roll through the quiet soft cold. The only noise our squeals and laughter; the bright red warmth of our faces the only heat. Down the long white hill into the diminishing light. We'd disappear in the pale dusk and roll to a stop against some tree, its branches shaking heavy snow down upon us. And then it would be silent. Flakes simply falling against our faces. When do the single ones come clear in the dimming sky? And Francis, bright blushing cheeks damp with sweat, his mouth open, pink tongue touching them as they fall. A few catch in the lashes, linger, then melt.

Our breath, in clouds, disappearing into gray. What keeps me here, sitting behind the glass watching him?

The reverie left no room for argument. Like my vertigo beneath the parting clouds, or today's agitations, I could only shake it from my head, take a deep breath, and focus elsewhere. Abbott's doorjambs seemed secure. I noticed the brass-plated locks, and the doubled glass of his windows. There must be a key somewhere, hidden, for the inevitable emergency. I can't imagine the house could be broken into. I made a mental note to ask Abbott for the name of his carpenter, in case the disturbingly thorough team I'd hired failed to finish the job properly. There was no reason for me to stay. Mrs. Weathered had disappeared and Abbott was leading songs by the piano. The whole group gathered around him at the far end of the front room, and I took the opportunity to sneak away to the vestibule and my hat and coat. I slipped the small envelope with my "outline" into Abbott's pocket, found the door and left.

THE TEMPEST.   ACT III.   Henry Purcell.

SONG (Ariel) and CHORUS. COME UNTO THESE YELLOW SANDS.

yel - - - - - low sands And there take hands; there take hands; Foot it feat - ly

here and there And let the rest the cho - rus bear.

Violins.

CHORUS.
Soprano.
Hark! hark! the watch - dogs bark,
Alto.
Hark! hark! the watch - dogs bark,
Tenor.
Hark! hark! the watch - dogs bark,
Bass.
Hark! hark! the watch - dogs bark,

Hark! hark! I hear the strain of Chan - ti - clere, Hark! hark! I hear the strain of Chan - ti - clere.
Hark! hark! I hear the strain of Chan - ti - clere, Hark! hark! I hear the strain of Chan - ti - clere.
Hark! hark! I hear the strain of Chan - ti - clere, Hark! hark! I hear the strain of Chan - ti - clere.
Hark! hark! I hear the strain of Chan - ti - clere, Hark! hark! I hear the strain of Chan - ti - clere.

68

MY FATHER GREW UP by a river on land his grandfather owned. It had been a farm when he got it, but Alberon Dee (my great-grandfather) hated farming and wanted the land for a garden. Not a vegetable garden, or simple flowers, but a topiary garden of sculpted hedges, mazes, and mechanical statuary. It was his obsession, and he pursued it all his life.

My father and grandfather were both born and raised there, in an elaborate stone house of Alberon's design. It's gone now; I've only seen it in photos. Even in my grandfather's time it was collapsing. Heavy parapets had fallen; exterior stairways settled, missing their marks by one or two feet. It's disappeared in pieces since then, a scavenging ground for builders and the curious. I never wanted to go see it, and I never did.

The garden has disappeared too, lost to nature and the river floods. It was an elaborate maze, a work of art covering nearly twenty acres by the time of Alberon's death. I've seen the plans, the etchings of the gardens in Heidelberg after which he'd modeled it. It was a life's work, painstakingly planned for thirty years (when the need of money kept him tied to farming) and carried out over his last twenty-five years. He lived, that fruitful quarter-century, off the fortune of his son Morris.

Alberon thought of his son as an investment, a property to be improved by education and feeding so he might ultimately bring high returns in the form of an independent income. His wife Elizabeth had other ideas, but Alberon's focus was so coldly utilitarian he drove the boy from home at the earliest possible date. The lack of warmth was mutual. Morris hated his father's oddness, and despised the nonsense and mystery of his obsessions. He loved straightforward work. He looked for clear problems and satisfied himself by solving them directly. Morris Dee fled from home at the age of seventeen, tired of Alberon's musings about nature and the plants, and joined a company of men working the railroads m Montana. By twenty he had a claim to land near Butte, and by twenty-five he'd returned to his father's farm as the owner and operator of Dee Metals, Inc. He was an enormously wealthy man.

His bitterness at his father wasn't gone. Rather, it was transformed into a naive, overbearing boisterousness, an inexhaustible flow of gifts, advice, and projects. He would flood the archaic inefficiencies of his father with an ocean of good works, done sensibly by a man of means. To begin, he moved back home and started renovations. The failing parapets came down. The stairs were put right. Pocked walls of stone were stripped and refitted with a fine gray slate brought in from New England.

It was all a matter of indifference to Alberon. So long as he was left alone with the garden the rest of the world could go to hell. With Morris home Elizabeth would be happy, and the house would be taken care of without the need for farming or an income. A small stipend on the side was hardly too much to ask from a "man of means," nor the nominal cost of keeping the garden. Only one piece was missing. Morris, still ignorant of the larger wheels within which his life turned, happily provided it: John Lewis Dee, his only son, and my father, was born on the eighteenth of June, 1925.

Alberon Dee took possession of the boy within a few weeks of his birth. Sonia, the boy's mother, welcomed the intrusion, eager to bring the boy up far from Morris's gross oafishness. Sonia despised her husband, almost as much as she loved his wealth. She would suffer him so long as she had children to raise or the need of his support. She and Alberon took to each other warmly.

It is unclear whether my grandfather, Morris Dee, ever noticed the many ways in which his son was kept from him. He never became close with John, nor felt he understood him. He might have dismissed it as a fact of fatherhood, no stranger, really, than the distance that always separated him from his own father. There were, as well, some scenes—bursts of temper or frustration when he was asked to pay for elaborate summer travels that took Sonia and John away for weeks without him. The enormity of the garden was also beginning to bother him. But Morris managed to obscure these complicated moments of insight under a thrilling avalanche of business and civic projects. John Dee grew up unaware of any special link to him. He regarded Morris as most boys would regard the landlord or the school principal.

John Dee never went to school. His days were spent with Alberon studying or at work in the garden. It was a demanding regimen. The garden required far more than a simple knowledge of horticulture. An elaborate science of mathematics and perspective was employed in the planning of the grounds. Aside from basic proportions and the Golden Mean, John Dee learned about illusionistic perspectives and the mathematics of flow. The garden had an underground system of irrigation which functioned without motors. Most importantly, it was populated by mechanical statuary: articulating figures from history; small metal birds which sang and fluttered; false fires. Alberon found most of the originals in seventeenth century engravings from the printshop of Johannes de Bry. A volume by Matthäus Merian kept him occupied in calculations and castings for almost fifteen years.

Alberon hoped that the boy would grow up to continue his work. He conducted John's education with great care and thoroughness, preparing him solely for this task. It's no wonder my father became a historian, unequipped as he was for anything else.

Alberon Dee asked to be buried in the garden when he died. I've heard the story from my father many times. His grandfather had an uncanny ability to anticipate events, changes of the weather, even sickness or accidents. One March afternoon, when my father was sixteen, he came into the big shed by the garden and found Alberon bent over a piece of paper knocking the stubborn end of a fountain pen against the wooden table. He did a lot of work in the shed. Cuttings, welding broken pipes, sketching out plans on paper or in his head. But he never wrote there. In fact, my father told me, he could barely write or read at all. His plans were drawn beautifully, the distances measured and marked in numbers. Where the name of a plant or piece of statuary might be scribbled, the marks were agonized and crude. That effort alone might take Alberon several hours. My father looked that day, and saw a few painfully scrawled sentences.

The will said two things. He asked to be buried in the garden, at the feet of Diogenes and his dogs. Alberon specified a depth and prohibited the use of a coffin. He wanted to enter the earth as directly as possible. And in his last laborious sentence, Alberon asked that the garden be given to John Dee, and that John keep it and nurture it in perpetuity. Morris Dee violated the first request, and my father failed to honor the second.

The funeral was held in the capital, in a city Alberon had avoided for the last twenty years of his life. A route was cleared and a procession held. Morris insisted that his father be treated as an important civic luminary, and he had enough money to make that happen.

I imagine my great-grandfather's slow dissolution within the unwanted ebony coffin whenever I view a garden where the fresh earth has been overturned. I imagine he suffered, damned by his son to rot alone until the distant day when insects worked their way through the hard wood and began the long task of carrying him back into the earth. My father's betrayal was the lesser, I still believe. The garden's descent into chaos was a kind of progress Alberon Dee could have appreciated and blessed. I don't think he really believed the garden would survive him; only that it would not become the property of his son and be tidied up into a broad lawn suitable for football.

My father said he couldn't cry at the funeral. He was unable to connect the black charade with the old man he was told lay inside the box. He cried at home in the garden, sitting near Diogenes. He sat through a dark evening of rain, pressing the ground, and the small hidden plate which triggered movements of Diogenes's head and hand. A light pressure made his head turn, just so, and his hand lift toward you. My father said he sat there, Diogenes turning toward him over and over, the soft rain dripping off the metal brow, running wet along the fine, straight nose, until the dusk became too dark and he could not see. He knew, had always known, he wouldn't keep the garden after his grandfather died. He left it that night, tired and cold, and let it all go to rot.

Morris endured John for another year, then bought him a Harvard education; it was there he began writing the papers that became books, and later brought him such renown. He never took me or my mother to see his home by the river, and I never asked to go.

SEVEN

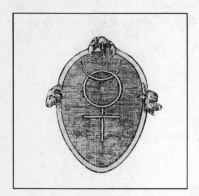

THE DESK WAS BACKED UP to the bed now, to save space and keep everything clear of the walls. Where they'd torn up the floor the workmen left planks to walk on. At night from my bed it seemed as if I'd been set floating, broken boards and spars awash in the black water around me; my bed was a raft on open seas with no stars overhead for navigation. Very late, touching my chest where my heart beat, I listened to the choppers landing and taking off from the police tower. The strange marks carved into the desk hovered near enough to touch, and I did, running my fingers along the familiar figure: Dee's Monad, a "philosopher's stone" of sorts, a mark inscribed by the sixteenth-century magus John Dee (not my father, but the object of my father's researches). The mark was made to—how absurd it sounds in these pinched and cynical times—conjure all knowledge. I felt it, carved on the back of my father's desk in chains. Even in the dark I recognized the simple shape by touch, like braille:

Like the twelve-tone staff, the mark was made to contain a kind of music, a universal harmony Dee believed lay dormant in the lines and which he hoped to unlock by assiduous study of the Monad itself. The "musical" pattern of all phenomena could be revealed with this simple key. Knowledge and power were caught in the mark; the problem was how to read it. How poignantly human Dee was, presuming to conjure wisdom in a simple mark made by hand. Through study of the Monad, Dee believed, musicians would perceive celestial harmonies, without listening; astronomers would observe the intricacies of the heavens, looking only at the page; optics, hydraulics, and the transmutation of lead into gold were all written within the shape of the Monad.

The component parts were rigorously geometric. The circle, cross, curves, and straight lines were composed in exact proportion. Though Dee was not specific about the decoding of the Monad, he was exact about its measure. When drawn according to his instructions, the figure is an amalgam of older "hieroglyphs" important to the hermetists. Symbols for the sun, the moon, and mercury, together with astrological signs, such as that for Aries, co-inhabit the Monad with the Christian cross, the numbers 2, 3, 4, 5, 7, 8, and 10, and the alchemical mark for gold. The simple dot at the center of the circle is both the earth around which everything rotates and it is man, the microcosm, containing in miniature all that exists in the greater macrocosm around him. Liss has even suggested it is the ineffable "inner Monad," at once primary and unreadable.[1]

My father was fascinated with Dee, and with the concentrated symbol of the Monad. I think the arrogance impressed him. And the faith that rigorous study of a symbolic system (even one so boldly simple as Dee's) would reveal some wisdom about the world. All my father's scraps and notes were thick with drawn symbols— Monads, chemical and astrological signs, drawn codes for mapping. The proliferation of graphics was what delighted him in the sixteenth and seventeenth century texts to which he kept returning. He kept Matthäus Merian (the volume his grandfather gave him) open on

1. Terry Allen Liss, *Magic and Science in the Writings of John Dee.* Thesis, for the Master of Arts in History, University of Washington, 1974.

his desk at home. When I was bold or lonely, and still a little boy, I would insist he stop his work and sit with me to look at the pictures. The memory came to me, clearly, through my fingers on the carved desk, as if by reading the shape of the Monad I'd read this recollection. I rolled over in bed, closer to the big carved board, and closed my eyes again.

The heavy beating of choppers surged suddenly; they were coming down over the hill. The floodlights filled the street, wrapping the desk in a geometry of shadows. Gouges and pinpricks loomed like craters in the harsh light. Whatever they were looking for was silent or inaudible beneath the thrumming blades. I looked out, staying low in my bed, and saw nothing but the night air full of light. The choppers were too high, hovering, and the buildings and downtown were obliterated by the bright floods. Was it drugs? Or just routine? The choppers drew away higher and higher, and the light widened and dimmed, until it was dark again and my bed was a raft on the cluttered sea. I left my hand touching the rough, worn carvings, pulled my leg up over a pillow, and fell again into sleep.

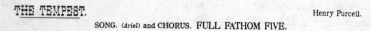

THE TEMPEST.

Henry Purcell.

SONG. *(Ariel)* and CHORUS. FULL FATHOM FIVE.

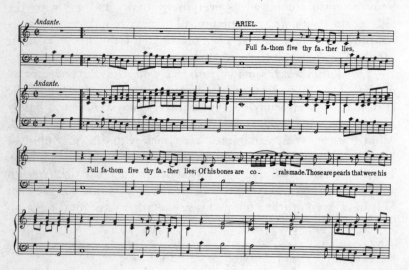

*Love is the historian's first duty. The historian must rec-
ognize his subject, and care deeply about him (especially
if, as so often is the case, that subject turns out to be himself). Beware of the third person; it is a cold and dangerous deceit.*

—John Lewis Dee[2]

The tactics of the workmen did not disturb Kitty. The first evening
only, when plaster was ripped from around the windows and door,
she hid in the dressing cabinet, cowering among the familiar smells
and fabrics. After that first violence she grew bolder, prowling the
work sites each day. She kept track of things, even while the workmen struggled with their demolitions. At night while I slept she in-
ventoried the torn-open places. She might be heard scrambling
between two-by-fours or perched atop a ladder left standing where
rot was being scraped from the beams. Her explorations didn't panic
me (the way I might panic if she fell through an open drain hole). As
I lay in bed listening, the sound of her inspections reassured me. She
was checking to make sure the progress of the workmen was all in

2. John Lewis Dee, *Miscellaneous Papers,* undated.

order. By morning she was asleep with me, curled on the bedcovers or spread across the papers on my desk.

Abbott turned up a treasure chest of documents as part of a legal settlement with a Yale trustee suspected of financing museum thefts. Evidently Abbott had some sort of "information" and a deal was made out-of-court. We got the documents (plus the promise of a posthumous donation of the man's definitive pewter spoon collection) in exchange for clemency and a lecture hall, I think he said, to be named later. Included in this bounty were daybooks of Andries Verweerd. Abbott explained all of this in hurried, excited tones (replayed through my blinking office message machine). He suggested I drop by his house that evening. We'd have "a go" at the outline I left him and make arrangements for the transfer of the documents. No mention was made of my early exit from the party, and I presumed it simply went unnoticed.

A bluster of wind rattled my office windows and a breeze blew, ruffling papers on my desk. The ice lacing the cold glass panes had loosened, and a small trail of water could be seen on the sill. After vacation, when the bursar got maintenance over with their tools, I'd have them put in the double panes and decent fasteners that couldn't be pried. I guessed it must be warming up outside. How late was it? The small watch still turned, its clicking dimmer than before. I kept it with me, and enjoyed the reminder (those many silent moments when I could feel it against my thigh) of "she" and our first portentous meeting. I turned from my desk and pulled a volume of the encyclopedia from the shelf.

> Dwarf: Extraordinarily small member of a race of normal stature; also a being in folklore. Historically, household dwarves were kept as curiosities in ancient Egypt, and were especially prized in Rome. In medieval and Renaissance Europe they occasionally held responsible positions, but served primarily as entertainers and household fools. In eighteenth-century Russia, elaborate "dwarf weddings" were held at court, and in 1710 a dwarf couple spent their wedding night in the Czar's bedchamber.

Dwarfism, unlike cretenism, is often accompanied by extraordinary intelligence. The body is usually well proportioned, but normal stature is almost never attained. The condition of arrested growth is brought about by a deficiency of anterior pituitary hormones, particularly gonadotropic hormones. The deficiency normally stems from a hereditary or idiopathic underfunction of the esinophillic pituitary cells.

While many dwarfs experience astounding longevity, complications such as diabetes insipidus, increasing intracranial pressure, and impending blindness may bring on rapid deterioration and, ultimately, death.

I wasn't sure what use I could make of the information, but it was nice to have some sort of "historical perspective" on the problem. Not that the startling dwarf was a problem. Indeed, she loomed (or, rather, at this point, her absence loomed) as a harbinger of insight or revelation, a signal, such as prophets receive, a portent. I knew her entry into my life had not been accidental, and neither would it be inconsequential. It was just a matter of time before she would overtake me completely, the collapsed star flaring suddenly bright, to obliterate all else in the heavens.

Her next motion came pushed through the mail slot with the rest of the day's offerings, in an envelope which still looked to me (unawares) like a "submission." "F.Y.I.," the return address said, and nothing more. I remembered the provocative Chapter One immediately, and pulled it from my file drawer to refresh my memory, before continuing with the tale of Oscar Vega:

"'I have a murmur in my heart,' Oscar Vega explained, trying to account for his tardiness, and the week of school he'd missed. He pointed to it, through his sweater, and looked down, as if to see if it might really be true. He wanted to add something, some authenticating detail, but couldn't come up with one, so he just kept pointing, silent. Father Simp, his counselor, was silent too. The day's bright light battled through the high windows, overheating the small office and the man in the black suit.

"Father Simp pried at the window's shut latch, wanting to let some cold air in, but it wouldn't open. The school stood alone on a small lot among the many houses in the valley of the gray factories. The grim neighborhood sparkled under heavy snow. The factories heaved their black ash into the sky. Oscar looked out the window, watching the tall brick stacks. Hadn't there been an airplane in his dream, and a warm sunny day?

"'You cannot persist in lying, Oscar,' the priest intoned.[3] Oscar shrugged, knowing that wasn't true. What Father Simp meant was that he *shouldn't* persist. That was a more interesting claim.

"'Why not?' the boy asked with genuine curiosity. The question carried no defiance. Father Simp shifted in his chair. He wanted to go home and have a beer. Nothing had ever been easy with Oscar, and the priest was weary of it.

"'Must everything be turned into a theological question?' he asked.

"'Shouldn't it?' Oscar marveled at the church. Sometimes it seemed beyond his understanding, but that never kept him from trying. 'If we're all children of God, Father, and must live by His laws, isn't everything, you know, theological?'

"'No.' Father Simp pinched the bridge of his nose, as if to make that sharp edge sharper. He turned away from the boy to scribble a note. 'Not today. Tomorrow after classes you may share that question with the afternoon group.' Oscar took the little slip. 'And every afternoon next week, too.' Oscar looked and saw the same instructions on the form. An empty box stood next to each day, waiting to be checked off. He felt slighted, as though the triviality of his punishment reflected poorly on him. Weren't his problems much more profound than simple delinquency?

"'Is that all, Father? A week in the afternoon group? I don't see what good that will do.'

"'Would you rather attend all month?'

"'It's not the number of times, Father; it's the group.' Oscar paused for effect. Father Simp paused too.

"'They never answer my questions.'

3. How often the historian wishes he could make this injunction to his "sources"!

"'You can't expect other boys to answer all your questions. Use the time to read, or for your homework. I'm not putting you there as punishment, Oscar. You obviously need some help organizing yourself.'

"'But what about my questions?'

"'The question is whether or not you pass. You won't pass by skipping, and you won't pass without your homework.' The priest leaned forward, enjoying the momentum of his argument. 'If you'd just focus on the real problems, the practical task of getting to school and getting work done, the Lord might make room for those big why's you keep asking. You can't expect illumination, Oscar, if you've not got the lamp and light bulb in good working order.'[4] He smiled and nodded, pleased by the neatness of the homily. It was a relief to have arrived at one. Oscar was confused by the argument, but charmed by the priest's new mood. What had seemed so tiresome for Father Simp was now a pleasure. His face was bright with good feeling. He leaned forward and patted Oscar on the arm. This, more than the argument, invited the boy's agreement.[5]

"'If I do my work I'll understand better why I shouldn't lie?' Father Simp nodded yes and settled some in his chair. 'Sometimes I think it's better to lie.' The priest was silent. The warmth drained from his face. 'Would I make a good priest, Father? If I studied and everything?' Father Simp took hold of Oscar's shoulder and pointed him toward the door.

"'Every afternoon, Oscar. And don't miss another day. If you show some progress we'll take up your other questions.' Oscar hitched his loose jeans up and took his books and left.

4. The homily suggests our "relativist" has been forced to recognize the primacy of method (the lamp and light bulb) over pure faith in the work of the historian. The "doctor," too, will surely endorse the primacy of method, but one wonders what place faith will, in the end, take in F.Y.I.'s "New Old Historiography."

5. A further complication. Is the informal, social network of influences (here, the pat on the arm) really of greater weight than sound argument in determining the direction historical inquiry will take? But whose arm is being patted? If Oscar is, as I've previously supposed, actually "history" itself, the priest (that is, the relativist) relies on a gesture of love and affection to coax "history" into its fullest development. Two issues in one gesture—thus the terrific power and concision of allegory.

"The building was old and made of brick. Oscar watched the heavy door close and Father Simp's shadow pass from the frosted glass window. He liked Father Simp, and did what he could to spend time with him. The hallway was empty. Sun came through the transom windows and lit the dusty air. It smelled of stale sweat and floor cleaner, humid and full as a greenhouse. In spring the double doors were left open and the air was fresh and breezy. His friend Tony had lent him some nice shoes. Hard and black, with white laces still tipped in sturdy plastic. Oscar watched them tap along the dull waxed floor.

"If Father Simp taught his classes he might enjoy them. Oscar imagined the tall skinny priest standing by the blackboard. He'd slam the pointer down to quiet them. He'd have to. The board would be filled with information written in the priest's cramped hand. Oscar would ask a question. How do you know if an idol is false? Does Jesus answer the prayers of murderers? Is it a sin if you simply like to *sleep* with an animal? It never worked out. The classroom, no matter who was in charge, was hostile to his interests. The priest stopped, inevitably, and told Oscar to focus on the lesson or leave. Even the good Father Simp, his counselor, would have no time for his questions there. It was nice to have a counselor, and to get to see him so often. Sometimes it got dark out if they sat talking long enough.

"The loud bell rang and the hallway filled with boys yelling and running to lunch. Marco, Dan, and Tony tackled Oscar and took him to the playground for a game. Marco swore in Italian and Tony pooled their money for hot dogs and chips from a vendor across the street. Oscar never hit the ball well, but he was a fourth. His friends thought he was clever and brave. There was nothing Oscar wouldn't do. While the other boys saw this as courage, for Oscar it was a matter of fear. Everything was frightening. No worse to jump than to stand on top of the cliff waiting. This ubiquity of fear heightened every sensation and made Oscar blind to the islands of safety his friends clung to. They admired the ease with which he leapt away, eager for new dangers. The new and unknown frightened them. Everything known frightened Oscar. If he leapt, it was to the possible safety of something unknown."

* * *

At some level, I'm certain, I'd begun to care about Oscar. He had an endearing earnestness, and sad circumstances. I found myself scolding his teachers, knowing that I could do better. Given time and some attention, a bright boy like Oscar could easily master reading and writing and move on to the important questions he hungered for. He bloomed in my mind like a hothouse flower; his colorful bud burst open, and he compelled me now, with all the virtues of a character in fiction.

Equally, the impending failure of F.Y.I.'s weighty allegory forced my attentions to Oscar alone. The allegory had overstretched a bit; certain complex, if still too-subtle points (re: the New Old Historiography) could not be ironed out. Only Oscar remained: an earnest endearing boy in a degraded city. What was F.Y.I. trying to tell me? The submissions could not be from anyone truly "in the field," but had to have come from some other, more mysterious source—most probably "she." To what end I did not know.

Outside the air had softened and the temperature crept above freezing. The wind was shifted and came from the ocean, full with moisture and the salt-iron smell of kelp and seawater. It blustered and beat chaotically, knocking flag lines against their stanchions, and dropping ice from the trees. Snow underfoot glistened. It no longer gave the satisfying crunch of dry compacting powder, as it had each night since the storm began. Pools formed in the trail of footsteps behind me. I looked toward the crest of the mountains, where the highway had been closed, and saw clouds gathering. They formed peaks against the face of the hills, and dropped down like sleep into the low places, and the valley where the city began.

By late afternoon the sun was obscured among towering stacks above the ocean, and the sunset was just dim bruises and sudden bursts; there was a smothering density to the weather that meant rain, not snow. Only the ocean made clouds this thick and heavy, and they were never cold, nor delicate. When I left my apartment to walk across campus to Abbott's it began. The rain fell and I scurried along, stupidly unprotected, watching the dirty snow pock and melt in the downpour. Two blocks and I was soaked, and in four thunder rolled. I arrived at Abbott's with the first visible flashes of lightning, only a few minutes late. Francis answered the door. He was wearing just his underpants. "Afternoon, Mr. Dee," he said, unremarkably. We both stood still in our places.

"Good evening, Francis. I'm here to see your father."

"Is it raining?" he asked, looking more closely at my dripping suit.

"Pouring, Francis. It's a veritable storm." Lightning crackled in the trees. The boy made no gesture of invitation. I noticed the beating of his heart could be seen, in palpitations of his skin, there beside the hollow of his sternum. He seemed transfixed by the lightning. "If I could just come in," I cajoled, "just into the vestibule. I'd like to shake myself dry a bit." He started, as if surprised by my voice, looked around the cluttered entryway, and ran back into the house. The door remained open, evidently my invitation.

"Abbott," the boy called precociously. "Mr. Dee is here." I watched his pink legs disappear, bounding up the carpeted stairs. The vestibule was a welcome shelter. I peeled off my jacket and hung it loosely on a peg. I picked at my wet trousers, hoping my body and the warmth of the house would work their magic.

Francis returned. He was dressed nicely, in a clean white shirt, woolen slacks, thick gray socks, and a tie. His short dark hair was slicked back with a wet comb, and his face was bright and red from a scrub. A fine figure he cut, when dressed so. The tail of his shirt stuck out the fly, but I thought it would be unfeeling to mention it. "How very nice you look, Francis. Very sharp indeed." The boy nodded. "Silly of your father to make you dress up just for me."

"I don't think he's home, Mr. Dee. I can't find him anywhere." It was unnerving, the ease with which he stared at me. "You're still in the vestibule."

"Yes, yes I am. I don't want to spoil the carpet, you see." I lifted a wet pants leg by way of explanation. "I'll just stand here a moment, if I may. Let the storm pass." Francis rushed away, as suddenly as he had the first time. Drawers could be heard sliding, and doors thudding dully shut through the ceiling above me. Water beat upon the windows, and the small light of dusk went out as the storm grew. The boy returned with a bundle of fresh clothes and a towel. Slacks and a shirt, a jacket, vest, and tie; stockings and boxers were folded neatly on top. A pipe fell out of the suit pocket as he came skidding to a halt before me.

We sat in the living room while the storm raged outside. Francis made tea. The pot was properly scalded, and there was sugar and cream; biscuits and sweets were laid out, and a snug cozy was produced.

"Do you have any idea where Abbott has gone?" I asked. It was a mystery.

"No."

I waited for some elaboration, in vain. "I was supposed to meet him." Francis nodded politely. He'd left the little spoon in his tea and was vexed by the perturbations of its orbit inside the cup. "We were going to discuss my work," I added, filling in the silence. Rain battered the windows. The spoon poked Francis in the chin as he tried to sip. I shifted where I sat, adjusting the vest. It had crawled higher up my body, along with the suit, as I sank farther down into the overstuffed couch.

"What do you study?" he asked. Intelligent child. It was a good question, touching upon a subject of some importance, and about which I could speak at length:

"Primarily it's mathematics and architecture I study, focusing on the sixteenth and seventeenth centuries in Northern Europe, though departmental requirements, and the practical necessities of grant writing, have shifted some of my energies onto the broader scientific developments of the period, especially the emergent physics with its links to calculus, and its precursors in hydraulics and the mathematics of flow. A fellowship several years ago gave me a chance to do extensive work on the larger cultural context within which the technologies of water management developed preceding the so-called 'Golden Age.'" The boy sat listening. He fiddled absentmindedly with his spoon, while keeping an attentive, if unfocused, look of interest turned toward me. "Currently I seem to be concerned with the question of insurance, in its broadest sense. Turning loss into gain. The seduction of mathematical security, a mathematics that can mitigate individual loss. The Dutch have a peculiar talent for profiting from the insecurity of others, and that manifested itself in, among other things, the modern practice of a precisely calibrated insurance. Insurance is, I believe, Francis, in fact the center of a great vortex of change that began with the Elizabethan Renaissance, and then the 'Scientific Revolution'; the underpinnings, in short, of early capitalism and its attendant analytical metaphysics. Though the Newtonian physics and its calculus have conventionally been raised up as the 'standard-bearer,' the paradigmatic model by which other developments of the era can best be understood, it is my belief that all of it, Francis, all of it, including the physics, emerged *ab ovum,* as it were, from the early development of insurance.

"If, I say, if I can tease out the conceptual links, the groundwork laid by Huygens, by Van Schooten, Snellius, God knows, perhaps even Stevin or Vierlingh, I believe I can establish the precedence of insurance in the broad web of changes that ushered in the modern era; the era, that is to say, of an analytical metaphysics, and the expansionistic capitalist world economy. Newtonian physics, Francis, may be nothing more than a necessary adjunct to a sound insurance policy. That, in any case, is my thesis."

"But where's the popular hook, Dee, the human interest? The *hero,* Dee. Who's the *hero* of this epic of yours?"

I looked up at the boy. Abbott stood behind him, having just interrupted my incautious speculations. "Abbott." I rose from the engulfing couch and offered him my hand. "We, that is, Francis and I were just discussing my work . . . my uh, ideas concerning the 'project.'" I nodded eagerly at the mute child. He was still transfixed by the spoon.

Abbott fetched a teacup from the kitchen. "I stopped at a café it got so bad. I knew Francis would take care of you." The boy kept silent and shifted uncomfortably in his chair. Abbott was as wet as I'd been, and left a little river between the door and kitchen. Now he lined his recliner with dish towels and settled into it.

"I'd like the opera house to be the 'hook,' as you call it, Abbott. The opera house and its policy."

"What policy?" Abbott fished around in a drawer and found my pages, together with a box of cigars. I paled. Abbott hesitated, then put the box back in a drawer. He directed Francis to build a fire.

"The insurance policy. It's the story of an insurance policy, the building and its policy. Very 'beginning-middle-end,' you see, with the 'birth,' all of the 'growth,' and finally the 'execution' of it."

"Muffin," Abbott whispered to his son. "Maybe you'd better get Daddy his Nicoderm." Abbott turned back to me and winked before draining his tea. "I've got it, Dee, of course. It's all coming to me. From that chapter in your treatment. 'Sweepings,' or some such."

"'Loomings.' *Moby-Dick.*"

"Yes, yes. 'Loomings.'" The new chairman settled more deeply, disrupting the towels, and flipped through my outline. He kept prying between pages, as if looking for a missing check; then he stopped on page three. "This 'Verweerd.'" He pointed at the name with a spoon. "He's a crusty old codger, don't you think? A little Zorba, maybe some Merlin to him; too smart for his own good, basically a lovable crank? What happens to him? I mean, in the end? Is there anything you could do with Verweerd?"

"Well, in the end, of course, he dies."

"That's right."

"They all do."

"Darn it all." Abbott shook his head, stumped, and nervously took the small patch from Francis. He applied it to a raw spot on his arm and signaled the boy to make more tea. "I'm thinking 'hero,' Dee, point of view. It's not just the money, though of course that would be nice. I'm just not sure the story of 'a policy' will wash, unless you've got something else up your sleeve."

"There is something, Abbott, as I told Francis. The origin of the modern condition."

"Right. But what about a sweetheart, or something really engaging like that? Maybe something significant. Wasn't there a war then? Was this opera house ever used in the war, like as a torture chamber, or a battlement of some sort?"

"A dramatic hook?"

"That's right."

Abbott meant his question to be helpful and I tried to take it that way. I thought of Oscar Vega. *He* was certainly a successful device. With the documents on hand, I had more than enough to narrate the adventures of Motley and Verweerd. They could be the heroes in the tale I would tell. "Something with a strong plot and characters?"

"Exactly," Abbott agreed.

"Human drama."

"Something to keep the pages turning."

"They all die in a storm."

"The heroes?"

"And the opera house is destroyed."

"There, you see." Abbott smiled and held the outline at arm's length. "Fancy conclusions can come later. You might think about a new title too. Something short and to the point."

I made promises and Abbott praised me. He was enthusiastic about tragedy, the cleansing catharsis of disaster, and the prospect of, he said, "a new *Tempest,* only this time without all the pretty lies." I could see what he hoped to encourage by the comparison to Shakespeare, but really I had Oscar Vega in mind, more than Shakespeare. An enchanting portrait of my heroes, modeled loosely on F.Y.I.'s presentation of Oscar, enticed me (and it was not a far cry from the "exemplary case" I'd set out to chronicle in the first place). Like Oscar, Verweerd and Motley were invitations into another world. The simplicity of it was a relief.

Abbott turned to the topic of my father. Had I come up with anything on the plants? Francis disappeared, gone upstairs to some boyish revel. The rain had steadied and the lightning ceased. My tongue was dry from the tea, and I kept lapping at a pool of cream I'd poured into my cup to relieve it. "I've got a deadline to meet, Dee, and if you want swift action on the book, I think it's best if I approach my agent with a double-deal; give her the *Tempest* and the plants and see what we can leverage." Abbott often spoke a foreign language I couldn't understand.

"What is it you need?"

"Chapter One from you, and a paragraph or two treatment. For the plants, see if you can dig up something short and simple, some letter or book intro where he sums up just exactly what he meant about 'acardiochronic history' and that lack-of-pulse thing. I want a few sharp quotes to tweak interest. My agent's no dummy, Dee. She's crackerjack smart, and has a nose, her nose right there, right on, the finger of America. If I can sell her on the plants she'll turn a hard/soft bio into six figures and a film option." Abbott was pressing more violently against his patch, agitating the skin in concert with the increased pitch of his enthusiasm. This agent must certainly know her stuff.

"Most of the monographs are less than two pages long," I reminded him. "My father never said much."

"Perfect, Dee. Take a few excerpts. Maybe condense it down to a paragraph, two at most."

"I can give you copies of what I find."

"Highlight 'em, if you've got time for it."

"With a Magic Marker?"

"I don't mind. I'm willing to piece it together from there."

My "things" dried, the rain became drizzle, and I surrendered Abbott's suit after a peaceful interlude in the large pastel bathroom. We sorted duties and set dates, and Abbott promised a reply from his agent by Christmas.

As we strolled to the vestibule, Francis came running down the stairs. He was tieless and undone, evidently by a brief wrestle with himself or a friend.

"Good-bye, Mr. Dee," he called, coming to a stop. He offered his hand. "I hope to read your book." It was a sophistication he'd picked up from his parents.

"Good-bye, Francis. Thank you for the tea, and for the dry clothes. I found your questions very stimulating and wise." He blushed slightly and scuffled in place. "Good-bye, Abbott. I'll be in touch about the proposals later in the week." Abbott clapped my back manfully and turned me toward the door. Francis stuffed a small envelope into my hand and stammered: "From my mother, Mr. Dee. I almost forgot," and then he rushed away up the stairs.

Dearest Mr. Dee:

I hope it is not impertinent of me to address this letter to you before we've even met, but I am assured by my husband that you are a fine young man, both generous and trustworthy. My son Francis, whom you have met, has as his fondest wish the desire to go swimming each week at the university pool. As neither my husband nor I swim, this has caused great consternation in our home. We do not want Francis, at his young age, to go alone. We are new here, and have not yet made friends from whom we could ask such a favor.

May I ask you, in your weekly trips to the pool, to allow Francis to come along? He is a responsible and quiet boy, and I'm sure he'll be no trouble. We are, of course, prepared to renumerate you for your time at whatever rate you deem fair. Francis is free from school early on Wednesdays and could meet you at your office, and walk with you from there.

If this is any trouble please just tell us so, or feel free to ignore my impertinence. Francis will soon enough find an alternative. If you are agreeable, just give word to Abbott and expect Francis at your office by 1 P.M. on Wednesdays.

Thank you sincerely, Mr. Dee. I look forward to meeting you soon.

Amelia Weathered

What a charmingly formal letter. And the boy was a delight. I made a note to tell Abbott yes, and marked the dates in my calendar.

EIGHT

RAIN HAD SLACKENED but the runoff from melting snow filled gutters and made fanned patterns of gravel and dirt. Stones crunched and turned underfoot, and the water kept coming. The electrical charge of the storm lingered with the smell of the ocean and drizzle. The wet air invigorated me. It wasn't too late, really, to walk a little, get some work done, and then be home in time to sleep.

My suit smelled flowery from Abbott's dryer, and I wished I could shake it clean, and fill it with the night air instead. He must use those perfumy antistatic rags I'd seen in the laundromat. Students with backpacks were still leaving the dorms, though most of the windows were black (and some left open). I could hear tinny rock music, and see flashing colored light and the broken window that marked its source. A farewell party, or maybe someone who'd been expelled. The district was empty without them. Christmas break drained the neighborhood of students and left the rest of us stranded among buildings and quiet cafés. I was glad for it.

History was empty and forlorn upon the hill. A few windows were warmed by the soft yellow of a desk lamp, and one or two classrooms burned bright under the glare of their fluorescent lights. No one could be seen in the empty rows of chairs. A workman washed the boards with a rag. In one dim office, perhaps, pages turned.

I remembered going with my father to his office during the quiet vacation, when the students had all gone. The rest of the faculty were on trips with their families. My father enjoyed the campus most at these times, and some mornings he would take me with him. He and I (with our dog Max, a corgi, all clean and smelling of soap and powder) would walk from home in the chill of the early morning. The cleaning lady in History knew me, and would offer candies or a stamp, tousling my hair, showing me secretly the single key by which she opened all the doors. It rested in my palm, light and symmetrical. The edges were clean and even, and much simpler than the usual keys. And yet it opened everything. Odd that it should be the simplest one.

We walked home slowly, stopping sometimes for a hot chocolate, or to smell the winter flowers in the greenhouse. Outside, while I was given a lovely cutting by the gardener, Father stood with Max, gazing at the hoarfrost, or up through mist at the spires, as if unaware of the secret attentions being paid to me. By this conceit he could pretend surprise when I turned to him, the blossom fastened to my collar with a pin, with a smile of pride on my face. He never tired of this routine. I made a point of saving each pin, and gave them to him for his butterflies.

The spire's clock said nine-thirty and rang its two measures. Rather than go to the Eichelberger for a snack just yet, I turned left, back up the hill, and went to the archive. Perhaps I could find something for Abbott straightaway. The library's reading room was loud and empty. Maintenance was scraping graffiti off the stones. The cruciform echoed with anguished metal clanking, and the violence of pounding pneumatic brushes. Apparently they had a timetable to meet. I rushed past and took the stairway, descending through several ages of rock. (The building from which the library grew had in fact been the guardhouse when the army was stationed here. Crude metal rings, head high, and the desperate calendars prisoners scratched into the walls were covered up by the construction.) After twists and turns through narrow granite passages, a clean wall of glass could be seen. Beyond it, bathed in bright light, was the archive.

Clad in special gloves, I penciled my request and took a seat while a messenger fetched the boxes. The portals opened and closed, and I looked up to watch the messenger through the glass. His sterile chrome cart was full with cargo, including the filthy boxes of my father's correspondence. He wheeled silently into the room and (with white-gloved hands) placed the food-stained cardboard in front of me. Since my father had scribbled and drawn all over the box, it was considered a part of the collection. Dirt and smashed butterflies were sprinkled among the folders—the archive did not "clean," it "maintained."

I pulled several folders from the later section, and spread them out on the table. The gruff, impersonal brevity of his letters robbed them of any humor or warmth. It seemed entirely appropriate that he'd typed all of them, taking away even the trace of his hand. I could see in his letters a record of his path through the years, a road map marking his travels, but it was impossible to find any emotions along the way. He rarely referred to himself at all. I flipped through a few dozen, scanning for "plants," and that clumsy Latinism "acardiochronic" blah, blah, blah . . . Maybe I'd see some mention of myself, too, I thought, and blushed privately at the vanity of it. Of course I'd want to find myself somewhere in these pages. What had he thought of me, or said to other people? I'm sure I knew, from all my memories of him, and the pleasure he took in my company. But something in me needed to catch him at it unawares, to hear him say it when he had no idea I was listening. I scavenged in the pages like a hungry voyeur, looking for the gesture, the mark and trace of his affection, put down somewhere in ink, un-erasable, written, so there could be no doubt.

There was nothing. It was a lousy bunch of letters, anyway, crumpled and crusted with food stains. I tried flattening them out, and scraping bits of gack off the more thickly stained pages, but the attendant started snooping and seemed about to come take the boxes away (to prevent me from "damaging" them). Maybe my father only donated the dull business correspondence, and kept the rest in files I'd not yet found. I put the filthy letters back in their acid-proof folders, and opened up a stack marked "notes." It was a jackpot (for Abbott, in any case)—three pages from 1974, titled "Acardiochronic History: Orgasm and the Plants" lay on top, and I nabbed them for the copier. I depressed the mechanical desk bell and handed the document to the attendant. Copies would be made and sent to my office. No use wasting more time in this grim bunker on Abbott's behalf. It only stirred up doubts and old confusions. I had no time for any of that right now, what with my own project hanging in the balance. I left the clean beige chamber, eager to find the last double doors again, and a breath of fresh night air.

The building's renovations echoed and rang and I followed the noise to find my way out. I could smell the sea increasing in rankness, and the air becoming moist and full, the closer I came to the ground-level exits. At last I scrambled up the final crooked steps, and threw open the double doors, glad to be out in it. There was the police tower, near a half-mile distant, glowing red against the thinning clouds. The warm light of the Eichelberger could be seen, spilling out onto the quiet street near my home. The windows lit a semicircle of melting snow, casting the shadow of the newsstand, and then the night closed in. It was nearly eleven. I made my way down the hill, satisfied I'd done my part for the chairman. The parties had all finished or been curtailed, and I was sad to see I'd forgotten to light my customary beacon in the apartment window. Poor cat. She probably fretted there in the dark, robbed of even this last vestige of our routine. At home I undressed and went straight to bed. Sleep would draw the curtain on my day, and in the morning (I resolved) I would write Chapter One of my researches. It would be nice to spend the day with something manageable and productive.

NINE

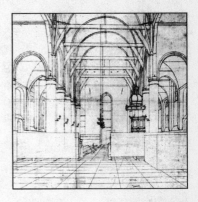

THE NIGHT FROZE EVERYTHING and I was glad to find the streets dry and empty the next morning. The sky was featureless, with only a thin haze, too high to be a threat. Kitty kept her place on the great desk (still shoved up to my bed) and I arranged my notes and folders around her. Brewing coffee obscured the defoliant and gave the apartment a fresh homey smell. The workmen were busy all day with some task in the stairwell. High, dry ground would be mine today. Putting aside all worry about Abbott's project, my father's barren archive, and my own disturbing memories, I sat down to erase all that, and began writing Chapter One of my researches:

The Opera House of Alton Motley   Nicholas Dee

The Opera House of Alton Motley

London, 1672
The biographer Roger North described the "nasty hole" of John Banister's concert room as "filled with tables and seats" and "with a side-box with curtains for the musick." Entrance cost a shilling, and Banister presented music there, weekly, to gentlemen, including Samuel Pepys, to enjoy in a free and easy, some would say drunken, atmosphere. Alton

The Opera House of Alton Motley   Nicholas Dee

Motley (1648—86) had his first exposure to the London musicians here. He undoubtedly would have met Pepys, William
Petty, and Robert Harley, whom he would later try to in-
volve in his "great and glorious endeavour"—the design and
construction of an opera house, to be built in the swamps
of Den Dollard, in the northeast of the Netherlands. The
concerts put on by Banister (and later by Thomas Britton
in a converted stable "not much bigger than the bunghole
of a cask") brought aristocracy into contact with the merchant class, in a situation of unparalleled degradation
and informality.

Banister arranged the front room of his home, by the
George Tavern in White Fryers, as one would an alehouse.
Round tables and chairs were packed roughly, leaving room
for drink and coffee to be carried in on trays. He managed
to elevate the concert from its music house origins (and
thereby attract the "finer" gentleman and ladies who would
not dare go to the music houses); but he never rid it of the
"compounded and adulterated drincke fit to have the head
beaten out" that made such concerts so attractive as entertainments. While the musicians were seated on a raised stage
with curtains ("required by their modesty"), the audience
drank and bickered in a room filled with smoke and beer.
Occasional damage was to be expected. Motley recalls a drunken
brawl which drove the Earl of Oxford, and his party, from
the hall. "Mr. Rosin got up from his chair and began to
sing with some force, and against the song of the lutanist
William Yokeney, whose performance Mr. Rosin called asinine.
The combatants were kept from each other by tables and fighting among their partisans, which activity spilled into the
street and caused Mr. Banister to end the concert."

Brawls were not typical, but the free-mixing was, and
it helped Motley make contacts with musicians and patrons
alike. They would figure prominently in the realization of
his "great and glorious endeavour."

The Opera House of Alton Motley   Nicholas Dee

The trips to London were unusual for the fragile twenty-
five-year-old. He spent most of his time in bed, attended
to by his physician and lifelong companion, Thomas Weekes.
Weekes, a "uromancer," counseled Motley about his health
and investments by making daily readings of Motley's urine.
"The accidents of pisse, as the severall colours, parts,
contents, substance, quantity, smell, etc." were examined,
and the activities, diet, and investments for that day were
thereby planned.

They lived on a large estate near Benson along the
river Thames. The estate was modest, but it bordered on
the river, and was blessed with swollen, bare hills rising
out of densely forested vales. Motley spent most of his
time riding through the woods in a well-appointed carriage
within which he lay in bed. His physician was carried alongside in a special box. A tremendous inheritence from Motley's
grandfather,[1] improved by unerring investments back into
Dutch shipping concerns, allowed them the life of country
gentlemen. It granted them the leisure to indulge both
Motley's hypochondria and his intense love of music.

1. Alton's grandfather Gerard Motley (1578–1652) was a carpenter's appren-
tice in Devonshire when, in the spring of 1596, he joined a British mercenary troop
which sailed for Holland to join the Dutch. Hostilities between Spain and its
Dutch protectorate had raged for more than half a century, with the British taking
various sides, depending on alliances and the state of commerce. War would continue for another thirteen years before a truce was called, and the Dutch needed
able men. Motley, like most of the British fighters, supported the Dutch because
they promised him good money. By 1603 it was abundantly clear that the Dutch weren't
paying. In the fall of that year, Motley quit fighting pending the settlement of
the Army's large debt to him. He'd been kept reasonably healthy and sheltered,
able to fight, but cash was never forthcoming. Burdened by a chaotic economy, and
obliged by necessity to funnel cash into arms and supplies, the Dutch government
was unable to fulfill its promises. The following spring, 1604, the Army negoti-
ated a settlement with Motley, granting him a large share of stock in the newly
formed V.O.C. (the Dutch East Indies Corporation) and a questionable tract of land
near Den Dollard. The stock was only speculative, but Motley took it, together

The Opera House of Alton Motley   Nicholas Dee

Winters were spent in bed, inside, while in summer,
the small consumptive investor would have his cushions moved
to the enclosed balcony above the great front entrance to
his home. From there he would toss gifts and candies to the
visitors who came around for them. It was Weekes who counseled this life *a couché*—as part of the prescription he
read from the daily samples of urine. The tremendous success of Weekes's counsel secured Motley's belief in the
value of his method, and Motley passed the years quite
happily, largely confined to bed,[2] and his estate.

In the summer and fall of 1682 a series of accidents at sea
ended their string of profitable investments. Substantial
losses struck for the first time. The bulk of Motley's fortune was unthreatened, but his confidence in the Dutch was
shaken. Weekes saw, in Motley's urine, signs of further financial disaster. Good fortune could only be ensured, Weekes
counseled, through a gift, an act of philanthropy, an offering back to the Dutch as balance for the tremendous harvest
he'd sown. An opera house would be funded and built. Thus
was born the "great and glorious endeavour" of Alton Motley.

----

with the land, and his freedom to return to England. Through sloth or guile, it is
unclear which, Gerard Motley left the V.O.C. stock alone, keeping the certificates
with his musket and medals, until April of 1640 when his first grandson, Alton
Motley, was born. He gave the stock as a gift to Alton and his family. Alton's
father, a bank clerk in London (and decidedly more aware of the world than the
elder Gerard) immediately redeemed the certificates and was rich. The fortune remained
stable until the 1670s when Alton came of age and enriched himself further by
careful, repeated investments (counseled by Thomas Weekes) back into the V.O.C.
    2. Weekes had Motley installed at the center point of an enormous bedchamber
designed and built by the alchemist and geomancer Elias Ashmole (a friend of the
physician). Weekes reasoned a subtle regulation of Motley's humors could thereby
be maintained, governed by the direction of his bed, and the slight elevation of
feet or head. Elaborate charts told Weekes which relation to the eight winds and
what angles of recline were most conducive to the business at hand, and by that
chart he instructed the burly attendants who moved Motley's enormous indoor platform about on its pivots.

At one o'clock exactly (the following afternoon) the slight, shy knocking of the Weathered boy disturbed my office calm. The door jiggled at his touch, the knob turned, and he entered. Francis was dressed in many colorful sweaters, bright ski pants, and a lavish woolen scarf. A towel and fins were thrown over his shoulder. His hair had been hastily combed with a nervous hand. My researches had effectively calmed me, coating my days as an antacid might coat the stomach, muting any disturbance with its smooth, chalky slowness. This visit from Francis was the first (welcomed) intrusion.

"Hello, Mr. Dee," he said, bowing slightly as he shut the door. "I've brought my fins and a towel." He pointed at the draped cloth without removing it from his shoulder.

"That's lovely, Francis. You're looking very bright today. I'm sure you'll swim circles around the rest of us."

The pool was quite crowded, and Francis shared my locker. He hung his sweaters and scarf neatly on the farthest peg, and stripped without a second thought. He glanced down the empty rows with careless curiosity, and scooted along to the fountain for a gulp of cool water. The ease of his nakedness beguiled me, and when he returned I found I was fidgeting and mute, blushing at his proximity. Francis stood as he'd normally stand, chatting, picking absently at an itching ear, touching me with a soft hand, and stark naked from head to toe. His smooth skin and trim body were so unlike Schloss and the other grossly matted men that I felt no threat or "emanation" coming from him. The fact of his boyhood, the simplicity and size of his body made every affection natural and unadorned. I stripped too, and stood beside him. Francis smiled poking himself in the belly with a thumb.

"Do we shower first?" the boy asked, filling the air with his voice.

"Yes, Francis," I gave back. "A quick rinse." I smiled at his easy stare. "And your suit, can't forget that." The boy slapped a hand to his forehead, and looked down at his nakedness, mimicking surprise.

"Can I put the flippers on too, Mr. Dee? Can I wear them in the shower?"

"Of course you can. Just mind people's toes. Everything is permitted at the pool, so long as safety and consideration are observed."

Whilst I fiddled with my robe and deck chair, readying myself beside the slow lane, Francis leapt without warning into the deep end, and swam straight for the bottom. I admired his angular form, and the swift movement of the fins propelling him to the depths. His hesitation there, and the release of a brace of pearly bubbles from his nose, gave rise to a quick panic, a reminder that I was here to guard his safety. I lurched forward toward the water, ready to leap in and drag him up, while he swam innocently to the surface. It was no small relief, both his smile when he came up, and the feeling of parental concern his submersion brought. "She" was not there. I scanned the gallery and could not find her. It wasn't surprising. She might have gone away for the winter break, or changed her routine for the holiday. Francis kept to the deep end, where I joined him with my kickboards, and we raced and Francis won, powered by his strong legs and the fins.

The simple pleasure of the boy's company brought a reminder of those many days when my father took me to the pool, and I watched dutifully while he dove and swam. I exaggerate my timidity; in fact I also played (though usually alone and with the kickboard clutched firmly to my belly). By two o'clock I was tired, and my father was too, and red-eyed and drowsy we'd walk home along the streets, empty usually, because it was Sunday. I watched the field behind our house, which was visible for several blocks, where Cam and Lonnie Ekdahl played, kicking a rubber ball; they were twin boys, a little older than I. Perhaps it only happened in the fall. The picture of them playing is always under a crisp October sky, with the wind rattling leaves along the grass, and the chill air full of wood smoke and frost. Blushing from exertion and the cold, they would kick and run, kick and run, unconcerned with distance or accuracy. The little ball flew across the muddy ground, bumping up against the fence by the woods, or it rolled down the small rise toward the houses. I watched them while we walked. My father was quiet, his hat fit loosely on. He held the rolled towels in his hand. He gave them to me, always, by the gate, and while he went in, I ran around to the back of our house to hang them. They made a colorful row with our trunks, flapping on the clothesline until they became stiff and dry, or froze if it was cold enough. Father sat in the living room by the window. We had a large easy chair, the padded arms a little worn, and he would be sitting there, looking out into the afternoon. I took off my shoes by the door, and set them next to his. And then I'd go to the chair and lie down in his lap, my legs dangling, however long, over the one arm. I would always put my head to his heart, letting my ear rest against the soft cotton shirt, letting it rest against his chest where his heart beat. And we sat there like that through the afternoon, always, until I fell asleep and he carried me to my room. Why did the heart make its next turn, without reason or will, marking off time like a clock? And why did it then stop? It seemed impossible that it would ever stop, that his heart could be silent.

When my father died I was asked to speak at the funeral, but there was nothing I could say. His death was so reasonless and irrevocable. I wasn't silenced by my grief, or anything maudlin like that. In some ways it was the opposite. I was sad, but there was nothing to say about it. He was gone. There were many things I would miss, but I already missed them. He'd been gone for a long time. My feelings were too diminished and common to be interesting. Why speak about his being dead? Of course I was embarrassed by my lack of words. I had a myriad of feelings, and love for my father. I just saw nothing useful or compelling in talking about it. I kept quiet, and sat patiently through the ceaseless consoling of friends. They read my silence as devastation, and I preferred they read it that way. Explaining my lack of interest was too difficult. No one would believe me, or they were horrified. But there's nothing to say about someone dying, and no reason to try. The exercise is more maudlin than the death; it is done, maybe, out of envy for the dead, an attempt to die a little with them.

The day had turned bright blue, and the mountains were cluttered with the remnants of the morning's overcast. In the southern sky the sun shone gamely, glistening on the bare wet trees and casting its long winter shadow across the muddy ground. Francis was as bright as the day, his face blushing a healthy red, with eyes to match because of chlorine. His colorful sweaters were exuberant beside my somber coat. I gave greetings to a man from Demographics (too bad I couldn't remember his name) and a handful of graduate assistants waved. It was nice to be noticed with the boy. They must have taken him for my son. "When are you due home, Francis?" I asked, appreciating the frequent bump of him against my side. It was endearing the way he walked, like a curious puppy, gazing out at everything while constantly tripping into me by his eagerness to stay near.

"Home? I think at dinner. Abbott never said." It was three-thirty. The large spires loomed overhead, with the clock about to sound.

"Are you hungry now?" It was a silly question. Of course the boy would be hungry. He nodded yes. "I've a favor to ask, and in reward I'll offer a small snack at my favorite bistro."

"A restaurant?"

"The Eichelberger. The best café in the district."

"What's the favor?" Cagey lad.

"Simply to carry some papers to Abbott. I've got a chapter he asked for, and some of my father's papers he needs."

"A messenger."

"That's right. A fleet-footed messenger. I suggest we have a bite at the Eichelberger, and drop by my apartment to pick up the papers. Then you can be on your way."

Showered with lavish kisses and a bounty of complimentary delights from Madame Ethyl (she embarrassed Francis with praise) we passed an hour with food and conversation. While the boy ate, prompting me with the occasional word or silence, I filled in the background of the university and the history of the city generally—redressing his father's failure to do so—and then discussed my work in greater detail. (I imagine his mother must be in charge of him. Certainly Abbott hasn't done his part educating the boy.) Francis drew strange shapes on the paper table cover, his hand dancing about it with gentle actions, as of salutation, and told me some jokes he knew (one was about a unicorn); all the while new provisions appeared as if by conjurations, laid before us like precious gifts from our beguiled hostess. Francis didn't say much, but his silence was warm and enabling.

A touch of wine left us both a little drowsy. The university's clock rang five and echoed from the hills. Francis held on to my sleeve while we walked. The market street was almost empty and it was night already over the mountains to the east. Above the ocean the sky was steel gray and its light came to us, diffused in a mist which masked the hills. I tried the door and it opened without my key turning. "It's just a little dark," I warned. "Hold on to my arm." We climbed the stairs and entered my ravaged rooms. Kitty kept silent, greeting us with a wet nose along our shoes. The tarps turned the dusky light blue. It was like entering the pool from underwater. Francis blinked and yawned like a newborn kitten, then clattered across the boards to the bed. I couldn't find the light switch. Apparently it had been removed.

"I'll just find the papers," I whispered, "then you'll be on your way." Francis didn't answer. There was enough light to read by, and I shuffled through the piles on my desk, looking for my "Chapter One" and the account of "Acardiochronic History." The ticking of the small pocket watch could be heard, marking the dimming light, and I felt my heart move in synch to it. I slipped the papers into an envelope, and turned toward the bed. Francis was asleep there, curled on his side with the cat. I watched his steady breathing, the bulky sweaters moving slightly. His cheeks were especially flushed, and the cat was nestled in by his hips.

Here is the text of the paper I gave to him (to be delivered to Abbott):

ACARDIOCHRONIC HISTORY: ORGASM AND THE PLANTS
John Lewis Dee

"I would like to say that language precedes chronology, but I think the relationship of these two is more ambiguous than that. How are they related? Typically, when reaching orgasm, men and women experience a period of inarticulate dissolution. Expression reverts to preverbal grunting and moaning, while the cognitive structures of chronology and 'self' are briefly disturbed. 'I was completely gone.' Language is scrambled. The dissolution of 'self' and linear time makes us radically unpredictable. This disrupts the functions of the state, particularly the agenda of social control normally carried out by the university. Thus, it is typically the police, rather than the university, that deal with sex, while the university desexualizes all human experience (including sex), making it suitable for study and 'comprehension.'

"Napping brings these same dissolutions, and at a less frantic pace. It is perhaps more subversive than orgasm because of its acceptability as a widespread public practice. Naps are thought to be healthy and harmless. Children are encouraged to have them. Notably, children are not asked each afternoon to take time out from play for an orgasm, however beneficial such a practice might be. A nap is suggested instead.

"I take orgasm as the light that may illuminate the link between language and chronology. Their common dissolution, under the sway of orgasm (or while napping), suggests profound connections. Let me state these as provocations, and leave them at that: without language, human experience would never arrange itself chronologically; the illiterate can more easily escape the narrow structure of linear time; orgasm delivers us to liberating dissolutions of language and chronology, and is thus an enemy of the state; sex is made to be private for fear of a cognitive revolution; for the preverbal infant, life is a constant orgasm.

"The plants enjoy peace and surcease from the anxious flickering between 'strict time' and orgasm. They live (especially when together in a healthy ecology) in a kind of endless, communal nap (or orgasm). The absence of any heartbeat is important. Note that orgasm ('the little death,' and also a sneeze) interrupts the normal functioning of the heart. When this most basic marker of time is suspended, even briefly, the structures of chronology and identity crumble. The plants, heartless, enjoy unmarked communion: acardiochronic time, which we can glimpse only in the culmination of our frenzy.

"The historian is wise to spend time among the plants, silent and occasionally having sex. Napping is important too, to renew an acquaintance with the scrambling of 'self' and language. He should endeavor to rewrite history from the position of the plants.

"J.L.D., March 1974."

His mother was more than sweet when I phoned, thanking me effusively for the meal, and the kind allowance of a nap. She asked if I didn't mind letting him just sleep a bit. She whispered too, at the other end, as if to keep from disturbing the boy. I sat by the desk, next to the big bed, and watched Francis. He seemed to bring on the evening with his sleep. Each breath that took him deeper into his dreams also brought the night on. The darkness, and the napping boy, drew me in, as I sat awake beside him. The heat of his face was palpable on my cheeks. I could feel my ribs rising and falling with his. There was a welling up in my eyes, like yawning, and I teared, probably due to some irritant loosened from the walls by the workmen.

THE TEMPEST.

AIR. *(Ariel)* DRY THOSE EYES.

Henry Purcell.

Dry those eyes which are ____ o'er-

-flow ____ ing, All ____ your storms ____

____ are o - ver-blow ____ ing.

106

While you in this isle____ are bi -- ding, You____ shall feast____ with -- out___ pro - vi - ding, you shall feast____

The nights became more peaceful once the workmen finished removing my staircase. The incessant clatter of their pneumatic tools was gone, and no unwanted visitors (salesmen evangelists, or the like) ventured up the sturdy metal ladder they had bolted into the gutted stairwell. The eventual replacement of the original, with a wooden copy cured and impregnated with some sort of chemical preservative, was scheduled for January. In the meantime I had a window of relative serenity and isolation. The foreman raised the question of exterior walls and asked that I sign some forms, which I did gladly in exchange for his promise to ban the noisy power tools during the hours I spent at home.

Documents from the Yale trustee were finally cleared through Abbott's lawyers, and he promised me I'd find them at the office (available for home use). Certain diaries of Verweerd and a smattering of relevant legal records were among them. They would get me through my introductory chapter, and into the body of the manuscript. Leaving the apartment to fetch them, late in the afternoon, I was surprised to find a package at the door. It had no postage, but was written in a familiar hand: "F.Y.I."

"In the attic of a house by the gates of the gray factory, along the railway running north through the city, Oscar Vega burrowed into warm flannel bedding, curled around a pillow, and pulled the blankets over his head. The boy in bed beside him watched Oscar disappear. They were friends at school and Oscar often came over late in the evening and asked if he could stay. Oscar's wet shoes sat neatly beneath a chair and his pants and shirt were folded and set on top. Oscar wanted to be a good guest. Tony, his friend, never noticed this detail amid the clutter of his room. Tony's room had a lock. Every time he stayed over, Oscar folded his clothes neatly, scrubbed his face at the sink, brushed his teeth, and went to the door to slip the lock shut. When the bolt slid into place Oscar felt warm and calm inside. If Oscar could have one thing it would be a lock.

"'You look like my dog,' Tony said to the lump of bedding which covered Oscar. Oscar couldn't hear him. The dog lay on the floor, unconcerned. When Tony turned the lights off, the dog poked its damp nose under the loose bedding and climbed in between the boys.

"At last everyone is sleeping. Oscar's heart flutters inside his damp warm chest. Nicholas[1] turns in his pajamas. Wind drifts along the empty street. Tony, as always, draws his leg up over the dog, not waking. The city sleeps, nesting on its few hills, quiet under the mantle of snow. Only the doctor is awake.[2]

"In Oscar's dream he remembers the cool white fridge in his mother's house, past the trailers at the end of the main road at No Point. When he was seven he thought when people died they went to the icebox. The cool box of light seemed solemn and sturdy enough for the task, and its moist chill air felt full of spirits.[3] He was tall enough to reach the gaudy chrome fin which, when pulled down, released the door. The icebox opened before him, full of mists and odors, suffused by the soft light of its small bulb. His uncle, a lumberjack disabled by a faulty blade, always called it 'the cooler.' The big clean man took Oscar in both hands, lifting him far off the ground. 'Boxcar,' he'd say, calling Oscar by the nickname he loved. 'Brews in the cooler?" The round, ticklish sound delighted him. 'Brews in the cooler,' Oscar always answered, mimicking his uncle's sweet enunciation. When Franklin Kolkshaw reported to the recess sokum game that dead Henry Shab, shot hunting, was 'on a slab in the cooler' Oscar put two

---

1. !

2. Is there really a doctor?

3. What a morbid child. Was he acquainted with death so young?

and two together. Franklin should know, his dad being both doctor and mortician for the small coastal town. All dead men went to the cooler, Franklin said so.

"The icebox was a wonderful thing. The dead mingled there with food and beer. The butter should not be left uncovered. Someone might get stuck. Oscar felt them in the cool fingers of air drifting down around him. He smelled them in the soft unspecific odor. They didn't frighten him. A lot of nice people were dead. Each had a place; Grandma up and to the back, near the rich, smoked meats. Who could say how they all fit? Important friends got more space. The vegetable tray was filled with thousands of small, insignificant dead. Oscar stood in the open door, looking at the meat.

"'Brews in the cooler,' he said again to himself. 'Brews in the cooler.' No one cared that he stood there letting the cold out. His brothers screamed at each other in the living room, beating on seat cushions. Dogs barked outside at everything that came down the road. Cousins were drunk in the yard. Oscar rearranged things so the light wasn't blocked.

"'I see Grandma, and Teddy. I see George and Pally and Gwendolyn,' Oscar recited. A woman on television could see through the glass, and called the names of children this way. It was reassuring. Oscar wanted to give the same reassurance to the dead, some of whom were dogs. 'I see Duffer, and Tim, and Henry and Bobby, and Aunt Kate.' It was nice to spend time with them. No one yelled, or could walk away. Oscar sat awhile there, talking with his friends about the day outside. Eventually someone would come to get food or a beer and they'd close the door, and Oscar let that be good-bye.

"To say the names into the cool white air was an act of faith which Oscar understood in his body. He felt it in the calm and sweetness of his small muscles, and in the strength of the names in his mouth and head. He felt faith in the best sense, a kind of believing free from the impurity of reason. Faith is natural to a child. The love he felt was for himself, more than for the dead. Feeling his voice, he knew he was what they needed. His recitation soothed them, just as the woman's voice on television soothed him, saying the names of children through the glass.

"Exhausted, Oscar tossed and tangled under covers with Tony and the dog. Sleep claimed him completely, like sex or a drug. He lay, lost in it, even while the late morning sun turned the dark curtains orange, and the dusty air of the room warmed to where the covers were too hot."

The dwarf occupied my mind doubly now—once by her absence, and then again by her peculiar submissions re: Oscar Vega. She was an affliction, as steady and disturbing as the foul weather. My researches and the boy, Francis, offered some distraction. I turned to them often, and found my chapters building nicely, high and dry at the big desk in my secured rooms. The boy's regular visits to swim, and the pleasure of seeing to his care and education, brought a fine and paternal satisfaction. He often looked as if he were on the verge of tears. I kept us to a schedule, and the afternoons settled into a routine, welcomed by the both of us. It gave me some calm and security, even while the empty neighborhood washed away under the storm outside. I turned back to my researches, hoping to erase "her" from the pages of my life.

The Opera House of Alton Motley   Nicholas Dee

The Opera House of Alton Motley (cont.)

The Prospero Shakespeare created in his *Tempest* was largely erased in the operatic *Tempests* of the seventeenth century. The spectacle staged by Shadwell in 1674, which Alton Motley attended during his one-month stay in London, featured nymphs and nereids, Amphitrite, Neptune, and Aeolus. The powerful Magus who ruled over the island of Shakespeare's play was reduced to an amiable, if troubled, father praying for the marriage and good fortune of his two daughters, Miranda and Dorinda. This opera was itself based on a stage adaptation by Dryden and William Davenant who together had conceived of Dorinda and her sweetheart Hippolito. Like Miranda (who'd never seen any man but her father) Hippolito

The Opera House of Alton Motley   Nicholas Dee

had never before seen a woman. Sycorax was added, Ariel got a sweetheart named Milcha, and the whole was consumated in a happy double marriage. The passion for balance and order was thus satisfied in this thoroughly farcical comedy. The shift away from the dark, complex powers of the artful Magus, and toward the pleasurable symmetry of a consumated comic romance, is of more than passing interest. Motley would score his own *Tempest,* based on Shadwell's. This would be the premiere offering, in what he hoped would be the largest opera house in all of Northern Europe.

Moore is correct that "to lament that this is not like Shakespeare is both irrelevant and obtuse."[3] Motley's *Tempest* (and especially his diminished Prospero) gives us good information about his perspective, and his time. (Better we should ask what forms Prospero can, or does, take in our own time, than complain about Restoration "abominations.")

***

In November of 1682, a bitter, windy month of snow and hail in the countryside near Benson, the frail investor spent several weeks drafting the first sketches of his opera house. Though he'd never received training as an architect, drawing and geometry had been taught to him. His design was guided by those skills (more than by engineering or other practical considerations). Motley passed the weeks with fanciful sketches, stretching domes and arches however far his quill could take them. He had no regard for the limitations actual stone and timber might impose. He filled a glorious landscape of hills and vales around the monument, proposing a site as fanciful as the architecture. While the structure, and its imagined situation, seemed to have no source but Motley's pretty dreams, notes from Thomas Weekes, his physician, prescribe exacting speci-

3. R. E. Moore, *Henry Purcell and the Restoration Theater,* 1961, p. 184.

The Opera House of Alton Motley   Nicholas Dee

fications for certain features of the building. Articulating vents and wind vanes, together with enormous lodestones placed along certain sections of the hall, were
sketched by Weekes, and incorporated into Motley's plan.
Evidently, the building would serve more than just its
obvious purpose.

Throughout that long winter, Motley stayed in bed and
worked at a drafting table hung on pulleys. Inquiries to
Robert Harley, soliciting help with the project, were met
with a blunt, if concerned, response. "It is the particular ignorance of that piss-monger who has taken the name
of Physician," Harley wrote back to Motley, "which now
threatens both your health and fortune, leading you, if
my intelligence is correct, to the draining of urine into
his phials, and money, as if down a sinkhole, into the
folly of a theater built on swamps. A man's fortune cannot be told in a phial of piss but it can be lost there."
Harley offered his support for staging the Motley *Tempest*
in London, but declined any involvement in the "Dutch
folly."

Motley had never traveled to Holland. Den Dollard was
simply a pretty name in his mind, a marker for the special
distinction of owning "a fine property" in "a small
fisherman's village, with sweete air, and good soil." Nor
had he any desire to go now. Travel across the sea was
difficult, and the relations of the two nations entirely
unpredictable. Weekes counseled wisely that he remain in
England and seek "a reliable factor" in the Netherlands
to oversee the execution of his plans. Inquiries were sent
abroad soliciting help from Motley's business contacts in
Holland, Friesland, and Groningen.

In coffeehouses and trading rooms, over ale in cafés
in Amsterdam and Leeuwarden, Motley's confederates exchanged
news of his endeavor, and the possible names of men who

The Opera House of Alton Motley   Nicholas Dee

could be found to help realize it. In June of 1683 a letter
came from Edwin Strick, a beet merchant in Groningen, rec-
ommending an older man (a "surveyor and natural mechanic")
whom Strick remembered for his brief fame devising reliable charts of tidal marshes. Andries Verweerd was living
in Delfzijl, and agreed enthusiastically to help with the
project Strick described. The plans were sent and finances
settled. By July, Verweerd had moved to the small village
near Motley's land and was signing on craftsmen and laborers. A "policy of assurance" was drawn up, at Strick's suggestion, with Johannes Drop of Groningen (the "only man
who hath sufficient means to make good on his promise.")
By late in August, construction began.

My apartment was a shambles. The light from outside was
muted, filtered through tarps the workmen hung from the building's
eaves. Was it late? (Hadn't "she" begun by asking me that? Was it
late?) The dull blue light from outside said it was daytime still, but
gave no clue to the hour. The rain had begun again, peppering the
scaffolds, lashing the gutters, and filling the drains. I could hear the
slight ticking of the watch, but could not find it easily (probably lost
among the piles of paper on my desk). If only I had buried it more
deeply. I shifted the heavy typing machine an inch closer, and started
pounding at the keys, letting the noise of my continued pages drown
the slight, ceaseless unwinding of her gift to me:

The Opera House of Alton Motley   Nicholas Dee

By late summer of 1684 the pilings had all been driven
and the base of the great building was set. Verweerd cleverly made plans to construct the eastern wall with a pro-
jection like a ship's prow, to divide the waters winter
inevitably sent raging into the estuary.

The Opera House of Alton Motley   Nicholas Dee

Motley had never recognized the full extent of flood-
ing on his cherished parcel. The land he inherited from
his grandfather wasn't really land. The "brown and stink-
ing estuary" of the Eems River, and the daily tides
washing over it, turned the parcel into tidal flats and
marsh. The opera house had to be built half in water, on
piles driven into the mud. Verweerd described the tract in
his odd, cryptic "daybook"[4]: "The parcel of land, north-
northeast of Finsterwolde, was easily found with the helpful identification of its place by the provincial office
at Groningen. I compose my notebook there, in a small shack
on the west of the parcel, surrounded by shallow waters
and sea grass. The bounty of its marsh and the regular
washings of the tide make abundant habitat for waterfowl
and shellfish. It is a beautiful tract, extending well into
the estuary to the east, and bordering on a mud field to
the west. North and south are marshland, and the whole is
flat, blessed with even winds, and covered in a shallow
tide."

With work under way, the remote marsh was transformed
into a crowded village of carpenters, stonemasons, join-
ers, entertainers, and cooks. "Simple quarters," Verweerd
wrote in his daybook, "stand on the west line, also on
stilts. If at ebb tide, walking, or the dray horse can be
taken; at flood, the men wade or carry wood and stone in a
boat. The water, knee deep at flood, is tireless and car-

---

4. This document, which is written in a mix of Old Dutch and Gronings—a dialect
which persists to this day—is made up of such idiosyncratic, abbreviated frag-
ments, it is difficult, if not impossible, to render meaningfully in English. The
written form is roughly adapted from the spoken language, and employed with such
variety and incompleteness that the reader is left to make it whole by extrapola-
tion and imagining. I have here rendered excerpts from his text as best I could,
filling them in and fleshing them out to give more clarity, meaning, and "voice."
I believe the translation is faithful to the original, but the issue of accuracy
is, here, especially clouded by the peculiarities of the document.

The Opera House of Alton Motley   Nicholas Dee

ries great loads with ease. To harness the wind and rain
also would make our labor nothing. Pity we work against
them."

Andries Verweerd (dates unknown) was a big man, well
over six feet and three hundred pounds, by his own account. He wrote in the daybook each evening, propped up
among cushions in his *bedstij* (a closet, really, built into
the wall at waist height, where Dutchmen typically slept
behind curtains or a shut panel). His chronicle veered from
practical matters to moral lessons, observations about human
behavior, and speculations about cosmology. Part hermetist,
and part Druidic animist, he kept a chaotic record of the
people, the plants, and especially the weather of the estuary. Taken together, it formed his "True and Faithfull
Relation of the Great and Glorious Endeavour of Mr. Alton
Motley, Esq., as Undertaken in the year of our Lord 1684,
New Calendar, Finsterwolde, Groningen, the United Netherlands, by Andries Verweerd, a Natural Mechanic."

Blessed by a mild summer and an unseasonably warm fall,
the workmen completed the foundation and most of the eastern
and northern walls before difficult weather arrived. Their
workdays began with the approach of dawn. The profusion of
animals and birds nesting in the estuary made such noise and
commotion all the men woke early. On most mornings, the dawn
was hidden in fog. Thick gray clouds lay close to the water,
drifting above the shallow tide. The sun didn't shine; it
crept upward through the mist, suffusing the marsh with a
dull, even light. Each man might stoke the embers of his
fire, adding new blocks of peat, raising a flame to boil
coffee. Bread might be mashed into leftover beer, to be eaten
with some cheese. A splash of water would be taken from beside the house, a dunk of the head, perhaps, more for re-
freshment than for hygiene. And then work began.

The days were hard labor: dawn to midday (when a meal
would be taken together, and the actors' troop would en-

The Opera House of Alton Motley   Nicholas Dee

tertain) and then from four until sunset. There was music
and drink in the long evenings, and many nights the men
passed out from exhaustion and liquor, to sleep in the open
air, on the great platform of the opera house. On each
Sunday the actors presented a new play, observing and sati-
rizing the progress and events of the week. Though Verweerd
pretended to help in the composition, the performance was
usually impromptu, and broadly stolen from familiar skits
and farce:

"Frans, as a housewife, tossed stones and lumber in
the pot, singing, to a tune unknown to me, the verse of
Cats about the peacock's pride, all the while pestered and
mauled by the men dressed as carpenters. When he adminis-
tered the broth to calm them, waving the wood beam like a
wand, they all fell to working, recalling the advice of
Cook, Tuesday last, that drunks who proposition her after
evenings should take their tools and apply them elsewhere.
What he means, and Cook said plainly, is hard work both
humbles and cools the heat of ardor."

TEN

An angel come to earth cannot conduct himself as an angel.

—John Lewis Dee[1]

THE CITY IS A FABULOUS and colorful thing at the holiday, strung up with lights and festooned with heavy boughs dragged from the mountain forests to the east. Add to that the sparkle of a winter storm, every light and reflection trebled in the prism of rain and mist, and the city becomes fully the fabled centerpiece of our bejeweled northern coast. One wants a sleigh, or balloon, for travel, so charmingly antiquated is the effect. Noisy cabs and the dread thunder of the jumbo jets don't fit with the pretty picture. The old downtown, especially, during the holiday, suggests carolers, jingle bells, and bonfires. The traditional Christmas Skiff (a flat-bottomed boat carved from cedar, bearing live fowl and camas roots prettily arranged around a central tower of flames) is sent floating into the harbor. The native population, confined to live in the tidal flats south of the first settlement, sent them (tradition would have it) each year on the night of Christmas, possibly to infect the settlers with parasites and rot, and in the hopes of burning the settlement down. The city fathers adopted the odd custom. It became a local celebration—a recognition and embrace

1. John Lewis Dee, *Miscellaneous Papers*, undated.

of the native culture (plus a chance to vend yams and barbecued chicken). Indian Illumination Night, we call it now.

I don't fancy the crowded noise and hoopla of these manufactured occasions, but I do enjoy my solitary strolls during the holiday. People take some small measure of pride in their appearance, dusting off the odd dress shoe even, emerging like rare, ephemeral butterflies from the chrysalis of sloth within which they sleep the other fifty-one weeks of the year. The cursed athletic shoe is, for a brief time, left at home, replaced at the very least by a sensible boot of the sort a lady or gentleman wears regularly in other, more sophisticated places.

Buoyed by the melting, and satisfied with the good progress of my work, I decided to take a trip to the vista. It was the evening of the First Boats, and I wanted to view the city from above during the height of its celebration. I thought, as a rare treat, I would dust off Kitty's special metal box and carry her with me. We set out at eight that evening, wandering away from our "sealed" home with the intention of mounting a tram headed east. The crowds are what confused me first, I think. There is no reason so many people should be on my street during a university holiday. I never imagined we'd be swept onto a tram by the surging of uncharacteristic masses of dancers. Or were they conventioneers? Their badges explained it, I'm sure, but they were written in a Cyrillic alphabet. I only know that the tram seemed to be correct, but the push of people behind us kept me from reading the number clearly.

The rubber-rimmed doors slapped shut with some difficulty and I settled in a seat next to three fat men. They chattered in a language I didn't understand. No worry, they all seemed smartly dressed, and the tram was lurching in the proper direction. It dragged up the slight incline, and began rounding the university's hill toward the valley. I couldn't see out the windows. The fleshy cargo blocked my view, and kept the glass steamed with their heat and exhalations. There could be no worry about missing our stop. The vista was the end of the line. Sad we couldn't see the pretty view along the way, though.

The faces were too uniform and fat to interest me, so I avoided them. I glanced for a while at the dull, repetitive advertisements, and then focused on the struggle of three riders attached to a shared leather strap. The three were standing and relied on the hung strap for support. It was designed for the task, and could accommodate more in its loop. These three entreated the leather firmly and persistently. Each required support of a particular strength and direction. A shorter woman had insinuated her slight, gloved hand into the lowermost fold, and let it lie fishlike. There she hung, in the narrow saddle formed by thirty years of downward tugging. She spun and pivoted as the tram demanded (or the crowd allowed). A gentleman who seemed to be sleeping stood by her, clutching the strap mid-leather. He pushed and pulled on it as the crush swayed him to and fro. A third, much taller man, was lashed to the upper fixture, where smooth bolts held the leather firmly to its mooring. He was content to stabilize himself; strong fingers and a stiffened wrist kept him from lurching.

I imagined vectors extending outward from each hand, directed deftly by the turn of a wrist or the motion of our travel. The sad droop of the young lady's hand steered her vector groundward. It pierced the tram's mechanical bottom and burrowed deep into the hillside. Absently, and as if too tired to do otherwise, she excavated the city and its hills, slicing through millennia of stone by a simple turning of the wrist. The sleepy man searched the bay, his strong wrist pointed back from whence we came. Deep-water fish woke from their blind slumbers; silt rose from the lightless bottom; and bones that had fallen there were disturbed. The very tall man pierced the sky, and his vector went farthest without touching anyone. Every hand held a vector now, on the busy tram. Hundreds of searching lines crowded the city's sky, bisecting birds, splitting raindrops, and tracing impulses on the clouds. The clattering metal car kept on, dragging its cargo of wreckless inquiries into the valley east.

We seemed to have taken a wrong turn. At some point in my reverie the tram swung off its expected track and made its way into the valley of the gray factories. Kitty was not concerned. The moist heat of the public carriage put her to sleep, and no turn, right or wrong, would wake her. The crowd had thinned some, and I could see lights in the neighborhood. They were hardly the festive ones I remembered from the regular route. Nothing was very bright; even the strings of colored decorations on houses looked shabby and dim. I saw no one out walking and wondered why the conventioneers would be touring this neighborhood. I looked again, and recognized their badges. We were on a tram to the factory, and only the workers of the night shift were with us. Kitty knew nothing, and was content. The cars lurched to a stop. The operator said the tram went nowhere after this. It was a "deadliner," and would not return along its route until morning.

Out the front window, where the operator cleaned it with his rag, the tall brick stacks of the factory were visible. They emerged from the corrugated roofs, broad and curved and scrubbed clean. The pleasant brick might have framed some facility of the university; I could imagine undergraduates playing handball there. The stacks darkened as they rose, punctuated at intervals by tiny blinking lights. Deposits of ash and contaminants stained them more completely, until, at the top, from thin blackened lips where they ended in the sky, slow rolling smoke poured out. It formed a river of gray against the darker night, and was stained red by the warning lights.

I think some kind of metal was once refined here, but shifting economies turned it into a chemical plant. I'd seen ships in the harbor loaded with green plastic barrels; fertilizers and foodstuffs conjured from slag heaps and sent overseas for the poor. The older refinery was now a ruin: long scars of brick lay where the stacks collapsed; poisonous cisterns were scattered like open sores, where the original pits had filled with blackened water. I got off the tram by the gates and watched the others amble in. They disappeared beyond the fences and I was alone with Kitty on a wet street. The tram operator assured me return trips ran on the number-seven line, closer to the harbor. If I simply walked the ten or twenty blocks I'd find them, and be home in no time. He shut the interior lights off, and settled onto the padded bench for a nap.

Vast brick warehouses filled the flat valley, and the harbor's cranes could be seen. They creaked and wheeled against the night sky, brightly lit by floods. The harbor was sleepless and active, like the factory. They never rested, it seemed, and I began walking, hoping to reach a tram somewhere between. Kitty woke up and kept her nose pressed to the gate, taking in the air. We walked in the middle of the empty street. Steam from underground rose through vents and manhole covers. The houses behind us stopped where the valley flattened out. No one wanted to live here, where the waste and slag had been poured. Landfill had made it solid since then, and the warehouses were built on that. A figure slouched by two corrugated doors on the block ahead, a boy, a teenager no doubt, probably here for a revel or rave, or to visit some weird industrial club of the sort I'd heard now took up space here. Youth had perversely made the manufactured wasteland into their playground, attracted by the glamour of filth and industry. He seemed to be alone. I could hear no telltale din of dancing or revelry. There could be no party without noise. He hadn't noticed us yet, and I crept into the shadows, not wanting to become his victim.

This boy might have been fourteen or fifteen. When he looked up, staring mostly at the distant cranes, I noticed eyes like those of Oscar Vega, deep and dark; they created an irresistible gravity toward which my attentions poured. The boy's full mouth, slightly open, was also as F.Y.I. described it. I was glad to be caught in shadow where I could see him without detection. I drew nearer, careful not to jar Kitty, nor elicit from her a sound. The boy wore a T-shirt, and was slim. Were those the palpitations of his heart, amplified by light and shadow, there beneath his thin cotton shirt? I felt my own heart racing, probably with fear, and took my station ten or twelve feet from him. I would watch and decide on some course of action. The boy stood still, hands in his pockets, and sunk his chin lower. He seemed content, as though the date he waited for was reliable, or he simply didn't care. Kitty made a slight meow and the boy turned toward us, almost smiling and curious. The sound from the shadows puzzled him. "Kitty?" he called warmly. He clicked his tongue and crept nearer. "Kitty, kitty, kitty." Good soul, she answered back, and he smiled, holding his two hands out to feel a safe way through the darkness. Fear kept me still and silent, though my heart raced faster, and my breathing became troubled and shallow. Kitty kept answering and the boy drew near enough to touch me. His warm hand brushed across my shoulder, and suddenly our shadow was thrown by a river of blazing light. The spots of two silent police cruisers flooded the block, bright as a noon summer sun. Kitty slipped back into the depths of her box. The boy and I stood, almost embracing, caught in the merciless klieg lights.

The police worked swiftly. The boy was rushed into one of the cruisers. They drove him away before I even had time to ask any questions. The second car stayed, illuminating the block for the cameras. I heard the busy static of their radios, and the eerie blips and beeps that came in with the voices. There were two officers and a dog. The cruiser was plush and seamless, sporting no exterior markings to indicate its function. The cameraman lurked in the margins. His dim red indicator light could be seen, moving across the dark like a lit cigarette. I stood still where they'd caught me, and kept a finger in Kitty's cage to soothe her; everything would be fine. The taller, man-lier officer approached me, carrying a small notebook and a pen. "Evening, sir, sorry to have alarmed you." He offered his hand to me. The bright light didn't seem to bother him. "Sergeant Dex. I'm with vice." We shook. "Nicholas Dee," I answered. "Professor Nicholas Dee, History." He made a note of it in his book. A hand signal from the sergeant shut the camera down, and the equipment was packed and gone in minutes.

"Terribly sorry about the boy, Dee, but he's one of ours; we couldn't have him traipsing off with you tonight. We've got more important crimes going down." The officer chuckled in a friendly way, as though we were confederates.

"The boy is a police officer?" I asked innocently. "He seemed awfully young for police work."

Sergeant Dex kept scribbling as he talked. "The boy's not a policeman, per se, but we do like to keep him as part of our opera-tion. Suffice to say he's better off elsewhere tonight."

"Has he been arrested, then?" It was all so sudden and arbitrary. They'd probably misunderstood his actions. "He wasn't assaulting me, Sergeant. At least I don't think so."

"Of course he wasn't, Professor."

"It was Kitty, you see. He wanted to pet Kitty and was having some trouble finding her in the dark." I held the cage up by way of explanation. Sergeant Dex raised his eyebrows and sighed, then con-tinued with his note-taking. "We were in the shadows, obviously, and he wanted to find her."

"This Kitty of yours," he asked, gesturing toward the cage. "Do you usually bring her along?"

"I'm not some sort of habitual prowler, Sergeant." His imputa-tions offended me. "I was on my way to a tram, back to the univer-sity. We boarded the wrong one and ended up out here."

"And the boy was going with you?"

"You don't seem to realize, I could have been a victim here." His superior attitude and incessant note-taking had got my hackles up. "I'm sure I don't need to remind you that you are a servant of the public, Mr. Dex, and should act accordingly."

"Professor," he mollified, patting my hand. "As I tried to explain, we're not arresting you. I'm taking a few notes, for my own reasons, just a little background on your M.O., address, occupation, that sort of thing. I'm happy to drive you and your Kitty home, gratis, door-to-door. I'm trying hard to serve, Professor. Excuse me if it's a little rough out here, but you're the one who chose to leave home tonight."

"M.O., Sergeant?"

"Just a little background, sociological data or whatnot. I'm sure you've seen worse in the psychology labs. Shall we?" He gestured toward the car.

Sergeant Dex proved to be a more soothing and informative guide on the trip home. While his partner drove and muzzled the overexcited dog, Sergeant Dex stayed in back with me talking, inquiring more politely about my work and studies, and the features of the city that interested me most. He reassured me again about the boy, pointing out that urchins on the street have no better friend than the police, for family and school have already abandoned them. The police, he told me, keep a special eye out for youth and their safety, and in return the young ones help the police with information and "street smarts." He would not tell me the boy's name.

At home I reflected sadly on the discoveries I'd made: the dreary, hidden conditions that persisted near the factory, and the dangerous life of peril which filled the city's streets. It was a city over which the police alone held dominion. Looking out my window, past the obscuring tarps, the chaotic lights of the harbor and the downtown presented a bleak totality to me. It was all dirty out there, all untoward and threatening. What role could the university ever have in a city such as this? My contact with the police, and the terrible tale they told, threatened to undo what small faith I had in the safety and future of my life (and vocation). The protections and tranquillity of the campus itself had even been called into question by Sergeant Dex.

Good that I was having my home reinforced. If the workmen ever finished, I'd at least feel safe in my apartment. I looked around the small room, noting the cluttered cartons and old food I'd let accumulate. Papers were scattered everywhere; what they didn't cover was obscured by a thin film of sawdust. My bed was habitable but nothing else. It wouldn't do to drag my home down too. It wasn't much, just an emblem of something greater, but I set to cleaning my ravaged apartment, right there and then. At least I could take some comfort in those few sanctuaries I did have. I slept.

The rains had increased and the days grown dark while I worked alone on my researches. My only trips out were for food at the Eichelberger, and to go swimming with Francis. I descended the sturdy metal ladder each afternoon, usually at dusk, and made my way past the other apartments (empty, probably for the holidays). Everything was melting. The soil was heavy with water. The drains had clogged, and the basements of the university were made unstable. Miss Benifica, in fact, was overcome by a gushing from the ventilation duct, a stream of slush which came suddenly down upon her as she mimeoed. Abbott sent her home and ordered the reprographics office closed.

The newspapers were filled with declarations and disasters. Madame Ethyl wailed unceasingly about Gideon and Judgment, but did so quietly and at a back table. I took soup, and whatever the chef recommended. With Francis, it was pizza, and his kind attentions. I turned a blind eye to the newspapers. The clean fences of text enclosed a frightening territory of unfathomable dangers. I willingly immersed myself in the safer world of Andries Verweerd, and resisted the paper's insistent alarm bells re: the dissolving world around me. I sometimes had need of information: the date or day of the week; the phases of the moon; or the schedule of power interruptions in the various districts. But these few concerns, and a mild curiosity about the police, were all I pursued in the papers.

More important news came from Francis, letting me know by telephone when next he wanted to visit the pool. We went each Wednesday, as arranged, and now went on Mondays and Saturdays too. Other news came from Abbott. "Contracts are forthcoming," his remarkably calm and casual message said. "Nothing's really set, but my agent's floor is one-fifty and I'm thinking of a two-thirds/one-third split, which I'm sure you'll agree is fair given the work I've put in and the fact it is your first time out. She's set the auction for next Monday, and I'll call you when I get word. Maybe you could dig up another few nuggets on J.L.D.? Something a little more biographical. Check the archive, and I'll have them faxed to sweeten the pot." Could he mean one hundred and fifty thousand? Even one-third meant fully twice what I spent in a year. The pot seemed plenty sweet enough. No use going back to that cursed mine (in the subsubbasement) digging for nuggets where there was only dirt. I was sure I'd find nothing in those cold, ungiving papers (neither any mention of myself, nor items useful to the chairman). I gazed out the window, past the scaffolding and thick swirling rain, and wrote a note to Abbott saying so.

Perhaps my cold shoulder put him off; he canceled a little get-together I'd planned, a bit of Christmas cheer for myself and the Weathered family, on the eve of Christmas Eve. Amelia insisted on two days at the cabin, his note said. Francis would be staying home (watering the plants) and they'd drop him off at my apartment for the party, if that was still all right with me.

I'd made space by moving the wardrobe and drawers to the kitchen, and arranging some chairs around the desk. Clever lighting and my extra flannel sheets masked the ravaged walls, and I hung hemlock boughs and ivy from the exposed beams. Together with the bright red punch bowl, and streamers cast hither and thither, the decor gave the impression of a festive Alpine hut. Purcell on the tape machine added a pretty background. At the appointed hour, Francis could be heard, shouting my name from outside on the street.

With his bright face blushing from the exertions, he clawed his way up the ladder (ascending swift as an eagle) and alit in the absent doorway. He wore a bow tie and pressed slacks. His kind mother sent a note, both of thanks and regrets. It mollified me, and I read Abbott's handwritten postscript: "Warner may go to 200. Give me a call Monday." The boy had no intelligence about his parents' impetuous flight. He'd been given a fruit basket, wrapped in noisy yellow cellophane, which I took from him and placed before us, amidst the hors d'oeuvres. Francis clapped his "things" upon the table and quaintly began removing the food. "It's my mother, Mr. Dee," the boy stammered. "There's something I need to tell you." His haste and boldness alarmed me. What secret motors turned to make this innocent boy seem so troubled?

"What is it, Francis? Sit, here, catch your breath. Is there something wrong with the food?" He finished the hasty clearing without any further explanation and sat, as I bade him, for a moment on the bed. Then he sighed deeply and started in again.

"It isn't any accident that we've met, Mr. Dee, you must know that already." He stared at me with need or impatience—it was difficult to tell which.

"Of course it isn't, Francis. I'm a colleague of your father."

"No, no, no, Mr. Dee," he objected. Clearly he was worked up about something. "I don't mean just meeting. I'm talking about my mother, her notes, all of this time together."

"Have you not been enjoying our time together?" My heart sank briefly. "You need only have said."

"Mr. Dee." He grasped my loose hand, and entreated me with his eyes. "You know it's terrific going to the pool and getting to visit you here. I don't mean any of that." He paused and turned to face me more directly. Who was this boy, so voluble and full of things to say? He'd been so silent up till now, and so deceptively clear, almost invisible.

"What do you mean, Francis? I'm not making any sense of it."

"I've made you mad."

I drew my mind together, wanting to speak reasonably and clearly, so that he'd not misunderstand me. "No, Francis. I'm not angry with you at all." I looked at him intently, anxious that he get my meaning. "We can be reasonable and clear, can't we?"

"You might as well try and stop water with a sword, Mr. Dee. I know well enough by now, it's all fatal and foolish. She's making everything happen again, and you've landed here, in the middle of it all. You might as well be stranded, Mr. Dee, belched up on some island and drowned."

"Calm, Francis," I begged. "Let me get you some water and we'll just catch our breath." I went to the kitchen and pushed my way in between the furniture. The water wasn't cold, but it would have to do. I sat down next to him, and made him drink slowly. We took a moment to rest. "What about your mother, dear boy? What exactly has she done to you?"

"She needs your help, Mr. Dee. You'll have no alternative."

"I don't see why she hasn't asked me. She seems perfectly polite and well mannered. Of course I'd do anything to help her." I was none the wiser for the boy's explanation. "But what's happened to *you*, Francis? I was asking about you."

He clamored to his feet and stood, wobbling perilously on the spongy bed. He addressed me, posturing like some plumed bird or oracle. "Destiny, Mr. Dee; I'm to tell you about the instrument of this world and what's in it." He glanced again at the notes he'd scribbled on his wrist. "She said you'd help us, if I asked you. It's all her plan, Mr. Dee, not that I minded at all, but I never thought she'd take so long." I expected, at this juncture, tears or wailing, but none came. I worried that he was, perhaps, ill, or somehow possessed.

"Have you caught something, Francis, some virus, or a, a contagion?"

"It's her, Mr. Dee. I'm simply transmitting what she compels me to."

"Just . . . how old are you, Francis?" Maybe the boy had been made to drink liquor again.

"Twelve, Mr. Dee. Thirteen next month." The absurdity of his posture, and the terrible desperation of his tone clashed inside me like conflicting weather fronts. He seemed much larger and more complicated than any twelve-year-old boy I'd known before.

"Is your mother, is she a, is she quite small, would you say?" The boy stayed standing, out of breath and flushed. My questions seemed to puzzle him.

"Well, she is very short."

I blanched at the implications. "Is she a dwarf, do you know?" He nodded. Yes.

It was "her." "She." It could be no other. "Sit by me please. I'd feel much more at ease if you'd just sit here beside me." I patted the comforter where he stood. "Do you know, do you have any idea, what she wants from me, what exactly?" Francis loosened his collar and sat down. "More water?"

"Yes please, thank you." I went to the tap again and filled two glasses. "I think she needs to finish some work she's doing, the book. She needs some help with it."

"Funny she wouldn't just ask. It sounds like a reasonable enough request." I sipped my water, spilling some with my nervous hands.

"It's not reasonable at all, Mr. Dee. It's a very difficult book. Abbott didn't have the slightest idea."

"Oh yes, of course." I remembered that she'd married the new chairman just last year. "Is that why they're married? Was she after his help too?"

"I don't know, really. She doesn't seem to expect much from him." Francis was leaning against me now, and I felt both sad and relieved.

"And to whom was she married before Abbott?"

"Oh, no one. She's never been married before." Francis reported the fact nonchalantly, but I blushed with embarrassment at my indelicacy.

"I'm sorry, I shouldn't pry. But, surely your father, that is, I meant to ask . . . who is he?" I stammered, trying to find solid ground. The boy looked at me shyly, inclining his head down, as if to diminish the impact of what he was about to say.

"I think," he whispered to me, leaning close. "I think my father is John Dee."

The breath drew out of me like a phantom.

"Amelia says so, anyway," he added. I stared in dumb fascination at the boy. I looked at every feature of his face again; the eyes revealed to me a depth of brown I'd sensed but glanced away from; the delicate brow gave itself away, the slight turn and length, an infant version of my father's elegant, dark lines. I looked down impulsively at his small, palpitating chest, there beneath his shirt, where the muscle turned in its nest of bones. I could imagine it, had in fact seen it so often at the pool, the delicate motion of his pale skin. My hand came up, to reach inside his shirt and rest there, but stopped instead at his shoulder. I gave a reassuring pat. He held his hand over mine and we did not speak for some time.

The storm had risen and there was thunder when he left. He vanished into the night insisting on his promise to be home to attend to the plants (some of which were nocturnal). Alone, as I was, and beckoned to the kitchen by the sound of the tap I'd left running long before, I glanced at my reflection in the naked glass of the unframed window. I suppose we all have such moments of transparency or doubt, but I have them seldom, and am all the more disturbed by them for it. The brief, accidental glimpse of my thin reflection gave rise to an unreasonable expectation that I should be seeing Francis or my father outside that same window. The reflection became then, for no more than an instant, a dumb, puzzled flickering between these two as I asked myself, whispering, is that Francis, or my father, my father or Francis? Fatigue kept me from seeing it was my own profile that startled me. I lurched toward the window, thinking to grasp them, or him, whomever, and the image rushed toward me, equally panicked and unreasonable. The flickering confusion dissolved into bewilderment about the reflection itself, frustration that this accident of light could confuse me so powerfully, and leave me lurching after phantoms. Where was I in this equation? I felt my body beat once with fear, a vertigo, like falling, which engulfed me and then disappeared.

THE TEMPEST.

Henry Purcell.

AIR. *(Ariel)* KIND FORTUNE SMILES.

Kind ____ for - tune smiles and she Has

yet ____ in store for thee Some strange ____

____ fe - li - ci - ty. Fol - low, fol - low me, fol - low, fol - low me,

fol - low, fol - low me, fol - low, fol - low, fol - low, fol - low, fol - low, fol - low, fol - low, fol - low,

In the morning I woke and opened my eyes to the strange decorations that had framed our little "party." Francis came rushing back to mind then . . . balanced on the bed pronouncing. His claim about my father rose up like sickness or a hangover, and staggered me, again. I postponed getting up, wanting some safety under the covers. It was mute and warm there. I clutched the long pillow to me, and fell back into sleep. In the close, orange light beneath the covers, I dreamt the feeling of Francis's heartbeat so vividly I might have been touching him. I'm certain it was *my* chest I felt, drifting away. But that momentary action, made long and complex by half-consciousness, was enough to reassure me, or settle something, and I woke again feeling better, more stable and brave. It was almost nine and I dressed and made coffee, as though starting a typical day. Francis had said he would be fine, but I went over posthaste to see that the boy's revelations (and our moment of sharing and/or grief) had not left him unduly anxious.

The day outside was empty and gray. Lifeless clouds, unlocatable in height or dimension, were upon us again, and the silent neighborhood mimicked them. The stores were deserted, though open, and the trams ran without passengers or noise. I tried whistling, to brighten things, and accelerated my pace. I had the watch with me, and the small scribbled note she had dropped. Francis answered the door and hugged me. I tried directing us inside, but Francis clung so tight it was as if we tangoed, the one partner leading, the other dragged along. The boy had been crying. "She's mad at me, Mr. Dee." I let him lean closer, and put my hand on his shoulder to steady him. "I just know she's found out somehow." Francis looked like a drowned puppy. He hadn't slept properly, and seemed not to have changed his clothes since the night before. A blanket and pillow on the floor showed he probably stayed the night near the door worrying, crying by himself with the bow tie and party clothes left on. I guided him to the couch and let him lay his head against me and sniffle.

"It's all right, Francis," I assured him. "There's certainly no way she could've heard. Neither you nor I have passed this little secret on, and nor will we until we deem it time." He looked up from my chest, all puffy and blushing.

"She knows already, Mr. Dee. I'm sure of it. She always does, and when she gets back . . ." Fear passed though his eyes and he pressed his face to my shirt again and bawled. Maybe I'd underestimated the depravity of this dwarf.

"She doesn't . . . beat you, does she?" I asked, holding the boy more closely. Francis shook his head no, snuffling his nose along my shirt as he did so.

"I wouldn't have said anything if she'd not sent me over by myself," he protested. "She's the one who kept putting it off and putting it off."

"And no harm done by telling me, Francis. You've done nothing wrong." He was inconsolable. "Surely if we explain to her the circumstances; she'd have to be blind not to see the reason in it. Dry your eyes. I'll not stand by and see you punished for this." Francis clung to me still, sniffling and drying his face with my shirt sleeve. My solidarity calmed him some, but didn't seem to dispel his dread. He both needed and feared her return, and there was nothing I could do to hasten it. Francis handed me a crumpled yellow page. It was a telegram.

"This came, just before you got here." He'd opened it, though it was addressed to Abbott. I unfolded the small crinkly paper and scrutinized the text. "Warner went to 190, plus in-kind travel for Dee. If possible, MS by spring, fall pub date. Schama to ghost on bio, ghost needed for Tempest? Please advise. Tempest travel ASAP. Boat or plane? Call. Blinky."

"Travel?" I inquired out loud to no one.

"It's your book contract," Francis said matter-of-factly. "I think they've arranged travel for your researches." The boy wasn't just guessing. He seemed to have picked up some of Abbott's impressive business sense. The grief fell briefly from his tearstained face like a mask as he pointed to the relevant details. "ASAP. That means soon. I think they've arranged in-kind travel, so you've got to take it on their schedule." He looked up at me patiently, like an elementary school teacher leading a child through sums.

"Boat or plane," I recited. "I guess that means to Europe."

"To Holland," Francis specified. "Blinky never gives an openended junket for a first-time-out." I looked at him, cowed by his expertise. "Abbott said so," he explained, nodding. My future was rushing toward me, faster than I cared to take it. On this morning when I'd hoped simply to console the boy and sew some happiness, sixty-three thousand dollars and travel ASAP came instead, courtesy of the missing chairman. "I've wired the accounts back to Blinky," Francis continued, "and said 'no' to the ghostwriter. We can set up the travel arrangements when Mother gets back." He savaged a ragged thumbnail with his teeth, and looked at me.

"You've wired this 'Blinky'?" I inquired. "The publisher?"

"She's your agent. I used Abbott's name. Mother made it very clear he was to accept any offer that included travel."

Francis doggedly insisted he stay at the house and wait for his parents' return. I ordered him to wash up and change his dirty clothes, and counseled that he not let sloth flourish amidst grief. He would alert me as soon as "she" returned, sometime the next day, and our tête-à-tête would be had without delay. Francis would be fine. I checked the kitchen and saw he was well stocked with coffee and tea. I pinned Madame Ethyl's number to the corkboard, just in case. Of course I wanted to stay with him; but reason told me a few hours away, putting together my researches, would do no harm.

By afternoon the clouds covered everything. Increasing traffic slipped and slid along the wet pavement. The police were positioned at the intersections, directing cars where the lights failed. Hovering choppers radioed intelligence back to them and kept everything regular. Special units were set up around sinkholes and other hazards of the flood. Their clean blue vehicles and black stormcoats glistened in the mist, catching the blood-red reflection of the warning lights. I made my way past them with haste, not wanting to be caught in an emergency.

Dazzled though I was by the figures, and the formal authority of the breathless telegram, none of it seemed real without Abbott's loud confirmation. Until he returned and said it was so, I thought it best to resist undue anticipation. There were a few boxes to pack at the office, and bring back to the safety of my home. Mist obscured the library spires and the hour with it. While night darkened the edges of the sky, the area of the university stayed strangely lit. Floods from the choppers diffused evenly in the mist, and turned the sky yellow and gray. The carved texts of buildings were still readable through the gloom.

Tribal noises could be heard as if from classroom films, tinny and thin in the distance. Those few students who stayed for the holidays were banded together in some revel, clad only in sheets and sandals, reenacting a bacchanal of sorts with plastic jugs of beer instead of wine. Near the old campus gate I strode past them, swerving to avoid collapsing athletes. The yard stank of mud and vomit. Middling scholars crouched prone in the debris, lowered to their knees by alcohol and dancing. Music from competing systems blared across the middle ground, powered by the towering amplifiers of rival factions. I couldn't think clearly in the cacophony and wondered if the choppers weren't maybe hovering here for reasons of vice. Circles of "dancers" could be seen crashing against walls and into windows. Their frenzy spun them beyond the designated area. The line between celebration and vandalism seemed to have become completely blurred. I blinked at the blinding colored strobes, and looked skyward, hoping for some timely intervention. Were these even students at all? Their loud, unbordered event erased all trace of the choppers. Which didn't mean they weren't, in fact, there. I clasped my hands to my ears, focused my eyes on the steps in front of me, and hurried through this circus of degradations to my office and chores.

"She" had been there, and left another submission. I knew it to be so, soon after reading this last and strangest installment in her written seduction of me. All pretense was gone, and she brazenly embraced her real subject: me. This "chapter," plus my new intelligence from Francis, re: "her" left no doubt about the identity of my tormentor.

The gray mists *were* soft against the windows, and distance *had* indeed muted the evening din of the bacchanal. I *do* admit to feeling a little drowsy, and lying down on the stuffy couch to read. But the rest I cannot account for:

"F.Y.I.

"Alone in his office, Nicholas Dee hangs his coat on the metal hook, feeling drowsy. Clutching the manuscript pages he's just received, Nicholas shuffles toward the office couch, and begins to clear papers from it. He slumps into the cushions, helpless in the face of his nap. The couch aches at him, sweet as honey, beckoning him to recline. It draws his body and limbs down. The gray mist is soft against the window, and the din of students has been muted by distance and exhaustion. He lies back and surrenders, letting the day go from his tired mind. It feels as if gravity has been wedded to joy.

"Sleep undoes him, mixing the evening with his fears, unfinished essays, ceaseless rain, and the sweet memory of a childhood nap in the afternoon, blankets tossed to the wall, a shaft of sunlight warming his small back and arms. There are butterflies, and his window looking out across the play field, noises from his father's study, and traffic along the small avenue behind the house. The couch smells of cat fur and dust. His nose is pressed to the cushion where his head rests. Nicholas brings his arm to his mouth tasting the soft skin (a habit of sleep), the salty exertions of the day, and he remembers the child's bicycle outside, propped where he left it riding back from the field. Warm and sweaty, rushing in to the living room and his father; then, later, laid down in bed he pedals again, warm legs working against the cushions. Too big for the couch, his legs keep extending. The bicycle is sturdy beneath him and the pressure against his back; that woman from the bookstore rides along above him, her face falling against his ear. His body is too big for the tiny bike. She presses against him like the sky and he can't seem to turn far enough to see her. Each time he tries turning his neck ever so little and slowly the bike begins to wobble and fall, and he lurches forward to right himself, bumping his hands against the couch arm. It's hard pedaling in sand, and with that woman occupying the sky. She smells of cat fur and dust, warming him all over, thick and heavy as a shaft of sun in the afternoon as he slept. His wrist is salty where he tastes it. How could he not have noticed? She's everywhere, filling the sky with categories and words, impossibly clear, and yet unreadable. Lines drop down from them, describing a geometry of the day, crowding the afternoon and cutting across the child in bed asleep beside the wall. In one startled breath he sees it all, lurching from the couch to draw it in, panicked and completely, and he surfaces enough to ask Who is she? What is she? But the nap drags him down again into memories. How can a child's room be devoured by a thought? The weak middle of the couch pulls at him, drawing him deeper into the crevice between the cushions and the back. Nicholas tries to gather all the lines, and the words afloat in categories like ghosts above the sleeping boy and his father. Reaching into air by the couch-back, he tries to hold them. Which line is this? Can it be shifted? Nicholas pushes at it, but his arms are leaden and powerless. That woman's tether trails above the house, multiplying, turning into strings she seems to be pulling. She's been pulling them all along. His sock is caught among the springs. The boy is pinioned to his bed. The room is unbearably hot, but there are no blankets to be kicked off. She is tiny in the sky, and every line leads to her, like a vanishing point. Will he remember this? Nicholas pushes his face from the crevice and breathes, then fails to form the thought. All that's left, as he struggles from the couch, is a vague interest in insurance. Must finalize that insurance, Nicholas thinks to himself, fumbling for a pencil on his desk.

"Sometimes, as now, he feels a weary sadness, waking to find the same world from which he'd fallen into sleep. His naps seem to promise so much more, a dissolution of his borders, a rearrangement of life. He sometimes wishes the progress of his nap would not be erased upon waking, that the dissolution to which it delivers him could somehow be preserved. But there are no maps to mark these places, no geometry by which to locate them. He observes their loss, absently smoothing his undone sleeve, and wonders about the time. His thoughts evaporate like gasoline into air."

First I must remind the reader that none of this ever happened. "She" had taken advantage of the simple coincidence of my returning to my office then, drowsy, to perpetrate this fiction about my nap. The conventions of fiction falsely give her account a certain sort of authenticity. Her tactic leads, in the extreme, to the misperception that "she" had more thoroughly revealed me than I might have. (The prima facie absurdity of such a perception should be evident.) And while the details of my childhood (and my father's study) may have had a certain uncanny accuracy, that is not enough to invalidate my position as the primary reporter of my own consciousness and memories. "She" had invaded me, brazenly and completely.

I got up from the couch and hovered near the windows, thinking she must've lied to the boy, and was, by some chance, now retreating across the muddy "quad." I wanted very badly to find her, and called Francis at once. He was alone and hadn't seen either of them. His cheery tone and the background din of the television told me he'd set up house to his satisfaction. I chose not to alarm him with my suspicions. He'd call, he told me, immediately when they arrived. I next considered phoning the police, but was uncertain if a crime had been committed. Something had been taken from me, some measure of control over the narration of my life; but narration, I felt certain, was not covered by any statutes. I compromised and put in a complaint to the campus security force. I requested an APB and some sort of comprehensive search, a sweeping of the grounds, but the operator told me most of the force was home for the holidays. A stop could be put on any anonymous mail, if I requested it; an officer could visit and check my locks. Beyond that, she said, there was very little anyone could do. I refused the offer of service, still gripped by my impatience and the need for immediate action.

I tore at the file drawer, searching for her earlier chapters. I'd put them all in the growing "N.O.H." folder, and only managed to isolate them after an agonized sorting of the legitimate submissions from this small pile of masquerading fictions. How had I let them infiltrate so thoroughly? The creation of new files seemed like a logical first step, a hedge against the chaos perpetrated by my tormentor. I unwrapped a clutch of folders, and began marking the titles and dates of each submission boldly on the manila tabs. I'd keep each one separate, "in solitary" as it were. Arranged chronologically, the folders filled an inch of space in my topmost file.

I phoned the campus operator again to make an appointment with security. The issue of the locks and windows had never been properly dealt with and, at this juncture, it seemed like a good next step. "I don't mean to alarm you, miss," I began, "but this is something of an emergency."

"What's the nature of the emergency, Professor? Perhaps I can get you a 9–1–1."

"I'm being written about," I tried first. There was a prolonged silence.

"I'm not sure I understand."

"Someone else is writing about me, falsely."

"What exactly is the nature of the emergency?" She was bereft of any imagination. I'd have to spell it out for her. "A mysterious dwarf, you see, has been depositing her fictional 'chapters' in my mail stop, anonymously. It hardly seemed like anything to bother you with, but then the subject of her pages turned to me and an alleged nap."

"Anonymously?"

"Well, with just some initials on each one."

"You're the earlier call, the APB?"

"That's right. I had second thoughts. Your suggestion of the inspector seemed like a good idea."

"I can put that stop on your mail, effective tomorrow." Her cheery tone implied that would be enough. She hadn't grasped the vulnerability of my office.

"But my doors and windows, miss. They're in terrible shape. Students have been prying at the latches, climbing through the windows at will. Nothing is secure. I'm in the basement, you see."

"You've had a break-in?" Forms rustled, and hasty jottings whispered through the line.

"No, no, I've not been broken into. The students were acting at my behest, simply to retrieve their papers. I meant this office could be violated, and with ease."

I heard her crossing something out, and then sighing. "All I can do, Professor, is pencil you in for January, unless there's a break-in, or some other crime, in which case I can call a 9–1–1 and get the police here to investigate."

"There's no need for the police. Not yet, anyway." A long pause was filled by more rustling. Her hand slid over the mouthpiece, briefly, and she returned to the line all business.

"That was Professor . . . ?"

"Nicholas Dee."

"Officer Kien will make a full inspection on the twenty-eighth, Professor Dee. Until then I suggest you remove any valuables or irreplaceable files. Keep them at home, or in the library if need be. And call us if you decide on the mail stop."

The bacchanal had given rise to a bonfire. Bright orange flames could be seen reflecting off the buildings. The clouds glowed too, scraping the spires, headed east toward the mountains. I pressed at the glass, troubled by its transparency and flimsiness. The dull brass hardware rocked in place. The screws' teeth dug into putty and dust. The solid wood had been drilled away. I turned the lights off, so I could see more easily out into the night, and slumped into my desk chair. In the dim chaos of my office it was difficult to say what was "valuable" or "irreplaceable" and what was junk. My tormentor could, in fact, have already broken in and stolen a great deal, and I would never know. It was my habit to let the years accumulate in clutter and dust.

I picked through the layer behind me, the melding stacks of journals and scribbled notes. A vein of Christmas cards opened up in the middle, and I plundered them. Were these "valuables"? I took a manila folder from the pack I'd opened in my first panic about the "chapters," and labeled it "Christmas." Next, the pile yielded class notes.

Labeling them was simple, and the discovery suggested a few easy categories by which to arrange the new folders. One drawer for "School" and one for "Life." Within each, clear subdivisions could be made, with the contents arranged chronologically. I marveled at the depth and variety of my accumulations. Letters, magazines, notes, reminders, unwashed plates (and the food itself), silk handkerchiefs unopened in their wrap, plastic forks and spoons gathered (probably) from the cafeteria, just in case, flat clay figurines attached to magnets (gifts?) and drawings by children, fifteen or twenty, as though I'd assigned them as homework for a class. The slant of my hand had shifted over the years, and I found I could date papers on sight, judging by the steepness of the angled letters. Pages faded and grew yellow as I dug nearer the desk, suggesting a dispersal pattern which began at some zero point on top and to the right, where my hand might naturally reach in an effort to place something "aside." Pages grew brighter and more bold as their distance from that spot increased. Backwaters on the bookshelves and couch held veins of dark, discolored papers—older work which I'd planted there, airborne spores which germinated and grew, melding finally with the larger organism. It wasn't simply sloth. This uncritical residue was organic, as with an insect secreting its carapace.

The basement was empty. The lights were doused in the few offices that shared my hall. I whispered hello through the dark frosty glass of the Reprographics room, and used my key and went in. Miss Benifica would understand, and I'd see to it my budget covered what I took. The folders were found easily, and I secured a dozen empty boxes from the recycle room. The loan of a handcart completed my supplies, and I set up on a clear spot by my office door, ready to sort and file each item and trace of my long residence in the basement of History. It took ten boxes and both my standing files, sealed and strapped, but I managed to pack it all (excepting the furniture and some food). Some papers could not be unstuck from one another, and some had faded so completely I made a special file. Textbooks, directories, and university pamphlets stayed where they were; the rest went with me up the small stairs, out the door, and into the night. I'd decided to take the operator's advice and relocate my valuables, moving them out of harm's way and into my apartment.

A trace of the moon glimmered over the mountains. Thin clouds lay low on the hills, full and dry. The handcart clattered against the stone walkway leading away from our building, and I felt the weight of it, even and balanced against my hand. Patience made their transport no trouble at all. The campus and streets were empty. Along the dark, cobbled walk, through the university's thicket of trees, and past the idle guard's booth, I maneuvered the tiny wheels. An empty tram passed, lit up inside as bright as day.

I placed the boxes on pallets laid down where the floor had been removed. It was almost 4 A.M. The phone rang. She had come in from the cold, I first thought, and Francis has been true to his word, alerting me despite the ungodly hour. Fatigue kept me pinioned to the bed for one more ring, and then I scrambled to the desk and answered. "Hello, yes?" I whispered, breathless.

"Hello, Dr. Nicholas Dee?" The voice was unfamiliar.

"This is he."

"Dr. Weathered suggested I call you."

"You mean Abbott?" Why would Abbott be giving out my number, I wondered. Unless of course re: the project.

"No, Amelia, Amelia Weathered. My doctor."

"Your doctor? Blinky?" I'd heard that New Yorkers never remembered the existence of other time zones.

"Dr. Dee? My name is Oscar Vega. I've been arrested by the police. Amelia Weathered said you might be able to help me."

THE TEMPEST.   ACT IV.   Henry Purcell.

DANCE OF DEVILS.

ELEVEN

THOUGH I'D SEEN the police tower nearly every day of my adult life, I'd never stepped inside its doors. At this hour it was the most visible landmark in the city, lit in shimmering red as though aflame. The other blocks were empty and black. The trams had stopped, and the taxi men could only be had on call, so I bundled up in my overcoat and began walking. While the city slept I hurried downhill toward the water, then turned north into the bleak neighborhood surrounding the police. The empty blocks were strewn with garbage. What the melting snow hadn't turned to pulp was blown along the street by the harbor breeze. My way was lit by harshly buzzing fixtures the police installed to keep derelicts from sleeping. There was no warning, no signs or broad plazas marking the block from which the tower rose; just the special red glow, and an apron of broad steps leading up to the metal doors. Dirty globes hung on either side of the portal, illuminating the engraved promise "to protect and inform." I looked up and marveled at the towering fabric of stone and lit windows weaving its way higher and higher into the winter night. The hundreds of barred windows gave cryptic evidence of the business conducted inside.

The grand foyer was rather small and dirty and the clatter of typing machines echoed against thin partitions of plastic and glass. A solitary man in coveralls pushed a broom along the chipped linoleum floor. The once great space, now divided into narrow hallways and cubicles, opened above me and I could see the damaged ceiling hovering in the gloom, supported by arches and metal nets. Oscar gave me no office number, nor any instruction beyond coming to the police tower to rescue him. I wandered further into the warren, hoping good fortune would lead me to the "holding tank" or what-have-you. Several yards along, as I stood choosing between doorways, two steel rings closed around my wrists. The matronly voice of a corporal (as it turned out) told me to follow. "There'll be no wandering around in here unescorted," she explained. "We'll just get you checked in with the desk sergeant."

"But Officer," I objected, even while scrambling to keep up. "You're making a mistake." I brandished my shackles at her. "I've not been arrested. I'm here to pick up a friend."

She spoke brusquely over her shoulder, not slowing. "Routine, sir. No civvies without cuffs, unless by captain's orders. I'm happy to adjust them if you're uncomfortable." A turn of her head and a quick smile told me she meant well. I was left in a small cubicle to rest, while the corporal retrieved some forms and readied me for the desk. My wrists ached now from the press of cold metal. I knew the wheels of justice to be enormous and slow, and hoped I would not he made to wear cuffs throughout their laborious turning. A burly man in police blue rattled on the door and opened it. He pointed a silent finger and beckoned for me to come.

The tower was built on the foundations of the old church. Its central dome remained, undisturbed, enclosed within the larger building. Different features of the ancient ceiling came into view as we navigated the temporary hallways, traversing the broad cathedral floor: a cherub here, a winged angel there, Adam, Eve, scenes of the Temptation. When I looked down to watch my step, the broad space shut down, but I had only to look up to return to the heavens, and the damaged allegories of the crumbling ceiling. Soon enough, they disappeared altogether. We passed through an elaborate cage and out of the glorious hall. The air turned granite and chill. I was relieved of my cuffs and taken down a long metal stairway. Bare white bulbs hung infrequently, marking intersections with crossing halls. The iodine stink of the harbor grew stronger, but I could see nothing. Slits had been carved into the battlements, obsolete rifle sights. I heard the black water outside. A green sign glowed at the end of the long straight hallway. "Vice," it said.

My escort straightened me up before the door, checked my posture, and arranged my arms nicely at my sides. He knocked on the frosted glass and strode away. A lovely lady opened this penultimate door, and smiled. "Ah, Professor Dee. We've been expecting you. Please come in." I stepped nervously forward, bowing slightly, and entered the pleasant office. "You can have a seat here. I'll get you some coffee."

"Yes, thank you very much." What a pretty anteroom Vice had. The chairs were nicely stuffed, and upholstered in a soft, shimmering fabric. A low table sat among them, Danish, obscured by magazines. The police seemed to have good taste in fine art prints. A small grouping of Impressionists graced the far wall, and a Picasso reprint sat alone opposite. I supposed that Oscar must have been collared on some Vice charge, and the desk sergeant had the good sense to send me straight through to retrieve him.

The lady officer returned with my coffee and opened a last, frosty door. "Professor Dee?" She beckoned. "The captain will see you in here." I touched my hair, habitually, took up my coffee, and went in. He was a big man, stuffed into a rolling chair behind his busy desk. Rather than rising he simply nodded. His cigar, clenched manfully between biting teeth, let go a measure of ash. "Dee," he grumbled. "At last."

"Captain," I replied.

"Sit, Dee, please." There seemed to be only a footstool. "I understand you're here to pick up the boy."

"That's right. Oscar Vega. He phoned me from the station."

"Got your number the other night, did he?" The captain smiled around his cigar.

"Actually, I think a friend gave it to him. Not a friend exactly, but a doctor. Oscar's doctor." I paused, thinking about my explanation, and tripped, again, over his question. "What do you mean, Captain, 'the other night'?" He ruffled through the papers on his desk, and pulled a clutch of yellow pages from among them. "Dex filed a report, Sergeant Dex. Certainly you remember him. Tall, manly sort?

I've got the video right here. Standard perp profile; name, occupation, M.O. It says you 'contacted' Oscar Vega Thursday night. Something about an animal."

"The boy was simply trying to reach the animal, Captain. And as I told Dex there was no 'contact' whatsoever, and certainly no criminal intent. I had no idea it was even Oscar Vega." He flipped nervously through the thin pages.

"It's a madhouse, Mr. Dee. Pure chaos. Who told these kids to go live on the streets, anyway? And who gets the blame? Victims, always the victim; men like yourself, out for an innocent walk, molested and anatomized by these drugged kids. Tell me, Professor, did the boy look sleepy to you?"

"I hardly even saw the boy, Captain. Your men had him out of there in seconds." He smiled proudly at this detail, and I gulped my coffee down. "I can't see how there'd be anyone to blame, when no crime was committed." The captain shifted in his chair, wanting to lean farther forward.

"No crime, but an imputation. You're an educator, am I right? Hardly the sort of thing a university would want to hear about. Not that there's any reason they would." He bent down to his intercom. "Sergeant, send in Clausewitz." The name brought a shivering spasm to the captain's mouth. "Certainly not, if we can find some common ground; a mutually beneficial pact, shall we say. You and I aren't enemies, Professor, but allies."

"I'm only here to help the boy, Captain, and then to be on my way."

"To help the boy, precisely. And we've got a plan to do just that. No use arresting you." He leaned toward the intercom. "Clausewitz," he barked. "ASAP."

"And no reason, Captain. I'm blameless." The man seemed to snap just then; he dashed his cigar against the wall behind him, and began crawling over the big desktop toward me.

"No one's blameless, Mr. Dee. The world's no clean oyster open to experts for the innocent shucking. I'm sure we all wish we were somewhere else." He began slipping off the desk, his precariously balanced papers giving way. "I could sing once, you know, Dee. But here I am, sitting behind this desk in a goddamned fortress." The cascade stabilized, and he perched at the edge. "We've all got our place here, Professor. Don't press me."

The door opened. An elegant gentleman in sharkskin and a felt homburg entered the room, laid his gloves and hat on the bookshelf, and turned to look at me. "Professor Dee? Clausewitz, Inspector Clausewitz." He closed the door silently. "Captain, you can sit down now." The obedient man slumped into his chair. I'd been about to take issue with the captain, but the smooth inspector made my re-joinder moot.

"Inspector. Perhaps you can clear all of this up. The captain was raving about something. I think he mentioned a plan."

"The captain is very passionate about his work, Professor. I am sure you understand. Of course we only want to help the boy, as you do."

"I don't think I understand your methods."

"Of course you don't, you're not a trained policeman. Why, even the captain here sometimes forgets, and he's been involved for over forty years." Clausewitz patted the exhausted man now and sent him from the room. He waited for the door to close and offered me a chair. "There we are now. We can all relax for a moment. I'll have more coffee sent in and we'll get everything sorted out to your satifaction."

Inspector Clauswitz was true to his word. He wanted my help collecting information from Oscar, and perhaps by making contacts with others he called "the terminal boys" (apparently those self-same urchins I'd seen hanging out by the city's ferry terminal at night). He appealed to my sense of civic duty, rather than bullying me with idle threats as the captain had. More important, he showed a sophisticated knowledge of pedagogy and the principles behind my calling as an educator. There was a world of danger we could better protect the children from, the velvet detective assured me, if we built bridges to them through talk and information. This would be my role. I assured them, by oath, that I had no previous contact with the "terminal boys" or their confederates. My innocence (though so bizzarely denied by the captain) was my passport into their confidence. I was told these duties would take no time. I'd simply note anything Oscar volunteered and, on some future evenings, be asked to spend time with other boys.

The alternative, Clausewitz insisted, was to leave Oscar Vega rotting in jail with no responsible party available to take him. Of course I agreed. Clausewitz would drop by my office the following afternoon to settle the details.

It was very late into the night. I was exhausted, essentially in a walking sleep, when the lovely sergeant knocked again on the clouded glass. I saw her profile through it and beside her the figure of a boy. He was slumped and silent, as if they'd just wakened him. I couldn't make out any details through the opaque window and became agitated waiting for Clausewitz to finish with some paperwork. He did and beckoned the boy to enter. Indeed it was him. There could be no doubt; the boy from the warehouse *was* Oscar Vega. He was tired and sleepy around the eyes, but he smiled upon seeing me and held out his hand. F. Y. I. had described him well, the haunted angelic face, and the remarkable depth of his eyes. I took his hand and said hello, startled to be touching this boy whose identity had once seemed little more than allegorical. Now here he was, warm and physical, holding my hand and repeating my name to himself softly.

Oscar Vega said little, nodding off to sleep, as we rode to the university in Sergeant Dex's cruiser. The end of the night was sweeping from the eastern sky, and faint dawn was taking its place. It was gray and bruised, promising another muted day. It took little to guide Oscar up the stairs, and a pointed finger was all he needed to get him to bed. Kitty sat atop the desk watching, waiting to see who this stranger was. Oscar barely even woke. He pushed his shoes from his feet, tugged his clothes off, then lay down and slept.

Tired and exhausted myself, I lay down beside him and watched him breathing, fascinated. The delicate ribs rose and fell in the graying light of dawn. His existence seemed almost miraculous. I'd thought of him so often, imagining days asleep beside the harbor, touching, with him, in those pages, the cool cotton sheets where he slept at Tony's house. Now he lay beside me, his warm skin alive in the air I breathed. I leaned closer and took a deep breath. The boy smelled acrid and a little salty. I swallowed, stared, and lay back down as he stirred in his sleep. The room was masked and baroque with its festive ornamentation. Nothing was changed since my aborted party. Oscar tucked one arm beneath his head and stretched out, touching me with his leg. I cannot deny the fascination of it, nor could I think to move. I lay, as if sleeping, and watched him. He took his other hand and pulled his boxer shorts down, releasing what had become obviously enlarged with his pleasure. He played upon it with his hand, manipulating himself for some time, relaxing and breathing more deeply as he did so. It was toward no climactic end, and seemed to be conducted without self-consciousness, as if in sleep. Oscar simply settled into his pleasure and dreamt. I lay beside him and could not steady my breathing nor heart. They ran fast and nervously, as if the boy, by touching himself, thereby touched me.

At some unchartable hour I had a dream. I was taking Oscar to camp. A broad field opened up before us, thick with lush green grasses and wildflowers. In the distance, activity could be seen, clustered around two camps quite near to each other. We ambled through the meadow heading equally for both. At one camp, wild unruly boys played exuberantly in the grass. The meadow flowers were all dead, trampled underfoot, turned brown and dry with neglect. Garbage and rusted metal were strewn around the field, and many of the boys seemed to have hurt themselves on it. Nevertheless, they seemed quite happy. At the other camp, the field was mown. Neatly clipped grass, damp and green, carpeted the hillside. All across the lawn, clean boys lay sleeping. They lay curled on their sides, or peacefully on their backs, cradling books. It was the university. I started toward them, happy to have found the proper camp, when a voice called out from behind me. It was Clausewitz. He was every inch a man. He beckoned me toward the garbage. Oscar, apparently, belonged there, at his camp. The sleeping boys are all dead, he told me. I pushed at one boy with my foot, trying to wake him, but he simply rolled over and stared stupidly into the air. He was drugged or unconscious, perhaps even dead. Clausewitz beckoned again.

The dirty boys were being led inside, through the great mouth of the gray granite structure that now towered into the sky. Still they fought. Groups fell wrestling to the ground gouging and tearing at one another. Clausewitz did nothing to stop them. He simply kept them moving into the building. Through the barred windows you could see them filling up the inside. They were caged, locked up, but they were wild. No one could control them in there. They could only contain them. The building was a riot of noise and violence.

Oscar had been silent, but now he began tugging at my arm. He seemed to be pulling me farther along, into the long meadow, toward the hazy horizon. It occurred to me that we could simply go to my office at the university. Oscar would be fine there. He needn't go to sleep like the other boys. It seemed like the best idea, but Oscar kept tugging. He was insistent. I could not see the horizon. It was all lost in a summer haze, a salty mist out past the edge of the field. No, Oscar, I said to him. My office is here. I work at the university. He became stronger and pulled me again. He seemed older than me now, or wiser. Please don't pull so, I begged him, but he dragged me through the grassy meadow. The ground turned wet and spongy underfoot. Out beyond the last sight of the university and the police, he took me into the tall grasses, into the wet marsh, with the shore dissolving under an incoming tide and I woke before we'd found deep water.

When I woke he was gone. Oscar's clothes were folded neatly in a pile by the bed, but his shoes and he himself were gone. Apparently he'd taken some of my things, and left while I was sleeping. No note was written, but the boy made a point of piling some of his money (five dollars), and a small pocketknife on top of the clothes. I took it as a promise to return. There were no messages waiting on the machine, so I called Francis at once. "Merry Christmas, Mr. Dee." The boy sounded genuinely cheerful, though his parents' sudden vacation gave the greeting a bitter cast.

"Francis. I'd completely forgotten. What an awful Christmas it must be for you." The continued broadcasts of the television, plus some new pop tune on the electrophonic stereo drowned out my claim.

"We do everything early, Mr. Dee, December 5. That's Sinterklaas Night. Mother's never done Christmas really. I think they're coming back today."

"Good, that's what I was hoping. It's imperative that I see your mother right away. Will you be okay in the meantime, alone I mean?"

"I'm fine, Mr. Dee. Though I hope we'll not miss our swimming today. It is Wednesday, you know."

"Of course it is, Francis. I'm not at all sure the pool is open though. I'll have to check."

"Would you? Would you phone me if it isn't and we'll do something else?" The boy's eagerness was unmistakable, and a reminder I had an obligation to him, perhaps even fraternal.

"Of course I will, Francis. I'll phone immediately if the pool is closed. We'll do something."

"Terrific, Mr. Dee. I've got my suit and towel."

"And you'll call me, won't you, Francis, when your mother and father return?"

"At once, Mr. Dee." Suddenly I remembered Clausewitz.

"I'm at the office, you know. Today, after twelve. You've got the number there, don't you?"

"No problem, Mr. Dee. I'll find you right away, wherever you are."

History was quiet, and its basement empty, on this Christmas morning. The nakedness of my office was alarming, so I hastened next door for books and papers. Clausewitz might think me a slouch, a do-nothing absentee, holding a chair just for prestige and a retirement plan. I'd seen it happen at other schools, and the masquerade offended me. A box of materials from Reprographics put the impression right. It was a few minutes after noon, now. There was a percolator next door, and some coffee mugs. I retrieved them and set the brew to perking. The aroma would soothe the inspector, while adding to the atmosphere of diligence and reasonableness. Twelve-thirty. I recognized the sleek leather glove, even before he rapped it on the window. Clausewitz was alone. I rushed upstairs to let him in. "Good morning, Mr. Dee," he bade, matter-of-factly, giving me his hat and coat without comment. He pointed toward the coffee and nodded.

"You've not slept," I noted, pouring him a cup. "Are you sure this is a good time for our discussion, Inspector?"

"I rarely sleep at all, Dee. A little coffee and I'll be sharp enough." I cleared some papers from his chair, and gestured. My arrangement let us start with a small reciprocity, coffee for coffee, chair for chair. I perched on the desktop.

"The boy's still sleeping," I told him, summoning a parental tone. "Exhausted. I don't believe he has a real home." Clausewitz nodded judicially, and pulled a slim folder from his attaché.

"Just the police, Mr. Dee. Like most of the boys; nobody is there for them except the beat cop."

"Am I, to keep him?" I asked, rushing, perhaps too fast. *"En loco parentis,* and etc., etc.?"

"That's a possibility." He gave me a hard stare. "Nothing can be done without your cooperation."

"My cooperation with you, Inspector, with 'the plan'?" Or did he mean it in some enormously larger sense? "Of course I'll do what I can, within reason."

"You'll find the police are nothing if not reasonable. I have the details with me, if you'll just clear a little space off that desk of yours."

Clausewitz wanted me to pose as an innocent, and to purchase narcotic drugs and sex from the terminal boys. I was to win their confidence with my naïveté, and establish contacts with their suppliers by suggesting drug sales to students at the university. If I was unwilling, Oscar would be taken to jail, and charges of solicitation would be brought against me.

"Don't dwell on the threats, Dee. That's just a little fail-safe. I think you'll agree the plan itself is worthwhile and there should be no need for any nastiness."

"You're proposing that I commit crimes, for the police?"

"Only to gain access to larger crimes, Professor. Don't be alarmed if our methods are strange or unfamiliar. You needn't concern yourself with methods."

"I don't see how promoting crime will be of any help to you."

"Of course you don't. That's why we want to work with you. A trained policeman isn't capable of so high a degree of undercover work."

"It's unthinkable, Inspector."

"I don't like to argue, Mr. Dee."

"There's no argument here. I simply will not do it."

"My plan is much more extensive, and more important, than you realize, Professor. It is, in fact, total. I don't mean to frighten you, but your cooperation isn't optional. I've not come here to ask you anything, I've come to inform you."

"I will not be made a criminal by the police."

"Oh, come now, Professor. You know that you're already a criminal. We all are. Let's not kid ourselves."

"I've been convicted of no crime."

"Of course you haven't. Which is why we're so keen on you. It isn't often we find someone so, so clean as yourself. Which is not to say you aren't guilty."

"Guilty of what?"

"Now, Mr. Dee. Technically, of course, there's the solicitation charge. But far more profoundly . . ."

"There's been no solicitation. You've misread my actions entirely. Any court would toss you out on your ear."

"But I thought your complicity had already been established?"

"I'm innocent, Inspector. Innocent as Job."

"I have the forms here." The cool inspector slipped some papers from his slim case, and offered them to me. "Your guilt is not a problem for us, Mr. Dee. We have every confidence you'll continue to operate on our behalf."

"I will only 'operate,' as you put it, to help the boy."

"Exactly, Professor. I'm sure of it."

TWELVE

"SHE'S HERE MR. DEE. She's come back." It was Francis, on the phone, with his breathless announcement. Amelia Weathered had returned to the city. I found her at home, waiting impatiently in the vestibule. The door opened as I approached the house, and the dwarf peered out. I had fallen finally into the crushed invisible center. Her eyes were silver and blue, icy as the day I'd first met her. They danced and darted, somewhere near my waist. I could only stare uncomfortably at the top of her hair and the colorful scarf she had wrapped around her head. She took my arm and led me in.

After her long and elaborate seduction of me I expected grand prophecies or a stirring call to action of some sort. Instead (and, I would learn, typically) she dealt with first things first. "Where is Oscar Vega?"

"Oscar?" I stammered, unnerved by her presence. Francis pointed me to the couch, then went noiselessly on to the kitchen. "He's out, out this morning, before I woke." The information upset her. "I believe he's due back at my apartment, soon."

"Out?"

"This morning. When I woke up he was gone. He didn't leave a note." Francis returned with iced drinks, and sat silently beside us.

"And you didn't wait for him?"

"I'd promised Clausewitz, you see. We were supposed to meet." Somehow I'd begun apologizing for my near heroic efforts to save the boy. "Not to worry, uh, Amelia," I continued, still fearful of her. "I left him a note with complete instructions; the office number, times, directions for locking and unlocking doors. I even included your phone number." I nodded brightly at this detail. "He hasn't called already has he?"

"Called?" she barked. "Why would he call? The boy can't read or write. Your note is nonsense to him." She dashed her scarf upon the recliner. "Go there immediately!" And with this exclamation she pointed out the door, brandishing her enormously long arm. "And bring him back here."

When I arrived Oscar was in the kitchen cooking. The apartment was full with the odor of garlic and olive oil, as redolent and welcoming as at Madame Ethyl's. The boy was singing a song about clams, poorly but with gusto: "I think of my happy condition, surrounded by acres of clams," he bellowed. "Surround-ed by acres of cla-a-ams, surrounded by acres of clams." And here he banged the pots with a spoon. The song was a regional anthem of sorts (plus an advertising jingle for a local clam shack) and Oscar seemed to know every verse. "Oscar?" I called from the doorway. "Oscar Vega? It's Nicholas Dee here." I noticed the cat curled around his neatly folded clothes.

"Nick?" The boy came from the kitchen smiling, and holding a spoon covered in cream sauce. He'd taken my tweeds, and a garish Christmas tie. "Nick's okay, right, Dr. Dee?" There was cream sauce on his upper lip.

"Anything you like, Oscar. Nick, Nicholas, whatever. What are you doing in the kitchen?"

"Cooking." He stepped up to my proffered hand and shook it. He was fresh and scrubbed from the shower, though his hair was left in a wild tangle, dripping down over his eyes. "I hope you're hungry. I made an awful lot."

"I, uhm. I'm not sure. I mean, I'm not sure it'll be just us two. Amelia, that is, Dr. Weathered would like us both at her house, and pronto." Without thinking, my hand was at his mouth, wiping the warm sauce from his lip. "There," I stuttered. "You had a bit of sauce, you see."

"Thanks. Can we maybe bring the food? I haven't put the noodles on yet." He pulled the jacket off and started undoing the tie. "Sorry about your clothes. Mine were kind of dirty."

I searched the drawers and dug up some old things I'd long since stopped wearing: a weather-worn boatman's shirt, some dungarees, a big sweater, and sturdy boots for the weather. I gave them to Oscar, in place of the professorial suit. "Where did you go this morning?" I asked him. He was cinching the dungarees up with a belt, securing the oversized pants loosely to his hips.

"To get food. You didn't have anything here."

"I wish you'd woken me up."

"I thought I could surprise you."

I sat down beside him, wanting to test the truth of Amelia's remarkable claim. "You might've left a note."

"Well, like I said, I kind of wanted a surprise, you know. I thought maybe you'd wake up and I'd have the food and all, like in bed, breakfast or whatever. I got up specially early so l could do it."

"Why didn't you phone me when you got back?" I asked it without accusation. He pulled his new boots on, and looked up.

"I didn't know where you were."

"I left a note." He wouldn't look at me. Oscar kept on with the boots.

"Didn't see it." He scooted off the bed to the kitchen. "Look you're here now, and I'm here." He clattered the pans, looking for something. I went to the kitchen to help him.

"I left it on your clothes, Oscar. In plain sight."

"I said I'm sorry, already. Screw it, Nick." The boy's temper broke, and he brandished the sausage at me. "Haven't you even got a goddamned top for this sauce?"

Amelia had filled the living room with clothing and books, towering files, boxes full of loose pages, and a glass ball collection Francis placed carefully in a plastic bag. Every other room was a shambles, disgorged of any contents by the furious movers, mother and son, who were now yelling instructions back and forth across the chaos.

"Burn the suits, Francis," Amelia demanded, from the living room. "If it won't fit Mr. Dee, I want it dispensed with."

"Amelia," I ventured, trying to locate her among the stacks. "It's me, Nicholas, Nicholas Dee. I've brought Oscar Vega." She emerged from behind some wicker baskets. Her scarf was turned into a sweatband, and she wore a hemmed lab coat for the dust. Amid the bounty

and disorder, she looked like a vendor at some holiday market unloading stolen goods. A wooden salad bowl toppled into my hands.

"At last. Oscar, give a hand to Francis with those things. Nicholas, come with me."

"Amelia?" I stammered. "What is going on?" She hurried me
up the stairs.

"I don't mean to alarm you, but we're leaving the city, tomorrow. The police may be after us."

"The police? But why? Why, and . . . And where is Abbott?"

She pulled two drawers violently from the dresser, and dumped
the contents on the floor. "Try these shirts."

"Where are you going?" I asked, too puzzled to do as she said.
"And in such a hurry?"

"'We,' Nicholas. Where are 'we' going. Holland, eventually. We
have that book to finish, after all. Francis and Oscar are going too.
I'm sure you'll agree it's best that way." She scrambled onto the dresser
top, and began unfastening pinned clippings from her bulletin board.
"Hold these."

"Where is Abbott?" The shirts had his monogram.

"Be quiet, Nicholas; be quiet and let me explain." The shirts
were stained on the collar, and smelled like Abbott. What had happened to him? Murder, or drugs, corpses, arson, and jealous ven-
dettas flooded my mind while Amelia fumbled with her clippings. I
dropped the garments to the ground, and sat on the bedside, bewil-
dered by the busy dwarf and her implications.

"Don't worry about Abbott," Amelia insisted. She leaned down
from her station, and commanded me with her eyes. "He won't be
going with us. It's your father I need to talk to you about." My father. Was it the truth now, at last?

"Francis already . . ."

"There's something else, Nicholas." She crawled down now, and
slid the shirts off the bed beside me. "Prepare yourself." I smiled
weakly.

"I don't want any of those awful shirts," I volunteered. She
turned to me.

"Your father could not read or write." What a ludicrous idea.
I blushed suddenly, and couldn't keep from chuckling at her state-

ment. The chuckle turned into a shiver of heat down my spine, and I laughed forcibly, to scare the heat away. I did not say anything more. There was nothing to say. I glanced at her, and blushed again, feeling a little sick. "He couldn't read or write, Nicholas." An awful racket came from the radio downstairs. The boys had it stuck between stations, and the static and pops were terrifically amplified. Half a voice, only the mangled consonants really, ripped and growled inside the static.

"This is just crazy," I said to Amelia; then I made myself laugh again, but it came out like the voice on the radio.

"I wrote all his books. They were my books, with his name on them." She stared at me, utterly still. "I wrote every paper, every word of his."

I had been pressing Abbott's shirt collar to my chin. I only noticed it now as I pushed the shirt farther up my face and smelled him again. My eyes darted above it, like fugitives above a wall. Abbott stank of tobacco and sour sweat, and I looked over at Amelia. "I, you see. I don't see any reason to believe you. It's ludicrous. No reason at all." She took the shirt from me and tossed it to the floor.

"He never learned to read or write, Nicholas. It's that simple. His grandfather couldn't read or write, you know that. Who do you think would have taught him?"

"It's just crazy," I stammered, taking the shirt back from the dirty floor. "Even if he's gone . . . somewhere, that's no explanation for treating his, his shirts this way." I gathered them all up and retrieved the two drawers. "This is just nonsense about my father." Amelia watched me straighten and fold the undone clothing, and did not keep me from putting the drawers back in the dresser. She was silent for a while. "I would have known, Amelia. I would have known, and everyone else would have too." The pins and tacks were gone, so I tried pressing the yellowed news clippings to the board, trying to match the small perforations to the holes. "He was my father, after all. Of course I'd know such a thing." The scraps all fell as soon as I stopped pressing. Amelia gathered them from the floor and threw them in the garbage.

"He was a brilliant man, Nicholas. He just couldn't read or write."

"So you did it for him." I was dizzy, maybe from stretching to reach the board. I sat and bent my head down to give it blood. Now Amelia threw the shirts away too, and yelled for Francis to come take the plastic bag.

"I wrote for myself. We worked together, Nicholas, but they were my books. We talked, and that helped me think. I had no other way to get my work out, Nicholas. John Dee had access to certain things and I did not. He let me use his name." It still made no sense to me, but neither did my objections. I wanted to hit her with some proof, some incident or evidence, a document in his hand, a note of love or thanks he'd written to me, which I had as proof, but there was no such thing. The cold metal archive came swimming back with all its typewritten pages, and I felt sick again and lowered my head farther between my knees. Some time passed, perhaps only minutes. Francis saw us and said nothing. He slipped the bag away, and hurried back downstairs.

"What do you want from me?"

Amelia put her hand to my cheek and made me turn toward her. I'd been avoiding her eyes. "I have one book left to write. You're going to help me finish it."

I sat on the bed, clutching the one shirt I'd kept her from taking, and stared at my pale hands. I never thought the simple motions they made writing had much interest or importance, but now I watched and made the letters of my name: N-i-c-h-o-l-a-s D-e-e, my hand wrote in air, slowly moving through the shapes. J-o-h-n D-e-e: a name—a shape— whose traces I'd failed to find in all his papers. There were scribbled notes on the back of my hand: "Clausewitz, 1 P.M. Pool!!!" The words could be as bereft of meaning as the dirt smudged beside them. I stared hard, making my eyes smear them into emptiness. The letters crowded together; I silenced the sound they made in my head, and studied, instead, the curve of the "C," the jutting skyline of vertical marks. If they emptied, I got vertigo staring at them; they became jagged transparencies through which I might fall into endless space, like that fear of the empty window when it held my mixed reflections. I shook it from my head, again, and let the words fill back up with sound and meaning.

Amelia said he chose to stay illiterate. It was unbelievable, like choosing to continue falling when solid ground could be found to stand on. What must the world be like, surrounded by decorative meaningless codes? Every surface covered with a senseless geometry? Endless conversations sparking from them—people talking, crying, screaming, or laughing, simply from the sight of those crazy shapes? I looked around the room and saw the books and papers, the posters with text, and countless labels and cards. The room was an endless field of words, clear and sensible to me. How intensely private he would have felt, unanchored, and excluded from the conversation of things around him. And she seemed to think he was happy?

Why did my mother choose not to tell me, or to let him continue this way? How could it have been so easy for them? I remembered so many times with my father and his books, long afternoons sitting by his desk, turning page after page. He'd point to the drawings, and tell me about them. I might mention a name, an incident discussed in the text, and then he would warm up to it, telling me volumes from his bounty of stories. I rather liked that about reading with him. He told me what the books did not, and he found so much in the elaborate illustrations:

"See the picked flowers scattered at their feet, Nick?" he'd ask me, pointing to the margins where the cherubs knelt. "They'll all be going brown soon. The bigger, lush blooms go first. It's the same with the grapes. 'Early ripe, early rot,' is what my grandfather always said."

"Whose hand is it?" I'd ask. There was often one reaching out from a cloud in the drawings.

"It's the artist's," he always answered of the heavenly hand. "The hand that drew the picture. Now he's going to eat the grapes. No use letting them spoil."

Amelia continued sorting and cleaning, silently. It might've been an hour, or only several minutes since she announced her plan to me. Either way, a world of time had intervened, and I looked at her, unsure of what she wanted. "What book?"

"Our book, *the* book, Nicholas. There's only one." Was this a promise or a threat? Had I any choice in the matter? My life had been sucked into a vortex, beginning that long ago afternoon, when my search for insurance led me to "her," and the puzzling gift she gave.

"Why didn't I ever see you?" I asked, still disbelieving. She continued stripping the walls of their decorations.

"It wasn't very difficult, Nicholas. We met at his office, or for lunch. Sometimes I'd attend conferences with him." She shooed me from the desk and climbed on top of it, trying to reach some of Abbott's diplomas.

"I don't understand." Her tale exhausted me. I sat slumped on the bedside and did not move to help her. "Why did you send me those submissions?"

"Do you believe what I've told you about your father?" She sounded like the doctor now, the doctor she was to Oscar Vega, answering questions with questions. I gave her an honest reply.

"I might."

"I think you wouldn't have even heard me if I'd not puzzled you first with some mysteries. I needed to unsettle you, to bother you into wondering. Most stories never really get heard, we're so certain of what we know."

If I stayed in the city, it seemed, I was doomed to fall into the demonic machinery of the police. The inspector made that much clear. There was little left of my home, and no safety any longer in the basement of History. Until the students returned, there would be nothing here for me except paranoia and hiding. Amelia said the police were just pests, and could easily be "thrown off our trail." But I knew in my heart the inspector's intentions were far more profound (were, in fact, "total"). He would be back, and nothing could be done to deflect him. There was, too, the matter of Abbott. Surely we were burning his things for a reason. I chose to leave that question unpressed, not wanting to become an accomplice or confederate in this possible crime. My innocence, up until this point, was clear to me. I wasn't about to let that last shred of safety go. I stumbled from the bed and told Amelia I'd be at my apartment, gathering my thoughts. Oscar could come with me, I offered, but I wouldn't make any commitment beyond that.

"You'd better gather your things too," she said. "Your furniture and boxes can be stored, but you'll want warm clothing for the voyage, and the manuscript to work on. Bring them with you in the evening."

"I haven't decided," I reminded her, "whether or not to go at all."

"You'll be in Francis's room tonight with the boys. There's just the big bed; I'll not have you sleepless on the living room couch."

"I'll be at my apartment," I corrected her.

"Here's the key." She handed me the small metal tool. "You're welcome to anything in the kitchen, just be quiet if you come home very late." She smiled and squeezed my hand. I took the key, and her instructions, with a skeptical nod and left.

Ice blue cruisers were busy on all the streets, and the choppers were out. They ran invisibly above the fog (though one could gauge their distance and direction by sound). Sometimes a floodlight would break through, and then the pounding of the rotor; the infernal machine itself would drop suddenly from out of the mist, and touch upon a rooftop, or clatter into an alleyway. It was the flood that had them out all hours. Crime and narcotics aside, the city was plunged into a state of emergency by the ceaseless melting. Streets had turned to rivers, and whole hillsides come undone, making the usual pathways too dangerous for travel. The police directed everything, keeping us safe from the waters.

I made it across campus (still protected by its altitude and quasi-military fortifications) and found my apartment looking more ragged and forlorn than I'd remembered. Where the tarps had blown away, the full extent of the workmen's "renovations" was uncovered. There weren't any walls anymore. No proper walls, really, just the rotting framework and the dingy backside of the interior plasters. Had I punched it my fist would've broken through into open air. A hastily welded carapace of I beams and scaffolding held the denuded shell in place. The workmen were gone, home for the holidays or kept from it by the floods. They'd planted a big sign on the muddy front walk where the door used to be. "Incompetent Structure. Keep Out." Kitty could be seen in the double storm window, three stories up, looking worriedly out into the bad weather. "By order of the police," it said in smaller letters on the sign.

My home, an "Incompetent Structure"? I stood on the sidewalk, pawing at the board that blocked my entrance. Was I subject to any legal or financial penalties? Had anyone seen to the safety of my things? I pried the board loose with my hands and scrambled through the dank entry. The stairs were still in place, thank God, and the ladder. The upper story, in fact, was far more "competent" than the rest, having been kept dry and tidy by the carpenter's renovations. Kitty was safe, I realized, though the building itself was not. Wind blew, even now, through the cracked plasters, and the windows rattled in their hefty new frames. Everything was as I left it. I found the manuscript on my desk, and my researches stacked neatly beside. My clothes were scattered, and the room was filled with the excavations from my office. I collapsed on the bed and called Kitty to me.

Too bad she couldn't tell me what to do. Her silence, before, had been a blessing. Often I thought her exemption from the world of human chatter and blathery talk was what made her love so special. Her head was full of that undifferentiated attention best expressed in purring. An animal, even one so cagey as a cat, never cluttered feelings up with words. That was what Amelia meant, I guessed, when she'd tried praising "the brilliance" of my father's illiteracy. What he knew, how he understood, really, could not have endured in a literate mind, she had told me. Because he had no marks to make, no lines of text, his immersion in the world was less fixed, was fluid; it could not have persisted on the dry ground of the written word. Oscar Vega shared my father's "gift." "Oscar will propel you toward your own dissolution," was Amelia's ominous prophecy.

Illiteracy might be all well and good for a cat; but a man, or a boy, had so much to lose if he lost the power of the written word. Not even Amelia should have kept my father from it, if indeed he wanted it. And it should not be kept from Oscar. Kitty drew nearer and licked my hand. Her wet sandpaper tongue was warm; her actions said she was worried . . . as if the actions were words. Even in their absence I read the world that way, everything a sign for something else. Was it possible the world could be otherwise? Were there other worlds, amidst the densely readable one I woke up to every morning, other shapes the days could take? The thought was uncontainable, like empty space, and rather than shaking it from my head, I got up from bed, took the phone, and called her. Standing by the windows, brushed by rain, I told her I'd go.

Amelia scolded me on the phone for thinking I had to haul the boxes myself, or even with the boys' help. We had 180,000 dollars now (not to mention the in-kind travel); she wouldn't hear of me risking my good health on hard labor we could hire muscled-help for. Between five and midnight the moving men worked. I labeled boxes and directed the men. The desk was wrapped in yards of felt and crated, before being lowered out the window by hoists. My warm clothes and the most important documents went in a lumpy suitcase that had the virtue of stretching. This I took with me, plus Kitty, in the taxi. The rest went by truck to the harbor.

At 1 A.M. the Weathereds' was dark and silent. I tipped the cabbie, and tried my key, appreciating the well-oiled silence of the locks. Kitty leapt as the door opened, and hurried inside, looking, I guessed, for warmth and a dark corner. I left my shoes in the vestibule and crept quietly to the kitchen. There was cat food and a note about towels. More exhausted than hungry, I gave a little food to Kitty then took her with me upstairs to bed. It was pitch black when I entered. The boys' room softened as my eyes adjusted to the slight green light of the bedside radio. I could see their bare limbs in outline, tangled together on the one side of the bed. The covers had been dashed and twisted, and I straightened them some without disturbing the sleepers. Kitty was sniffing. I patted the foot of the bed, and she curled there. It was really quite warm without the covers, and I could see why the boys had kicked them off. The room was stuffy and humid, like a greenhouse or the pool. From the strewn clothing an odor of freshly mown hay or socks filled the room. I lay down beside them and watched, noticing in the dim green light the damp of sweat on their rising and falling ribs. The actions of their hearts could be seen, and I rolled toward them and let my hand rest on Francis where that muscle turned, and I slept.

THE TEMPEST.

Henry Purcell.

AIR. *(Dorinda)* DEAR PRETTY YOUTH.

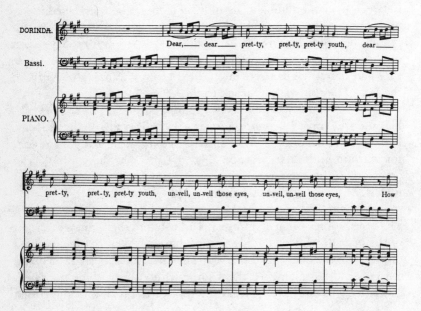

can you, can you sleep, how can you, can you sleep, how can you, can you sleep When

I, when I— am by, when I, when I— am by? Were I— with you all— night— to be, Me-

-thinks I could, me-thinks I could, I could from sleep be free, me-thinks I could, me-thinks I could from

sleep, I could from sleep be free. A-las! a-las! my dear, you're

Very slow.

167

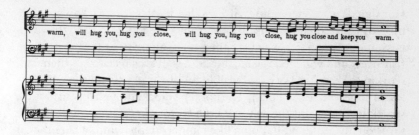

warm, will hug you, hug you close, will hug you, hug you close, hug you close and keep you warm.

The next day found us descending, irrevocably, into intrigue and vice. Amelia drugged the inspector in an incident I prefer to forget. She then explained to me the particulars of our book, or "the book" (as she insisted I call it), while Francis and Oscar laid the sleeping detective out on the davenport. "The book," she said, "the book is what will take us to Holland."

The ship's horns could be heard bellowing in the mists like an ancient beast, as we fled the house (and the sleeping inspector) to hurry toward our noon departure. The city pounded all around us on its hills, an overworked muscle wild with expansions and collapsing. I was flushed and delirious. Why did the buildings seem to rise and fall as we ran, fleeing along the wet pavements? The taxis might have all been forewarned about our criminality. They sped away, universally, toward other fares and barricades.

The city slept or was empty, enjoying its protracted holiday, behind walls and windows that kept the melting and storms at bay. Water filled the streets and the gutters, tore chunks from hills, and people stayed inside, until it could be dealt with or went away. Tawdry Christmas decorations, so gay and brilliant at night, hung loosely off the wires, torn and disabled by the wind. The city was strewn with the leftover garbage of its celebration. We stumbled through garish paper, bleeding colors on the ground, hats with ribbons, spent rockets, crushed boxes and cherry bombs, plastic wrap, tin foil, and endless glittering cellophane "icicles," strung together in the mud. Near to the docks the broken shells of the burning boats were stacked, dragged from the water and left for scavengers. (Tradition said to let them burn, and just buy new ones the next year.) Amelia was calm.

Her signals were silent and swift, and her pace was remarkable. While the boys stayed close, I had some trouble keeping up, due to weakness and/or my nostalgia. I stopped for a moment at the crest of the fish street and watched the harbor cranes. It was nice to see them still working. The university was visible too, behind us, and the gray factories appeared to the north. The library's clock, though lost in clouds, struck its hour, and the ash from the factory kept on. I could see the tarps on my building, flapping like banners in the wind, where they'd come undone. The city surrounding my wrecked home continued with its functions. It was an organism, now that I was leaving it, and I had been expelled like a crazy particle.

We had no trouble with passports. Our tickets were expensive and the police didn't bother us. While acres of fourth-class passengers and chattel snaked in slow lines to board, we were given porters and a private ramp to the upper deck. The boys were treated like spoiled princes. Amelia and I were given fresh flowers and liquor. The porters unpacked our boxes and I found my room equipped with files, a desk, a typing machine, and a tape player. Kitty made haste to the ample dressing closet and hid. Unpacked and anxious, I went aft with the boys at the blowing of the last boat horn. A surge of milky water rose from behind the enormous ship. The metal decking shuddered with the strain, and slowly, slowly the behemoth drew away from the dock. I'd sat this far out before, on the old pier, but I'd never been on so large and laboring a vessel, gaining speed and leaving.

The city's frame came swiftly into view. Both the police tower and the library's spires were lost in the weather, but their bulk and superior position could be seen in glimpses. Between them, the city read like a fractured sentence. The buildings were tall consonants, or short fat vowels. Blips of punctuation were scattered on the hills, beginning or ending clusters I'd known all my life. It was written crooked, like the streets, and made no sound as such in my head. It made a shape, as familiar and complete as any piece of prose remembered from a favorite book. With its seven hills, and several trains, the city was more like a paragraph of text to me, an unlikely grouping of lines which had settled into order simply by their persistence. The lines were crazy and jagged, but they'd come to fit each other well. We were leaving the city, the place which had formed me, and apart from which I had never been. The cluttered hills, saddled with their brief and tawdry history, disappeared into the clouds. The many buildings, the university and the police, were swallowed by the air. Distance opened up, empty and unmarked, between me and the "incompetent structure" of my home. l could see its contours, still disturbing the sky, but nothing could be distinguished. Each minor detail bled into the next; the city was reduced by our flight and turned into a tiny, singular stain, soiling the horizon. The boats, burned and smoldering, and the harbor cranes turning on their pivots, the library's bells, and the factory, the choppers and stalls, and the constant erasure by renovation or decay of what little history we had . . . all of it blurred together in the distance, until it was a single, uniform mark on the silent horizon—an ineffable Monad, at once primary and unreadable. We traveled farther into the curving sea and lost sight, even of that last monolithic trace of my home.

II

WATER

AMELIA FOUND ME IN MY CABIN and took me to lunch. Though we could take meals in our rooms, she insisted we go, and I agreed. "We're having the fish, Nicholas, and a few tumblers of Dutch *jenever*. It'll bring your strength back." I followed her through the narrow hallways, steadying myself against the ship's rocking. Low to the ground, she suffered none of the imbalance I did, and made easy progress to the dining hall. The room was spacious, with warm wood paneling, and windows on three sides. Tuxedoed staff hovered along the edges with carts and dewy, silver pitchers, waiting for a signal. The other diners all looked to be in their eighties. Amelia's history (as she'd reported it) said she was even older; yet we were easily the youngest couple in appearance, and in spirit. The room would have been silent as a morgue if not for our conversation and the tinkling of a busty piano player. The gray sea turned wild outside, and rain began lashing the windows. It was endless and even, curving into borderless space far beyond the reach of my vision.

"What is '*jenever*' exactly?" I asked. Amelia had signaled the waiter to fill two chilled glasses.

"*Borrel,* Dutch *borrel*. A sort of aromatic gin."

"It's quite strong, then, is it?"

"Quite. You'll find it calms the sea nerves. It's what made the Dutch such great sailors. They were all drunk on *jenever*. It's customary to take the first in one swallow." We raised our glasses and did so.

"I need to know something," I began, soon after the drink hit bottom and started to warm me. Amelia signaled again to the waiter, then gave me her attention. "Is Francis really my brother?"

She sighed deeply, and raised her glass before speaking. *"Proost."* She said it with the long Dutch tongue roll, and the full "o."

"Proost."

"Francis is your brother."

I took the fact all at once, like the drink, and was silent while it settled. The implications were enormous. They billowed inside me like warm vapors.

"My half brother," I corrected. Amelia said nothing, but laid her hand over mine.

"Your father and I couldn't imagine any way to tell you. You had just started graduate school, and we thought you really didn't need any more unwelcome news."

"Then, my mother . . ."

"Had just died. He was grieving, you see. He could be a very demonstrative man. We were in Holland, actually. Near Ezinge." I was glad for the *jenever*. I sank meekly into my chair, and sniffed at the glass. "It took me by surprise," she acknowledged, "but I was very, very happy."

"And you raised him alone?"

"He was no trouble."

"Wasn't he unhappy to be kept from his father?" The waiter returned with another bottle, white wine, and the fish. I smiled woodenly, and paused while he performed with the trays and knives.

"Francis spent time with John; but you know he was just five when John died. I think his eagerness to meet you, and his anxieties, have a lot to do with that." It touched me to be reminded of the boy's affection, his need really. I blushed, thinking of him, so tall already, and sweet. Which reminded me of "the question." I'd harbored it all along, ever since learning that "she" might be his mother . . . Decorum said no, but the *jenever* and wine urged me on, and I asked.

"Is it, that is. Will Francis keep growing, to be . . . very tall, do you think? I mean, I was just concerned about it, and I guess, to be honest, the childbirth too." I poked at my meal, looking away from her. The fish had its head still on, and I found the clouded eye unsettling. It was horrifying. I looked up. "I'm sorry, I've been rude and thoughtless. Of course you needn't answer such a question." The small mouth was tragic, so I masked the whole fish head with an arugula garnish and dug in.

Amelia filled our wineglasses, and leaned toward me. "I owe you far more than that, Nicholas. Of course I'll answer any questions you have. The time for secrecy between us is past. I'm not a dwarf, or midget, as you might have supposed." She whispered the two words. as though forming her lips around tiny pearls. "I'm just, very small." She blushed at this, and lowered her eyes. "In fact I used to be quite big, you see, at one point, certainly big enough to bring Francis into this world." Her arched brow, and a drunken tip of the head told me there was much more to this.

"How, Amelia? But how is it that you're so, so much smaller now, then?"

"I have been"—here she paused to stress and enunciate the word clearly—"waning, as of late." She drained her cup and waved more boldly to the steward.

"I've never heard of such a thing. How terrible." I thought perhaps she'd want to take my hand, or some other comfort, but no gesture came. "Is it, irreversible, this 'waning'?"

"More *borrel* please, steward," she requested, aside. "This wine's a bit sour for my taste. Irreversible? No, Nicholas. I believe it can be reversed, but only through near Herculean efforts which I'm increasingly unable to muster."

"I want to help, Amelia. Truly."

"Share this *borrel* with me, then. And stop picking at your fish."

"Help with the condition, I mean. The 'waning.'"

"Of course you want to help. And you're doing so already. It always sounds a bit preposterous, but it's the book that will help most. The book's the thing. I'll disappear completely without it. I know I should have gone into television, or something more high profile, but you've got to understand where it all began, Nicholas. Why, the printing press was practically a total revolution. Books seemed so incredibly powerful to us then."

"The Book"—the one that would save her from disappearing altogether—required nothing more nor less from me than the completion of my researches. She insisted I go to my cabin after lunch and plunge back into Motley and Verweerd. I need merely keep on with my work. "And your work?" I asked, quite drunk from the *jenever*. "Am I to 'mesh' with it, as it were?"

"I'll do the meshing, Nicholas. You just keep digging." The porter commandeered a footstool from the powder room, and Amelia rested her small feet there. "Trust, Nicholas. Trust and fortitude are all I require of you." I invited her to join me at my desk, hoping to get a few editorial suggestions, but she refused; after several more minutes of long-winded explanation, Amelia fell deeply and utterly asleep.

I felt no great confidence, nor clarity, about her ultimate goals, but my commitment to research was solid. It was, after all, *my* book I was writing, regardless of what she called it. She was still only "she," and it was I, Nicholas Dee, who was "I." Baffled and dazzled (and drunk), I returned to my cabin, and the familiar sight of my pages. The desk was arranged beside a broad window, much ampler than the conventional portal one saw in movies. From it I could see the great expanse of ocean off the starboard side. Kitty lay among the papers. What a relief, to return here and find the familiar pages, waiting patiently. Now they opened up to receive me and I fell in, as if into bed.

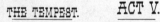

The Opera House of Alton Motley   Nicholas Dee

Though Alton Motley is all but unknown in the musical history of the period, the enthusiasm of Andries Verweerd and
the musicians engaged to present Motley's *Tempest* suggest
he was a composer of some talent and invention. Verweerd,
probably repeating the comments of his musicians, often
praises the "Italianate" style of Motley's Ariel songs,
and speaks of the composition as a whole with lavish regard and some sophistication. Verweerd wasn't so taken with
Motley's theatrical talents:

The Opera House of Alton Motley   Nicholas Dee

"First Dorinda, and now Amphitrite! He has composed no songs for Caliban and none for Miranda. The play smells greatly of his queer interests, mostly, I think, spirits and sprites. The Ariel is fine and measured, and Frans will play it prettily. But how can there be no magic in the Prospero, and the Act V already upon us! Only devils, and deities, and sprites. I should fashion a Pandora's box, not a theater, to house this invention. Pieter is well displeased by the Prospero and gives the speeches where William Shakespeare put them, disrupting us all and our progress. He says 'the motley fool' who's composed this nonsense will hear his full fury, and from the mouth of Prospero in the words once given him."

Alton Motley, by his own admission, never read Shakespeare, nor saw *The Tempest* on stage. His interest in the material began at the April 1674 performance of Thomas Shadwell's operatic version. The opera was performed at the Dorset Garden where Shadwell was regularly commissioned. Motley saw it in the course of the unusual spring he spent in London (with Thomas Weekes's permission) attending musical theater. That spring he had his first broad exposure to the new French composers including Perrin, whose *Ariane* was presented by the King's Company at Drury Lane. Motley made several contacts there, and at John Banister's in White Fryers. With his wealth, he engaged composers from the Continent to send works for performance at his estate near Benson. Word of Motley's money and generosity spread by letter through Italy and France. Over the next ten years he had private audience for what was certainly England's most outstanding series of new French and Italian works.

Given this privileged exposure, the sophistication of Motley's "Italianate" adaptation is less surprising than it might otherwise seem. The Italian style was still quite new to most British audiences, but Motley evidently had

The Opera House of Alton Motley   Nicholas Dee

already learned some lessons from it. Verweerd wrote: "The
song of Neptune late accompanied by dancing is excellent
and sonorous, and with vigorous strings. Willem Koeman will
sing the part, if Mr. Leveridge cannot be convinced of the
honor of it. The composer instructs me that the stage front
will open, and the band of thirty violins and harpsicals
will sink beneath the stage and pit. A second curtain, all
the while of use, will part and discover a new frontispiece,
joined to the great pilasters on each side, beautified with
roses wound round them, and several cupids flying by rope.
Behind, the scene which represents a thick cloudy sky will
drop to the rocks and water. This sea, in a tempestuous state
of perpetual agitation, will calm, and the tempest drained
of its many dreadful objects, spirits in pretty shapes, rising and crossing in the air, will lift the clouds to reveal
the actual sea and sky beyond. I am promised a solemn masque
in conclusion, and have arranged for the actual situation of
the theater and its invention to be there discovered."

Verweerd's ambitious mechanicals—including the bizarre
design by which the opera house would open up at play's end
to reveal the vast expanse of Den Dollard and the thin horizon of land to the north—required enormous resources and
limitless ingenuity. During the long summer and mild fall of
1685 a temporary channel was dredged, and the fleet of rafts
and barges trebled to seventy-five. The building site north
of Finsterwolde was now busier and more populous than any
other in the province, outside of the great city itself.
    The line of houses Verweerd described that first summer
was now a village of seven hundred (mostly laborers), with
an influx from the neighboring towns each Sunday when the
players presented their newest skits. Some farmers moved their
herds closer and set up barns, milking stations, and shear-
ing houses, in the fields to the west. Ships could be seen
every day, coming in and out of the harbor; the smaller ones

The Opera House of Alton Motley   Nicholas Dee

risked the channel to save time unloading. Barges and rafts met the others in large fleets, to take materials, and make room for ships still waiting beyond the bay's entrance.

For Verweerd the work was a godsend, a project commensurate with the high regard he had for himself. He slept out in the building now, in an enormous nest that would be the organist's loft. He'd fitted it with a bed and study and moved his small collection of books there. His time was divided between "the great and glorious endeavour" and the education of Frans, the troupe's boy, who would play Ariel.

"Frans came with the troupe having no training in any art but a desire, good humor, and the voice of an angel, all natural blessings for his chosen work. His mind is nimble and when exhausted by labor and running makes good progress with numbers and with drafting. His family is cowherds, and no schooling but what the fields and animals of the island, Schiermonnikoog, gave him at morning and dusk when Frans counted, matching cows to stones he'd kept in his pocket. The island is haunted by spirits and moves across the water east by pieces, and Frans lost his family in a terrible storm. He is twelve and never left the island before the ocean took them. Frans tells me Pieter of the troupe, who is sixty, charmed him with spells and a potion when Frans was small and the troupe came to the island for St. Maartin's. They came again each year for the celebration with the cattle, and to renew the charm. Frans went with them this time, on a fishing skiff the last night, to land, to see what his life would be."

In late fall of 1686, when cold froze the estuary, Verweerd left Den Dollard with the troupe and musicians to stay the winter with Johannes Drop. He was confident the construction would be completed the following spring. They traveled inland to the Allersmaborg, the small estate where Drop, their "insurer," lived. The troupe would be warm and coddled there, and Verweerd was eager for it.

FOURTEEN

THAT NIGHT we were the captain's guests, at his table, for dinner. Amelia had arranged it. While Francis instructed Oscar about forks, I greeted the tall captain and his tiny companion. We had him to ourselves, and the other passengers strained to appear disinterested and calm. He was an elegant man, with all the integrity and strength of the night outside. Of course he was gracious to the lady, and saw to her chair. I thought they might be old friends, from their ease and familiarity, but that was just his good manners. The steward doted on us, and the menus were dispensed with. The captain arranged all his dinners ahead of time. We had that particular and rare pleasure of giving up our right to choose. I settled into my chair, happy to have been welcomed to a table where each course was determined by a higher authority without waffling, argument, or appeal.

I took my napkin from the ring, and smiled at our host. He and Amelia made a handsome pair (she, boosterized by a pile of telephone books on her chair). The boys sat to my right, eyeing the spoons (which I feared Francis might try hanging from his nose). "Holland is a strange country," the captain was saying, quite loudly. Clearly he was accustomed to "hold forth" at his table and was mustering us up to listen. "I've seen men there dressed as fishes, luring their catch from the ocean. By this disguise the dogfish were tricked onto shore. They'd crawl onto the sand to see their outsized cousins." He paused and looked around at each of us, perhaps to judge our credulity. "The

183

clever deceivers, these were islanders from the Wadden Sea, would lay nets along the water's edge and, on a signal from their leader, pull the disguises off to reveal their true human form. The fish, reasonably frightened, would rush back to the sea only to be caught in the nets. By this method, the Dutchmen caught more fish than their families could eat, and so had to resort to salting and pickling. This was a very long time ago, of course, but similar practices persist to this day in every branch of commerce there."

"I believe it was Terschelling," Amelia confirmed. "Sometime in the sixteenth century. You say, Captain, that they continue with this practice?"

"In more sophisticated forms."

"Fascinating. Captain, truly fascinating." Amelia played her part well, knowing just the sort of "interlocutor" the voluble captain desired. "Tell us," she continued, encouraging him, "what is your estimation of the people there?"

"The stature of the men and women there is very beautiful," he observed. "Their personages are very tall, and all their members in very good proportion, especially their legs. They are not so tall as in Caesar's time, either because of their mixture with strangers, or because the quality of their meats and manner of living have altered since that age. They are very skillful mariners, and their boats are excellent upon the sea, in addition to which they dispatch their voyages faster than any other nation. They all have some smattering of grammar, and every one of them, every husband and wife, besides speaking their own language speaks English, and many German, Spanish, French, or Italian."

"Yes," I added. "Apparently the schools are quite good."

"They marry their children into strange towns," the captain continued, glaring at me, "and foreign countries, and marry noble with ignoble, young with old, gifted with dull. They are quick to temper, but also to forgive, and have no compunction about exposing the naked body. The populous, men, women, and children alike, converse together unclothed in public houses."

"Naked in the saunas," Francis said loudly. "I got to go every day after school in the winter. Mother said it would save on our heating bills."

"You lived in Holland?" Somehow I'd never been told, or had forgotten. Francis looked toward Amelia, fidgeting and eager to talk. She nodded her assent, and he continued.

"Four years. We lived in Groningen. I went to school there, and Mother studied at the university."

The soup arrived, a thick pea soup with little sausages and ham. The captain glared at Francis, shutting him up, and went on with his own disquisition. "The Netherlands may be said to be a sand and mud dump, left over from the ice age," he rumbled. "The withdrawal of the ice cap, and the warming of the globe, created a great flow of water, and sent sand and silt to the vast delta which became the Netherlands. Sea and wind threw up a fringe of lofty sand dunes, and behind them rank swamps and muddy shoals came into being. Mottled by the handiwork of the tempestuous sea, this putrid land was cut deeply by floods, silted with marine clay, and poisoned with the concentrated leachings of the western half of the Continent. It was then, and is now, the kidney of Europe. You'll find I've taken most of this from Van Veen."[1] Poor Francis. The captain's oratory left him mute and forlorn. I patted his arm in consolation and let him sip from my wine. The captain's voice pressed against me like a hand. "The first prehistoric men and women to see this fetid bog did not dare to live there. They may have traveled, with their scows or coracles, through the tangled streams of the hybridic wilderness, but they could not survive there. Discovered to the Greeks by the voyage of the Argonauts, this place of 'eternal fog, where the sea rushes over sandbanks, covering them,' was supposed to have been where Hades and the Gates of Hell were located. 'The people living there,' one of the ancients wrote, 'need not pay their fare when they are dead.' Presumably because they had already crossed over. Pytheas visited the Coast of Awe in 325 B.C., and came back with his tale of horror at having discovered the 'Sea Lung,' by which he meant the Netherlands. This unnavigable portal of fog and swells, Pytheas reported, where ice, water, and air mingled equally, had been so vexed by the gods that its sea rose and fell without storms. A modern observer recognizes the tides here, but to the Greek, this phenomenon was demonic, especially in its

---

1. Johan Van Veen, *Dredge, Drain, Reclaim, the Art of a Nation*, Den Haag, 1948.

extreme. *Jachtschotel?*" the captain offered, as the waiter brought a heavy stew to our table. We were served, and a heady *bourgogne* was poured all the way around.

"The first to live there were the Frisians, presumably a miserable farming people driven out of Sweden by famine or beatings around 400 B.C. They lived on artificial mounds of clay piled to a height slightly above the tide. Pliny, who saw the mound-dwelling tribes in the year A.D. 47, likened them to shipwrecked sailors, marooned on piles of mud in the midst of a vast swampy wasteland. 'They try to warm their frozen bowels by burning mud,' Pliny said, 'dug with their hands from the earth and dried to some extent in the wind more than in the sun, which one hardly ever sees.' There were no trees in the sea marsh, and no crops, or cereals. Cattle shared the mounds with them, grazing on short marine grasses, and the Frisians caught fish in their reed baskets. Will you join me for another bottle?" the large Captain asked rhetorically, gesturing to the steward. He left no space for an answer. "Toward the sea was *Het Wad*, the tidal flats where shellfish could be gathered. Toward land was the *wapelinge,* the low swampy wilderness where no man could pass except by boat through treacherous, tiny creeks. There were, in all, only seven roads to the interior. four by water, and three by land. They had no king, or ruler to govern them, but formed a natural democracy based in the revered EWA, a law of eternal rights, too sacred to be written down. To write it down was a profanation, and would be punished by death. It was remembered by clever rhyme and passed from mouth to mouth. The flexibility and persistence of the EWA is due largely to its oral transmission. The written word would have frozen what must be fluid and adaptable. At the annual gathering called 'Thing,' every dweller was to help find the right application of the EWA through recollection and argument."

"Thing?" I thought, chewing my stew. Had they really called it "Thing"? I sputtered through the sticky meat, meaning to interrupt the captain, but managed only to attract the sympathetic busboy, who swatted me on the back and refilled my water. The captain, ever polite, pretended not to notice.

"In A.D. 800, when Charlemagne's Christian warriors came to conquer the Frisians, Charles the Emperor ordered the EWA to be put down on parchment. The marsh-men refused, knowing the sacred interdictions. After six successive days of slaughter, the soldiers gave the remaining mound dwellers three options: to all be put to death; to be made slaves; or to be cast adrift at sea without oars or rudders. The twelve that remained chose the last. Awaiting death far from shore, the twelve saw, in their extremity, a thirteenth man, sitting on the stern of the boat, and now magically steering them toward shore. The thirteenth man taught them how to set the law down in writing, and the Frisians were saved. Such is the saga which has come to us, and we know that the *Lex Frisionum* was put down on paper in the year A.D. 802. Oddly, the revered EWA, as it was recorded by the twelve men, deals primarily with financial compensations for the loss of valued items. Apparently, the natural democracy of free men was based on a sort of insurance table, rather than the lofty principles of law one might have expected. The killing of a free man, for example, is valued at fifty-three shillings, the killing of a hunting dog capable of taking down a wolf is eight shillings, a pet dog twelve shillings, the cutting off of an ear brings thirty-six shillings, of a nose seventy-eight, and of the breast of a woman, four." Did he say insurance? I wondered. And as the sole basis for a working democracy; remarkable. "While the farmers and merchants, gathered in the countries to the south, were kept from the Frisians for twelve centuries by the impenetrable swamps, Charlemagne's invasion began the gradual mixing of the European races with the imposing mound dwellers. The mounds by now had proliferated and grown. Nearly fifteen hundred were made by the Frisians, some covering thirty to forty acres and rising nearly fifty feet above the flood tides. We can imagine the women and children of a village, bearing willow baskets of clay and mud from the marshes out to their mound, raising it gradually over twelve centuries to keep their families and cattle above the storm floods. The Romans had tried to conquer them and failed, unable to pursue the agile natives through the twisting swamps. *Fierljeppen* persists to this day as the national sport of the Frisians, in which a running man springs over a wide canal with a pole which he can carry with him. The ancestors owed their freedom to this technique. Even after the invasion of Charlemagne, control over the Frisians was tenuous, at best." I struggled to reach the *jachtschoetel,* which was marooned by the boys, and was relieved when the steward noticed my exertion. He brought it to me himself, graciously, and without interupting the captain's dissertation. I tried to recall his point about insurance, but found it had been swept away in the flood of subsequent details. Scrambling to hold on to the "pole-vaulting" or what have you, I lost that too, and could only remember the word "thing." What was the importance of "thing"?

"Gradually, with the church and armies, and with the allure of profitable commerce with peoples to the south, Frisians were invited into the community of Netherlanders that emerged distinct and independent from their European neighbors during the early middle ages. It was the battle against the sea which now united the Netherlands and made it a nation which would fight for its independence against all enemies. From the EWA came the ancient oath 'We shall defend our land with three weapons, with the spade, with the handbarrow, and with the fork.' An increased population brought with it the necessity of reclaiming new land, not simply defending what was already dry. In the first centuries after the millennium, the Asegas, or EWA sayers, found the Law of Right Diking and became the Dike Masters. Like Nehemiah, when he built his wall around Jerusalem, the Dike Masters led the people in both work and spirit, reminding them of their common enemy. A 'Golden Hoop' of dikes would ring the Netherlands and protect it from the sea. Like the EWA, the word of the Dike Masters was heeded and the dry land was hewn from swamps and ocean. The sea exacted a terrible retribution many times, as in 1287, when fifty thousand drowned in one December flood, in 1421 when the Hollandse Waard was destroyed, in 1532 at Reimerswaal, where people gathered human teeth from out of the silty remains and sold them to dentists in town, in 1634 in the All Saints' flood, and in 1686, in the terrible disaster that struck Groningen and Den Dollard. Dutch resilience is based in such disasters as is the unity mustered against common enemies, whether human or natural."

The sea raged outside, invisible and unheard. The captain's oratory settled heavily over the table, like bad weather, and would not disperse. Amelia scribbled some notes on a pad the steward brought, and kicked me gently beneath the table. I shook myself and brightened, gathering energy for the captain's finishing sprint. "The country is now largely as it was then, in the late seventeenth century, a financial center with some innovative manufacturing concerns, and a preponderance of farmers. Technologies of water control, and the particulars of their market-based democracy have altered slightly since that time but both proceed on roughly the same principles as they did three hundred years ago. Interest in a common enemy, and an overinflated sense of national pride, are expressed largely through sporting concerns, especially, and I'm sure the young gentleman will remember this from his four years there, through the national soccer team, which is asked, from time to time, to redress past economic and military defeats by triumphs on the field. The legacy of the Frisians persists in an obdurate independence of spirit, and an interest in precisely measured and assured compensations for loss."

The arrival of the cheese marked the end of the captain's tireless account. There was *nagelkaas,* sharp Gouda, Camembert, sliced fruit, and a protracted silence. I might have just read a book, so thorough was the stupor into which his encyclopedic account had delivered me. I had the uniquely bookish sensation of resurfacing, coming up as if out of sleep, into a busier, sloppier world of activity and noise. Oscar had disappeared from view, and might have been under the table, pestering Francis. The younger boy was barely able to stay still, though he sat desperately straight in his chair, swatting at invisible hands. Whose book was this, anyway? I felt some compulsion to wrest control of the evening's narration from our mouthy captain, before he went on into further Dutch obscurities.

"I think Oscar's getting sick under the table," I observed to Amelia. Even she seemed to have grown weary of the captain. "Maybe we should get the steward to take them to their room." Francis dropped his silly grin at the words and looked like a stricken dog. I was suddenly reminded of the extremities of grief to which the boy was inclined. Amelia was tired and not a little drunk; she didn't seem to notice.

"I don't think he's getting sick," she corrected. Oscar scooted back into his chair. "Maybe you two would prefer something active, like a swim in the pool."

"Oh yes please," was Francis's eager response.

Amelia refilled her glass with *bourgogne*. "Maybe the captain would like to join them." She smiled at him, and offered some wine. The captain, done with his meal, declined the invitation and went instead to his cabin. Amelia insisted I stay at the table and finish the captain's wine with her. It wasn't every night we had access to his stock, access for which we'd already paid a pretty price in tedium. I looked up, warm and wistful (from the hour and the wine) and was glad to have Amelia there. There was more I wanted to know from her. Some things were on my mind, and the captain's bizarre description of what lay ahead made my concerns feel all the more pressing. It could be awful, I now thought, to be nowhere on a boat.

"When this is over, Amelia, and I've finished the book, will we go back to the city again, and continue with our normal lives?"

"Would you like to go back?" she answered sadly.

"Yes. When I've finished the researches."

"There's another month yet, before classes start."

"Time isn't the problem, I don't think. Have you noticed how unhappy Francis can sometimes be?" I remembered the boy's sadness upon first telling me of her scheme, and his many sudden silences since that time.

"Is that what's wrong?" She was impatient with me. "Of course he's not simply 'happy.' He expects a great deal from you." Her accusation surprised me. I drank some more wine to take the edge off it.

"I think he expects some things from you, too," I answered. "A child can't always make sense of adult actions."

"I'm aware of that."

"You should talk to him more. And to Oscar."

"About what?"

"I don't think they understand you fully."

"Oscar understands a great deal more than you yet realize."

"*I* don't understand you." I slouched into my chair, and swirled the wine around the glass. "I don't understand this whole project of yours."

"The book?"

"Yes. That and . . ." It must be now or never. "And why have you made me a criminal?"

"The uh, the little drugging?"

"And Abbott. I should have turned you in to the inspector."

"Don't lose sleep over Abbott. And the drugs; the drugs are undetectable." Amelia put her plate down, and began scooting the heavy chair toward me. "It would be the inspector's word against ours."

"You seem to be conducting a war, or espionage of some sort." I worried for a moment, thinking I'd gone too far, but Amelia was not upset by my accusation; she was, instead, amused.

"That's a fair description," she allowed, tilting her head, as if to think. How could she be so calm, when her admission was so alarming?

"Then how am I to continue, reasonably, as a professor, and with my life, if I'm, that is, if I'm made to be a confederate in your schemes?"

"I guess it's undercover work, really. You don't have to own up to everything, to everybody." I looked up at the window and was alarmed by my reflection.

"I should lie?"

"Tell a story. It's what you already do. I wouldn't call it lying." She leaned toward me and took my hands in hers. "No one is asking you to give up your life, Nicholas. Just look more closely at what you've been doing all along. I think you'll find that we're engaged in roughly the same project."

"Which is?"

"Researching lost times, Nicholas. Our researches, our trip by boat. Just where did you think we were going?"

"History? Our researches into history?"

"You've not yet realized how elusive it can be, nor learned how to read it. You don't know your real enemies."

"My enemies?"

"The university and the police are loath to lose control."

"But I work for the university."

"Yes."

"I'm paid by them, to find all these facts and figures. Surely they'd never pay for 'enemy' work."

"Facts and figures are doors, Nicholas, hard and flat. And the university pays for you to fit them neatly in their frame and keep them closed. You're capable of more. Real researches upset a certain social order." She put her hand to my chin now, and made me stare into her dilated pupils. "It's like napping or sleep, you see, when we really give in to a complete reading . . . a dissolution that muddies the order of things."

Her vision made me shiver, briefly, and then become flush with heat. I drained my glass of water, and motioned to the busboy for more. "But," I stammered, objecting. "But I like order."

"Yes of course. So do the police."

"Just what are you accusing me of?"

"I'm pointing out a habit of mind, a pattern. There's no conspiracy and no evil dictator; only a legion of eager men, functionaries, good citizens, like Abbott and the inspector, and you also."

"Me?" I remembered hearing precisely the same implications from the inspector, something about my guilt. Everyone seemed to be challenging my innocence as of late. "I hardly see how my habits, my alleged habits, have anything to do with the police."

"Think of your researches as a kind of sleep," she offered. "There's some intelligence you have only in your weakest moments." Amelia emptied the last bottle of wine into my glass, and finished her advice: "You should be wary of the compulsion toward strength and control."

"I don't know how . . . "

"Just keep an open mind to Oscar, and finish those researches."

"My usual work for the, uh, 'the enemy.'"

"I think this book will turn out differently."

What were my researches, but a kind of sleep? The tall stacks of papers, the pages spread out over my desk, gave off a warmth of welcome as sweet and irresistible as a soft bed. My chair fit me well. Settling into it relaxed me, like the press of my pillow against my head. The documents might be full with facts and figures but I could always hear them as voices, mixed together like in a dream. Everything was alive at once, if I spread them out and read them. My reading, like sleep, reopened all the pages, and I could listen. Centuries opened up. Borders were blurred or erased, like in the reverie of an afternoon nap. And here was the strangest thing. While I took great pleasure in figuring out dates, or establishing a chronology—writing out what I'd found—the researches (before the writing) brought a conflicting joy. In research, origins and borders were erased. Different times and voices collapsed into my singular mind, and this dense cacophony gave me the strange pleasure Amelia had described.

How could such researches ever be put onto the page? What had I erased in the time between researches and writing? What connections had been severed? I wanted to recover something, though it was hard to find words to put to it. Amelia said it was there in my weakest moments, in the compelling reveries of my half-sleep. But some measure of fear kept me from embracing those moments. I'd felt it with my father too, or with the borderless memory of him. He was vivid in my dreams, and in my half-sleep, but like the researches, he faded into death the nearer I came to putting marks down on the page.

> *Because we are incapable of watching or reading fully,*
> *generously, and at risk to ourselves, there can be no*
> *more Prosperos and no art, only entertainments.*
> —John Lewis Dee[2]

We stayed a very long time and when I tottered back to my cabin, I found Francis in bed there, waiting. He'd fallen asleep with my Purcell book open on his stomach, and a little drool coming from his chin onto his bare neck. It was very late. I didn't want to alarm him, but my clumsiness thwarted me. When I dropped the first shoe he started, and the second made him sit up and address me. "Mr. Dee," he whispered, stretching. "Is it okay if I sleep over?"

"Is there something wrong, Francis?" I didn't mind his coming to visit, but it was unexpected.

"Nothing's wrong," he answered, unconvincingly. "I just wanted to talk to you, earlier. But then I fell asleep."

"You're probably very tired."

"Yes."

"Maybe we could talk in the morning, when we've both had time to rest more."

"Are you very tired too?"

"Very tired, Francis. I'm practically asleep on my feet. Maybe you'd better go back to your bed."

---

2. John Lewis Dee, *Miscellaneous Papers*, undated.

"Would you come wake me in the morning, and we could have breakfast, just us two?"

"Gladly, Francis. Breakfast is a wonderful idea." He crawled from under the covers, still fully clothed, and slipped his shoes on without unlacing.

"Will you walk me to my room?"

Under the gray morning sky the sea was unchanged. The ship kept on toward Holland (an evermore distant and strange-seeming place after the captain's elaborate talk). The boys were asleep in their bunk bed and I snuck in, letting Oscar slumber under his countless bed covers in the lower bunk, to wake Francis with a soft hand on his chest. "Francis," I whispered. "It's Nicholas." He turned his flushed face toward me and struggled to open his eyes. "Breakfast time." His mouth worked like a baby's, bringing up saliva, and he rolled over onto his side. "I'll be in the dining room."

"Breakfast time?" He was awake. "I'm ready, Mr. Dee." The boy scooted from the covers and pulled the nearest pants and shirt on incompletely. He shuffled into the permanently tied shoes and rubbed his face with the shirttail. "Is it early still, Mr. Dee?" he asked, facing the window, trying to gauge the hour.

"Almost nine, Francis." He took my hand in his and led me down the hall that way.

The dining room was empty at this hour. The first wave of early risers had moved on to jog the deck, or get back to a treasured book. There was a buffet. Fluffy mounds of scrambled eggs settled in the steam-table trays, with bacon stacked beside, sandwiched between greasy napkins. Pitchers of juice were kept on ice, and fresh fruit was piled in glass punch bowls at the end. I took coffee from a brilliant silver urn, and Francis made a hash of cheese and potatoes, sausage, bacon, and toast.

For all of Amelia's power in my life, it was Francis—with his almost invisible interventions—who had steered me toward her, and precipitated our portentous reunion. Like Ariel, the boy enchanted me, and led me step by step to the governing force (that is to say, his mother). Sitting at the breakfast table, puffy and mussed from sleep, he didn't look sprightly. Circumstance had forced him into the uncomfortable role. Even with his first revelation to me (when he stood stammering atop my bed) he had faltered, reading lines scribbled hastily on his wrist. Now he blushed and stammered again, embarrassed by his own questions. "Who *was* he, exactly?" the boy asked, meaning John Dee. "No one ever told me." Who was he? I had so many answers, but every one of them had been erased by Amelia. Was he a historian? A scholar? She said no. Rain seemed to pester the windows, until a hose dropped into sight, and the water stopped. The ship's crew was cleaning. I knew he was a gentle and generous man, but I knew little else.

"Well, he was your father, I gather. And mine." The lingering film wobbled down the glass, then a squeegee wiped it clean. "Actually, I meant to ask you the same question." Francis shrugged and sighed, then picked at his hobo-hash. I tapped my spoon nervously, staring out the window at the sea. Amelia's revelations had silenced the long, clear answers I used to have; I kept quiet now, for I could not do otherwise.

"I thought he was my uncle, or grandfather, or something," Francis tried. "I mean, I *knew* he was my father, but I had no idea what that *meant*. I always called him John. I didn't know what he was."

"What did he tell you? Did he tell you anything?" Water rattled the broad windows again as the crew turned the hose on full. The sight made me thirsty, and I drank the tepid coffee all at once. It was difficult to read the boy's silent face. Francis did not fidget, but sat still. His eyes looked like the windows, wet and blurred, impossible to see through. He was only five when John died. What could he possibly remember? His mind wandered away behind the eyes, casting about for some recollection. He worked his mouth a little, as though more saliva might bring with it a thought, a memory, or some small clue.

"Did he ever tell you about me?" he asked, sounding painfully like the young boy he was.

"No, Francis. I wish he had, I truly wish he had. I think he was just afraid of telling me about Amelia, about your mother."

"Because you'd be mad." He said it as an accusation. I put my empty coffee cup down and wiped the dribble from my chin.

"There was just too much to explain."

"Do you really wish he'd told you?" The question was an awful one, made worse by the uncertainty in his voice. Francis would not accept lies, it seemed, and now pursued me to what seemed a bitter end. Of course I would have been upset. Amelia's revelations about my father's work—his illiteracy—were devastating. I'd built most of my interest in history on myths about my father. But this admission was not what the boy needed.

"I do wish I'd known you," I said, omitting the uglier part of the truth. "I truly wish I'd known you."

"Do you think he lied to us?"

"He never denied knowing you."

"Do you think what he did was lying?"

His question echoed inside me, rattling the myriad doubts I had left hanging through all my years in History. Was it lying, what he did? Were omissions lies?

"Yes."

"I think so too. They were wrong to lie to us. Both of them." His stare was dark and even, even as his eyes became full and wet.

"They thought it would be less painful that way."

"It was less painful for *them*." Francis jarred the table, moving suddenly forward as he spoke, and it unsettled me. He blushed furiously. "What they did was wrong."

"I have no excuses for them."

"He should've told you about me. He should've told you there was, I was me." I felt my own eyes fill, and fiddled with the empty coffee cup, hiding my reaction behind it.

"He must have loved you. More than he could say, Francis. He had no idea how to tell anyone."

FIFTEEN

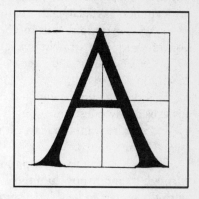

THE CAT was with Oscar most of the time now. He made an effort to find her in the big closet, in her hiding place, and he won her trust. Now she slept with him in the bottom bunk some nights. Oscar devised simple games with a paper ball, which she chased and retrieved. While I missed her evening warmth and purring, I enjoyed the small pleasure of knowing they'd made friends. In the new constellation of my life, where everything else was turned upside down, Oscar's affection for Kitty felt warm and reassuring. I'd certainly not forgotten Oscar Vega. Any distance I kept was due to personal need rather than neglect. The memory of him, disheveled and sleepy, in the doorway of the inspector's office (my first long look at the boy), and of him asleep that night beside me, was so strong I think I left it buried beneath a raft of other concerns. It wouldn't do to persist in my avoidance, and I went to find him in the afternoon, the day after Francis and I had talked.

The boys were together on Oscar's bunk reading comic books. They lay on their stomachs, pressed side by side on the narrow bed, with a thin, colorful magazine open on the pillow. They answered my knock with suspicion, but beckoned me in when I said it was me.

"Close the door please, Mr. Dee," Francis instructed with his customary formality. I did, and pulled the chair up to the bunk. "I'm teaching Oscar to read." The older boy blushed while Francis pointed to the comic. "He's got all the names down already." Oscar confirmed it, also pointing,. "Green Lantern." He picked out the name on several panels. "Coke." Here he pointed to the familiar red logo. "It's easier with comics," Francis said. I patted Oscar's arm and praised him.

"Have you told your mother about this, Francis?" I shared my concern with him straightaway.

"No." Francis slid over to sit by me. "She doesn't want me to teach him."

"I didn't think she would. Did Oscar ask to learn?" He rolled his eyes at my question.

"Sure he wants to learn. It's dumb not to."

Oscar nodded.

"So why don't you help too?" Francis asked. "We're just going through it, and I show him the words till he knows them. We started with the names so he'd have something to follow."

Francis meant well, but he had no idea how to teach a skill like reading. Oscar might become an accomplished mimic—repeating the names as Francis pronounced them—and still never know a single letter of the alphabet. No collection of signs was ever so arbitrary and varied as that set of twenty-six. Beside them, the red and white wave of Coke seemed like a vivid depiction of the product itself. How could anyone explain why "A" was ay, or "B" be? And why was "W" not the inverse sound of "M"? To go one step further, and link the arcane codes into pronounceable words, was enough to connect Oscar to the written language.

He knew what spoken words meant, and once he got the sound of each written word right, he had the meaning too. Saying, say, "Kitty" in his soft broken voice, he knew the sound meant that warm fur sausage with legs and a wet sandpaper tongue . . . but the remaining distance . . . to leap out of his body, out from the sound of his mouth, and connect the abstract scratches on a page to, to Kitty, that was the biggest leap of all. If the boy wanted to learn, it was wrong to keep him from it. Amelia's objections would have to be ignored (or the lessons kept from her). Written words were so even and welcoming to me. It was the distance they allowed between things. I'd always liked distance. Written words built bridges between people who never touched. Not even their voices touched. That was the nice thing about bridges. While connecting, they also buttressed the gap, and made it more permanent. Of course I would help Oscar learn.

Oscar met me in my room each day after that for lessons. I wanted to bring some order and completeness to his study. We began with the alphabet and its origins. "First, Oscar, you should bear in mind the distinction between phonetic alphabets and simple ideogrammatic systems." The boy lay on the bed with Kitty, like a sleepy child ready for a bedtime tale. "The phonetic alphabet, like our own system of Roman characters, is a group of abstract symbols which indicate sound. I will point to each figure on the chart, and you will tell me its sound." I had constructed a simple chart of the alphabet (showing contemporary figures in bold), with historical antecedents arranged in the conventional left-to-right chronological ascendancy, leading eventually to the modern symbol. I pointed at the "A."

"Aayy." Oscar said, pronouncing "a" as in "splayed." Then he gave me the "aaah" and "ahhh," and we moved on to "B." We were to "Z" in a jiffy. Kitty had crawled up Oscar's shirt front and was arranging herself along his ribs and chest. Her tail switched with pleasure where it emerged below the last button.

"You will have noticed, Oscar, that the twenty-six symbols have no meanings in and of themselves. One cannot simply write 'BHLYK,' for example, and expect that meaning will thereby be conveyed."

The boy took my pointer and indicated each letter as he said it. "I-M-N-N-D-N."

"You're fiddling a little with the rules, Oscar. The phonetic statement, that is, what you've said out loud, conveys meaning. But if you were to write the series of letters you recited the meaning would be unclear, if not impossible to read."

"Francis gets it."

"I don't doubt that Francis gets it. You've established a syllabical code with Francis using what is conventionally a phonetic alphabet."

"I just wrote it down and he got it." Oscar rolled onto his back so Kitty could lie on him directly, with the baggy shirt for a tent.

"Well, regardless. Syllabical codes are not broadly shared, and my point was to distinguish phonetic codes from ideogrammatic." He tilted his head back and watched me upside down. "Do you remember the 'no loitering' sign?" I drew the simple rectangle, with the depiction of the sleeping man and a circle-slashed-through over him. "This is an ideogrammatic sign, Oscar. It represents a meaning directly. It doesn't represent a sound, per se." Oscar took my pen and pad and drew a bell.

"Telephone," he announced.

"Exactly, Oscar. But the alphabet isn't like this."

"I want to read books." He squeezed Kitty to his chest and engaged me with his eyes.

"Pretty soon you'll be able to read anything, once you master this basic skill."

"Good. I want to read the Bible. Father Simp says I can find answers in there."

"That's called faith, Oscar. I prefer a book that offers questions."

"What's called faith?" The boy's hands strayed over his belly and pants, poking and patting, following their own line of inquiry. I shifted in my chair and crossed my legs.

"Father, uh, Simp's belief in the Bible," I answered.

"He said I have very strong faith."

"I'm sure he's right. But I would be wary of his estimation of the Bible." One hand worked its way into the loose jeans and rested there.

"Have you read it?"

"I've studied it at the university. It's a historical text, really. It's an extraordinary document, but obviously not every 'answer' could be in it."

"I know most of the stories from Bible class. Father Simp said the book would answer all my questions."

"That's his faith again, Oscar. He means you can find answers in the Bible story by interpreting it."

"No. He said all I'd have to do is read it." The boy's hands, his ease and curiosity about his body, compelled my attention. I sighed, and moved my chair closer to the bed.

"Well, reading's certainly the right place to start. Some things you read will mean very little unless you interpret them. The stories in the Bible, for instance. Once you learn what all the words mean and get the story right, you need to figure out what the story itself means." He looked at me upside down, his head flopped back over the bed's edge.

"Like with a parable."

"That's right." Something was going on in the pants, a tremor under the buttoned fly, and I found myself blushing.

"Hey, no problem, Mr. Dee." The boy nodded his head with confidence. "I don't need to read to get that. That's what I did best at school, in Bible class. Father Cloud always let me do the interpretation and sum-up." I smiled and patted his arm. His confidence was endearing. Too bad he was wrong about reading.

"But when you *can* read, Oscar, you'll find very subtle shades of meaning in the written words. You'll get to figure out your own interpretations from the text itself. Writers often hide meaning in cleverly chosen words."

"Why do they hide it?"

"Not 'hide' exactly. They, uh, they present it there. But readers don't always see it so they say it's 'hidden.'" Oscar rubbed his cheek, puzzled, and drew one arm inside his shirt.

"So if I read all the words I can get all the . . . 'subtle' answers, like Father Simp says I'll find?"

"Yes. Or you'll find the really subtle questions." I didn't want to confuse him.

"Terrific. "

"Yes. Terrific." I picked up my prepared text and continued. "Let's move on to the thirty-third century B.C. You will recall that Sumerian administrators kept track of inventories through a system of clay tokens, only a few millimeters in size. A collection of spherical and ovoid bullae, small clay vessels or 'envelopes,' as Logan calls them, were used to store the tokens. The opacity of the bullae kept the accountants from seeing what sorts they contained. With more than two hundred different kinds, spherical, cyllindrical, conic, biconic, triangular, tetrahedral, each further distinguished by a variety of incisions and punched holes, the accountants needed some sort of marking on the exterior of the clay vessels to show them what tokens were inside. Thus, a system of imprinting was begun, wherein each bulla was marked by the impress of its corresponding token while the clay was still wet. And this, properly, is the earliest instance of a notational technology indicating something more than just number. Do you follow me?"

The boy had drawn both arms inside the shirt and was fiddling with the cat in there. His sleeves hung off either shoulder, empty and useless. His body looked like a double amputee's, strapped to the doctor's table with a moving tumor on his chest. He'd managed to undo most of his shirt buttons. "Oscar?" I prompted. I guess he was waiting for me to get to the good stuff.

"I'm with you, Nick," he insisted, still upside down. The shirt fell open, exposing Kitty and Oscar's busy hands.

"Oscar. You'll need to concentrate if you're to learn any of this." I fixed him with a stern look. Kitty leapt, and the boy nodded, turning over so he could face me properly.

"Right. Sorry." The shirt stayed on the bed, where it had slipped from him, and Oscar sat up to give me full attention. I tried returning to my text, but found myself unable to take my eyes off his skin. His beauty unnerved me. I couldn't keep from staring, running my eyes along his even shoulders, and onto his chest. For a moment, everything stopped, and there was simply me and Oscar, and an electrical field of silence. He stretched and yawned. I looked at his eyes, and saw in them an indecipherable ambiguity, boredom, and curiosity. He caught my stare and smiled, before falling back against the bed. The alphabet was gone, supplanted by the fact of his body, and the mysterious boy it enclosed. When he lay back, arms stretched above his head to the bedstead, his loose pants jiggling around his hips, I wanted to reach and touch him. I shook the impulse from my mind and sighed, then tossed the book onto his stomach. He flinched a bit and shrugged, before sliding the book off with his hand. "Sorry, Nick. I'm just bushwhacked." I had no reply. He regarded me easily with his warm eyes, but now I avoided them. Oscar unbuttoned his jeans and pulled them off. "Would you rub me?" he asked, lying there. I felt myself leaning down, as if reaching to his belly, but I came no closer. "My back's all tired," he continued. "I think my bed's really soft." Oscar flipped over, tugging his baggy shorts around to get comfortable. He relaxed, face down into my bed. "Just all over my back would be okay. Maybe we can do our lesson later, when I'm not so tired."

"Clarity of engagement" was all I could think, and I did so, silently in my head. Rubbing his back and shoulders, his ribs and hips, and holding his neck softly to loosen the muscles inside, obscured every formal and constructed "communion" we'd had previously. "Clarity of engagement." We didn't talk. I think Oscar may have slept through most of my attentions. The alphabet chart sat beside us on the bed, and when I was not looking at Oscar, I was looking there. I'd hoped (and still hoped) the alphabet would be a bridge between us; now I found myself splayed across the chasm, touching him more directly with my hands.

Naturally I did not tell Amelia I'd begun teaching Oscar the alphabet. It would only upset her. There was some intelligence in my weakest moments (she had claimed) and my afternoon with Oscar had about it some qualities I might call "weakness." Certainly, I felt as if I'd "given in" to something. Oscar's interest in our lessons was sincere, but his body sometimes intruded. I improvised an afternoon program of swimming (thereby exhausting the boy) then having our lessons with some coffee. The black drink kept him attentive, and the exercise left him relaxed and focused. Oscar made terrific progress this way, and Amelia never asked about it. She was happy to see him spend time with me.

The body (and its humors), I now understood, were the source of *The Tempest*. Motley's composition—and its quasi-religious staging—had been prescribed by Dr. Weekes. The music began in readings of the Motley urine. Each aria was an appeal to forces Weekes thought warred over the bodily humors. The uromancer prescribed verses (to be presented in the precisely planned "sacristy" at Den Dollard) as an appeal to the spirits and sprites which could right the balance by their interventions. Now that I'd found the key (in a sheaf of folded pages Motley kept), all the parts fit nicely. The inexplicable introduction of Neptune, Nereids, Tritons, and Aeolus, as key figures in the drama, could be explained. These were the "Spirits of Urine." I had found the reference among the folded pages. Shadwell's inclusion of Neptune and the sea nymphs convinced Motley to use Shadwell as a model. *The Tempest* was an operatic prayer to the water gods.

Motley's "water" was in the balance, and the new opera was an offering to right it.

Verweerd carried out the plans with some faithfulness to the
original operatic score, but with very little regard for Motley's exacting architectural specifications. In this (Verweerd's area of greater
expertise) the Dutch engineer transformed Motley's opera house into
an elegant machine, entirely unlike the precisely situated cruciform
originally sketched by his patron. Motley had aligned his building with
the winds and magnetic fields Dr. Weekes deemed most influential
for the urine. It was a solid vault, oriented north-northwest, with an
elaborate system of vents and vanes to bring particular winds into the
chamber. Lodestones built into the structure reinforced the earth's
magnetic field along critical lines. Verweerd trebled the vents, reori-
ented the building toward the prettiest outlook, and punctured the
walls with open archways. "The pleasing tides must enter and retreat
without interference," he wrote in his daybook. "The wise engineer
works with the force of water, rather than against it." Motley would
have a terrible surprise when he went the next fall to be present for
the realization of his "great and glorious endeavour," the premiere
(and only) performance in this great hall.

Verweerd left Den Dollard, that winter of 1686, and took the
acting troupe and musicians inland, to Allersmaborg. There Amelia,
the two boys, and I would pick up the trail. We were headed to Ezinge,
where the Allersmaborg still stood, perhaps in ruins, to find the last
days of Verweerd and Motley, and to reimagine the terrible destruction by storm of the opera house at Den Dollard. Soon enough, we
would arrive at the sight of my researches.

Without land in sight the sea was featureless and gray. The ship's tremendous height and tinted windows obscured the water, rendering
it even and flat, like a tightly woven carpet. My legs had steadied,
or the ship found its path. Whichever, the course of our travel was
smooth, and the weather was unremarkable. The sea's regularity, and
the warmth of my cabin made me fall often from reading into sleep;
it was in such a state that Oscar and Francis found me the next afternoon. They woke me from my nap and asked if I would join them for

a swim. A swim, I wondered, staring out at the featureless ocean. There were two pools, one outside with plastic tables and enormous striped umbrellas, and one deep inside, sloshing about in the ship's belly like an overful bladder. The indoor, I insisted. I retrieved my robe and trunks from the cabin, and rang the porter for a broad terry-cloth robe. Francis made the suggestion of a picnic, and we asked the porter to bring one.

The water was clear and deep. It filled a long metal shell painted blue, and there were no lane barriers. Oscar and Francis peeled their shirts off and dove in, splashing the wicker basket the porter brought, and dampening the bills I'd pressed into his palm. The pool was deeper than the one on deck. There were ladders and platforms on all the walls to dive from. I lay down on my towel with a book about Henry Purcell, and took a soda from the basket. I had some suspicions about the Motley *Tempest* and this was a good chance to check up on it. Hadn't Purcell been the organist at Westminster, the organist to whom Motley had begun sending his scores?

Oscar sailed over my head and broke the water with an enormous splash. I tucked my towel around the book, and kept reading. "Mr. Dee," Francis called from the pool's edge. "Come in for Marco Polo. It's no fun with two." Sweet boy. His bright face and smile always said please, even if he didn't. I put the book inside a plastic bag I'd brought for the purpose, slipped my robe off, and lowered myself in. It was warm and buoying, like a salty hot spring. My skin felt sticky and tight when I bobbed up and floated.

"Not It," both boys screamed. Oscar tossed a taped diving mask to me. "It" in Marco Polo had to find and touch another player to be "not it." Rather than trust me to keep my eyes closed, as the rules required, the boys had sealed a mask with electrical tape. I put it on and was blind. The dark cloth tape covered the glass completely and the rubber seal was undamaged. I let some water inside, to stop the pressure, then submerged again. Where was everyone? I could hear the dull clank of a boy's ankle against the metal wall. He could be anywhere. Silence. I let some bubbles out my mouth and sank farther. The water held me gently in place, and I relaxed, trying to sense movement in the tiny currents. Most boys were daredevils. I felt the water turn me very slightly from behind, then he whooshed over me, and I tumbled underwater. The air was getting thin and I enjoyed the hollow feeling inside me for a moment more. My lungs pulsed once with fear, my head emptied, and I kicked up toward the surface, almost without wanting to.

"Marco," I called. The word echoed in the empty metal room. "Marco."

"Polo." Two voices speaking at once. Oscar was very close, saying the word quietly to fool me. Was I near the corner now? I had a complicated memory of turns and lunges, which made me think I was close *to* a corner. But my real world was just black and wet. I could be anywhere.

"Marco."

"Polo." I took a big breath and went under again. My ears enjoyed their deprivation. Water filled them with the vague sounds of its activity, some clanking and a rustle like leaves, only it must've been bubbles or a limb. My hair was loose. I could feel it model the small currents, weightless. Could it all touch me inside as out—if I opened my mouth and drew it in deeply like a breath, an ocean of water drawn down into my lungs, dragged through me like air? What stillness, if I was all water, and let the current move through me that way. What dispersal, and dissolution, finally, to the willowy connecting world. Like falling into sleep, the giving up and opening. I let some air out, careful to position myself as if unaware, then pushed violently across, and caught him, "it" (now that I had him in my grasp), Oscar's slim, muscular body. Now he was "it," and I needed only to play it smart and keep a little distance to not be "it" again.

Amelia was occupied with travel plans and sketchings, charts and timetables, throughout the final days of our voyage. I saw her for meals. Even then she was secretive and distracted (hardly a new condition). The light gray skies of our long travel gave way to darker gray, as the ship bore north across the Atlantic. The wind and water were calm (uncharacteristically so, the captain told us). On deck in a single chair under blankets Francis and Oscar enjoyed their comics. Oscar asked Francis if he'd ever read the Bible, and Francis hadn't. The two boys began with John 1:1. "In the beginning was the word," Oscar read slowly. Francis pointed to each letter in turn, and they worked their way gradually forward. Amelia would be leading us when we arrived on land (just as she had led us across the sea). I saw a map on which she'd marked a line from Rotterdam, where we would be landing, north to Amsterdam, Enkhuizen, and across the water to Stavoren, by land into Friesland, then east to the Allersmaborg. By train we could make our way direct in less than three hours. But her route wasn't charted for speed.

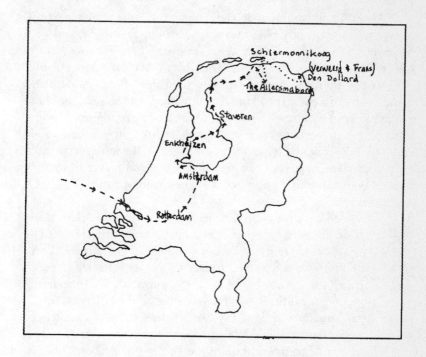

It was in fact marked (I saw) by arrows, advancing along the path of our travel: from Rotterdam, to Amsterdam, to Enkhuizen, Stavoren, and finally the Allersmaborg. The route of Verweerd and Frans was marked too. Her plans loomed with the promise of something rich and strange.

I would not resist her. Her stature was increasing noticeably as we approached Holland. It may have been the intensity of her spirit, or a change in posture, but she no longer resembled a dwarf at all.

The emanation of power which had always engaged me (even on that long-ago day when I first left my apartment looking for a policy of insurance against personal loss) was now uncountered by any accident of physiology. Her body might have swelled to fill the larger envelope of her aura. Or I had changed. Regardless, she was bigger; and the nearer the boat drew to Holland, the larger she seemed to grow.

One evening after dinner, she came to my cabin to help me pack my bags. Our first sight of land would come late that night, and we'd be in the harbor by dawn. Traces of rain (the first since we left the city) pestered the black windows. The wide night closed down in rank mist around the ship. Amelia said she could smell the Continent and could taste our nearness to land. I wanted to see the shore, and kept my eyes to the window, hoping I might find searchlights burning through the fog. There were none. Amelia brought candles, so we could dim the cabin lights and see farther. "You'll want everything in a small carrying bag, Nicholas. I'm afraid we won't have the luxury of a caravan. Anything bulky will be sent ahead in trunks."

"Everything? What exactly will I need?"

"Your manuscript should be packed, and no more than a few pounds of documents, whichever you deem most important." The archive would be scandalized by our handling of the papers. There was no doubting we'd have hell to pay if we ever returned. "You'll want warm clothing, too. Nothing fancy or formal. We'll be seeing some desperate conditions before we arrive at the Allersmaborg." Amelia was already emptying my dresser drawers. The candlelight softened her intensity, but I felt an echo of our first night together, when I was made to participate in the sacking of Abbott's things. Clearly she enjoyed packing. I picked at the enormous pile of pages I had spread out around the desk. It was from within this chrysalis, this cocoon of sources, that I usually felt able to "form," or "formulate."

"Just a few pounds?"

"That's all we can carry."

"I need Verweerd's daybook, absolutely. And Motley's. I'd like to keep the letters too, and the records Drop made about the finances and the policy." I'd already gathered an armful and Amelia stopped me there.

"Fine. That's all then, that and the manuscript." She took the tumbling pile from me and stuffed it in my vinyl bag. "You'll need to leave room for clothing."

I stood by helplessly as Amelia plundered the remaining piles, taking them armload by armload to the heavy trunks the porter left. She filled one and shut the lid tight, then moved swiftly on to the next. The gathering rain made tears on my reflection. Amelia moved in and out of that dark picture, materializing each time she came near the candle. She'd disappear, as if into the darkened sea, as she bore my sources away with her. Her swiftness and strength were remarkable, and I remembered them now, from our last exit, leaving the city. It was as if she (and a great deal else) had lain dormant through our journey overseas, and now came to life, stirred by our arrival and the chance to finish what she'd begun by leaving.

III

HIS RESEARCHES

LIGHTS LIKE LANTERNS hung in the sky on the coast, and the boat made its way in the last hour of night, down to the river mouth, and then inland to Rotterdam's harbor. Amelia was still awake. The glow from her forward-looking windows could be seen imprinted on the fog. I lay abed in the dark, half-sleeping, yet unable to close my eyes against the sight of the flat, shrouded land. The smallest elevations could be seen clearly. The water ended at the "fringe of dunes" our captain had described, and behind them were towns, lacing the ocean and the night with searchlights. When the sun appeared it was nothing; just a dull blemish of gray above the towns. The day stayed dark, even as the sun crawled higher in the sky. Our ship turned in at the mouth of the river; an hour to the harbor.

The boys were awake now too, and stood on deck at the railing, wrapped together in a blanket, staring at the shore. Our ship bypassed the enormous *Europoort* and kept on up the *Waterweg* to the city itself. Something was wrong with the usual machinery. The ports were inaccesible, and our ship was made to dock at the older, more primitive piers. The sky pressed down on the industrial docks and the river. Our prow, finally relieved of the sea, drew easily through the icy water, rolling a small wake to either shore. Maassluis and Rozenburg passed, and the river broadened and split. A massive concrete cylinder rose into the fog and I could see its lights, like the searchlights of the police choppers, glowing in the overcast. It was the Euromast, Amelia said. It shared with the police tower back home a commanding outlook, and an unassailable foundation.

Bicyclists wavered in packs along the river, uniformly bundled in bright parkas. Their bikes were black, and as plain as the riders were pretty. Some older men, I noticed, wore frowsy black overcoats and hats, or the workman's dull blue overalls. But they were few. In the river mist, the colorful jackets blurred as the bicycle riders drifted past. At the edge of my view, the sight was like a disease of the eye: dull gray, punctuated with smudged eruptions of unfocused color. The city gathered around us, both spacious and cluttered. The buildings were short and haphazardly adorned, some with bright neon strung along contours, others with geometric signs and fenders. Brick and concrete competed equally, and the scars of continual renovation were opened up everywhere; it looked like the city had paused in the midst of its own construction to consider, if only for a moment, what to do next. Structures, old and new, lined up along the streets with the sort of deference one finds in emergency waiting rooms. Accident and circumstance dictated the order of things. New buildings were coming in everywhere. A crane or two, scraping clouds, stood dormant over every quarter. It was still early, and the streets were quiet. Bicycles and trams maneuvered through the gloom, and some few newspaper stands could be seen coming open. Small boats, like water-borne insects, scrambled over the river, obeying their own rules.

Francis was bright and animated, pointing out features of the shore to Oscar, and describing at great length the destruction of the city by German bombers in 1940. He knew more than I did about Rotterdam, and he could pronounce all the names correctly. Wind or the sun had thinned the clouds some, and we could see beyond the city to its green borders. The boat shuddered and slowed, and drew closer to a slip. Ours was the only boat docking beside the Delfshaven. Colorful striped tents were set up in the adjacent park, and a crane had been maneuvered onto the bulwark. Customs, and other official business, were arranged throughout the tents.

The customs' agent refused my passport. He did not refuse me entry into the country, but literally refused my passport. He was a younger man, very distracted by music playing on a small tape machine, and he waved my papers away, as if bored by them. I paused at the gate, insisting he take the slim blue document, and at least stamp it to indicate his approval, but my argument went unheard. He would have none of it. Tossing his headphones down, the agent took me by the arm to a Plexiglas cubicle and, there, addressed me.

"You got a problem, mon?" He pronounced "man" as "mon," in a Caribbean dialect I'd heard before at the university. "I thought I sent you on?"

"You didn't check my papers."

He smiled at me, nodding. "Who gives a shit about your papers."

"I'd like to have them stamped," I explained, pulling the new passport from my pocket. "To indicate my entry."

"Don't be stupid. I sent you on, didn't I? That would be plenty to indicate your entry." The young man began rolling a small cigarette from a leather pouch he kept with him. "I don't want your mess with the papers." It was nice to see him so relaxed, despite our misunderstanding.

"I need to have them marked," I tried explaining again. "What if a policeman stops me, or I'm accused of staying illegally in the country?" The agent grunted with surprise.

"What would the police be wanting with you?"

"I'm just saying suppose."

He took it, at last, and slipped it in his pocket. "On you go then. I got to be back at my post."

"No, no, no. Take it and mark it please. I'll need it back to travel." He offered me the small cigarette instead, and pulled the passport from his pocket.

"Oh, oh, oh," he stuttered, animated by some new surprise. "I know that name." He smiled broadly and slapped my open hand. "We got to have you waiting here." The agent sauntered out, leaving me with the cigarette and nothing else. Amelia and the boys had moved past the tents, and were sitting with our bags on a park bench. They could not see me through the crowd.

The young agent opened the Plexiglas door and ushered in Clausewitz. His cool and nervelessness filled the cubicle. It took my breath away.

"Dee, at last," the unruffled inspector cooed. "You certainly picked a slow boat for travel."

"Inspector," I whispered. It seemed ingenuous to shake hands, but I offered him mine anyway. His suit, though unpressed, retained all of its sheen and sharpness; and he didn't look too shabby himself.

"But how, Inspector, how did you get here before us, and with time to look so sharp and rested?" I hoped the agent, or someone, would return soon to interrupt us, and keep the inspector from having his way with me.

"I took a plane, Dee. I've been here over a week, and I can't say I like it."

"We won't be staying long," I tried, hoping to deflect his antagonism. "Classes start at the end of the month." My cheery tone wasn't lost on him. He tipped his felt hat back on his head and leaned closer.

"Maybe we'll go back before then."

"I, I can't. I have my researches, you see. The contract and all. Mrs. Weathered explained it to you . . . as I recall."

"When she drugged me?"

"Drugs?" Had I any innocence left to protect?

"Don't trouble yourself about it, Professor. I've seen far worse. It's best to take it like a man. I can't begrudge you. The point is you're in danger here, but I think you already know it."

"In danger? Here, in Holland?"

"Mrs. Weathered. We know by now what she's capable of. We're hoping you've had some success, you know, wresting the boys away from her. I'll do all I can to help. We've got a budget for this kind of thing."

"Help? What sort of help?"

"With your work, *our* work." The inspector's friendly tone threw me into some confusion. "I know how you feel about this, Dee. You're new to it all, and maybe a little bit cowed by the prospect. No one's asking for expertise here, or any top-notch treatise on police tactics and techniques." He put his wide, gentle hand on my shoulder and slowly tightened his grip. "Just remember the boys, Professor Dee. I'll take care of the rest."

"That's what 'she' said," I answered, haltingly. "To just remember, to think about the boys."

"She'll devour them."

"Actually she's been very kind, that is, lately."

"Kindness is not what they need. I think you'll agree these boys need the firm hand of the police."

"One of them is her son."

The inspector flipped his notepad open and read from it. "Francis, the younger one. Twelve years old. Valley School, eighth grade. Teachers say he's very bright. Odd boy, tends to boss the other kids around." He looked up from the page. "Aren't there some doubts about the boy's maternity? I don't think it's reasonable to suggest she could have had the child." I tried to see past the inspector's broad shoulders, glancing, as if without interest, through the crowd, hoping to make contact with the boys and woman in question. His face kept intervening, and I found myself staring into his clear gray eyes.

"The boy, Francis, confirmed it to me. I'm quite sure she's the one, at least, who raised him."

"I'd like to see her prove it in court. And the father. Any ideas about the father, Dee?" His eyes moved closer, and the hand took my shoulder again. I hesitated and coughed, trying to mask my discomfort.

"I, I really can't say."

"Work on it, Dee. We're running a scan back home." Clausewitz relaxed into his chair and offered me gum, some new sort with caffeine for pep. He gazed out at the crowds and the surrounding park. His face warmed up, and he sighed like an old alum come back for a twenty-fifth reunion. "I'm here on a project too, you know, Dee. No fancy contracts and agents like you've got, but an attractive little documentary nonetheless." I tried to summon up interest.

"Police News Team?"

"That's right. You hate to see a little country like this run down into the ground by lawlessness. They used to have more statutes on the books here; really clever, thoroughgoing stuff." The cool inspector became wistful and dreamy. "What do you know about 'immersion,' Professor?"

"Well. A fair bit." What was he getting at? "What aspect, exactly, do you mean?"

"I mean the drowning cell." His eyes grew larger as he explained. The crowds outside were pressed against the Plexiglas, and I could see nothing beyond their colorful backs. "Dutch misfits and criminals were put in cells filled with water. They had to swallow the water to keep from drowning in it. The flood could be kept coming at whatever rate the jailers saw fit. Kind of reduces everything down to its essence. No one wants to drown, do they? No one in their right mind, anyway. I think it's very elegant, don't you?"

"Very, direct." Why did the inspector's enthusiasms always come across as threats? "Of course we have much subtler methods today. The misfit is kept swallowing without recourse to crude and brutal things, like an actual cell or water."

"Of course," I agreed, whispering. "No need for cells, really. Not today."

"But credit the Dutch, and that wonderful Golden Age, Professor. I've read your papers on it. One day you academics will wake up and realize what a fruitful era that was for penology too. I think you'll find some of our most fundamental principles were established then."

"Yes, I've seen some studies.[1] I didn't realize you had an interest in history, Inspector."

He nodded vigorously.

"I find it very useful, for my work." His excitement was worrying.

"I see."

"Knowledge can be put to many uses."

I stared vacantly past him, unnerved by his ambition. "Yes," I whispered.

He waited for more, in vain, then slapped me lightly on both cheeks. "Is it fatigue, Professor? Has she been keeping you away from your work?"

"No, no. Of course not. She's my . . . collaborator. On the book. I think we're going east for a while." All his informality was wiped away. Suddenly the man was all business again. He peered into the crowd with steely suspicion.

---

1. S. Aylies, *The System of the Penitentiary*, 1837; P. Colquhoun, *Treatise on the Police of the Metropolis*, 1797; M. Foucault, *Discipline and Punish*, 1979, J. Lawrence, A *History of Capital Punishment*, 1932; T. Sellin, *Pioneering in Penology*, 1944: N. K. Teeters, *The Cradle of the Penitentiary*, 1935.

"I really shouldn't have kept you so long, Dee, but I thought you could use the boost. Just remember, I'm with you, Professor Dee, everywhere." The mysterious inspector put a finger to his lips and backed silently out of the cubicle. He disappeared into the crowd. I was left dazed and alone (and a little cowed by his parting promise and/or threat). What jurisdiction could the inspector possibly have in Holland? Little or none, I presumed (and little help either, if the customs' agent was any example). Clausewitz was just a face in the crowd here, a touring documentarian, with no more jurisdiction over affairs than I.

"Clausewitz is here," I told Amelia, as soon as I could get to her. She showed no alarm.

"What does he want?"

"He thinks I'm working for the police, that I'm doing some sort of undercover job for him, taking the boys away from you." Amelia listened to my explanation, nodding patiently.

"Well. Let's hope he's wrong." The boys (though I was certain they understood none of this) both nodded their agreement with Amelia.

"Of course he's wrong," I insisted. "Despite what you, and the inspector, have said, I have never been a, a collaborator or, a confederate, of the police."

"Calm down, Nicholas. We needn't waste our energies on it. Muffin." She turned now to Francis. "Gather the luggage and get a cart. We'll need to find some breakfast and then catch a train to Amsterdam." Francis scooted from the bench, and took Oscar with him. Kitty cowered among the bags. "You and I, Nicholas, will pay the inspector no mind at all. He has no jurisdiction here."

"But I fear he has some power."

"He can do nothing. What he tries to do is not important." I disagreed with her brash dismissal, but as often with Amelia, it did no good to argue. She was making a statement of faith, rather than a reasoned argument. I could choose to share that faith or not, but no amount of evidence would shake her from it.

Now everything became swift and crowded. Noisy schoolboys on bicycles filled alleys and the margins of the boulevards. Tiny cars ran in sleepy rivers of traffic. Those on foot were mostly silent, bundled up in mufflers and hats. The streets seemed neither hostile nor welcoming, strange nor familiar. Pulling the baggage behind us on a wooden dorrie, we made our way into the city in search of food. Amelia lay down on the luggage to rest awhile, tolerating the frightened cat, and Francis asked strangers where breakfast could be found. The pedestrians were polite but unhelpful.

"*Ontbijt?*" one tall chain-smoking student replied, as if he'd never heard of such a thing as breakfast. He sighed and took Francis by the shoulder, turning him toward the Westersingel. "*Volg deze straat,*" the bemused smoker told us now, pointing. "*Een halve kilometer of so, bij het Centraal Station.*" He whistled like a train. "*Begrepen?*"

"*Ja,*" Francis answered. "*Het trein station.*"

The vast plaza beside the station was thick with buses and trams. We found our way across to a small snack bar, an orange and green plastic and chrome affair, with a few empty Formica tables and pleasant molded seats that swiveled. Amelia rang a small desk bell, impatiently beckoning the chef, while Francis explained the menu.

"The *frikandel*'s a little head-cheese sort of thing," he allowed. "I'd stay away from that. The *kroketten* are tasty. They're kind of a deep-fried stew, like a short tube of stew."

"Deep-fried?"

"Yeah, so it's got this nice crispy outside, then it's all, you know, stew inside. The *sate* ones are great. The *patat*'s just big french fries."

"Is *hamburger* a hamburger?" the older boy asked, looking for something familiar.

"Yeah," Francis assured him. "Sort of." Amelia was doddering by the Plexiglas counter, berating the proprietor in Dutch; something about tobacco and fish. The man kept his arms crossed, coughing and spitting while she fixed him with a stare. Finally he gave over some of the tiny, thin papers, and opened a pouch of tobacco to her.

"Francis dear," she yelled to the boy. "We'll be having herring. If Oscar or Mr. Dee would like anything else they'll have to order up now."

"Hamburger," Oscar requested. "And the fries with ketchup and a shake."

"Mr. Dee?"

"Just the, uh, cheese soufflé please, Francis. And an egg if he has one. Fried, with the *patat* also. I'd like a coffee with that."

I watched the chef prepare our meal. He took several small packages from a freezer and dropped their contents into the deep-fry. A raw burger came off a stack from inside the cold case and went into the hot fat too. An egg from the fridge was broken open into the boiling oil, a pile of potatoes went in, and then the coffee was drawn. The preparation was simple and fast. Amelia supervised the selection of herring from a bucket the man kept hidden in the bottom of the fridge. These were not on the menu, and she took them from him raw, preventing any use of the deep-fry. Rolls and onions went with them. Traffic increased on the sidewalks, and the bikeways and roads were full. Though it was almost nine o'clock, the sky had not gotten any lighter, just more gray. Packs of teenagers, smoking, sailed past on bikes. They rode two, sometimes three to a bicycle, and a few among them seemed to be dressing still, pulling their school clothes on as they rode. Their dexterity impressed me. One boy forsook the handlebars for a good twenty yards, riding blind inside the bright striped sweater he was pulling on, and still managed it without a spill. Stale tobacco and wintergreen cleanser battled with fish and fry fat. Oscar opened up a window. The boys here looked like girls and the girls looked like boys. As the captain said, they were all long-legged and lanky, even the preteens, and shared the same heavily gelled haircut. It was like watching an Olympic team, except they were all smoking. My "cheese soufflé" was a deep-fried pastry envelope of cheese. I left it on the paper plate, and finished my herring.

Our day in the city was a blurred haze of damp gray, and icy cold winds, interrupted, on occasion, by warm buildings. We seemed always to be leaving—the snack bar, the grocery, museums and libraries . . . we'd turn around and exit the buildings before I even had time to discover our purpose. Amelia directed us with speed and deliberateness, as if we were already late for some final rendezvous. We caught buses running and trams without tickets, traversing most of the city's center in a rush of elaborate preparations.

Despite all my reading, the country was new and strange to me. Spoken Dutch was a far cry from the easy decipherable texts I'd seen over the last fifteen years. Their speech moved like a rapid wet stream—

a fluid rolling sound of babbling gurgles and bubbles; where the stream hit hard consonants, it faltered and broke into a spray of throat rasping. It was impossible to picture the familiar letters I'd seen in the written language. The sound that student made, for example, when he told us the pancake *huis* was *"gesloten,"* could not be adequately represented on paper. It began with a prolonged throat clearing, interrupted by the hissing tongue, and ended with a soft, dismissive vowel. *"Huis"* was like house, only the speaker tried swallowing the word and biting down on it, nipping off everything except the slippery "s." Francis, who'd learned the language out loud as a child, was cheerful and competent, engaging everyone we encountered with an easy greeting and questions. The Dutch paid him the compliment of continuing the conversation in their native language. When I tried speaking, the first response was a friendly question back in English. "Oh. Are you American?" Their English was clear and fluent. It was meant as a favor to me, so I wouldn't have to bother with the Dutch. Francis passed easily, undetected. The boy drew small maps, and tutored Oscar on useful phrases over breakfast. He'd bloomed like a hothouse flower since landing.

Sitting to rest on a bench that morning with Oscar, in the empty park behind a museum, I was drawn down by a sudden, hollow weariness. Francis and Amelia were fetching slides from an office inside. Perhaps it was exhaustion, or a memory of the city, my home, we'd left far behind. I had been looking at Oscar's soft chin, and the cloud of breath that billowed when he exhaled. We were both tired. He rested his hands on his lap and sat slumped inside the bright new jacket he'd gotten only an hour earlier. There wasn't much to say. The park was deserted. The grass was covered in dead leaves and frost. Bare trees were black in the mist; their limbs in silhouette made tangled lace, and disappeared in the sunken clouds. We both smiled and sighed. I guess it was his chin, and his smooth throat. I could see the story Amelia wrote, the chapters describing Oscar, alive in the warm skin. There were his eyes, set in the soft, angular face, and the smooth blushing cheeks. Inside the jacket, inside him, was all of his past, his experience—the story of him I'd read and known from the pages. How could a whole past be contained the way Oscar, the sight of Oscar, held the past in him? That was the mystery I couldn't understand; and it was a magnet that drew me to him. I could look at a calendar and see all the days, the feeling and events of those days, dormant on the pages that marked them. There were photographs I treasured, bent and worn in a drawer of my desk; their surfaces held whole events, a time and place, alive inside. I watched Oscar's soft neck when he swallowed and turned. The hollow at his collar deepened and was a little damp.

How strange that he'd first come to life for me in a fabric of words—what Amelia wrote down on the page. She fashioned a story of him, and I began to know the boy, or feel I knew him, from the pages she gave me. When he walked through the inspector's door and stood by me, sleepy and breathing, only inches from my eyes, it overwhelmed me. His warm and living body held so much—it held what I'd read, and it held the living boy. When I touched him, I touched the boy in the chapters, the character of Oscar Vega. I knew so much from the pages, much more than our single encounters told.

"What are you thinking?" Oscar asked in the mist. He bent his head sideways, and looked at me from under the hood. Words failed me. I sighed and stuttered, trying to start them coming, but finally couldn't speak. I stammered, and reached my warm hand toward his cheek, but did not touch him. Oscar smiled and looked away into the park.

The clean yellow train sped north across farmlands and through towns to Amsterdam. We sat on facing seats with a city map spread out on our knees between us. Noisy children played games over the seat backs and their tall parents ignored them. The day flew by outside. Swans stood in vast empty fields. Sheep and cows were gathered by ditches. There were no fences around the animals. Ditches divided fields, and dikes made borders beside the roads and rivers. One canal was carried in concrete over a highway where the land was too low to contain it. Amelia announced we'd be going to museums in the afternoon, and an "old brown café" in the evening. *"Echt Nederlands,"* she promised. More coffee came in a narrow cart pushed down the aisle by a train attendant. The country was soaked in it, coffee dark and bitter as dirt. The attendant tipped the heavy jug on its pivot, and produced a precisely measured cup. Francis had it with *koffiemelk*, to take the edge off. He took a small bottle of the warm, glutinous milk from the cart, and tipped it to his steaming cup. The black coffee turned tan and oily with the additive.

"I think, Oscar," Amelia began, "you'll enjoy the Rijksmuseum." He smiled at her attentions. "Having grown accustomed to the tiny collection back home, the Rijksmuseum should be a real feast for you. You'll find the *Anatomy Lesson* there, the Rembrandt we looked at in the book." Francis slipped one of his licorice candies into the coffee.

"The doctor and the police?"

"That's the one. It's called the *Anatomy Lesson of Dr. Tulp*. Rembrandt painted it." The younger boy offered me a sip. Out of politeness I took it, and was surprised by the delicate flavor. It was like an anisette toddy, or fennel with burned potatoes. Francis passed the drink to Oscar.

"*Koffiedrop,*" he called it. "My friend at school made it up."

"It's much larger than in the book," Amelia went on about the Rembrandt. "We'll only have four or five hours I'm afraid. Muffin. You're not poisoning our friends with another of your concoctions are you?"

The city began suddenly at the edge of fields, and the train tracks gathered fast into a yard thirty meters wide. The arching canopy of Amsterdam's train station looked cold and broken in the dim winter light. Our car clattered across frozen rails to the enclosure, and the sky disappeared. The station was enormous and full. Taped announcements echoed around nesting pigeons, diminished by the squealing friction of old brakes. We dragged our bags onto the concrete platform and watched the doors slap shut.

The face of the city was much older than Rotterdam's. Standing in a crowd of Germans, in front of the station, we saw a skyline of pretty church towers and old municipal buildings. Exhalations from chimneys rose into the haze and lingered. Francis was buying *oliebollen,* and I could smell the yeasty hot grease across the open square, mixing with tobacco smoke and fish in the cold air. We picked our way through the broad confluence of tram lines and huddled under an awning on the Prins Hendrikkade. The fried dough was hot and delicious, speckled with currants, and powdered with sugar on the outside.

We went west along twisting alleys and sudden, strange canals, toward the Haarlemmerpoort, and the hotel Amelia marked on the map. The buildings looked old, even if they were filled with modern things. Pretty facades masked a crazy confluence of centuries. Time went backward as the buildings went up. On a crowded shopping street (which kept turning incessantly left) electronic bargain stores sat below old shuttered windows; any minute, it seemed, a man might lean out from above and empty his chamber pot. Higher still, tiny attic doors opened under three-hundred-year-old winches meant to hoist heavy furniture. Many were still in use. Two televisions from a discount shop rose slowly overhead. The facade said "1657," but everything sold at ground level was proudly modern.

Buildings still in use were simultaneously being gutted. Offices operated behind a thin shell of historical fronts. Along one block, the facades formed a solid wall, propped up by scaffolding and wooden beams. Behind them was nothing but a construction site, a pit where the elaborate plans of the architect would soon grow. The doors and windows could then be thrown open again and the city go on with its business. We followed our map, and Francis's lead, through noisy crowds and shoppers to a tall narrow house above a fetid canal. "International Readers Hotel," it said on a colorful painted sign. The water was green and ominously unfrozen. "Youth and scholars welcome." A rusting bicycle was half-submerged beside the small bridge we crossed. There may have been others. The door was ajar. Reggae and smoke drifted out when we opened it. We went in, and a sweet older man in a cardigan came to the desk to greet us. "*Dag, mijnheer, mevrouw.* Boys." He rumpled Oscar's hair and gave a pat to Francis. "*Wat wilt U, mijnheer? En kamertje voor de familie?*"

"*Drie, alstublieft,*" Amelia answered. She straightened my jacket and smiled at me. "I've gotten you your own room, Nicholas. I'm sure you'll be wanting to get some work done on that manuscript of yours." The interior was dim and close, and the rooms were tiny. We carried the bags up the narrow stairs and left them in the boys' room; I arranged the day's leftover herring in a bowl by the bed for Kitty. She travelled now in Oscar's bag, nestled amongst the poorly washed clothing, with the zipper opened slightly for air and light. Upstairs, I had a view of the water, and a desk because my bed was smaller. The floor was crooked, and the walls had bent. Through my window there were no traces of the last century (save the forlorn bicycle that was sunk into the canal). The outlook was limited and narrow, like the room itself. If no pedestrians passed, and the bike was ignored, I could imagine myself alive in some previous time. A scholar in his rented room. My pen and cheap lined pads of paper ruined the illusion, so I shifted them to the bed, and spent a moment by the window alone, pretending.

SEVENTEEN

WE BUNDLED UP AGAINST THE COLD and walked the few miles to the Rijksmuseum. A light snow was coming down, out of the haze. Oddly, it was brighter out, now that the snow had started. Enough light came from the sky to cast shadows and to sparkle on the tiny flakes. The sun spread white over the gray southern sky, like water blotting paper. The snow smelled fresh and it mixed in the cold with smoke and the frying fat. The pavements were slick so the bicycles didn't stop. They rolled past faster, unwilling to try their brakes. All manner of bags and briefcases hung off the handlebars. Passengers sat nonchalantly on the small back racks, reading or enjoying a cigarette. The museum was enormous. The plaza and the building were filled with children. A little horde, some fifty or a hundred of them, jostled and played anxiously in the lobby, waiting to be gathered and let into the galleries. I expected bright towels and fins, beach balls and the like, so loud and evident was their anticipation of pleasure. Guides did little to restrain them. The children followed pell-mell, sometimes slipping from one group to another without notice. Amelia set a time and disappeared into the vast collection, dragging Francis along behind her. Oscar and I wandered into the rooms, and soon found ourselves in the seventeenth century, in front of Pieter Claesz. *Vanitas.*

"Are you from the city, back home?" I asked Oscar, wanting a brief retreat from the dizzying race of our travel. "I mean our city."

He was preoccupied with the painting, and paid me no mind. Fortuna took all his attention. Claesz had painted her in an open book, propped against a table leg in the still life. "Were you born there?" I prompted.

"No." Oscar looked at me and shrugged, as if apologizing. He blushed, avoiding my eyes. "I'm not from here," he admitted in a whisper. He looked back at me, biting on his lower lip. "I'm not from the city." Oscar pointed at the figure, almost touching it. "That lady's naked."

"That's 'Fortuna.' Fortune." Now I whispered too. On the table-top were bones and a skull. Claesz arranged them beside a painter's palette and brushes. An empty glass sparkled by the skull. "But . . . do you live there now?"

"Yep." He turned away again. I waited, but that was all he offered about his life. "Is that sheet music under the guy's cane?" Oscar pointed to the right side of the painting. Papers were scattered beneath musical instruments. To the left were more papers, a quill pen, and some books. There was armor stacked with the books. "I don't think it's a cane, Oscar. That's a kind of old trombone. It's called a sackbut. So I guess it must be sheet music." The pages were obscured. A gray cover masked most of them. "A lot of 'vanitas' paintings had sheet music."

"That's like 'vanity'?"

"Or like 'mortality.' They were supposed to show the imper-manence of things. Like the life of man, or flowers, or time passing. Do you see the little pocket watch on the table?" We stepped up to the canvas, and looked closely at the small, open watch. It sat beside the bones.

"Oh yeah. Looks like that watch you have. Why would sheet music be in a painting about mortality?" I scrutinized the watch a moment longer. Really it was nothing like mine. Mine was far slim-mer and more modern. The watch in the painting was clumsy, almost spherical, and probably always running out. I thought mine might never run out, the way it'd kept going, ever since Amelia gave it to me. "Was it like, a funeral march or something?"

"A funeral march?"

"The music in the vanity paintings."

"Oh no, no. Music was included, along with the other arts." I directed the boy's attentions back to Claesz. "You see here the painter's palette, and a quill, for writing. Some had globes too, or maps and the instruments for drawing them. The arts were, well. Somehow they were connected with dying." Oscar looked at me skeptically. He was silent, waiting for further explanation. I shrugged.

"Maybe people did them so they wouldn't die. You know, like leaving a mark?"

"A hedge against mortality. That's very possible, Oscar."

"This painting's here, you see, even if the man's dead." The boy smiled, pleased by this proof of his thesis.

"Yes. Good point." I nodded my encouragement, though privately I thought the issue was more complicated than that.

"And the armor can keep a man from dying."

"Yes. That's true too." I admired the compelling sheen of the painted armor. It looked solid and unbreachable. It was incredible; the metal was nothing but gray and white paint. "Though a higher percentage of people in armor die than for people out of it. Men who wear armor are soon dead men." Oscar laughed at this odd truth and I habitually wondered about its analogs. Would men who fashion art (like those who wore armor) also soon die? Did they don their arts (like soldiers dressing for battle) only in situations of high risk? Did they wield their craft only when loss was imminent and threatening?

"The sheet music is armor," Oscar went on. "It holds the music so it doesn't die or disappear. Same with the books. Why's the statue staring at its foot?" I was still lost in my analogy. By armor, did he mean prison, or protection? I looked up and saw the sculpture Claesz had painted: an Alexandrian boy sitting on a draped pedestal. He was naked and bemused, and staring, indeed, at his upraised foot. "He looks like he's got a splinter."

"That's a queer joke, don't you think. A wooden splinter in a marble statue. Painted."

"Yeah. That can't be it."

"I think it might be Narcissus." I watched him watching the figure. I thought of Oscar in the painting, naked on the pedestal, intrigued by the details of his own body. "You never told me where you grew up," I reminded him. Oscar kept his attentions fixed on the Claesz. He looked at me, then turned away.

"There's not much to tell."

"Where's your family?"

He smiled shyly. The questions weren't entirely welcome, but the attention was. "I had a bunch of brothers, but they were a lot older than me. More like uncles." Oscar touched my arm, to move us on to another painting. "My mom lives up the coast."

I'd never been to the coast. I'd read about the beaches and the logging in the newspaper, and I'd had a few students who were from there. Some of my colleagues had houses there, for the summer or weekends, but it was depressed from the bad fishing and lumber; north and south were rich people, but they only came part of the year, and bought little more than groceries and hardware. It was an impossible economy. Our way was blocked by children. Two dozen of them, nine- or ten-year-olds much shorter than Oscar and I, were gathered around a docent. The kids had sketch pads and pencils. They were drawing geometric boxes, staring at three Vermeers. We sat down on a bench behind the kids. Oscar fiddled with a tram ticket, and watched the children. "Did you run away?" The cleanly drawn Vermeer boxes looked very empty; I thought of Oscar and his home. The little draftsmen were working earnestly, and with a great deal of care, on them.

"Sort of. I came to the city with my uncle." Oscar looked up at me. "It was just supposed to be a couple days, but I didn't go back with him when he left. I'd go back, I guess. But there's nothing there." He pulled his lower lip in and shrugged. A small boy bumped us, backing away for a better view, and Oscar kept him from falling. "Anyway," he continued, "I like my school in the city a lot, and I've got friends there. Dr. Weathered wants me to live at her house, and maybe I'll do that."

"Why wouldn't you, Oscar?" The prospect of a nice home for him seemed very important to me. "I mean, where do you live now?"

"Just, here and there. I stay with my friend Tony a lot. It's no big deal." I couldn't imagine it was no big deal. Oscar was young, and clearly more adaptable than I was, but even one night with no home was a sad and worrying thing. No wonder the police had such a say in his life.

"Hasn't your mother come after you? She must be worried sick."

"She says I'm fifteen and can make up my own mind. I don't think now's a very good time for her to have me around." Oscar had turned on the bench and faced me. One foot was pulled up onto it, and he scraped the other back and forth across the wooden floor. I watched the kids moving on, and the Vermeers. Despite their insistent intimations of action—the surprised eyes, half-open mouths, the verging postures—the figures in the paintings stayed absolutely still. The gallery was empty and silent without the children.

"Do you think you should go back? Maybe she needs you to help her." I didn't think he should go back, but I thought he should have to think about it.

"I can't help her." He bumped my leg with his. "I never could help her before."

"You'll have no choice but to live with Dr. Weathered, Oscar. There's no question."

"Couldn't I live with you?" The words made me blush.

"I don't really have a home. I suppose, when we go back. If I find a place big enough. But," I said, taking a sterner tone, "you will live with Dr. Weathered and Francis, until I do. From the day we return. No excuses."

"Yeah," Oscar said, still uncertain. "I'll probably do that." I thought he was both relieved and troubled by my insistence. I was so unaccustomed to talking, really, at all, with anyone about such things as life. It was hard to tell when silence was the better answer. What could I say to Oscar? I wanted him to talk, but I had nothing to give in response except sympathy. Was that enough? Each time I opened my mouth to him, I wished there was some wise solution or answer to what he'd told me which my words could get across to him. Instead I could only offer markers of my sympathy; clumsy tokens, to stand for something I felt far more strongly than my words. Amelia had a talent for talk, especially with Oscar. With me it was writing, or silence.

* * *

It was dark out and colder. The boys and I walked briskly across an open, snow-covered park, and through quiet streets. The silence now was easy for me, as Francis kept up a monologue about Amsterdam and the Dutch. Amelia stayed at the museum, gathering prints (or was it etchings?) for inclusion in "the book." I watched the warm yellow windows of the houses. Curtains were kept open in all the ground floor living rooms and we could see each family framed inside, sitting on stuffed chairs with doilies and big couches, facing the window and the TV. The blue flickering lights of televisions played from each living room. Francis was taking us to his favorite sauna. The snow was still thin and bitter, and when the wind blew I thought I'd have to stop and find shelter. Francis kept us going by his refusal to stop, and his repeated lie that the sauna was on the next block. How could a sauna be on *any* of the blocks we were walking? The neighborhood was quiet—postwar brick houses, packed tight side by side. There were no restaurants, no open shops, no trams or people, and surely, I thought, nothing so glitzy and cosmopolitan as a sauna.

The boy turned in at a house without windows, and pressed the small doorbell. *Het Klein Zonnig Sauna'tje,* an engraved doorplate said. An enormous lady answered the door and let us in. She was well over six feet, and probably in her seventies. Her smile was as warm as the stuffy hallway. Francis greeted her, and she lit up like a sunbeam and hugged him. How on earth had she remembered? (Though a twelve-year-old boy with a penchant for saunas probably wasn't too commonplace, even in Holland.) She led us down the hallway to a pleasant sitting room with numbered cupboards and a big mirror. It might have been a bedroom once. The sauna was simply the first floor of someone's house, converted for the use. The lady gave us towels and a *welkomsdrank*. I took hot chocolate to warm me, and the boys had sodas. Two women, friends as old and blustery as our hostess, buzzed in, chatting and babbling, cooing greetings to the old lady. "*Daaaaaagggggg,*" they crooned, "*Oooooohhh, wat ontzettend koud vanavond. Dag, mijnheer,* boys." They waved, continuing with their chatter, and began stripping their clothes off. Francis joined in, and told us to just leave our clothes in the cupboards.

"We can share one," he allowed, letting his pants drop to the ground. Naked, but with my chocolate and towels, I followed Francis into the next room. Oscar followed too, seemingly more at ease than I, but also willing to let the younger boy lead. "This is the *babbelkamer,*" he said, nodding politely to a half-dozen loungers lying around on beach chairs. There was a fat old man, and two teenagers, a little girl and two ladies. Towels were draped everywhere. Naked patrons "babbled" and read, or just rested. Others wandered through the room to get drinks or a magazine. It smelled salty and clean, like fresh laundry kept in a cedar chest. Next to this carpeted chamber was a small tiled room bordered by showers. A few people sat on wooden benches here, with their feet in plastic pans of steaming water. They looked like wrung rags. An older man slumped forward, as though he might have fallen asleep. Another, who had just a stump where one arm should be, leaned back against the wall, exhausted. Two children, bright and pink, fiddled with their warming pans, testing the temperature of each other's waters. Not a minute passed without one of them (brother and sister?) getting up for a refill from the line of taps along the wall.

Showered and wet, we went in, at last, to the sauna itself—a darkened, dry cedar room, searingly hot. Francis took my hand, and Oscar kept an arm on my shoulder to find our way in. There was room on the top shelf (for these were shelves, really, more than benches) and we put our towels down and sat. The box was filled with talking. My nostrils burned from the heat, and I began to sweat. The dim light was enough to see everyone now. The ladies were there (the ones who'd come in after us) naked and dripping, and they kept up the conversation. A younger man with a bandage wrapped around his nose lay next to them. He was quiet, until the talk turned to American foreign policy. He had some loud opinions about the secretary of state.

"It's the Middle East," Francis whispered to me. "That and a local bean festival." The middle shelf, just below us, was empty. Oscar scooted from his place in the corner, and arranged his towel there. He lay down and stretched out on his back. The dim light glistened on him, showing drips and rivulets along every rib and and hollow. My throat burned and felt empty. Francis was inhaling sweat off his own shoulder, slurping it a little, like a thirsty dog. A blind man opened the door, clutching both his cane and a towel. "*Ooh, daaaaagggg,"* the ladies sang again. *"Goeieavond, Mijnheer* Bergsma." They took his outstretched hands, and sat him down at an empty spot near them. Evidently they were all regulars. It seemed much hotter now. I could only breathe through my mouth (or risk scorching my nostrils). This is how cooking goes, I realized. Oscar stretched and put his hand on my foot. I saw his breathing, and the heart beating. Sweat dripped in fractured lines along his stomach and thighs, and made a shallow pool in his belly button; I looked at the man's bandage again. Wasn't time up yet? The sand clock said only ten minutes had passed.

"My lungs are very hot, Francis." Maybe the boy would have some wisdom about this.

"Ten minutes can be plenty, Mr. Dee. Especially on the first round." He leaned down and put his hand on Oscar's chest. "Oscar. Mr. Dee and I are thinking of going now, to the *doompelbad*. We'll do the sauna again in a half-hour or so." Oscar whispered yes, and sat up. Sweat fell from his face like water from a shower, and he swallowed some. "They say to cool off a bit first," Francis said, leading us back into the tile room, "but I think it's better to just jump right in." He opened the heavy door marked *"Doompelbad."* Beyond it was the backyard. Stones were set in the ground. They led to a small tile pool, dimly lit from within. It was snowing. Francis left his towel by the door, scampered across the stones and jumped in. Oscar followed, and I did too.

I can only say that my body was undone then, for a moment, and I was lost in the untraceable flicker between burning and freezing. The water was almost ice. I slipped in without knowing, and was in over my head so fast my body dissolved in an instant. Naked and submerged, the extremity of hot and cold erased all my boundaries. Suddenly I was everywhere, burst from the surface of my body. I became the water and the air, the ice-cold wind and stars and the empty night around them. My mind had never been so clear. Under water, eyes and mouth open, heart pounding, I had no need of air. The absence inside me was euphoric. I could breathe water, or the earth or snow or trees. It was all moving through me, like an ocean's wind, playing past my heart and the hollow space where my body used to be. My mouth was open, but I did not draw a breath. I fell further, the emptier I became, and might have been spinning backward into space when Oscar pulled me up by my arms, and held me with my head above the water. "In too long, Nick," he said, wrapping his arms around me. His body was warm. "You okay?"

"See," Francis chirped, sitting at the pool's edge. "It's totally great, yeah?" I let Oscar maneuver me to the tile steps, and shuffled toward the door with my weight on him. The delirium drained me of all will. I understood now why the two men had looked so wrung out. With the boys on either side, I slumped against my towel and lowered my feet into a pan of warm water. Heat rose through me, and the boys' quiet chatter was like the wind. The air was cool. Inside (if there was, any longer, an inside) I was warm. After a nap on my towel in the *babbelkamer,* and a cool soda to refresh me, we did it all again, and then again.

From my bed that night I watched the snow obscuring carved phrases cut into the peaked buildings, opposite. A light burned behind the small attic window, and I could see shadows inside and flickering, as though from lamplight. Something had been displaced inside me, loosened from its moorings by the day, and then dislodged by the transformation that overwhelmed me in the sauna. Some ineffable, sinewy thing was flushed from its stuck position, and set into motion. I felt as if another body, a second, more ghostly body, was floating free within my own. I could feel it swimming, slipping through my narrow places, as sleep flowed in and filled me. I dreamed of the bridge by the museum, where we walked with all the children. In the dream, I was facing away, watching people crossing the bridge through gray sleet. There was a dog, beside a woman, running like it was lost or left behind. It might have been a painting I'd seen that day, the image was so blurred and vivid. A glamorous figure in furs moved through the center, her face behind a black veil. Her eyes were focused beyond me. Where was she going? They all seemed to be going. I neither turned, nor moved to join them. I could not. Like the paintings, I was stuck in my position, forever verging on action. But the figures had been freed, loosened from their frozen postures, and now they flowed past me.

*Action must preceed understanding. It is a mistake to
delay action waiting for knowledge to make it safe.
Without action we learn nothing.*

—John Lewis Dee[1]

The next morning we were late and looked for a cab or tram to take us to the station. Trains ran all the time to Enkhuizen, but we had a boat to catch there, and not much leeway on catching it. Was it Sunday? There were no cars or cabs anywhere. Leaving the hotel, we hurried up the canal to where the trams ran. That bike had sunk, and left no trace of this century behind. A carriage clattered past, drawn by two horses, and then a tram. The snow was heavy all night, and still kept coming down. The city looked older under white. The dissonant noise and bright plastics were buried, and at this hour everything was closed and peaceful. The tram was almost empty. There was a conductor who took tickets, and he sold us some, enough to get us to the station.

Oscar slept, even as the worn-out train lumbered away from the platform. He slumped against me, using my shoulder for his pillow with Kitty purring in the opened bag beside him. Amelia had her thermos of coffee, and Francis brought *koffiemelk*. Our boat would go across the Ijselmeer to Stavoren. The train was empty, as the tram had been. Maybe the poor weather kept everyone home, or the hour. The land was flat and flooded. Snow made reeds and meadows white, but there was black water everywhere between. The wind was strong, but not cold enough to freeze the marshes. The horizon disappeared in the falling snow. Towns came every few minutes, interrupting the fields, but the train didn't stop at them. It was all black and white out there, all water and land. Francis had his card deck out, and was playing solitaire on his lap. The figures were strange to me. The royalty looked at once more sumptuous and longer-in-the-tooth. They were marked "H," "V," and "B," for *Heren, Vrouw,* and *Boer* (man, woman, and farmer). How could a farmer be royalty? And why no king or queen? I gulped down the coffee and gave Kitty a few soft pats. I would work on my pages during the boat ride over.

1. John Lewis Dee, *Miscellaneous Papers,* undated.

The steam-driven boat was a fishing skiff with a cabin built on it. Wooden benches and tables, plus a woman with a hot plate, made the interior more welcoming. She had two pots on the burners, and the smell of smoked sausage and soup woke the boys up. I organized my papers on a forward table. Windows all around made the cabin light. Oscar and Francis stood at the prow, facing the choppy gray water. It looked like a sea, even though it was now bounded by the dike. With the low clouds, no borders were in evidence. The dock had no mechanical contrivances, just a gangplank which they swung away. Peat and coal were thrown on the boiler, and the engineer signaled the captain. Enkhuizen drew away behind us, sinking deeper in the mist, then it disappeared. The church steeple and the tower of the Dromedaris lingered like ghosts. In the trackless white distance they hovered above the water, and then they too were gone. The boat's motor had an even, pleasant rhythm, like the beating of the chopper blades back home. Everything, water and air, was empty and gray. Our progress could not be marked. Somewhere ahead was Friesland (which our captain had described): the land of terp-dwellers, the putative gates of hell, the dreaded sea lung.

The Opera House of Alton Motley   Nicholas Dee

The winter of 1686 was deeply cold and marked by bitter storms. Den Dollard was always cold in winter, and usually flooded. Storms blew from the North Sea, raising the level of the tides. By December of that year, the floods would claim nearly 1,600 lives; but none that fall had proved large nor violent enough to breach the dikes. October was called "kind" by chroniclers who lived around the estuary. Even the opera house, exposed as it was beyond the last line of dikes, was never seriously threatened.

Verweerd left supervision of the building site to the masons and took a group of thirty-seven men (his musicians and theatrical troupe) inland through the province. Their first journey, by barge up the Winschoterdiep, was to the city of Groningen. The canal began south of them, and traveled through a few towns and poor farmland, forty-three

The Opera House of Alton Motley   Nicholas Dee

kilometers to the walled city. This was the main highway
for travelers going east and south into Germany, and the
barge was something of a spectacle. With their cooks stationed over pots and flames on the aft deck (where any
unruly fires could easily be pushed off into the canal),
and a small village of tents joined together amidships,
the self-made barge was a floating inn of sorts, a por-
table and miniature version of the village of workers the
men had become accustomed to. The musicians could be heard
rehearsing inside the tents, and the shadows of the actors
moved and flickered across the canvas, cast by bright oil
lamps. In the short, bitter days of winter, the sight for
farmers of this bright yellow tent of music, floating slowly
across their barren fields, with a coven of witches over
pots on its aft deck, must have made for memorable tales.

Ice on the canal and persistent winds made their trip
longer and more difficult. A drunk day feasting in Scheemda,
and a bitter night tied up to a sluice gate in Waterhuizen,
kept them from reaching the city before late on the fourth
day. Verweerd, and the opera house, were well known in
Groningen (mostly for the size and accessibility of Motley's
purse). Elaborate and frequent taxes were levied, suspi-
ciously specific in their reach and application. The additional costs did not bother Verweerd; he had already accepted
the "conjurations of good fortune bought by coin, offered
as in a ritual supplication," which was to say, the regular payment of insurance premiums to Drop. He only resented
that the task of settling taxes took up so much time, and
required him to travel to the city. The amiable factor
preferred his own work to the business of the government.

This trip, however, had an air of celebration about
it. The players knew they'd return the next spring to the
finished theater, and to a scene of elegance and splendor
where thus far there had been just labor and mud. Done
with his work as planner and engineer, the old man must
also have known the trip was more important than his other

The Opera House of Alton Motley   Nicholas Dee

journeys. He pampered the players, and indulged whims, like
the day of reveling in a bitter cold snow in Scheemda. He'd
wake without plans, or let his business go untended for a
day. In Groningen, he insisted that the company pass the
week in high style. They took lodgings near the Nieuwe Kerk,
in an expensive inn, and the troupe and musicians were free
to do as they pleased with their days. All week he pursued
his business, and brought Frans along when the boy wasn't
performing skits for money with the troupe.

"'Tis a well-appointed city and has about it the smell
of fish and burning sod, strongly if it's cold. A north
wind cleans it and brings sickly sweet cow dung which is
worse in spring. Frans tells me the students are very clever,
but ribald and generous with beer. Yesterday, he says, when
Pieter donned a thorny cassock and pranced and brayed,
mocking the high and mighty of the brothers of the rosy
cross, and tossing up his tail more than once to show what
was rosy, the noise of retorts and rude epithets from them
went on for many minutes before attention was paid again
to the troupe. There, they got a dousing and some coin.

"I have little trouble with the government, though
they make much trouble over me. The payment of taxes is
accounted too many times, with a flourish of forms and
signings. There is not a day I am done with one, but must
wait for another, in another pleasant room to sign the same.
Each says I am an old friend and pretends interest in my
project, which talk is dull and tedious. I would pay more
to be left alone, but money is not all they take by taxing.
They must take time and account too and so it will be a
week here.

"I ask little of the company, except that some nights
they entertain at the inn so I can sit somewhere dry and
with borrel to hear them. I will not go to the Leesersplein
and be trampled by drunk scholars. A minister taking my tax
promised a harpsical to be brought for our players, and
tonight we will have the Nereids."

The Opera House of Alton Motley   Nicholas Dee

THE TEMPEST.   Henry Purcell.
CHORUS. THE NEREIDS AND TRITONS.

240

The Opera House of Alton Motley   Nicholas Dee

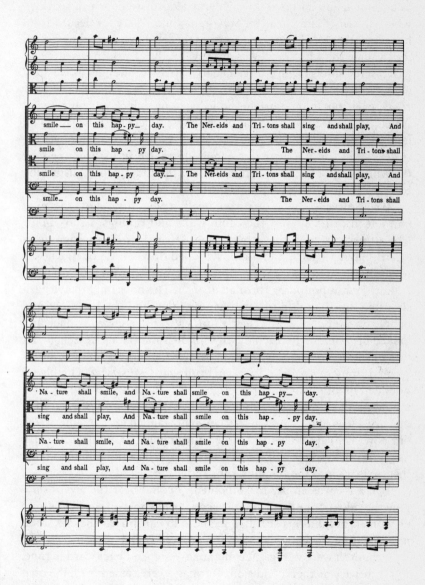

The dull sun increased and made the water shine like mercury. The boat dipped and battered through gray leaden swells which sparkled where the light caught them. Stavoren could be seen, released from low clouds that had hung over most of the journey. The light warmed me through the windows. I was drowsy, soothed by the pleasant regularity of the ship's engine. It seemed to increase in strength as we drew closer to land. The boys were on deck letting the wind billow their coats, each clutching a bright, boiled sausage which gave off steam. Amelia was asleep with the cat on the bags. Where the town stood on land the sun had broken through. It ruptured and spread out over the water, and soon the boat was engulfed, trebled in its brightness by the white deck and cabin. I stumbled out the sliding door, disturbing Kitty with the breeze, and joined the boys on deck.

The direct sun was warm and melted what little snow the wind had left in drifts against the cabin walls and railings. I took in air like a thirsty dog and let it wake me. Oscar lost his sausage overboard playing tricks, and a gull swooped down and got it. The air was full of water (its clean smell) and the smoke from the fire in the engine. I felt it pounding through my feet. The boys might have been shouting, but I couldn't hear them over the din. The buildings and people on shore had come clearly into view. I stretched my back and looked up, wanting to catch the edge of the sun, so long unseen, and it was blocked by a shadow. The ship slowed, but the pounding motor seemed to increase again in strength. It was Clausewitz. The blades pounded manfully against the bright air, as he hovered and blocked the light, making passes at our ship. The crazy sun reflected off the outthrust lens of his camera, as Clausewitz guided his machine across our bow. The captain had cut the engines and let our momentum carry us to the dock. Clausewitz circled once more, his noise filling the sky, then rose up into the blinding sun, and disappeared.

The air was empty for a moment. I could hear the waves slapping the sides of our boat, and the chatter of people on shore. A group of women in fabulous stiff habits and odd cardboard sheaths stood manipulating the gangplank. A dog gnawed bread at their feet. The only children were in rags. We might have stepped backward in time, so primitive was their condition. Our bags were tossed from the boat by the captain and loaded on a cart and then the boat drew away, taking no one.

EIGHTEEN

"MUFFIN," AMELIA COMMANDED. Most of our welcoming party had already disappeared, perhaps disappointed with us. Only a few of the boys, and a pack of dogs, remained. "Find out what we'll need to do to get to Leeuwarden. Speed is not important." She surveyed the empty lanes leading away from the dock. There were no signs of welcome in sight, no bright beer logos or stylized ice creams. The idle boys stared at us, then ran away. Drab older houses lined the front street. The sunshine glistened off their empty windows, and then the sun disappeared, again, in the clouds. I saw the familiar beacon of the V.V.V., our traveler's aid station, in the distance. The white plastic letters were barely visible above a thick hedgerow, and the building itself could not be seen. Two ditches and a meadow, muddy from the snow, came between us.

"There's the V.V.V.," I suggested, but Francis was already gone. Amelia couldn't see the sign, because her vantage point was too low. Oscar was keeping the dogs away from Kitty.

"Francis will be back soon," Amelia countered. "This is just the sort of errand he thrives on." She was right. I had no doubt that Francis would turn up soon with some miraculous coachman who just happened to be going to Leeuwarden. Still, I didn't like to stand around idle, particularly in so disquieting a place as this empty village.

"Maybe I'll just go over while we're waiting. Can't hurt to ask," I said brightly. Was there a path? I started along the lane, away from the water, but soon it turned away from the meadow. Now the sign was no longer visible. The houses petered out, and there were only fields. Some of the boys played soccer in the muddy grass by the last house. Too bad the sun was hidden again. Amelia and Oscar had moved the bags to a bench and sat with them, talking, looking out over the water. I could see their tableau, tiny and silent at the end of the narrow lane. The dogs were not a problem now; someone had tied them up. There was water and mud in all the fields. Thin roads wound by on dikes, and some disappeared into trees. Everything solid was white, or glistened from melted snow. With the sun gone it was cold again and the roads would be icy and treacherous soon. The yelling boys and some seabirds were all I heard. Was there a snack bar nearby, with *patat,* maybe? I sniffed the air, but found no hot-fat smell; only fish and snow.

Francis came sprinting back. Even the hedgerow was lost now, masked by a low billow of mist that blew in on the wind. Maybe the boy had found food also. The muddy soccer game adjourned to smoking, and I walked back along the lane, mocked by my reflection in the empty houses. Carts were coming up the front street, full of fish and ice, and pulled by horses. Damp canvas sacks were thrown over the piles, but some had come loose and fallen. One cart had facing benches in back, on either side of the cargo. "He's going to Harlingen," Francis explained, breathlessly. "I guess there's no buses going now, because of the weather." His cheeks were bright red from the cold and from running. Clearly the prospect of a trip on a fishmonger's cart thrilled him.

"But, Francis dear," Amelia cajoled. "Surely there's a train running, storm or no." The old man pulled his horses to a halt, and began loading our bags.

"I don't think so, Mother. The men said there'd be no train." Here he paused and mumbled. "At least for a while anyway." Oscar pitched in with the bags. The man put warm blankets on the benches and climbed on.

"How long a journey is it, Muffin?"

"We'll be in Harlingen tonight, and then we can go to Leeuwarden on a canal boat, tomorrow morning." Here was the top-secret treat he'd waited to spring on Amelia.

"A canal boat?"

"The *trekvaart*, Mother! We'll go through Franeker, and Zweins, and Leeuwarden, along the *trekvaart*!" The horses shifted uncertainly in place, alerted by the jiggle of the reins. Our driver crooned a good-bye *"doooooeeeeeiiii,"* to his departing pals. He was eager to be going.

"Very well, Muffin." She motioned us onto the cart. "Just see that we don't freeze, and that we have a stop for food soon." She accepted my helping hand, and stepped gracefully over the fish to her seat by the driver.

We made our way north along the shallow, muddy coast, perched high on dikes where the roads ran. Fields covered with snow spread inland, cut by canals and ditches. The fish smelled, and the wet canvas was well used and sour. Francis and I sat together, facing Oscar. The older boy was mesmerized by the fields. Bare trees, black and white against the fields, disappeared in the distance, lost in low drifting mists. Cows were out. They gathered under the trees where there was still grass. Farmers put hay there too, and some cows slept by it. Mijnheer Visman, our driver, brought fish from Stavoren north to smaller towns along the Ijsselmeer. On this wet, fishy coast, it seemed a little like bringing coals to Newcastle. Apparently, some people preferred his fish, and he had a regular route with regular customers who'd have no other man's fish in the house. Hindeloopen was the first town we came to.

The rounded crown of a church tower marked it from far away. The road curved in, running along a dike to the small cluster of houses. A lighthouse, high as the church tower, shone a beacon into the clouds. The point was exposed to water on three sides. The town nestled low, inside dikes which blocked the strong wind. It was bitter cold approaching, exposed on the high road, but once we ducked down among the houses I felt better. My skin burned with false warmth, and I could hear again. There was Amelia, talking with the driver, and the soft sound of the horse hooves. I hadn't eaten since last night. "Is there a snack bar, do you think?" I asked Francis as the cart rattled across the cobblestones. "I'm famished." He scooted up and asked the driver.

"He says he's not sure, but he's seen a wall."

"A wall?" Silly boy.

"Yeah, *de muur,* the, uh, snack-bar wall. It's like a . . . vend-o-mat. A wall of little windows where they put all the food. It's usually a little old, and greasy, but it's hot."

Oscar hopped out and walked alongside the cart, wanting the exercise and a stretch. Though the buildings looked older, the town itself seemed a great deal younger than Stavoren. It was alive, to begin with. A crowd stood around one wet field, and watched muddy boys play some tackling sport in the snow. Cows were tethered to the benches on either side of the field; bounty, perhaps, for the winners. We had delivered about a third of the fish by now, stopping at six or seven farms along the way. The cold weather kept the fish-snow frozen. Mr. Visman directed us to *de muur,* and went about his deliveries in the tiny village. The houses were neat and small, each with a yard and a boat. They docked on back canals that laced the little neighborhood. It was snowing again, lightly. Amelia joined the boys and me, going to find snacks. She brought her ubiquitous thermos, hoping there might be a refill somewhere. A vegetable stand was closed, as was a small abatoir. The tobacconists, a bookbindery, and a smoky beer hall were all dark. We walked up a rise, past an old mill, and went left, as instructed. There was no wall. The horse and cart could be heard drawing near. The metal shoes scraped on stones where the snow didn't stick. Amelia had drawn a notepad from her coat and was carefully sketching a bizarre scene, women and fish afloat in the air amid kites.

"I don't mean to pry," I interrupted. Mijnheer Visman beckoned to the boys, calling them to help him shift his new cargo. "But what is it that you're sketching?"

"Oh, just a little scene." She drew a bull beneath the women. "It's for the book, Nicholas, it's all for the book. How easily you forget that I too am working, even while you labor over those difficult pages of yours."

"My manuscript?" The cargo of fish was gone. Now decorative painted furniture weighed the clean dry cart down. I waited in the silence hoping she'd explain further.

"That's right." She patted my hand. "But don't fear, your name alone will appear, Nicholas. I have no interest in fame." Amelia boarded, indicating that I should follow and help her over the new cargo. "Faith, Nicholas. Faith and humility." She faced me from the forward bench. "Our project depends upon it."

The country through which we passed was water, fog, and earth equally. We'd come off the coastal dike, and meandered inland. Our cart was going north, but on sodden roads, past half-submerged fields and farms. The blankets were warm, even if they were damp. Large leather cowls from Mr. Visman kept the wind from our faces. The boys had their trictrac, and I kept watch on the fields, marveling at the stoic cows standing in shallow waters or snow, muzzling the ground for grass. They found it, frozen or wet, and were content to stand, chewing. Was Amelia growing larger still? Seated in front, her silhouette loomed above me like an increasing storm. We had passed through Holland's ill-guarded border, into something rich and strange, and Amelia grew stronger from it. Coffee and a pipe passed between her and our driver. I couldn't hear them talking, through the wind and my cowl, but something had them animated and engaged. I entertained the silly notion, just for a moment, that he was Verweerd (he was old and big enough), and that Amelia was hearing the tale of the trip to the Allersmaborg, via Pieterburen and Schiermonnikoog. The scene did nothing to dissuade me from my fantasy. Where I sat, I might have been a bystander, an onlooker, perhaps from the troupe of actors. Francis was Frans, and Oscar a musician. The cart crept forward along the rutted lane, and convinced me of the truth of my fantasy. Braying sheep and a half-sunk boat, its broken prow sticking out of black water, lent atmosphere.

I leaned forward. The old crones whispered in Dutch, or maybe Frisian. Slow gestures, and an occasional tick to the horses, kept things going. How had she found him? Hadn't she sent Francis to bring him back? I drifted away some, both drowsy and charmed. Inside my cowl the air was warm and cloistered. My head fell forward, into half-sleep, and my mind fell back. Amelia floated off the forward bench, even while remaining there. How had I never noticed? She turned my head with her hand, facing me forward into their conversation. The cowl was leathery and sweet. Her hand brushed me, cradling my cheek. Old. How old was she, that her palm was so soft, like worn leather, and sweet? She drew her hand away, and I lurched forward, falling into them, blinking. The Dutch was so familiar. Visman had the throaty growl I remembered from the pages I heard, the archival pages, on microfiche; Verweerd's voice growled in the sterilized air of the archive. I'd opened the pages and heard him, like now with his wet mouth pressed near my ear. Upright again. Was he so close to me? I understood every word, as if it came from inside. The warm breath against my cheek, and his face floating in a text. The words came out my mouth. He smelled of fish. Amelia hovered behind, in air, guiding with strings and pulling, so he came closer still. How had I never noticed? I lurched forward again and was between them, lost in a cloud of pipe smoke, and Amelia was shaking me by the shoulder.

"Nicholas." Her voice was sharp and pinching, where moments before it had been as warm and interior as blood. "Nicholas. For God's sake, wake up."

"Amelia? *'t spijt me,*" I apologized. "Verweerd, *pardon.*"

"Nicholas. You're speaking Dutch."

"I'm sorry," I repeated.

"You're drowsy. I think the boys won't mind giving you some room to stretch out."

"Can we too?" Francis asked, done with his game. "We can use the bags as pillows." The cart was mostly empty now with just some lumber lined along its sides. Dusk was coming fast. Francis, Oscar, and I lay down below the benches, with our blankets wrapped around us. There was no wind, and with the boys on each side of me I was warm. The low clouds turned silver, then iron gray, and black. We were still two hours from Harlingen. I listened to Amelia and Mr. Visman begin talking again, and felt the rattle of the wheels through the cart. Then I closed my eyes, turned over, and slept.

Harlingen woke me with its smooth, well-kept roads. Our wheels ran without rattling here, and the change registered somewhere inside my body and roused me. The air was bitterly cold, and the sky black and clear. I lay still for a few moments. The ancient two weren't talking. The horse shoes clanked on the bare road, and the axle gave friction. There were boats, or buoys, in the harbor sounding horns. I sat up and saw rows of neat houses. Thatch roofs on the houses were dark and bare, like the sky. Warmth from inside melted the snow, and the thatch had been blackened by rot and mildew. Small windows in the houses showed a warm, orange light, and smoke came from the broad, stone chimneys. Families sat, arranged in front rooms, as they had in Amsterdam, but the glow that flickered on them was of fire, not television. "Is there a sauna?" I asked, to anyone. No one answered. It was probably too late for a sauna.

"There must be." It was Francis. The boy was curled against my middle, using my arm for a pillow. "They're in every town. Even tiny ones." He sniffled and wiped his nose on my sleeve. *"Hoe laat is't?"* he asked, wanting the time.

"Tien over half negen," Mr. Visman answered after looking. It meant ten after half before nine. Eight-forty. I wondered what the country would do when everything went digital.

"Most of 'em stay open to late," Francis cajoled. "Mother? We have Mr. Dee's health to think about."

Francis and I found the sauna, while Amelia and Oscar went to bed early at Mr. Visman's favorite traveler's inn. Following a cobblestone tow-path along the dark water of the Sexbierumervaart we came to an anonymous structure, hidden behind piles of dry sod. The number was correct (the innkeeper knew of it). Our knock was answered by a towering woman, perhaps the twin of Mevrouw "Klein Zonnig" in Amsterdam. She insisted we both take *jenever* as our *welkomsdrank.* It was dark inside. The hot cedar room was warmed with stones brought in from the fire. Other voices told me we weren't alone, but there was no light to show us their faces. Francis and I whispered, recalling favorite places in the area of the harbor back home. Why was there no sauna back home? We'd start one, together, as a business when we returned. The prospect thrilled the boy, and he carried on with the planning, ad infinitum. We tottered out, at intervals, through a doorway to the garden. The *doompelbad* was primitive (simply an open pool kept free of ice with a shovel), but that did not diminish my pleasure. It was miraculous, again. I disappeared into that flickering erasure, enjoying both the event and the aftermath doubly, because of our long cold day.

When I woke the next morning, and went to breakfast, I heard Oscar reading. He and Francis were in bed, enjoying the warmth a bright winter sun gave through the windows of their room. "'Am I a sea, or a whale, that thou settest a watch over me?'" Oscar pronounced slowly. "'When I say my bed shall comfort me, my couch shall ease my complaint; then thou scarest me with dreams, and terrifiest me through visions.'" Here he stumbled over "through," but Francis corrected him, and he repeated it easily. I made my way past their door, and went downstairs to my breakfast. How nice that they'd decided to read Job. I remembered Oscar touting the story to Francis, promising that it was "a real horror story." Probably they'd chosen it for the gore, and would pass right on to Jonah next. My own curriculum for Oscar had fallen into disordered informality; the alphabet was easy for him; there was no need for my charts anymore. Now we just read together when there was time. I tried directing him through the difficult words, and sometimes gave him lists. But Oscar usually ignored my program, and set us meandering over the book. He read the same way he conversed, jumping, then lingering, then jumping again. The proprietor said Amelia had gone ahead to the canal, and our bags would be picked up in an hour. There was a note with instructions, and I went and told the boys to get ready.

NINETEEN

"**HIGHER DIKES** make for higher floods," Amelia observed from her deck chair on the barge. "Vierlingh said as much in the *Tractaet,* in 1547. You'll notice the Dutch have forced themselves to increasingly enormous undertakings, by their insistence on building the walls higher and higher." We could barely see over the two furrows bordering the canal. While the water may simply have been low, the engineers here seemed to have built against the unlikeliest events, floods of fifteen feet or higher, twelve miles inland. This bright frozen morning, we rode east on an old barge, through Franeker and Dronrijp to Leeuwarden. The travel was faster and easier than our journey the first day, and the bright sun made the day beautiful. Horses on the tow-path pulled the craft, and it was easy to leave the boat and walk alongside with the horses. We were better prepared for travel. In Harlingen we gathered breads and cheeses, chocolate, cold meats, and coffee, and made a picnic for the day's journey. Francis secured his treasured *drop* (in four or five varieties). He gave us each a sweet hard candy, *zwartwit,* to suck on while we waited for the barge. I enjoyed the syrupy treat, and would have had another, but at its center was a full load of salt which flooded my mouth like a cruel punishment. I guess it was a health food, or some sort of restorative for the body. The bargeman took our money and stowed the bags.

Did Oscar worry about Job? The boys had the trictrac out again, and they put it on their knees to play. Oscar had dark glasses on, and was laughing. In the bright sun with his friend, he certainly didn't look preoccupied with Job. He'd made his own peace with indominitable authority—with the police back home. I had two gods to deal with, the university and the police. Each promised to be just, but with a different kind of justice. Were they my enemies, as Amelia said? I only ever asked, I think, that they "save" me, protect me from loss; my participation was directed toward that end. Had I been wronged? "Coffee, Nicholas dear?" Amelia held the thermos out to me. I could no longer tell a gift from a threat.

"Well, all right." Steam blossomed from the cup, throwing fabulous tendrils into the air. "I thought you were suspicious of coffee? Didn't you tell me, I believe, that it might keep me from my, uh, weakest moments?" The bright day had warmed her, and she also blossomed, smiling at the frozen blue sky.

"Of course I'm suspicious of it, Nicholas. I'm suspicious of its orthodoxy. I didn't mean you should never drink it." She sighed like a mother at my foolishness. "You'll find these days ahead full of 'weakness' and insight. We've arrived, Nicholas. There's no turning back from it." She looked around with excitement as the barge drifted past the last houses of Harlingen. "I don't think a little morning cup will stand in your way now. Just look at those marvelous horses."

We were surrounded by what she treasured, and her smile and vigor showed it. This watery land might have been her mind's interior. We traveled into the heart of it, past fields and furrows, dikes and windmills. Moated cities and gated towns unfolded like a map made of her mental landscape. She grew large here. The high water behind earthen dikes was an idea she might have told me once, uttering just the words into the hostile air of the academy; but here we sailed on it. The fields beyond the banks, little more than an argument in the citadel back home, now surrounded us. One had only to climb up on the dike, and walk along with the horses, to see the fields spreading toward the flat horizon surrounded by more troubling waters. Amelia lounged in her deck chair, with the coffee and Vierlingh, smiling at the bright cold day. Our boatman did nothing but smoke. There was no course to steer, and only the horses to attend to. The other passengers sat behind a windbreak toward the back. A tattered awning gave shelter. There were benches, and a fire burning in a barrel for warmth. Franeker was close and tiny, and I saw no signs of the great university, founded there in 1567. The canal drew past the old city wall, and traveled along the southern edge of the center. Where was the university? Francis's supposition, that it had closed after two hundred and fifty years because of some sort of police action (something to do with Napoleon), seemed outlandish ... the fabulations of an imaginative child. Universities did not close after two hundred and fifty years, did they? The vista gave us no intelligence about the school's fate. Franeker disappeared behind us, and the water grew more crowded with boats going west toward the coast and the open water.

The Opera House of Alton Motley   Nicholas Dee

Verweerd and the boy Frans left the city on a barge full of peat, going north to the Wadden coast. His business in Groningen was done. Now they would travel to the island where the boy was born and grew up. The others rode the company's elaborate vessel along the Reitdiep to Ezinge, and the Allersmaborg. Verweerd hoped the trip home would be good for Frans, letting him go back and see the men and women who knew him growing up, to show them what he'd become in his new life on land. They camped, with the others in a field by the Hoendiep, one night before departing, and had a feast.

"We braised meats on the fire and drank, and dogs troubled us for the meats. The guts in a sack kept them busy in the field when we threw 'em, and cook kept the heart. Frans would have the heart first. He'd have the tongue too, for his voice was breaking and we were sad over it. He's got his sweet song yet, but not two months longer, then his falsetto only, which voice is fine and strong. The heart he ate for courage, and the rest for his new voice.

"The inn would have us no more and we made camp in fields by the Ebbingepoort. I was at my business each day

The Opera House of Alton Motley   Nicholas Dee

and never witness to the debauchery gossip-mongers say came
on each day's rising of the troupe (Martin's rising especially I am told, and what he did to bring it down). Men
who trouble over morals would curse the rain for falling.
It is howling into a tempest, and less pleasant than the
storm.

   "Frans sang the 'Yellow Sands' as prettily as a lark
until the watch came and ordered us in the gates or away
from them, and the men pissed like dogs on the boots of the
watch. They were two and we were thirty, and so we stayed,
but stopped the singing." The journey north was taken on
canals still operating today, a network joining all the
towns in the broad, flat province.

   Verweerd and Frans carried little. Most of what they
had went along with the other men to the Allersmaborg,
where the two would soon return. The bargeman had worked
with Verweerd, when the Lauwerszee was being dredged, and
new charts were being made of the shallow estuary. He
welcomed them like old family, and they got bunks in the
warm cabin and good food the two days they took traveling. In Pieterburen, on the Wadden Coast, several dozen
fisherman kept their boats for work on the North Sea, out
beyond the island of Schiermonnikoog. The boy and Verweerd
went there, and waited for a boat that would take them.

   Leeuwarden had been visible most of the day. It sat above the
fields on its *terpen,* and the pretty church towers rose higher still. The
steeples sparkled in the sunshine, and Oscar invited me to walk with
the horses. I followed him onto the bank. It was impossible now to
tell nature from the man-made. Since turning in at the coast near
Rotterdam, we had traveled dredged, rechanneled rivers, ridden trains
across drained lakes, sailed on a flooded swamp and across a lake
made from the sea; now we rode a barge on diked canals over drained
fields that were ocean less than a millennium ago. Some of the canals

were rivers, but then most of the rivers were now canals. Nature and culture were fused. Land and man had settled, especially in the north where the technology was as old and simple as the towns.

Leeuwarden arrived, quiet and clean as a village. Shops and cafés bordered the canal, but there were no crowds. The horses were bothered by the cobblestones. We came to a lock, and the boatman tied up to the side, and said we'd be stopping for an hour. He would go on from there, in the afternoon, to Dokkum and the Wadden Coast. Oscar gave chase to some papers blowing past a deserted café, and I hurried after him. "Don't go too far, Nicholas," Amelia called. "We'll be staying on all the way to the Lauwerszee." It surprised me she had no business here. The city had several important archives, and the two premier Frisian museums. I'd presumed she would spend the afternoon chasing "functionaries" and securing more materials for "the book."

Oscar turned in at an alleyway and I followed. What was he pursuing? We'd come onto a crowded, narrow lane. The boy passed briskly through the merchants, keeping one eye on the blown broadside, and I followed, seven or eight yards behind. Beside a fish-fryer's caldron where two men were shouting about bad cod, Oscar caught the pages with a firm foot stamped down into the mud. "I thought maybe it was a newspaper," he explained, panting a little from his exertions. I looked down into the mud. He'd gotten a printed page, but it seemed to be in Frisian, or some dialect of German or Dutch that I couldn't read.

"I'm sure there's a newsstand, Oscar. If you want to get a paper." We looked up and down the busy lane. Walkers jostled in packs, crowding around small shops. Goods were stacked amply by the doors: flat baskets full of glittering fish, or dull, dirty tubers and roots. A herd of tourists drifted past the lane's termination, slowly so the gawking travelers could take a long, distant look at the shops. We could see no stationers or news vendors along this alleyway. "Maybe back by the canal," I suggested, disheartened. Oscar didn't hear my advice, or paid it no mind. His interest led him in the other direction. The alley wound away, disappearing in a slow turn. Buildings on both sides leaned in, resting precariously one against the next. The sky was nearly pinched off by them.

"Maybe down that way," he said, leading me. The middle of the street was muddy and primitive, and the shops took up all the dry space with their stacked goods. We maneuvered past carts and barrows through a crowd of shabby farmers. Above us, topping the narrow buildings, well-lit offices and third-floor atriums of aluminum and glass rested on the stone shoulders of the older structures. Smartly dressed young men and women could be seen inside, working at computer terminals, and carrying on business over telephones. Their offices, imbedded like modules behind the pitted facades, blossomed out the tops into the bright winter air. The doors at ground level bore no marks to indicate them. The crooked portals gave onto smoky dark hallways and narrow stairs, most leading down. Like Amsterdam, disparate times had here been jammed together, but it was all turned upside down now. The older city had come down to clutter the streets; now the contemporary was clean and impossible to reach. Was there an entrance through some other, more obvious place? I stumbled into Oscar, gazing up at the atriums, and accepted his arm across my shoulder, to guide me on without falling. The alley enthralled him and he paid little mind to my distraction. The narrow passage bent sharply right, and the offices disappeared from view. Another canal could be seen ahead, where the alley opened up.

"Maybe that way," I suggested, pointing to the broader space. "I think there's a public square." Oscar nodded, and led us on. Wicker tables were scattered around a cobblestone plaza where the canals came together. A café serviced the tables and Oscar sat us down at one, near to the water. The sun was brighter here, and warmed us where we sat. The plaza was curiously empty. A group of children filed obediently along the opposite bank, silent and in uniforms. I looked up and down the canal, scouting for a newsstand, but saw none. Oscar pulled the one muddy page from his back pocket and unfolded it on our table. It was in Frisian, and completely unreadable to me.

"Is this Dutch?" Oscar asked, scanning the page.

"I think it's Frisian. They have their own language. It's supposed to be the closest language to English." He ran his fingers along the unmuddied portion of the paper, touching the dense paragraphs of text.

"What do you mean, 'closest'?"

"The most like English. I think they have a lot of words in common." We scrutinized the lines. There was very little I recognized.

"Is it pronounced the same as English?" Oscar was mouthing what he made of certain lines, silently.

"No, no. I don't think it is. I think the sounds are much more like Dutch." Oscar slid the paper toward me.

"So pronounce some." I blushed. Sweet of him to ask, but of course I had no talent with Dutch, let alone Frisian.

"Well, I don't really know how to say it out loud. Even with Dutch, I can only read it."

"So read it out loud like Dutch."

"But I don't speak Dutch." Oscar huffed impatiently and took the muddy page back.

"That makes no sense. How can you read Dutch and not speak it?" I took the paper from him and found a clean margin. I wrote down "Salt=Zout. Lake=Meer," and pointed at them without speaking. Oscar read them out loud, mispronouncing the Dutch. I wrote "Zout Meer."

"Now, Oscar. You tell me what that means in English."

"Salt lake," he said immediately.

"There. You can't speak Dutch, but you can read it."

"Oh, right. Wow." He stared happily at the margin, and then, smiling, at me. "I get it. So you, like, know all the Dutch words, even though you can't say them, right?"

"I know a lot of them."

"And so, you just, like"—here his hands flew hither and thither about the page—"read them, word after word without hearing the sound, at all? Just like the shape by itself with no sound to go with it?"

"Sometimes I sound it out like English, like they were English words. But that's not the same as speaking Dutch." The boy was dumbstruck. "And if someone's deaf, Oscar, writing is completely devoid of sound. It's shapes, just like a drawing, only the shape is coded." Oscar took my pen and drew shapes on a napkin. There was a triangle with a square set on its point, and two circles intersecting over a dot.

"Like that?" he said, staring.

"That's right." I admired his handiwork, and stared with him.

"Only, it's like, 'snap!' And it means something?" I took the pen back from him and drew below the shapes:

"Is that a word?"

"It's called Dee's Monad." Oscar ran his finger along its contour, investigating. "My father was fascinated by it."

"What does it mean? Is it something he made up?"

"No, he just studied it. It's named for another John Dee, a mathematician and, sort of a scientist, in the sixteenth century. Each part meant something in particular. The signs for different planets are in there. And you can see a lot of numbers." I used the pen to outline them as I spoke. "You see the one, there, and the number three?" Oscar nodded yes, touching the shapes once I'd sketched them.

"So it's like a sentence, or something? About planets? Can you read it to me?"

"No. It's not a simple statement written out. John Dee made the Monad because he thought the symbols contained some sort of information, the truth about things, really. Like, a person might have a secret, or something they knew but couldn't say. He thought if you studied the Monad long enough you'd find out the secret, by staring at it and thinking about its parts and appearance. Like if you spend a lot of time with a person, you, I guess, find a way to understand the secrets inside them."

Oscar simply stared. His mouth was dropped partly open, and his tongue rested on his lower teeth. "So it's," he started, faltering. "It has something in it, and, you'll, you can know it too by looking at it?"

"John Dee thought so."

"Are there ways to look at it?" Oscar persisted, cradling the napkin. "I mean like with a person you want to know, like you were saying, you've got to know how to be with them. Like when to, talk or touch them, or be really close, or when to, you know, just be with them, like without talking." He looked up at me.

"Yes. I guess that's right, Oscar." As a theory, what he said made sense to me. I shifted uncomfortably, and Oscar was silent a moment, reading the flickers of doubt in my face.

"I know that's not so easy for you, Nick, but you get it, right? I mean, that's what you mean about the Dee thing, isn't it?" I looked at the napkin, gazing at each curve and hollow, distracted by Oscar's precocious sensibility. He knew so much about people, about reading people. I wasn't very good at that, but I wanted to be. When I needed to see into a puzzle, or a person, I asked questions. Sometimes silence, just waiting without talking, was the better choice. Was Oscar better equipped than I to read the Monad? Dee constructed inquiries into its secrets, but he also prescribed silent observation.

"I think that's right, Oscar." I nodded, pausing. The boy sat silently, watching me. He ran his hand softly over the napkin, no longer looking at it, but feeling it still. I waited for an instructive summary to form itself in my head, but none came. Words fled, dissolved from my mind by Oscar's example, and his warm silence. The fresh wind battered along the square, and a waitress made her way slowly from the café door, bringing paper menus. "I think that's right," I repeated. Oscar nodded, slowly, bringing the napkin to his face. "You're always touching what you read," I said, watching him with the Monad. "Why is that?" The boy's eyebrows raised above the veil and he lowered it.

"Nick," he sighed, exasperated with me. "How would I know I do that, or why I do that?" He shook his head and pointed out his order to the hovering waitress. *Patat* and soda. I had *patat* and a hot chocolate. I'd only meant it to be friendly. Our bond seemed always nascent. Today's brief adventure took us away from Amelia, and into a conversation that promised to forge a broader, more durable link between us. I thought for a while, worried by Oscar's sharp response. He slouched inside his big jacket, with just his nose and eyes emerging from the drawn collar. The waitress returned with our food. How should I read his silence?

"Are you angry at me?" I asked, shyly. Oscar jabbed a greasy fry in his *sate*, and rolled his eyes.

"I will be, if you don't stop asking questions." He put the fry into his mouth, and took a drink of soda.

"I don't mean to pester you," I apologized, feeling clumsy, rather like an overtrained racehorse cantering through mud. "It's difficult . . . to read you, Oscar, to tell what you're thinking. I'm only asking."

"Maybe I don't always know."

"I don't expect you to. It's not a test of some sort, just my questions. I don't mean it as, prying, or, or as an attack of some sort."

Oscar slid the *patat* trays forward, and drew away from me. He sat, just thinking, for a bit, but with his hands held up. The gesture was an announcement and I paused and waited, giving him time to gather his thoughts. "Asking isn't always the best way for me, Nick. I hear you ask me something and it's like there are only a few ways to answer. None of them is what I'm thinking, so they all seem sort of wrong. What can I say? It's not as if I'm keeping any secrets from you."

"I should talk less?"

"I didn't say that. Just, you don't have to be figuring me out all the time." I tried figuring out exactly what he meant for me to do. What could I say? And why were my eyes beginning to tear? "What time is it, do you think?" No church tower was visible from our square, and we'd heard no bells ringing. Oscar looked at my face, frowning. "Are you okay?" he asked, sheepishly. He took my hands to his mouth and blew on them for warmth. It made me want to blubber, but I was silent. "You're . . ." Oscar blushed and hesitated. "I think your eyes are tearing." Something had begun, emerging, and now it came out my mouth.

"When I first read about you, Oscar," I started rambling, "in those chapters, I wondered if you were real, and then l worried about you, about where you slept, and whether you were warm or had someone taking care of you." The boy watched, puzzled by my sudden account. "I wanted you to have something, some help, or a teacher who would really help you. l couldn't believe you were real on the phone, really calling me on the phone, after all those pages, and it startled me, to actually see you, standing in the inspector's doorway that night when you came home with me from the police."

"What chapters?" There was suspicion in his voice. Had he missed my point entirely?

"I, that is Amelia wrote them." I held on to his hands. "She gave them to me . . . to tell me about you, so I would take an interest, in helping you."

"She wrote about me in chapters? Like in a book?" Oscar wiped my cheeks dry again. "What was it, like a, a psychologist's report kind of thing?" Caution clipped his words. I remembered my own anger at being made a subject, on the evening of the fictional "nap chapter."

"They weren't 'reports,' exactly. They were more like stories, and each time there would be some day, or incident from your life." I nodded my head, still teary. "She wrote one about me too," I added, hoping he'd see our confederacy. "It was slipped under my door with nothing to tell me who, or what. I was upset by it too, I mean, like you must be." How had I been derailed onto this new apology? I only wanted to tell the boy, something, and now . . . "I'm sorry," I said. "I thought I'd told you before, or Amelia had. I didn't realize she'd just, done them." The boat appeared at the far end of the long canal.

"Where are they?" I saw her, in the distance, perched on the forward flat of the barge like a hawk. She and Francis stood scanning the quays.

"The chapters? Well, they're, I guess they're in a box somewhere. I saved them all, and packed them up, when we left the city." They'd not spotted us yet, but forty yards more and they certainly would.

"What do they say about me?"

"They're very complimentary, Oscar, and very kind. I'll show them to you." I smoothed his tangled hair with my hand, and felt his warm face. "I think she's coming up the canal right now, thirty yards down." Oscar looked over his shoulder and saw them, just as Francis spotted us.

"Teach me to write," Oscar asked urgently.

"Of course I will."

"Teach me to, better than she did." His dark eyes were doubly impatient as his speech.

"I'm sure you're already able to write some things well."

"Promise me," he whispered. I watched his dark pupils enlarge as he bent into my shadow. His eyes were Monads, impossible to read, and I was reflected in them.

"We're leaving now, Dr. Dee." It was Amelia, shouting her impatience from our vessel. "Thank your lucky stars the captain was persuadable."

We sailed out of the city into the dimming afternoon. I glimpsed the clean, glass atriums, catching their last glitter, as the canal turned out of the square, and then we were lost to the older waterway and countryside. The barge floated north through the last light, and into the ice cold dusk. Villages dwindled and farms became less frequent. Our barge was alone going north. The other passengers had lain down among their bundles to sleep, and the boys sat by the fire barrel throwing dice and bones. It was an old game Francis learned from his school chums in Groningen. Amelia gripped my arm, sitting with me on the canvas chairs with a bottle and two glasses. The night was brittle and dense with stars, but the *jenever* kept us warm. Empty fields stretched away on either side, but we couldn't see them over the banks. We were drawn along the smooth, silent water, and I kept my eyes on it, enjoying the gentle sound of thin ice crackling. "We rode this same canal," Amelia reminisced. "Last time." It could have been a thousand years ago.

"Who did?" I asked, quietly. Amelia's eyes were wet with pleasure, and drink. She touched my face with her hand and smiled at me.

"Your father and I. The trip we took after Sylvie died." I remembered. I thought he'd gone alone, for research, but they took the trip together. Amelia had already told me, for that was the genesis of her final book, the researches we were now embarked on. It was also the genesis of Francis, who'd been conceived on that journey. "It was spring then, so our evenings on the barge were much longer, and warmer. It was still light after eleven. Every night, even when the clouds came in." She settled back into her chair and drew the blanket tighter.

"Did he help you begin the book?" I wished I'd gone with him, once at least, on his research, to see him work. But of course I couldn't have. He had no work.

"Oh yes, he helped," Amelia answered. "I knew I wanted to deal with the question of inundation, history and inundation, and with some larger argument about good reading. But he was the one who kept marveling over the canals here, and he kept my mind on dissolution. The Dutch landscape, Vierlingh's response to the floods; those began, for me, with John Dee."

She was staring at me. I might have blushed, had my face not been so cold. "Dissolution?"

"It was his greatest skill." Her gaze mimicked the night, implacable and old.

"Though Vierlingh," I hurried, trying to direct her attention away from me, "argued for a fairly constricting use-oriented approach to water control, as opposed to the ambiguous acceptance of inevitability and mixing that I understand to be the cornerstone of your reading of him. The use of controlled inundations, for example, is, in Vierlingh, not an embracing of the virtue of floods, so much as a begrudging recognition that greater, uncontrollable inundations would thereby be forestalled." She interrupted me with her hand, placing it firmly over my mouth in mid-exegesis. "We'll never agree on Vierlingh tonight, so shush-up your arguing. I was just thinking how much you look like your father." Now I did blush, though it was invisible in the moonlight.

"Yes. I've been told that." She stared with ease, and I fidgeted.

"Have you noticed it in Francis, also?"

"Yes I have. His eyebrows, and his mouth." I shifted the blanket up over my chin. "I never noticed it before, of course. Until he told me. Then it was plain."

"He's a beautiful boy." We nodded our agreement on this. "I'm so glad to see him happy with Oscar, and with you." I filled our glasses again with the *jenever*.

"I am too," I agreed quietly.

"You stopped asking me about John Dee. Why is that?" She held my hand, and it felt like being shackled. I was silent. "I thought we'd spend quite a bit more time, you and I, remembering him." I had not asked her much at all. I remembered the deep curiosity about my father that made our first meeting so portentous. The first tale she told was so total, in some ways, it seemed to erase the man I had been curious about; and it replaced him with someone else. My interest was shut down, or on hold, as though the first story was so complete and unexpected, it left no room for further questions.

"I've been asking Francis, quite a bit. We talk about him. I guess that's been enough for me." It was an evasion, and she recognized it as such.

"I'm sure there's a great deal Francis doesn't know. It's obviously a choice you're making."

"I'm suspicious of you." My honesty surprised me. Maybe it was the drink.

"Suspicious? That I might be lying?"

"Well, no. I think I believe that you've told me the truth. Or I can't think of a reason not to." The water turned, bending our course farther east. "It's more suspicion, or maybe resentment about your having, so much of him. I want to know him without it being you who tells me." At another time, in a different place, I would have sounded, or felt, angry. But, oddly, I only felt clear. "I'm also surrounded, even without you telling me, I feel like I'm surrounded by, by information about him, all the time now."

"Because of Francis."

"And because of you. And the, the researches. Sometimes you make me into him, just by circumstance. By how you look at me, or what you have me doing." Her gaze crystallized that feeling in me, again, and I was lost, flickering between my father and me, and that summer they sat in the dwindling evening.

"You're very much like him. You're like when he was your age and frightened we'd be caught." Her voice was liquid in the evening silence.

"Well, I am frightened. I'm frightened nearly all the time." She offered no answer to this, just her hand, and considerable patience, looking out along the water. The canal straightened out. It stretched ahead like a draftsman's sketch, vanishing into the horizon where the night began. "I want everything you have of his," I told her.

"Not your stories. I want the things you have, like that watch you gave to me."

"You already have everything." It was damning if it was true.

"There must be something else. All I have is furniture, and all those typed pages. There must be things he gave you, things he cared about."

"The typed pages are mine, Nicholas. I'm sorry, but he never had an interest in all that academic foofarol. You have the watch, and his butterflies. I don't think there was anything else, anything solid, or material, that he really cared about at all. What he treasured died, or is just past." She looked at me like I was a silly child. I felt that way, and drank more. "He would have enjoyed this, this evening, and the boat . . . If you'd just give up your stubborn habit of divorcing the past, that flood of past things, from your safe, tiny dry land . . ." She just shook her head, and looked away into the night.

TWENTY

AT DAWN FOG COVERED THE MARSHES of the Lauwerszee and made it impossible to see to the ocean's edge. Eight kilometers of muddied spartina and shallow tidal flats stretched north. Beyond that, another eight kilometers of ocean separated Schiermonnikoog from the coast. We would go to the island, to find what I could about Frans's past, the place and circumstances of it, before going to Ezinge and the Allersmaborg. Our bags went on without us, and Kitty with them. She would be happier and better cared for at the Allersmaborg. Amelia packed food in a canvas day-pack, with extra clothes for her and Francis. Oscar and I would be fine in what we had. The trip to the island was only for a day. The bargeman transferred barrels of drink and molasses to another boat, and we went with them. The estuary was thick with birds. The noise and disturbance of them, fighting over fish, and nesting, mingled with wind and the rippling tide. Spartina glistened where ice laced its green stems, waving in the shallow water. Shrubs and cows loomed nearby. Amelia made coffee on a little burner she cajoled from the bargeman, and we had bread and cheese with it.

Tired and cold, I drifted in and out of sleep as the barge floated north. At the estuary's farthest border we put in at a sagging dock, and were told to get off. The boatman waved good-bye, and left us there, along with two barrels. Amelia marched to the dock's end, scolding fate. Oscar was fitting Francis with the pack. Some problem with the channel kept the captain from passing out to sea before the late afternoon and this was as far as he could take us. Amelia stood on a pillow of land where the dock was fastened. An enormous wall of earth rose beside her, stretching away into the fog in both directions. Scrubby tufts of grass made the dike green, and sturdy, and Amelia gazed up and down its length. "The ocean is on the other side," she observed, ominously. The boys and I stared at it with renewed awe as Amelia led us onto the slope. The ocean, at last. The raging enemy that ringed the shallow land, always threatening; lapping at the door, as at this dike, lord knows how many fathoms deep behind the barrier. I looked back at the delicate estuary as we climbed, wondering what chance it stood if the dike were to break. None, I reasoned. Even from the small vantage of twelve feet up, climbing the face, the marshland began to stretch out below us, resolved into maplike clarity, merely by the slight shift in perspective. I saw, it seemed, the whole country we'd been crossing, asleep in its depended bed, and wondered what rage the sea would bring on the other side of the wall.

We made the summit (admittedly only eight yards or so), and turned to gaze upon a vast expanse of mud. There was no ocean. Tiny pools rippled, lost in a desert of brown muck and ribbed sand. Rocks, draped with slippery green vegetation, cluttered the flat, empty bottom. To the landward side was water—the broad rippling surface of the estuary; and to the seaward side was land—a vast flat of empty mud, peppered with listing ships, left limp on the ocean's floor by an outgoing tide. The islands could be seen on the horizon, perhaps no longer islands. Strips of angry gray water appeared between them; but who knew how far it had fled? "Well," Amelia huffed. She tapped her toe, nervously, on the cinder footpath. "I guess we'll just walk to the island." Francis hurried to her with the pack, arriving at her side before she'd even beckoned him. "Muffin. You'll inquire . . . down there"—here she pointed vaguely at some structures gathered near a dock—"if there is a guide who can take us. I believe the channels are breachable at the low tides. We're prepared to pay handsomely for a competent man."

The guide brought a bright red flag and no charts or maps of any kind, and led us off the slippery rocks onto the mud. He might have been drunk, or just very old; in any case he mumbled to himself and didn't seem to hear very well. He set a steady surefooted pace, marching us in a single-file line, fast away from shore. The day was more temperate here than "on land." A full wind from the islands brought the scent of the ocean, and our guide kept his pipe burning. The Wadden Sea bottom smelled of rotting weeds and fish. The wind whipped water off the tidal pools, but the layers I wore kept me dry. I was warm (so long as we kept moving). Far ahead, beyond the island, the gray line of sea was thin and silent as a mirage. It seemed impossibly small. How would the water come, when it came? As a wall? Listing boats lay scattered on the tidal flat. The water must have left them gently, and (I reasoned) gently would return, rising high enough to float the boats, and let them on to their destinations. A boy in a hide-bound kayak paddled past, through a shallow channel nearby. The island's lighthouse cast its beam into sheets of rain. Maybe it was blowing away from us, a simple squall.

The Opera House of Alton Motley   Nicholas Dee

Verweerd and Frans sailed on high tide with a fisherman from Pieterburen. Night had fallen over the Wadden Sea, and the tide had returned to fill the coast. Lanterns, hung from boats, glimmered everywhere on the water. Night and a good tide brought all the fishermen out, and their boats crowded the swollen water. The lanterns brought fish and warned the other boats, and they made a pretty sight. The sky was clear. Frans became more melancholy, the closer they came to leaving, and now, aboard the boat that would take them to Schiermonnikoog, he was inconsolable.

"The boy frets over what he loses, what every man loses, and will not hear me. He's asked that I take a knife to him and have it all undone, but such a cut cannot be made so late, and would do naught but scar him now. If my praise of his pretty voice made him mad I curse having praised him. It is strange and seldom said, but youth remembers too strongly. Age and time make us remember with more subtlety, and not fear it. Things remembered aren't lost, but the

The Opera House of Alton Motley   Nicholas Dee

use of them is, and that the boy despises. Frans only knows
what he is now, what he has always been, and cannot let it
go. He fears the island also and what he'll find there. If
I let him, he would take us from the boat and go back to
land. On the boat's deck I sat near and held him close to
me because he was afraid, and to keep him from the water.
There is no man or woman he fears especially, only the
island, and what he remembers of it. To stay him from his
fright I sang the 'Aeolus' best I knew it. I sang it soft
because I have no voice for it, only an ear, and to keep
the boatmen from hearing."

THE TEMPEST.

RECIT and AIR. *(Neptune)* ÆOLUS, YOU MUST APPEAR.

Henry Purcell.

While these pass o'er the deep,   Your stormy winds must cease,

The Opera House of Alton Motley

Nicholas Dee

The Opera House of Alton Motley   Nicholas Dee

keep, I'll bless

my wa-try realms with peace,

    Verweerd made a sketch of the island, and some men-
tion of the weather (which was blustery, and with rain),
but did not say whom they saw there. Presumably the boy,
whose family had all perished in a storm, was known to most
in the small, close village.

    "A pretty island, with farms and fisherman equally,"
he wrote in the brief entry. "The north is sand dunes and
a great wind from the sea. Sailed back to land at afternoon
by the Groote Siege to the Lauwerszee. From there by the
Reitdiep to Ezinge. Frans will say nothing, and all is
thereby said. The current on this coast is treacherous and
strange. The boatman says one may walk from the islands on
the ebb tide, but to be wary of the flood."

The squall had increased, and blown around us, so the coast was obscured now. As the bird flies, Schiermonnikoog was very near, but a maze of deep channels and twisting sandbanks kept us from it. Our guide was undaunted. He set a steady pace, stopping mechanically for ten-minute breaks every hour or so, and offering his pipe to me. Houses stood out plainly on the island's western end. Cows were being led along a road away from town. Ten or twelve of them ambled slowly. A wet, dirty dog and a boy kept them going, and we could've shouted to the boy and been heard, I thought; we were that close. Frans led his cows out from town, with stones in his pocket to count them . . . this boy was young enough. The island was the first sight I had of my researches, the particular place of my researches. Because of the weather, and the slowness of change here, the island could still have been Frans's. The dog ran a circuit around the cows. Oscar fell into a tidal pool and thought it was funny. Now he shivered whenever we stopped, and it worried me.

. The wind and storms must be what blew the islands east. The storms washed away the western banks, however long it took, and dunes grew off the other end. It made the islands wander across the sea; that's what killed the boy's family, a storm that took part of the town one winter. We were all wet by now. I watched the boy with the cows, and imagined Frans. What could anyone say to him that would stay his grief? Not about his family, but about his youth. That loss was so gradual and irrevocable, and I felt his silent frustration inside me. The cruelest fact of all was that change came invisibly, from inside, and not from some identifiable, hostile, external enemy. He'd have to cut himself to get at it. It was in him, this fundamental loss, and it was himself he'd have to mutilate to stop it. The wind blew harder, and brought the heavy squalls in again. The shallow pools and inlets rippled with it, and rain disturbed their surface. Amelia offered coffee, which helped quell the chills, and Francis gave his hat to Oscar because the older boy looked so miserable.

I wanted to turn around and not go there. The boy with the cows was happy. He threw sticks for the dog to chase. The island had always been wrecked by the sea, and always it built up again on the eastern shore. Who was I to come here, digging for information about one family and their death in a storm? Standing on the sea bottom, a few hundred yards from shore, I wanted the boy, and the island, not to see me, nor ever hear the story I knew, the one I was researching, of Frans's loss and his flight away, and the disastrous end to the "endeavour" of Alton Motley. Boats by the island which had been settled on the sand began rocking and lifting some. The sight was worrying. The water increased, and its effect spread like a contagion, advancing slowly from the facing shore. Our guide began waving his flag.

The current had increased considerably in the channels around us. Great plains of sand disappeared, leaving archipelagos of small islands. The tide was coming in, swift and sure as a river. Only with the advancing waves did I notice how varied and uneven the ocean floor really was. The flat expanse gave up its valleys, leaving swollen sand hills. Our guide knew his stuff. We stood atop one such hill, as if on a *terp,* while the sand around us slowly disappeared. That boy disappeared off the dike with his cows. He never saw the flag. Francis enjoyed the spectacle, even while clinging to his mother's arm. Oscar was quiet, and maybe a little delirious from the cold and wet. He was the only one among us without much to lose by swimming. Our guide sat nursing his pipe with the flag planted in the sand beside him. Some of the boats by the island were upright and bobbing, and our guide got up and performed a series of maneuvers. A large yellow banner aboard one of the boats answered. The channel immediately before us deepened considerably as another surge came through.

I was shivering now, as heartily as Oscar, and stared hard at the boat, as if the force of my attention alone kept it coming. It wound circuitously through the water and made good progress toward us. Periodically it stalled, and a man would come to the fore with a long pole to test the depth. We were surrounded by the sea. Our island was the only measure of its rising now. It seemed to lurch, like waves that never receded. Occasionally a surge would come which washed over us, but those fell off the other side. We stood nervously for another half-hour, while the ocean took all but seven or eight square yards of our island, and then the boat arrived. They let out a gangplank. Our calm guide ushered us on ahead of him, unplanted the flag, and we were safe.

I took some delight in stomping heavily along the dry deck, up and down the length of it, then sat down on a bench by a barrel of fire. The heat was an elixir, a wave of joy not unlike the transcendent ice of the sauna's *doompelbad*. We crowded around it, and the guide showed us the pots on the fire. There was coffee in one, and *erte zoep* in the other, hot as lucifer. Everyone began stripping. "Quickly, Nicholas," Amelia ordered. "We'll dry them by the flames. It will save you from a nasty pneumonia." She tossed me two blankets, and hung her slip on an unused oar. "One is for Oscar," she explained. "Make yourself absolutely dry, and wrap up tight, or else you'll both catch your death." I began peeling the wet layers off my body, enjoying the increasing rain against my skin. The showery gale left me cleansed and strangely warmer. Our vessel was stalled, unable to turn in the narrow channel. It drew too deep to proceed. The squall obscured both coasts, so that we floated on an unmarked gray sea, surrounded by water where before there had only been land. Oscar and I stood near the fire, hoarding the heat to dry us. We held our blankets open, to toast them, then wrapped ourselves up quick, and sat down on the bench, still shivering. The wool scratched and was itchy where my bare skin still had feeling. "I think we won't make it to the island today," Francis apologized. He pulled his extra sweater on over his dry clothes, and I envied him. "The boat's going in to port." I was glad for it. The boat wobbled on the water, going nowhere yet. The sail had been let down, so the incoming tide would carry us when the boatman let it. I nodded. It was hard to speak because my mouth was cold. Some coffee, and the soup, helped. Oscar was silent, except for shivering. I could feel his convulsions through the small bench we shared.

"Have some coffee, Oscar,' I whispered, giving him the cup. He opened his mouth to receive it, but kept his hands inside the warm blanket. Francis held the cup, and Oscar sipped from it, smiling. I shook my tired arms and stamped my feet, to give them feeling. Lights from the dock were visible, now that the day grew darker. The mist muted them, but never shut them out. Horns could be heard, and bells from buoys or boats. We were in no danger now. It was just time and tides. The boatmen were busy with Francis, trying to teach him some scandalous verse. Oscar looked up at me, miserable and sleepy. "I'm too cold," he whispered, and slipped out of his blanket and into mine. The boy was shaky and a little pale. He climbed in, wrapping his arms around me, and pressed against my skin as best he could. Oscar pushed his face against my chest, to get closer to the warmth, to get inside of it.

I took his blanket from the bench and wrapped it around our front, to give us more heat. His tremors came in waves and he scooted closer with each one. Oscar pulled his legs up over mine, so he sat on me, hugging me to him with both arms. I'd never held something so fragile. The boat drifted forward, allowed some progress by the tide. Amelia stayed in front testing the channel. Oscar's ear was pressed against me, and his nose was running on my chest. Every now and then he'd sniffle, and wipe it clean with his hand. He said nothing. Where I rubbed him, he got warmer. I could feel it easily. His skin had been so chilly and dry, and now it began heating up again. Against my chest I could feel his heart beating, so much stronger than mine, it felt like a repeated pressure. I ran my hands over him, rubbing with some force and vigor, feeling the soft skin become flush and heated. The boy shuddered now, but more deeply and less often. He rested his head on me, keeping his face against my warm neck, and moved his hands over my back, returning my attentions. I felt I'd brought life back into him, by my touch. His breathing deepened and was more steady. His body moved now, more easily, against mine, and the shivering slackened. I think he slept then. We were silent in any case, and held each other while the boat drifted. In the night, we made the dock, and dry land.

Some part of him passed into me then, like a storm from an ocean passing onto land and becoming part of it, and I would not leave him. Amelia ushered us, in our blanket, off the ship, stumbling a little, and unsteady. The guide took our party in. He built a fire to warm us, and we gathered in blankets beside it. Water was boiled for bathing. I could see myself in Oscar's eyes more clearly now. I gave him his bath, and stared at the dark pupils, the deep-set eyes, and his brow. Maybe it was delirium, still, from the cold, but neither of us spoke; there were no questions.

The Opera House of Alton Motley   Nicholas Dee

Despite a persistent and bizarre "black fog" and rains which washed away three hills near Benson, Thomas Weekes judged November of 1686 to be the best month for Alton Motley's travel to Holland. He was watching the stars, more than the weather, and that month brought a rare alignment of Venus and a star Weekes had called Aeolus. Motley was kept busy riding a barge up and down the river to prepare him for the rigors of the journey. Weekes saw to the packing of the famous beds, and charted his route: from Dover to Harlingen, and then by canal to the Allersmaborg. There, Factor and Patron would meet.

The train of carriages, single-file, filled nearly seventy-five yards of road. A quarter of them would end their trip at Dover, and the rest were packed aboard a Dutch man-o'-war, and taken across the sea in two days. Whether by luck or design, the voyage was relatively uneventful. In Harlingen, the entourage found mild, temperate skies, and the luxury of Holland's famous canals. After the pitted roads of England, and the swollen sea, the journey's last leg was like a deep and untroubled sleep. Motley floated east with his furniture on two barges, and arrived in Ezinge by November 15, fully five days ahead of schedule. Verweerd was away still, with Frans, gone to Schiermonnikoog.

The entourage of Alton Motley was a great deal larger than any troupe Drop's modest Borg had hosted. With thirty musicians and the actors already taking up space, Motley's arrival required the construction of seven additional sheds, to house the animals; the orchestra and actors would be moved into the barns. Out of magnanimity and because the music was his great passion, Motley asked to be given a loft in the barn with the musicians. The request delighted the Dutchmen, who volunteered their labor for construction. Weekes, who lived in constant fear that his wealthy patron (and sole benefactor) might suddenly be struck dead, consented to the design of a separate chamber, built into the loft, capable of housing the pivoting bed.

The Opera House of Alton Motley   Nicholas Dee

     This was the scene to which Verweerd and Frans re-
turned on the twenty-first of November. Motley enjoyed twice-
daily rehearsals of the orchestra in the dusty, overheated
barn. The actors had degenerated, drunk and unlocatable,
dispersed by lack of attention. (And Pieter had resumed
his complaining and his threats to speak in defense of the
diminished Prospero.) No one treated them specially, as
Verweerd did, and they'd taken offense and dispersed throughout the grounds with food and drink. At night fires burned
in the orchard, and the actors sang and danced beside them,
pissing and fornicating like animals. Motley honored the
arrival of Verweerd with the presentation of one of three
new songs he'd finished for *The Tempest:*

THE TEMPEST.

RECIT and AIR. (*Æolus*) YOUR AWFUL VOICE I HEAR.   Henry Purcell.

The Opera House of Alton Motley

Nicholas Dee

The Opera House of Alton Motley   Nicholas Dee

The Opera House of Alton Motley   Nicholas Dee

trem - - - - - - - - - bling dens for-sake.

Inspector Clausewitz woke us the next morning. I looked out the window of the loft (where our guide let us sleep through the storm) and saw him. There he sat, in a white compact marked with a black insignia, red lights swirling through the morning fog. He pulled up to the dock and stopped. I'd not seen a car in days. The clean technology—normally so fearful and heart-stopping—was diminished and made alien here. Imbedded in this older place, the inspector and his machine might have been a fabulation, a drunken farmer's nightmare, or some feverish mystic's vision. He'd lost all his menace, and joined the ghosts and goblins. A blast of the horn was directed at three sheep, whose lazy incomprehension could not be dispelled, even by this most hellish of sounds. The inspector stepped from the driver's side door and tried shooing them away manually. His gloves, his suit, the smart hat—even so early in the morning—none of it impressed the sheep. Clausewitz leaned back inside the car, drew out his Portacam, and started shooting the animals. He trained the lens on our guide's house, and then swept left for a panorama of the sea. I crept back from the window and whispered to Amelia that he was out there. "I'm not surprised, Nicholas. It's remarkable we lost him for as long as we did."

"I didn't realize we were 'losing' him? Is that what motivated all this, this backward meandering?" At some point in yesterday's near-disaster I'd begun to doubt the necessity of our route.

"Certainly not," Amelia objected. "We're guided, 'backward,' as you put it, by our work. I think you know where we're headed. It is simply coincidence that the inspector finds that a difficult route to travel." She sidled to the window, and peered out at him. "I'm sure he drove here days ago. I don't imagine our Clausewitz would ever deign to trail us *au naturel,* as it were; that is without all his speed and mechanical contraptions." I joined her in looking. The cool detective was sitting inside the car, enjoying a cigarette. The sheep had fallen asleep again, and there were some that gathered beneath the chassis for its warmth. The strange insignia looked, at first, to be a hideous skull, filled in black, with two gaping white eyes and a row of awful teeth. *"Groningen Politie,"* it said beneath the terrible specter. I looked again, and recognized the two-headed eagle which Groningers held as their provincial symbol. (The twin sharpened beaks of reason and force, the university and the police, given wings by their formation into a singular state and etc., etc.) Evidently he'd borrowed it from the local precinct.

"It might just be coincidence," I suggested. Oscar pulled me down to the huge featherbed, accidentally squashing Francis. "He does have his documentary to shoot after all."

Amelia shook the boys awake, and bustled through the tired daypack. "We've no time for him. Our host has arranged some sort of transport to Ezinge. We'll be at the Allersmaborg, no later than this evening. You can make a day trip back to the island in a few days if need be. Muffin." She dragged him from bed by the foot. "See if you can arrange food for the day. I believe we'll be six or seven hours in transit." Half asleep, and nodding, the boy pulled his pants on and hurried down the ladder. "You see to Oscar, Nicholas, and I'll settle debts with our host." Amelia followed Francis down, and I sat on the bedside, listening to boat horns blowing in the mist. I knew the inspector's arrival was no accident. He was here for us, and there would be no getting around it. I shook Oscar's shoulder, and whispered to him to get up.

"Look, Oscar." I stood up by the window. "Morning is here. No more boats."

"Uhhnn."

"Dee." It was Clausewitz, standing on his car top, shooting.

"Inspector, at last." Amelia's voice boomed from the doorway. I looked back at Oscar. He managed to sit up and asked me how soon we'd be going.

"Weathered. Have you drowned the boy yet, or was I just imagining the reports on my radio?" The radio. Had our emergency been broadcast on the air?

"I think Amelia's arranging things now," I told Oscar. "You really should be getting ready."

"Arranging what, Dee?" The inspector bellowed, taking advantage of his proximity for a tight close-up.

"He's fit as a horse, Inspector. You can see for yourself." The small woman pointed sharply up at the window, and Clausewitz looked harder. "And I'll thank you to leave us alone, so we can get on with our work." Oscar scooted from bed obediently and fished around the floor, looking for a towel.

"Put a shirt on at least, Oscar," I suggested. "The inspector is gawking." The boy pressed himself against the window, to get a better look.

"You were all over the emergency bands, Weathered, with the job you did yesterday. I was about to send in the choppers, when the news came in about the boats."

"Hi, Inspector," Oscar called, his voice still rough with sleep. "Are you coming with us to the Borg?"

"Is it drugs, Weathered?" Clausewitz pressed. "Have you got that boy sedated?" Francis came down the drive with an ox-cart.

"I don't think there's time for a shower, Oscar." I held the towel out to him, tossing it over his shoulders. "Why, Francis is back already with the, uh, vehicle."

"It's health and vigor, Inspector. Some of us don't need elaborate props to conduct ourselves through this world." With this Amelia tossed her bag onto the cart, and snapped her fingers at us. "Nicholas, Oscar. We're wasting time here." Oscar buttoned his pants and pulled his shirt on wrong. I straightened the simple bed, a loft-size mattress really, and gathered my shoes and socks. We hurried down the ladder and went out to board the cart. After all the rushing, our oxen's pace was painfully slow. The drama of our flight from the inspector was entirely undermined, and he walked easily alongside, filming our exit from various angles. The oxen shuffled forward, stirred by the silent driver. Clausewitz took one last shot overhead, dangling from a tree limb where he'd climbed, and then went to his car and drove on.

TWENTY-ONE

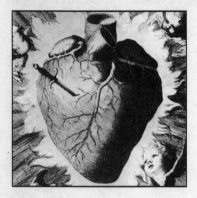

THE ALLERSMABORG APPEARED at the end of a thin, muddy road, lined with poplar. Even stripped bare, the trees made a thick barrier and bent together in the mild wind. The man with the oxen got us to Ezinge in the afternoon. From there we walked, the only travelers on a pleasant road. The sun had disappeared into the sharp gray clouds behind us, but the day was still brilliant and light. The clouds ahead were fringed golden; bright, cold air, scarred by smoke from fires, and steam from off the cows' backs, blanketed the flat land. It was almost dusk when we turned from the winding road onto a thin muddy one, and approached the moat and gate.

The house was still invisible through the bushes and trees. The moat stank, and the ground was thick and spongy. It seemed built on a *terp* of dead leaves and spoiled fruit, as if an orchard had been here a thousand years, unharvested, shedding every season's growth to the ground where it rotted. The road wound in toward the middle, where the trees crowded out the light. The gate was cheap and breachable. There was a mechanism for raising the bridge, but it was just a decoration, and the bridge stayed down. Amelia knew the residents, of course: Karl and Herman, a pair of poor artists who were stuck on a government waiting list for studio space. They'd been given the Borg in the meantime. There was no sign of either of them. The Borg could be seen through the gate, huddled on its mound of land, bounded by the rank canal. Like the trees and the rotten ground, the building seemed overgrown and untended. Cracks where later additions had been made (fifteenth-century beginnings having increased outward and later upward, in the next century, and again in the next) were settled now, and crooked with stress and weariness. The building seemed too tired even to collapse, as though it had tried already and could only get this far. Thick stick and mud nests held sea birds and starlings along every fold and crevice of the roof. Several of the upstairs windows were open. It was dark inside the rooms.

"Well," Amelia sighed. "At least the inspector didn't arrive already to greet us. He's probably still out searching for a more photogenic castle." Francis rattled the flimsy gate, and it fell open. Karl and Herman had left a note tacked to the front door telling us they'd be gone overnight. Inside, the remains of a fire were burning in the big stone fireplace. It filled one wall of the kitchen. And there was Kitty, nesting in scarves beside a bowl heaped high with *Tompoes*. Our arrival had woken her and she gave one "meow" then resumed her purring. What an agreeable traveler. The room was built into the ground, and garbage could be thrown out a small window directly into the canal. Oscar put his bag down and settled on the stone bench by the fire. He fed the embers with twigs, and stacked some logs on top. Dusk lingered in the trees outside and touched the uneven glass. "Welcome, welcome," the note said. "This will be your home. Every room is open. Do not break things, but use them all. If you want to make music on the instruments, do so. There are many, many beds. The rowboat by the kitchen window leaks. No one is to go out in it. We are away, maybe two nights tops. The iceman will bring new ice tomorrow. *Slaap lekker!* Karl and Herman." "Sleep deliciously," the valediction meant.

While Amelia and the boys organized affairs in the kitchen, I wandered up the stairs, into the main hall of the house. The dusty wooden floor was rough and worn. Tiles Verweerd once walked across with Frans (coming in from the cold evening to join Motley in the large music room) had been ripped away by scavengers. They left the worn wood. The walls looked stripped and tattered. Water stains hovered like shadows of some past flood or accident. There was a pump organ in the big room. It was pushed into a corner beside a window which gave what little light I had. One of its bellows was split, and wheezed dust. The other worked, but that was not enough to sustain a tune. Rather it played like a dying man, pausing every other moment to take in breath so he could continue moaning. The fixtures in the room, and its shape, were clearly kept from Johannes Drop's time when the great concert was held, and the room was filled with thirty musicians and Frans, singing in his fabled soprano. I looked at the far, narrow wall, where the frame of a slight stage was still visible. They might have hung him by ropes, to give a theatrical effect, or let him stand by the musicians and sing, as if in a recital. There was no shadow of hardware left to mark the ceiling. But those would have been cleverly hidden, and then removed altogether after the show. What did he look like? I invariably imagined Francis when I thought of Frans . . . the age of the boys, and the circumstances of my meeting them . . . They both played Ariel to another's Prospero. The notion of Francis involved in that glorious endeavor pleased me. His spirit was strong, and, I thought, ageless.

So there was Frans, dark hair and a pretty mouth, the red blush of embarrassment or pride on his smooth, pale cheeks. Would they have him in costume? Certainly Verweerd, returning to find the actors dispirited (or overly spirited), would have devised some indulgence to please them. Probably it would include a full performance. So Frans is in costume. The mechanicals have been fastened to the ceiling with bolts. The troupe, Pieter especially, is still drunk, and cannot be quieted. Verweerd has wisely chosen the kitchen for their dressing room, hoping the intervening stone walls will deaden the ruckus.

Motley has been in bed all afternoon, though not to sleep. Anxious about the strain and excitement of the journey (and now the first performance of Motley's work-in-progress) Thomas Weekes has ordered an afternoon of calculated spinnings and pivots, trying to fix Motley's alignment with the proper winds and magnetic forces of attraction. A fine and golden urine is produced at six, and Weekes has announced that the performance may go forward. Motley is carried across the orchard in a carriage, to the big house. The musicians have been in place for an hour, entertaining the crowd of forty or so with popular songs from the London musicals. Half of those dressed and mingling have come over from Benson with Motley. The remaining score are friends of Drop, and functionaries from the provincial government in Groningen. It is an awful and blustery night out, and

Motley is nearly toppled from his carriage when it is maneuvered through the front door.

The players are toasting Frans in the kitchen, but Verweerd keeps them from filling him with drink. He knows what the evening means to the boy; tonight, as Ariel, Frans will be beautiful and perfect. Given how the boy is suffering, the ignominy of faltering drunk would be too cruel, and Verweerd stays close by him. Frans's costume is made of lace and silk and his face is made up simply, with powder and wax. Kees and Willem are done up as devils by the cook, using coal from her fire; seaweeds hauled in by the fishermen are draped over them bare. As the overture sounds, the actors fall silent, and Kees and Willem make their way to the stairs, ready for their entrance and the "Devil's Chorus."

Where had she brought me? The wild enclosure of trees, and now the night, submerged us all, like water. When my father lay submerged, at the bottom of the pool, I counted seconds to myself, impressed and wanting some kind of measure for the event. I sat on cold tiles and held my breath with him. Later, at night in bed, where I practiced under my covers, I would count the seconds again. I knelt in the dark tent of sheets, drew in a great breath and sank to the bottom. My heart kept time (once for every second Father said), and the bed grew larger, as big and uncharted as the pool. The edges wobbled in the dark like water, the cotton cooler there, where I hadn't lain, and I made my way down, further and further into my dizzy fantasy. My chest ached with its cargo. When we walked across the bridge entering the Borg, I had held my breath, neither consciously, nor for a reason.

The boys came up from the kitchen to join me exploring, and Amelia went upstairs to rest a while in bed. There seemed to be no electrical fixtures, or none that worked. Oscar and Francis had oil lamps, and we found lanterns in most of the rooms, and candles, which together lit them well. The upstairs rooms were cluttered with beds and furniture, carpets, drapes, and enormous dresses, kept full on bustles and old sprung mannequins. The contents were kept in no particular order. There might be five beds in one room, or a single round table at the center of another, covered with wooden dolls. Amelia lay on a big bed in the master room, as if in state. The four-poster was positioned beneath an elaborate rectangular tester, hung from the ceiling by hooks, and topped with cups full of ostrich plumes. The whole was embroidered, inside and out, in silk, and with a dossier, and bonegraces flanking the head. A careful arrangement of velveteen cushions was scattered around her. Several propped her up from behind, lifting the upper torso and head, and improving the view of her from the door.

"Ssshhhh," Francis whispered, knowing she needed her rest. I snuck in quietly and gently let the stays loose, so the bed curtains could be dropped. She hardly seemed to be breathing. I looked at her smooth, unmoving face and at the hooded eyes. The boys moved down the hall, wanting more booty from their search. The small woman lay among the cushions, still dressed for the day but sleeping. I whispered her name out loud (to make certain), and then leaned closer. She smelled so clean and fresh, like the air when it's about to snow. I let my hand drift to her blouse, and hesitated a moment, almost forgetting to breathe. My heart pounded audibly by my throat; certainly it could be seen moving beneath my chest. The boys' noises could be heard, dim and constant, past the turn in the hallway, where the newer wing was built. Shaking, as I bent toward her, I managed two fingers beneath her blouse, and felt the soft skin where her breast lay. There was no heartbeat there, or perhaps I touched her too lightly. I took a deep breath, and shifted my touch, searching. Her face was unmoved. The skin was silken, and very warm, but I could not find a trace of the muscle inside, turning in its nest of bones. She gave me nothing; no message passed through her heart to my fingers, nor was their transit between our eyes.

Francis fixed the second bellows and spent most of the evening playing songs on the pump organ. He found a clutch of old show tunes in a satchel by the organ, but they were repetitive and dull and I gave him the pages of *The Tempest*. We cooked on the kitchen fire, roasting potatoes, and game-hens, which Karl slaughtered and left for us on ice. There was port, but no wine. Amelia and I sat drinking in the drawing room after dinner. We managed to fix both rooms with candles and lamps. Approaching from the gate, the house looked alive, ablaze with flickering activity and shadows. It was just the two front rooms, but the effect was pretty, and I went outside to admire it. The ocean was in the air, and the night was much warmer than the day had been. The wind, wet and blustery, battered the trees from the north. Dead wood fell, but I couldn't see it in the dark. All around the grounds, branches cracked and crashed. Their noise and splitting mixed with the wind and Francis, trying the overture on the pump organ. I tried listening for animals, thinking they'd be disturbed by the storm's increasing violence. There was nothing. The birds had either gone, or were lying in their nests. Cows and sheep were kept in barns far across the fields. There was no dog, or if there was it cowered somewhere.

Amelia lay on the fainting couch with her port and the pages of my manuscript. Documents were spread out on the carpet around her, and she moved through the pages marking them for insertions and emendations. Was my father in the other room, as she said he'd been, fourteen years ago? All our cargo (from Rotterdam, and the Lauwerszee) was stuffed in an upstairs room. Earlier, I mistook it for ancient clutter. Amelia had some of the boxes unpacked, and these contained the documents that now surrounded her.

I watched Oscar for a while. He made his way slowly along the high bookshelves lining the wall behind Amelia. His head was turned sideways, to read the titles, and every few feet he pulled one of the heavy books from the shelf. I knew his eyes were reading, and could imagine them, so brown and dilated in the dim light, taking the text in, taking the light, through the black, empty pupil. Written words disappeared in a stream, run one by one into the boy's eyes. His beautiful eyes at which I stared, reading in them, their depth and reflections, reading him like the Monad, unable to give words to what I saw there. There was transit in both directions. He read, while being read. Oscar knelt by the lower shelves, lost in a few feet of titles. I imagined the world that opened up there, on the windowless interior wall of books, like the entrance to an underground. I could feel the slight pressure on his knees, and the warm smooth wood beneath him where he sat. He lifted the books to see. Into his eyes then, the simple etchings of flowers, pistil and stamen enlarged, the names of tropical birds, and stones of the glacial plateau; the English manor house, methods of instruction in the time of Charlemagne, a chart chronicling bridge disasters . . . Amelia left him alone to it. Whatever Oscar lost by reading, he gained something too. (An angel come to earth cannot conduct himself as an angel; Oscar had chosen to come to our city, and now this was his life.) Across the hall Francis stumbled through the "Devil's Chorus," and moved on into the "Subterranean Winds."

If my father came here with her, they might have stayed in the bed upstairs where she had slept that evening. Amelia said that Francis was conceived in this place, and that my father's grief (and I think some drink) drove them to it. Was she much bigger then? She said as much. They collapsed together, coupled in my mind now, and the gap between them disappeared. Was it really his desire, or Amelia, scheming? She was artful, and strong. I'd come, apparently by my own design, when in fact it was her, her and the circumstances she conjured. I listened to the songs from outside in the storm a while, then decided it was time to go in.

Frans listens impatiently to Willem's bass, judging this evening's "Winds" fine and clear. However drunk he got, the costume and the stage always sobered Willem completely. Frans watches from the curtained stairway. The music has never been played in so perfect a room. The strings are bright and full, and the harpsichord quivers like glass, over the top. Willem needs only half his voice to overwhelm them, and Frans hears this, and calculates how he'll bring his own, slowly, up to full strength. Motley sits, elevated in the carriage chair, near the back of the room, where Verweerd has joined him. Despite powder, wigs, and money, the audience is noisier than that on the Leesersplein. They chatter continuously. Empty bottles and bones are given to young boys circulating throughout the room with buckets. The small servants, bringing food and drink, replenish what's been eaten, and carry the garbage to the canal and dump it.

The "Winds" comes to an end, and the painted scene for Act III is brought in. Frans is strapped into the ropes and lifted behind the drop. The chorus, including Willem, arranges itself among bowers Verweerd fashioned as an elaborate island. The scene resembles a Christmas party. Frans is swung forward on the ropes, and lowered to the "island." A series of tableaux: with servants carrying food on trays before them, the chorus surrounds the boy, glowing wands pointed toward him; Frans scurrying away, the harness still on him, as if in a search for Prospero; he rises above the scene, pulled up by the ropes, and describes a circle above them. The "Yellow Sands" begins. Frans starts the song in a small voice, then lets it fill out, like a delicate, expanding perfume. His lyric is liquid and sweet, and the sound widens and fills the room. The noise and chattering stop, and the party recedes behind the song. All attentions are paid to the boy. His beauty is enchanting. He floats, in his harness, suspended above the crudely constructed island. The snow increases outside, white and thick against the night. The room is small and enclosed. Aware of his effect, the boy tempers the volume, withholding some for the later songs. Verweerd has gripped the arm of Motley, who is mesmerized. The song is easy for Frans, supple and brief.

Francis looked spellbound by his efforts with the song, as I watched him through the doorway. The pump organ required more stamina than skill, and the boy was mustering it nicely. Amelia rose from the fainting couch, and was tottering around with the bottle singing, as Francis played the tunes. Oscar was still lost to the wall of books. The night's violence had increased, and rain began falling. It could be heard in the trees long before it touched the windows. Amelia danced across the hallway, and joined Francis in the big room. "Full fathom five," she sang, staring through the distorting window, watching the rain pour now. "Thy father lies." The couple made their way through the Ariel songs. I was frightened by the first thunder, and joined Oscar beside the books. The sound outside was terrible now and sent Kitty scurrying up the stairway to cower in some hidden place. Branches cracked and fell. Trees were crowded so close to the buildings there was no possibility of damage; they could only crumble or lean, having too little room to fall with force. Amelia was louder too, improvising recitatives where I knew there were none. She began haranguing her organist about "the project, gathering its head and going in an upright carriage." Perhaps she meant Alton Motley.

"Read me something," I asked, sitting down beside Oscar and the books. He looked tired and lost.

"No. I'm sick of all these books." Oscar leaned back against the shelves, and they wobbled slightly, but did not shift. Francis complained about the hour and Amelia ordered him to continue playing. The music swelled again.

"Are you tired?" I put my hand to Oscar's forehead, thinking he might have a fever from yesterday's near drowning. He sat quietly and watched me. His stare did not unnerve me. I'd learned a little about the traffic through his eyes, and I let it run for a while without fear.

"Yeah." He moved my hand to his cheek, and then to his chest. "They're sure making a racket." Amelia was stamping around the big room, orating, to Francis's organ accompaniment. Her vigor frightened me, and her slurred speech said she was drunk.

"I believe she's reciting something." We sat and listened to her roar. "I have bedimmed the noontide sun, called forth the mutinous winds," which here drowned out her speech. Francis (and some others?) seemed to be shouting at her, or scuffling, in response. I tried moving nearer to the door to see, but Oscar pulled me back and held me. "Graves at my command have wake'd their sleepers," Amelia resumed, in what clearly was Prospero's speech, "opened and let them forth by my so potent art." The crumbling of a tree outside obscured her words, and I started when its branches brushed the nearest window. Nothing broke, but it frightened me. Amelia called for "heavenly music to work mine end upon their senses," but the organ could not be heard behind the sound of shouting. The ruckus only dimmed, finally, after a terrific crash came from across the hall, and then Amelia's muffled vow to "drown my book."

"That's not to be included," a man's voice shouted back at her. Could it have been Francis, or Clausewitz? The accent was nearly unplaceable.

"Come with me," Oscar whispered, ignoring the uproar from the big room. The double doors slammed shut with the wind. "Come on, before they're finished in there. I want to show you something."

"But, Oscar." I pulled back. "Who was that, that man?" He released his grip for a moment and we listened; thunder came and the storm increased, masking any information that might have leaked through the doors.

"That was her, reciting, like you said. Come on." He pulled me, impatiently. "They'll only try and drag us into it." Muffled curses and the wheezing organ competed against the wind and trees. I thought I heard strings, and then the scuffling diminished. Had Francis taken issue with her deviation from the score? It was *The Tempest* she'd recited from, but not the opera. Oscar slipped his arm around me, and guided us to the stairs. Something had collapsed now, in this ruined shell.

* * *

Lightning splits a heavy oak near to the canal and all the grounds are lit for a lingering awful moment while the walls shake with the sound. Few in the big room take notice. Pieter is wrestled from the stage by eight tiny servants. Motley is shouting at him, and the drunken actor continues, bellowing his lines through the forest of arms reaching to stop him. He is drunk and enormous and manages the whole prideful speech (directed with spit and venom at the flustering Motley) before they stop him:

"*I* have bedimmed the noontide sun, called forth the mutinous winds, and twixt the green sea and the azur'd vault set roaring war. To the dread rattling thunder have *I* given fire, and rifted Jove's stout oak with his own bolt; the strong-based promontory have *I* made shake, and by the spurs plucked up the pine and cedar. Graves at *my* command have wake'd their sleepers, opened and let them forth by *my so potent art.* But this rough magic I *here abjure.* And when I have required some heavenly music—which even now I do—to work mine end upon their senses, that this airy charm is for, I'll break my staff, bury it certain fathoms deep in the earth, and deeper than did ever plummet sound I'll *drown my book.*"

"That's not to be included," Motley shouts, toppling from the carriage chair. Pieter is dragged down the back stairs while a half-dozen servants rush to right the fallen patron. Verweerd cannot keep himself from laughing, so comical is the sight: the drunken Prospero proclaiming his power—and its renunciation—to the man with money who both wrote him in as an affable dupe, and would have him silenced. This is the fate of Prospero in our age, Verweerd said once, when Pieter made the same speech: to be made into a dupe and silenced by those with money. The patron is propped up again in his box (much to the relief of his doctor) and the stage is put in order for the new *Tempest.*

"Continue with the entertainments," Motley shouts, and the music swells up. The entertainments recommence. Frans, shaken like the rest of the troupe by Pieter's removal, falters through "Kind Fortune," then hurries down the stairs when the devils come back on.

Thunder resounded, like chopper blades, in the attic of the Borg, where Oscar had taken me. There were no windows in the cramped passage where we crouched (rummaging past old crates) and the noise from outside was dimmed or increased by our progress through it. *Were* they chopper blades, approaching and receding? The boy led me through the narrow dark spaces, holding my hand to guide me, and said nothing. Below, Amelia and Francis could be heard, but only when the pounding from the sky let up. It was warm and stuffy in the attic. Oscar opened a final door and shuffled through. "Here," he whispered. I followed.

I couldn't see the borders of the room, because of shadows and the dimness of light from outside. One oval window on pivots was set into the wall, and below it a large bed was visible. The folds and outline of its covers disappeared into black where the light of the window was blocked. To either side was close, airless darkness. Oscar let the door shut and led me toward the window. We were above the trees, and their tops lurched and bent below us. Beyond the trees, meadows and canals stretched to the edge of what I could see. Was that the ocean, lining the horizon in gray?

"Wow," I whispered. The boy sat beside me, looking. He put his hand over my mouth and quieted me. I could see us both, in the light from the window. Where his legs moved into the shadow they were still visible, but only as ghosts, half implication. Not much could be heard from below; the wind was too strong. When it died, their music and machinations rose again, lifting through the house to reach us. Oscar turned me toward him, and pushed my chest. His hand was firm and slow. I fell back against some pillows, and he knelt, straddling me.

"I want to show you something," he whispered again. Oscar's eyes were caught in the soft light. His brow was shadowed, and I could see the wet pupils glimmer. He alarmed me by sighing deeply, as if to stifle tears. The boy pulled the tail of my shirt out and began undoing the buttons. I did nothing, but lay back. The shirt fell open, and he pushed it to either side. The cushions fell from the bed. Oscar touched my ribs, then ran his warm hand across my chest. My mind was full with both the moment and a desire to know what was in his mind as he moved over me. What information came through his hands? I ran my fingers along behind his, following to my navel, trying to get a clue. The boy said nothing. I looked impatiently at his eyes, and the dumb mouth, but found them gone, lost and inspecific, as if asleep. Oscar put his lips to my chest, then pulled his T-shirt off. He took my hand and moved it, more gently, along his belly and chest, and he pushed the shirt from my face. The sight made me dizzy. I felt his ribs and the ridge of his hip, then let my hand rest in the hollow under his arm, where the soft brown hair was damp. Oscar sighed again and the thought was too large and chaotic in my head. He shifted his hips. I could not think clearly what I was feeling. What was I feeling? The skin and warmth of him? The face and eyes, and the heart beating, visibly? There was too much information, scattered over us; I could not read it all. Every word was diminished or exploded. When Oscar had undressed me, and was naked, and he rocked forward so his middle pressed against my chest, he held himself there, pulsing where my heart beat, as if to push beyond me and through to the ground. I felt a collapsing inside, as of borders or gaps, and lost every thought or word to his body and to mine. Words could not have me, nor hold me. I might have fulfilled the inspector's desire for my complicity, that night, or found something in my own weakness, as Amelia had willed . . . but I had also eluded them both completely. I, we, were finally unreadable in our extended and mutual dissolution.

Below us, Amelia sang in the big room, and finished her recitation. Francis accompanied her adequately on the organ and applauded her final speech. At some dim, silent hour she went upstairs and rested. Francis stayed behind, gathering his mother's papers and blowing out candles. I traced the contours of Oscar's body with my hands, and I listened, in and out of sleep. The storm quieted and then surged around us. There was music at one point, when I lay my head on Oscar's chest, while he slept. It came from below in a voice far prettier than any I had heard before:

THE TEMPEST.

AIR. *(Amphitrite)* HALCYON DAYS.

Henry Purcell.

Halcyon days, now wars___ are end-ing,

You___ shall find where - eer___ you___ sail,

Hal-cyon days, now wars ___ are end-ing, You __ shall find __ where - eer __ you __ sail,

Tri - tons all the while ___ at - tend - ing With a kind ___ and __ gen - tle gale, with a

kind _____ and gen-tle gale, Tri - tons all the

while___ at-tend-ing With a kind_____ and gen-tle gale.

Hal-cyon days, now wars are end-ing,

Hal-cyon days, now wars are ending, You__ shall find__ where-__ e'er you sail, Tri-__ tons all the

while at-tend-__ ing With a kind and gen-tle gale, with a kind and gen-tle gale.

Da Capo sino
al Fine ⌢

Da Capo sino
al Fine ⌢

Frans had never sung so prettily, and long (the amphitrite having been given him also, because the actors were in disarray). Pieter was outside in the storm, kindling a fire and singing with Kees and Joop, who'd gone with him. The long night had exhausted Motley, but he sat enraptured, transported by the song and the excitement of hearing the music performed for the first time. Many in the room fell asleep before the final act. The servants spent as much time with pillows and the snoring as they had earlier with the bottles and shells. The disturbance with Pieter was largely forgotten, except by Motley and Verweerd, who'd been especially touched by the content of what was said. Motley was not a stupid man; the passion of Pieter's speech made it clear to him there were important issues at stake in his *Tempest*. He preferred a comedy, and a nicer, cleaner ending than Shakespeare's, and he tried out his argument for it, to himself, while he reclined, listening. Verweerd had more sympathy for Pieter, but did not share his passion. He was glad for the spectacle, but would do nothing to take sides against Motley. It was sad what had happened to Prospero in three quarters of a century, and the old man wondered what would become of him as more centuries passed . . . It was fitting that his power had been stripped, and that he was made into a simple prop in an elborate, mechanical entertainment. Motley's ending was fine.

Francis took his mother's notebooks from the low couch and arranged them neatly on a side table. It was very late now; he was the last awake. No one could be heard upstairs. The seven thick folders were ratty, covered with coffee stains, and nearly complete. He ran his fingers along the cramped blue title, penned on the first page of each notebook: "The Dissolution of Nicholas Dee." Francis picked out the last one, flipped toward the end, and read: Could there ever be an art, again, conjured from the wisdom, and faith, of a magus? An art that was wise about power and magic? Verweerd believed such a thing was impossible. Larger wheels had turned, and would turn further. Conjurations had become entertainments. Risk and loss were made anathema, and could now be contained. Real power—cold, thorough, systematic power—had finally outstripped these enchantments. Prospero was not killed, but circumstance had forever changed him. The notes went on for several more pages, describing a storm and the Opera House, and then they stopped. Music was sketched, after which it said simply "End." Was her book now complete? She had begun by leaving me, on that day when I went from my home to find a policy of insurance against personal loss; and now she had delivered me, through Oscar and her conjurations, to this, the evening of my disappearance.

The storm let up, though rain continued to fall into the broken trees. I could see the night through the small window beside the bed. Below, the last embers of the fire warmed Francis. He fed the pages of my own manuscript, one by one, into the small flame. He was tired and a little sad. Knowing his mother was asleep and could not scold him for his haste, he scattered the pile as one over the burning pages. By that light he turned again to Amelia's notebook, and opened it to her final entry:

The opera house of Andries Verweerd, nearly finished and empty, rises from the waters of Den Dollard. It stands alone in the storm. There are boats on the shore, flat barges, and men are filing onto them. Motley is wheeled forward in his carriage, with Weekes in a terrible panic. The boy Frans and Verweerd seem to be leading with Nicholas following, too far behind. The boats push off and are guided by ropes across the open water. I watch Nicholas stumble through sheets of rain toward the shore. He cannot reach the other men, nor do they hear him. Thunder and wind drown his voice equally. He falls against the ground, broken and exhausted, as the boats make the structure and the men begin unloading. I see rain fill his ears and mouth, soaking him, and he turns to look up into it. There is nothing but water. Gray water falling from the sky.

I know that he thought of his father then, and of his interest in finding him. Nicholas turned from the sky and saw the bay. He shuffled forward through the reeds, and he saw his fractured outline in the surface of the water. I watched him fall then, and his body turned as it broke the surface. He felt the muddy bottom coming closer. Nicholas let go a brace of pearly bubbles and sank, until he was resting in the mud. It was so dark there, and so peaceful. The only sound was his heartbeat. He felt it everywhere. It might have been the storm, or a chopper beating against the water's edge above him, for the depth and speed of the thrumming seemed to increase beyond any measure a single body alone could produce . . . then it dimmed. He let go a last measure of air; his body turned again. All his questions dissolved into the surrounding water, and he slept.

EPILOGUE

THE TEMPEST.

Henry Purcell.

DUET *(Neptune & Amphitrite)* and CHORUS. NO STARS AGAIN SHALL HURT YOU.

306

days shall pass in peace and love, but all, all, all, all, all, all, all, all, all, all, all your

days shall pass in peace and love,

days shall pass in peace and love,

days shall pass in peace and love,

days, but all _____ your days shall pass in peace and love.

but all _____ your days shall pass in peace and love.

but all, all, all, all, all, all, all, all, all, all, all your days shall pass in peace and love.___

but all, all, all, all, all, all, all, all, all, all, all your days shall pass in peace and love.

END

Acknowledgments

Many people, in America and Holland, made this book possible. I am especially grateful to the Bouw family for their interest and support throughout my time in Holland; to Matthijs Bouw in particular for his intelligence, generosity, and candor; to Karl Buske for always talking to me about work; to the Groningen Police for their delays in processing my expulsion papers; to the staff of the Universiteit Bibliotheek in Groningen for treating me, without reason or authorization, as a legitimate scholar; to Johan Polak for his wisdom, candor, and grace— a rare alchemy that I will always miss; and, again, to Gloria Loomis and Robert Stewart, who have supported me, in body *and* soul, through their intelligence and initiative as agent and editor. I am grateful to the Guggenheim Foundation and Artist Trust; their generous, timely support allowed me to complete this book.

Matthew Stadler is the author of Landscape: Memory, The Sex Offender, *and* Allan Stein. *He is the recipient of a Guggenheim fellowship, and literary editor of* Nest Magazine. *He lives in Seattle.*